LINES OF
DEPARTURE

BY MARKO KLOOS

Terms of Enlistment

Lines of Departure

LINES OF DEPARTURE

MARKO KLOOS

Text copyright © 2014 Marko Kloos

Published by 47North, Seattle

www.apub.com

ISBN-13: 9781477817407
ISBN-10: 1477817409

Cover illustration: Marc Simonetti
Cover Design: Sam Dawson

Library of Congress Number: 2013948462

Printed in the United States of America

For Lyra and Quinn.
No matter how many novels I write,
you two will always be my biggest accomplishment.

LINES OF DEPARTURE

PROLOGUE

Sometimes, the old sergeants talk about the Good Old Days.

There once was a blessed and mythical time when military service was a desirable job—a ticket to a low-risk career, access to decent food, and tolerable benefits. The military was selective, but when you got in, you were a member of a privileged class for the rest of your life.

Naturally, the Good Old Days came to an end about ten minutes after I signed my enlistment papers.

We've been fighting a new enemy for almost five years now, and we can't even agree on a name for them. The xenobiologists came up with an unpronounceable Latin designation that nobody uses outside of a textbook. The infantry grunts, known for prosaicness, call them Lankies or Big Uglies. The Sino-Russians didn't even *have* a name for them for the first year of the war, because they believed the North American Commonwealth was spinning tall tales to cover up terraforming disasters or natural calamities on the colonies we lost one by one.

Then the Lankies took SRA-settled Novaya Rossiya, just past the Thirty. One hundred thirty thousand dead colonists later, their scientists finally started to compare notes with ours.

1

These aliens are eighty feet tall and incredibly thick-skinned, and they roam around in groups. It takes heavy antiarmor munitions to put a dent in a Lanky, and their mile-high terraforming structures won't budge for anything less than a ten-kiloton tactical nuke. The only way to scrape them off a colony planet is to glass all their atmo exchangers and settlements with a few hundred megatons from orbit, and that sort of treatment makes the place unfit for human resettlement. Once the Lanky seed ships enter the orbit of a colony, that place is no longer ours, one way or the other. To us, it may be a war—to them, it's just pest control.

When I joined the military, humanity had a few hundred colonies between the SRA and the NAC, from the old settlement on Luna to the newly terraformed New Caledonia just short of the seventy-light-year line. Then the Lankies appeared and kicked us off a colony planet called Willoughby, and five years later we don't have a single colony left beyond the thirty-light-year line that used to mark the boundary between the inner and outer colonies.

We're down to sixty-nine colonies, and the number drops by a dozen or more every year. The Lankies show up, exterminate the big settlements, tear down our expensive terraforming stations, raise a fully functioning, superefficient terraforming network in less time than it takes us to send reinforcements through the nearest Alcubierre chute, and make the place their own. Once they're in orbit, our people on the ground can only scatter and wait for the navy's evac force to show up, because there's not a damn thing the garrison marines can do against the Lankies.

When I was a kid, I used to watch the corny military adventure vids on the Networks. I remember the more optimistic ones, where Earth gets invaded by some species even more violent and territorial than our own, and the nations of Earth forget their old differences and stand shoulder to shoulder against the outside threat.

In reality, not even the threat of alien invasion of their colonies could keep the SRA from messing with us and sneaking around behind our backs to take advantage of the fact that three-quarters of our military strength was suddenly diverted to hold the line against the Lankies. On the fringes, we had to dig in to defend our colonies, using garrison battalions and regiments where we had companies and platoons before. On the inner colonies, we suddenly had to deal with increasingly bold SRA raids again, having to pry the Sino-Russians off of colonies that had been secure NAC property for over fifty years.

All in all, the last five years have been anything but low-risk for people in uniform.

Back home, the colony flights have stopped, which has made Earth an even more unpleasant place than it was when I joined up. These flights had two purposes: Relieve the population pressure back home, and give some sort of hope for a better future to everyone who didn't have a ticket for the colonies yet. A slot on a colony ship was the ultimate lottery win, and as long as there was the chance of scoring one, the restless masses were not completely without prospects. Now even that remote chance is gone, and we have more welfare riots in a month than we used to have in a year. What's worse, the perpetually cash-strapped government of the NAC is now well and truly broke.

Space colonization is a hideously expensive undertaking, and we lost trillions of dollars in equipment on the colonies the Lankies took away from us. There's no more ore being mined on those worlds, no more raw materials coming in to offset the expense of colonization, and none of the private corporations are willing to extend loans or take on colony contracts anymore. To top it all off, the military was geared and organized to fight other militaries, and there's no money left in the budget to refit ten marine divisions

3

and five hundred starships to fight spacefaring eighty-foot creatures instead of Chinese or Russian marines.

Once upon a time, the military may have been a great career.
Now we're an overextended, underfunded, and unappreciated
force. Behind us, we have the restless masses of our overpopulated
homeworld, and in front of us, we have a new enemy who's phys-
ically and technologically far above us. Only a nutcase would want
to get into the service at this point, and you have to have a mental
defect to want to stay in after your enlistment contract is up.

Naturally, when the time came for me to sign my name again
or pack my things and become a civilian once more, I signed on
the dotted line.

CHAPTER 1
REENLISTING

"I solemnly swear and affirm to loyally serve the North American Commonwealth, and to bravely defend its laws and the freedom of its citizens."

I signed my reenlistment form yesterday in the captain's office, so my butt is already public property for the next five years, but the military likes ritual. We're in one of the briefing rooms, and the captain and XO are standing on either side of the briefing lectern. Someone dragged out a wrinkled North American Commonwealth flag and draped it over the wall display, and I have my hand in the air as I repeat the oath of service for the second time in my military career. A corporal from the fleet news service is recording the event for whatever reason. Even with our recent troubles, the military still has a 90 percent retention rate after the first term of enlistment, so a re-up ceremony isn't exactly an uncommon event.

"Congratulations, Staff Sergeant Grayson," the captain says after I complete the oath. "You're back in the fold for another five years."

What else was I going to do, anyway? I think.

"Thank you, sir," I say, and take the entirely ceremonial reenlistment certificate from his outstretched hand. This means a bonus in my account, which has been growing steadily since my first day of Basic five years ago, but Commonwealth currency is becoming increasingly worthless. By the time I get out, the money in my government account will probably just be enough to pay for a breakfast and a train ride home to the welfare section of Boston.

I didn't reenlist for the money, of course. I reenlisted because I didn't know what the hell else to do. All my professional skills revolve around blowing things up or working classified neural-network systems, which makes me pretty much useless in the civilian world. I don't much feel like going back to Earth and claiming a welfare apartment until I die early. I haven't been back to Terra since the day I left Navy Indoc at Great Lakes for Fleet School on Luna, but from what I hear over the MilNet, the old homeworld isn't doing so well. Some guys who have been there on leave recently say that the worst thing we could do to the Lankies would be to let them take the place.

Earth's population crested at thirty billion people two years ago, and three billion of them are crammed into North America. Terra is an ant hive, teeming with hungry, discontented, and antisocial ants, and I have no desire to add to the population headcount. At least the military still feeds its people, which is more than can be said for the NAC's civil administration. Mom makes it down to the civil building for net access once a month or so, and in her last message she mentioned that the Basic Nutritional Allowance has been cut to thirteen thousand calories per person per week. It looks like they're running out of shit and soy down there.

I didn't need to think very long about reenlisting, that's for sure. Of course, my girlfriend Halley also reenlisted, so I really didn't have much of a choice.

"So it's done," Halley says. The video feed is a bit grainy, but I have no problem seeing the dark rings under her eyes. She's had a long day at Combat Flight School, teaching new pilots how to dodge

Chinese portable surface-to-air missiles and Lanky bio-mines. We're in the same system for a change—my ship is part of a task force that is practicing stealth insertions on one of Saturn's many moons, and we can both tap into the orbital relay above Mars, which has enough spare bandwidth for a few minutes of vid chat.

"Yeah, it's done. Had no choice, since you went ahead and just re-upped before me."

"I thought we had decided we'd both sign again," she says. "Remember? You crunched the numbers and said that both our bonuses were spare change at this point."

"Yeah, I know. Just ribbin' you. Having fun at Flight School?"

"Don't get me started," she says, rolling her eyes. "I can't fucking wait to get back into the fleet. I mean, it's nice not to be shot at for a few months, but I'd swear an oath that some of these rookies work for the other team. I've almost gotten killed three times this week alone."

"Hey, you're grooming the next batch of hero pilots. That's important work."

"Grooming the next batch of coffin liners," she says darkly. "Our SRA friends have some new portable surface-to-air missile. Nuclear warhead in the fifty-microton range. Just enough to blot out a flight of drop ships without making a mess on the ground."

"Shit," I say. "Say what you want about the Lankies, but at least they don't fuck around with nukes just yet."

"They don't *need* nukes, Andrew. They're kicking our asses well enough without."

Other than the ever-present risk of sudden and violent death, Halley has been the only constant in my life since we met in Basic Training Platoon 1066 back at NACRD Orem. We've managed to keep a sort of long-distance relationship going, months apart interspersed with short leaves spent together in run-down navy rec facilities, or on backwater colonies. We've both moved up in our respective career fields—she's a first lieutenant in command of a brand-new top-of-the-line attack drop ship, and I'm in my second year as a combat controller after volunteering for what Halley called "the nutcase track."

The job of a combat controller is to jump into the thick of the action with the frontline grunts on critical missions, but carrying a bunch of radios and a target designator instead of cutting-edge weaponry. It was a logical progression when I wanted to move up from Neural Networks, since I was already trained on all the fleet information systems. They were looking for volunteers, and I was looking for a more exciting job than watching progress bars in a Neural Networks control room. They got their volunteer, and I got excitement in spades.

I passed selection for the combat controller track, and spent almost the entire third year of my service term in training. In the meantime, Halley racked up two hundred combat missions, thousands of flight hours, and a Distinguished Flying Cross for some seriously insane flying while snatching a recon team from the embrace of a company of SRA marines in the middle of a hot-and-heavy firefight. We both think the other has the more dangerous job, and we're both right, depending on the mission of the week.

"Going planetside again in a few days," I tell Halley. Even through the secure comms link, I'm not supposed to give out operational details. The filtering software runs the connection on a three-second delay beyond the normal lag, to chop the feed if it detects that I'm talking about planets, ship names, or star systems.

"Lankies or SRA?" she asks.

"Lankies. I'm dropping in with a recon team. We're going to look for something worth dropping a few kilotons on."

"Just a team? That's not a lot of guns."

"Well, the idea is to avoid them if we can. Besides, I'm going in with Recon. I'll be fine."

"Yeah, well, even recon guys die," Halley says. "I've showed up at more than one scheduled pickup without anyone there because the whole team got greased."

"If we run into trouble, I'll let Recon do the shooting while I run the other way. I'm just a walking radio farm."

"For being complete shit magnets, we're actually pretty lucky, you know?" Halley muses, and we both laugh.

"You have a weird definition of 'lucky,'" I say, but I know she's right. We're doing some of the most dangerous work in the Fleet Arm, and we've managed to survive almost four years of combat deployments without any serious scrapes. We only had twelve graduates in our platoon at the end of Basic Training, and four of them have died in combat. Strangely enough, all the members of our chow-hall table are still alive, and I'm the only member of our little group who managed to get hurt enough for a Purple Heart. Halley's Distinguished Flying Cross makes her the most highly decorated of us, and since she was the only graduate of our platoon to snatch an officer-track slot, she's also the highest-ranking member of Chow Hall Table 5.

"Well, we've made it this far," Halley says, as if she just had the same thoughts. "What's another five years of dodging ground fire?"

"Hey, it could be worse," I reply. "We could be back on Earth right now."

My current ship is the NACS *Intrepid*, fleet carrier and one of three ships of the new Essex class. The Essex carriers are fast, well armed, and the last new hardware in the fleet for the foreseeable future. The ships were ordered before the war with the Lankies broke out, and they hurriedly specified some refits to accommodate the new tactical situation before the three ships of the class were even out of the construction dock. The navy had ordered seven more, ten ships in total to form the new backbone of the

NAC carrier force, but then they ran out of money, so the three Essex carriers form a rather short backbone. They're not nearly as big as the Navigator-class supercarriers that preceded them, but they're faster and fitted with a better sensor suite, which has proven a bigger asset against the Lankies than sheer size or armor-belt thickness. The Essex carriers are always in demand, and always in the thick of things.

I like serving on a carrier, because the big bird farms have a lot more space than the little tin cans I usually pulled when I was still a Neural Networks administrator. As one of three combat controllers on the *Intrepid*, I get my own single-person berth, a luxury usually reserved for senior NCOs and staff officers. That means I get to vid-chat in private, without a bunch of my peers half-listening over my shoulder. Combat controllers are always in demand as well, since there are so few of us, and we get certain privileges above our rank and pay grade. The entire fleet only has two hundred of us, so we never have much idle time.

Since graduating from the pipeline and putting on the scarlet beret, I've been hopping from one star system to the next, fighting the SRA one month and the Lankies the next. If the fleet paid a cent for every million miles traveled, I'd be the richest individual in the history of the planet. Because Fleet Arm ships need downtime for refits and rearming, I tend to hop ships every six months or so, because we combat controllers are too few to go around to have as much downtime as the hardware. Before the *Intrepid*, I was on the *Atlas*, the *Tecumseh*, the *New Hampshire*, and a half dozen other ships whose names I can't even recall without consulting my personnel and transfer record.

In the end, it's all the same business, anyway—launching from a carrier or cruiser with a stern-faced and tight-lipped unit of Commonwealth grunts, going into battle against Russians or Chinese or Lankies, and calling down the wrath of the gods on our enemies when needed. The grunts have rifles, rocket launchers, and tactical nuclear mortars. I have something much more fearsome than that—a set of radios that can talk to the attack ships of the task force in orbit, and a computer that can just about remote-control that task force.

When the grunts bump into a minor problem, they use their rifles and rockets. For bigger problems, they lob half-kiloton nukes. For really big problems, they call on me, and I direct in a wing of Shrikes loaded with ordnance, or an orbital fifty-megaton strike that will turn an entire Lanky settlement into a few hundred square miles of abstract art rendered in glowing slag. One of my fellow combat controllers has the words *Planetary Remodeling Kit* written on the lid of his tactical control deck, and that joke is not too much of an exaggeration.

In between the hours and days of excitement, stress, and outright terror, however, there are days and weeks of boredom, thanks to the mechanics of interstellar travel. My next mission, a little less than eight days away, will be on a planet called New Wales, in orbit around the fourth planet of the Theta Persei system. The trip to the solar-system end of the Alcubierre chute to Theta Persei will take seven days, and the transition across the intervening thirty-seven light years only twelve hours.

Once we get there, we will do battle with the Lankies. I don't know yet what's waiting for us on New Wales, but a few factors have been a reliable constant for the last few years. We will be outgunned, outnumbered, and always just on the brink of utter defeat as we try to hold the line, try to keep our ever-contracting little bubble of colonized space from shrinking any further.

We're the corps. This is what we do. The Commonwealth— *humanity*—is in deep shit, and we're the people with the shovels. The trouble is that it's a huge pile of shit, and they're very small shovels.

CHAPTER 2
—————— NEW WALES ——————

You can always tell the efficient officers by the way they hold their briefings. The Fleet Arm's cap-ship guys and console jockeys tend to blather on and go through the briefing protocol by the book, and everyone in the briefing room usually zones out after being told the same information six different ways. The recon officers cut right down to the chase, and by the time their briefings are finished, the mid-rat sandwiches in the briefing room aren't even halfway gone yet.

"Today's mission will be a drop-and-shop run," Major Gomez says once we're all in our seats. As the sole combat controller assigned to this mission, I am the only Fleet Arm guy in the room. The rest of the troops are Spaceborne Infantry Force Recon, a team I've dropped with a few times before.

"New Wales has been Lanky real estate for right around a year now," the major continues. "Chances are good you'll find some major settlement clusters down there. They've had plenty of time to dig in and make themselves at home."

Behind the major, the wall-mounted holographic briefing screen cycles through a series of three-dimensional renderings of our target planet. As always, we have a rough idea where the Lanky population centers are located, but as always, our rough idea isn't good enough for orbital strike coordinates. The Lanky minefield around the planet won't let any fleet recon unit close enough for good targeting data. This, in turn, creates job opportunities for the Force Recon teams.

"We have the usual shit soup down there, which fucks with the sensors as always, but the recon drone got a decent IR fix on the northern hemisphere before they blew it out of space. They set up shop not too far from the old colony capital."

The map behind the major zooms in to magnify the target area, projecting the tactical symbol for "unconfirmed settlement" over the topographical data. New Wales had been colonized for over fifteen years before the Lankies showed up and seized the place, so there was quite a bit of decent vegetation and agriculture on the ground before the ratio of oxygen and carbon dioxide in the atmosphere got flipped around in the span of just a month and a half. Now it's the usual Lanky neighborhood—hot, humid, and certain death for any human not in a vacsuit.

"Primary target area is designated 'Normandy.' If the cannon cockers launch our pods reasonably straight, you'll be on the ground between twenty and fifty klicks from the edge of our suspected main settlement. Hoof it in, mark the atmo exchangers and whatever other high-value gear you see on your way in, and let the fleet guy do his job once you have eyeballs on Lanky City down there."

Since we started taking the fight to the Lankies, 80 percent of my missions have been what we coined drop-and-shop runs. Because the aliens secure their new colonies with super-dense orbital minefields, none of our fleet units can get close enough to a Lanky-occupied world for accurate targeting data or reliable controlling of remote drones. The Linebacker space-defense cruisers can clear a section of the minefield big enough for a strike package or a salvo of nuclear space-to-ground missiles, but the recon teams need to go in ahead of time to get a definite fix, so the

Linebackers won't waste their limited loads of very expensive missiles. We drop, tag everything worth bombing in the target zone, and upload the information to the ships waiting out of reach. The Linebackers blow open a window, the carrier sends in a strike package or ten, and then the retrieval boats come to pick us up.

The tricky part of a drop-and-shop mission is always the ingress. The Lanky proximity mines nail everything man-made beyond a certain size threshold, and drop ships are too big and too man-made to make it through. That's why recon teams get onto alien-controlled worlds by express delivery—ballistic drop pods, fired from the big missile tubes of capital ships. It's one hell of an exciting way to commute to work.

"Suiting up at 0700 Zulu. Launch is at 0830 Zulu," the major says, concluding the briefing. "You've all done this a few dozen times, so you know the drill top to bottom. Report any suit issues to the armorer, so we can plug in someone from the standby crew if needed. Good hunting, people. *Dismissed.*"

"How many drops is this for you, Grayson?" the recon team leader, Lieutenant Graff, asks me as we file out of the briefing room.

"Oh, hell, I sort of lost count," I tell him, even though I know exactly how many times I've been fired into space in a bio-pod. Drop counts are a main measure of prowess among the Spaceborne Infantry grunts, and being blasé about one's drop count marks one as a hardened SI trooper. "I think it's close to two hundred now."

"*Damn.* They really oughta come up with some new level for the drop badge. Platinum or titanium or something. You got gold four times over by now."

"What about you, LT?"

"This'll be number sixty-nine."

"You counting the training drops, too?" I tease.

"Well, we can't all be in demand like you, Grayson."

"Be glad you're not. I haven't had any real leave since Combat Controller School. Would have been nice to trade some of those drops for some time off. I haven't seen my mom in person since I shipped out for Basic."

"You're not missing much," Lieutenant Graff says. "Next leave you get, make it a colony, or one of the rec centers. Earth ain't much to look at these days."

"You been Earthside recently? Where you from, anyway?"

"Houston metroplex. I went home on leave three months ago. It's a fucking war zone now. You?"

"PRC Boston-Seven," I say. "It was a war zone already when I left."

"Kind of wrong, isn't it? We bust our asses to keep Earth safe, and they shoot at us when we show up down there in uniform. Makes you wonder what we're fighting for."

I don't have to wonder. I fight because the only alternative is to suck down recycled shit for food in a welfare city on Earth somewhere, and wait for the inevitable day when the Lankies conclude their interstellar pest control campaign against us by hopping into Earth's orbit and nerve-gassing our filthy little ant hive of a planet.

I fight because it's the only way I have to control my destiny at least a little bit.

———

It takes about thirty minutes to suit up in a Hostile Environment Battle Armor suit.

The HEBA suits are new hardware, relatively speaking. They were designed for offensive missions on Lanky worlds, and they're so stuffed with state-of-the-art tech that regular old battle armor looks like a medieval suit of dented plate in comparison. The regular battle armor works on Lanky worlds, too, but their built-in oxygen tanks are too small, and their filtration systems get overwhelmed by the amount of biological contaminants in the air. The Lankies seed some sort of pollen into the atmosphere to kick-start their own version of agriculture, and a normal suit's filters clog up in just a few hours.

The new HEBA suits have custom-tailored filters and a new oxygen storage system that lets a grunt carry enough breathable air for a few days of heavy physical activity. The armor is less resistant to small-arms fire than the standard infantry armor, but more flexible, and only half as heavy. The sensor package built into the helmet is advanced enough to navigate a starship: infrared, thermal imaging, millimeter-wave radar, ultrasound.

There's a built-in trauma kit, and a superfast tactical computer to tie all the information streams together. Whoever designed the armor figured out that the visor is the weak spot in a helmet, and that keeping one from fogging up on a high-CO_2 world is an unnecessary energy expense, so the new helmets don't have visors. The lack of visible eyes, combined with the little bumps for the helmet's sensor arrays, gives the wearer an insectoid appearance, so it took about five seconds after they released the first HEBA suits into the corps before someone coined the obvious nickname: *bug suits.*

The bug suits are custom-fitted to each wearer, and hideously expensive. The defense budget being what it is, they're strictly limited issue. Only personnel with frequent business on Lanky worlds get one—recon, combat control, drop-ship pilots, and Spaceborne Rescue specialists. All in all, there are maybe three thousand troops in the entire corps who have a fitted bug suit. They're strictly off-limits for missions against the SRA, because Command doesn't want the tech to fall into Russian or Chinese hands.

I have a sort of love-hate relationship with my bug suit. It's very comfortable, and the wealth of sensor input projected onto the inside of the helmet makes me feel almost omniscient. On the other hand, putting one on means I'm about to head out into Lanky country.

"Suits all check out," the lieutenant announces. "We are ready for business. Weapons check, please."

We all aim our rifles at the diagnostics target on the bulkhead and let the computers do the talking over the wireless network. Everyone's carrying the new M-80 rifles, which are also specialized gear for use against Lankies. The old M-66 fléchette rifles are still in service, but only used against the Sino-Russians. The little tungsten needles fired from the M-66s don't do much against the tough-skinned Lankies, so the new rifles fire twenty-five-millimeter dual-purpose rounds, a super-dense uranium penetrator piggy-backing on an explosive payload. The velocities needed for the penetrator to punch through a Lanky's hide means a lot of caseless propellant, which in turn means monstrous recoil. It also means that the new rifles are vertically stacked twin barrels without magazines, because the recoil impulse is so strong that a multi-shot action would be impractically big and heavy. With only two rounds in the gun, the new rifles are damn near useless against the SRA, but they work quite well against the Lankies.

"All right," the lieutenant says when we have finished the final weapons check. "Let's go mess us up some Big Uglies."

———————

The recon team is four troopers strong: Lieutenant Graff, Staff Sergeant Humphrey, Sergeant Keller, and Corporal Lavoie. I'm the fifth wheel on this particular wagon, but nobody minds having me around, because I carry the radios that call down the thunder if there's a need for it. We all drop in individual pods, to make sure the entire team isn't wiped out if the launch crew miscalculates our ingress timing and shoots a pod right into the path of a Lanky proximity mine. The artillery people are good—the chance for a catastrophic pod-to-mine interface at ingress is only 1 percent—but two hundred missions mean rolling that particular set of dice two hundred times.

I strap into my bio-pod, which looks like an artillery shell carved out of rock. The mines don't trigger for small, spaceborne inert objects such as asteroids, so our pods are designed to be a fair imitation of one. So far, they've worked as designed, but I worry before every launch that this particular one will be the drop where the Lankies have figured out how our recon teams get dirtside, and that my pod will be the first one to be blotted out of its trajectory by a newly updated mine.

"Final comms check," the lieutenant says over the team channel. "Sound off, people. Give me a go/no-go."

I listen to the team responding to the lieutenant's challenge and add my own acknowledgment when everyone else is finished.

"Echo Five, copy and go for launch."

"Echo One, copy we are go for launch. Comms go dark after this transmission until we are down in the dirt. I'll see everyone on the ground in thirty. Echo One out."

I give the launch tech standing next to my pod the thumbs-up sign. He returns the gesture and closes the lid of my pod. Immediately, my helmet's low-light vision kicks in to compensate for the sudden darkness. There's nothing to see in here except for the smooth inner surface of the pod's lid, so I manually turn off the visual feed to conserve battery power.

The pod is loaded into the launch tube by an automatic feeder mechanism. At this point, I'm just like any other space-to-ground ordnance in the carrier's magazines, except for the fact that I'm a biological weapon rather than a chemical or nuclear one. Ten of the *Intrepid's* 144 launch tubes have been converted for bio-pod launches, so an entire squad can be launched at the same time. For the next twenty-odd minutes, my life will be entirely in the hands of the ship's automated systems—the ballistic computer that calculates the proper trajectory for my pod to weave through the Lanky minefield and get to the target zone, and the launch mechanism that will fire my pod out of the tube at just the right velocity. One computer glitch, one power surge or bump at the wrong moment, one misplaced decimal point in a programming subroutine, and I'll end up shooting past the planet into deep space, or finely dispersed in a cloud of organic matter in the upper layers of the planet's atmosphere.

The worst part is always the moment just before the launch, when the pod's bumpy ride on the ordnance carousel stops and you know you're now chambered in a titanium-alloy missile tube like a cartridge in a rifle barrel. It's the moment before the plunge, the last few seconds before the electric firing mechanism shoots the pod out into the cold darkness of space and right into the teeth of the enemy's orbital defenses. Once the pod is on the way, my fear always subsides a little, but in those few heartbeats before a pod launch, I'm always nearly scared enough to shit my pants.

The launcher tube hums as the electric field is activated; there's a loud whooshing sound made by the air rushing out of the depressurizing launch tube, and then I am pushed back into my cradle as the pod accelerates out of the tube at eight gravities.

I always hold my breath during a launch—not a difficult task at all, with the weight of the acceleration on my chest like a drop ship's landing skid—and I only allow myself to breathe again when I feel the sensation of weight dropping away as the pod leaves the artificial gravity field of the carrier.

Some troopers start up their helmet displays on the way down, to bring up the tactical screen that shows them the precise location of their pod on the planned trajectory and the exact moment it will pass through the Lanky minefield.

I prefer to ride it out in darkness. I don't want to know the exact window of my possible sudden death. If I crash into a mine, or one fires its yard-long armor-piercing penetrators at my pod, I'll be dead in a blink. If I make it through, I'll know by the sound of superheated air roaring past my pod as I hurtle through the upper layers of the atmosphere.

For the next few minutes, my pod streaks through the hostile vacuum between the carrier and the planet, and I'm in total isolation—sightless, deaf, weightless, and feeling like the loneliest person in the galaxy. There's nothing to see, nothing to feel, no sensations to distract from the fear. Then my pod gets buffeted a little, and I hear the familiar muted roar of air rushing past the outer skin of my one-way ride. Five more minutes, and the main drag chute will deploy. I will drop onto a strange and hostile world for the 192nd time in my new career. Once more, I've won the roll against death and cheated my way past clusters of antiship mines that can turn a frigate into scrap instantly.

Of course, the ingress is the easy part of the mission. I'm about to set foot onto a Lanky-colonized world, and there are many ways to die a quick death down there.

CHAPTER 3
—NUCLEAR PEST CONTROL—

I know that this drop has gone wrong even before my pod hits the ground. As I descend on my drag chute, I turn on the helmet display to get my bearings, and flinch when I see that our trajectory has carried us right into the target zone. We were supposed to drop a few dozen miles away from the big red square on the map; but our pods are about to touch down twenty-five miles inside of it. Someone else is already on the ground and looking around, because my tactical screen suddenly updates with target markers and threat vectors all around me.

My pod hits the ground with a bone-jarring impact. The lid of the pod blows off automatically, and I see the familiar lead-colored sky of a Lanky-terraformed world overhead. The Lankies like it gloomy—it's all clouds, rain, and fog, all the time. My pod has adopted a weird nose-down attitude, and as I hit the release buckle of my harness and sit up, I see that our pods came down on a steeply sloped hillside.

"Echo Five is dirtside," I report on the team channel. "Everything's in one piece."

"Fabulous," Lieutenant Graff replies at once. "Grab your stuff and form up on me. Looks like Arty screwed the pooch on this one."

I take my rifle out of its storage bracket, check to make sure the barrels are both loaded, and check my computer-augmented field of view for the rest of my team. As far as dispersion goes, the aim of the launch team was outstanding—we're all within a quarter kilometer of each other. They shot a tight group from a quarter million kilometers away, but they missed the target altogether. As I trot down the hillside to join my team leader, I see a Lanky atmosphere exchanger towering above us not ten klicks away, and a cluster of the weirdly organic Lanky buildings less than two kilometers to our right. Instead of sneaking up to the settled area, we dropped right into it, and unless the locals are asleep or dead, we'll have a welcoming committee on top of us before too long. The only bright spot so far is the fact that we're all down and alive. I've been on a few missions where someone's chutes failed to deploy, and the results of a pod impact from high orbit are usually a ten-foot impact crater and some bits and pieces of organic matter mixed in with the mangled wreckage at the bottom. Most of the time, there's not even enough left to collect dog tags.

We all converge on the lieutenant's position. There's no cover nearby, and I feel very exposed on this hillside, in plain view of the nearby Lanky buildings. They're two kilometers away, but an eighty-foot creature has a very long stride, and we've seen the Lankies cover a kilometer in three minutes without seeming in a particular hurry. Thankfully, the lieutenant shares my misgivings.

"We're sticking out like glowing billboards out here," he says as we gather around him. "Let's get off this slope and then figure out how to unfuck this mess."

"There's a ravine at ten o'clock, down at the base of the hill," Corporal Lavoie says. "We can get away from those buildings and stay out of sight."

"Good enough. Let's haul ass, people. Dispersed formation, hundred-meter intervals."

_____

We haven't covered half a kilometer down the rocky slope when we see movement from the direction of the asymmetrical latticework spires of the Lanky buildings. A few moments later, we see the distinct shapes of three Lankies ambling toward our drop zone with slow and measured strides. Lankies never seem to be in a hurry, but once you have one coming after you, there's no way to outrun it without a vehicle.

"Three incoming from four o'clock, bearing one-ten," Sergeant Humphrey says in her terse and businesslike Canadian accent. We all had the symbols for "hostile troops" on our displays the moment one of us spotted the Lankies, but ingrained training dies hard. My tactical computer, ever helpful, calculates speeds and movement vectors, and informs me that we will reach the ravine just barely before the welcoming committee arrives at the hillside.

"Double-time," the lieutenant orders, quite unnecessarily. We run down the hillside as fast as our hundred-pound loads of gear and weapons will allow.

"Turn on the camo, everyone. We hit the ditch, you spread out and lay low."

Our suits have a brand-new polychromatic camouflage system. It's an array of tiny electro-optical projectors, designed to blend us in with any terrain. It won't turn us invisible, but it works well enough that you have to be pretty close to a trooper in polychrome camo to spot them. We don't know if the Lankies see the way humans do—we don't even know if they can "see" at all—but the few times where troopers in bug suits have turned on their PC camo to hide from nearby Lankies, nobody has gotten killed. The projector systems drain the batteries of our suits, so we're only supposed to use them in dire emergencies. As far as I'm concerned, our current malaise qualifies for the classification.

The ravine looks like a desert wadi. It's twenty meters wide, with a flat bottom that's smooth and sandy from whatever seasonal torrents sweep through it a few times a year. The edges are steep and craggy, ten feet or more of almost vertical drop to the ravine bottom. We help each other down to the bottom. There are plenty of rocks and boulders of all sizes lining the sides of the ravine, but it occurs to me that the place will be a trap if the Lankies figure out our location, because there's no quick way back out of here. Down at the bottom, my suit's sensors no longer have an exact fix on the approaching Lankies, but by the time we have dispersed and ducked behind cover, they're so close that I don't need millimeter-wave radar to know they're almost on top of us.

A hundred meters behind us, a towering gray mass appears above the ravine. I barely dare to move my head as the Lanky pauses at the edge of the ravine and then steps across it in a single stride. As always, when a Lanky is within a quarter of a kilometer, the earth quakes from the impacts of their slow steps. Nobody has ever managed to airlift an entire Lanky body back to a fleet ship for dissection, but we've salvaged their corpses in bits and pieces after battles, and our science people estimate that the average Lanky weighs close to a thousand metric tons.

As the Lanky disappears from sight and walks up the hill toward our discarded pods, a second one shows up at the edge of the ravine. This one is even closer than the first, maybe eighty yards, and it doesn't follow the first one across. Instead, it pauses at the ledge and turns its head to look down into the ravine. Lankies have no visible eyes in their massive skulls, but I can almost feel the Lanky's gaze on me as it seems to study the depression in the terrain. Then it turns to the right and starts walking along the ledge, toward the spot where we are trying to blend in with the local geology.

"Don't anybody start shooting yet," the lieutenant warns us over the team channel in a low voice. "He reaches into the ravine, we light him up. He walks past, we sit tight. Weapons *hold*."

I watch as the Lanky ambles toward us, its huge head swinging slowly from side to side. Even after a few years of seeing them close up, they still look utterly alien and unsettling to me. Some of the SI troopers think the Lankies look like an evolved version of pre-historic Earth dinosaurs, with their toothless mouths and shield-like protrusions on the backs of their skulls.

By now, the Lanky is so close to us that his red and my blue icon are overlapping on my tactical display. The impacts of his three-toed feet on the rocky ground shake loose cascades of sand on the far side of the ravine. If he discovers us at this range and decides to stomp on us, we won't have much time to get our weapons into play, but a preemptive burst of rifle and rocket fire would bring the other Lankies down on us in a flash. It's a gamble, but the odds are better for us if we sit tight and play rocks until the last possible moment.

The Lanky ambles past our position and walks along the ravine for a few more moments. Then he steps across the ravine fifty meters in front of our position and continues up the hill. I can feel his progress up the hillside by the tremors underneath my feet. If there's a good thing about opponents that are eighty feet tall, it's that they can't sneak up and surprise you.

"Let's move. Down the ravine, double-time."

We gather our stuff and start running, away from the landing spot that has become a local Lanky attraction. We were discovered, which is the worst possible start for a recon mission, but we're still alive, which is far from the worst outcome. Every kilometer we put between us and the drop site will increase our odds of staying alive.

"You know, this shit would be a lot easier if we could take some wheels along for the drop," Sergeant Keller pants as we trot down the ravine with all our heavy gear. Nobody argues the point.

The ravine runs out into the rocky plain three kilometers from the hillside. Our landing site is now far away, so Sergeant Humphrey chances a few sweeps with the millimeter-wave radar to check the area for Lankies. Half a dozen red icons pop up on our tactical screens, all clustered on the hillside. The nearest Lanky is roaming the area between the ravine and the drop pods, two and a half kilometers from our position. For now, we're in the clear, but if the Lankies figure out our egress route, they can catch up with us in a hurry.

"Well, that almost went into the pants, didn't it?" the lieutenant says. "Haven't gotten that close to one of them in a while."

"We're in a bad spot, LT," I say. "Too close to that atmo exchanger. We have no weather to hide in."

The area around the Lanky terraforming tower is mostly featureless and devoid of vegetation. The Lankies have their own fast-growing plant life, but they never grow anything close to their own atmo exchangers. Lanky worlds are foggy and rainy, but there's always a clear area around the mile-high terraforming towers, like the eye in a hurricane.

"Let's get to the weather line and then head north from there," the lieutenant orders. "North-northwest, looks like ten klicks. If we haul ass, we can be in the soup in an hour and a half."

We move out in dispersed formation, a hundred meters between each trooper, so we can't all get taken out as a group by a mine or a lucky Lanky. So far, we haven't done any fighting, just a lot of running and hiding, but that's the usual breakdown of activities on a typical recon drop—brief periods of sheer terror punctuating long stretches of running around. Any mission where we bring back our full ammo issue is a good one, because it means we didn't get spotted.

We make it back into the weather without any contact. The Lankies milling about on the distant hillside don't seem to be interested in looking for the passengers of those empty drop pods, which suits us fine. If the situation were reversed, and one of our SI garrisons stumbled across an empty Lanky conveyance on one of our colony planets, every trooper on that rock would be combing the place for the infiltrators, but the Lankies don't think like we do. Whenever they take over a colony, they just drop nerve gas on the population centers, but they rarely bother individuals or small groups. It's as if we're insignificant to them in small numbers, much like we would smoke out an ant hive in the wrong spot but not bother hunting down stray ants one by one.

Back in the fog and rain, we take a short break, and I take the time to send a status update to the fleet via encrypted burst transmission—contact reports and targeting markers for the atmo exchanger and the nearby cluster of buildings.

"Okay, people. We are still go, unless Fleet has any objections," Lieutenant Graff says. He outranks me by several pay grades, and he is in charge on the ground, but on the few drops I've done with him, he has usually sought my input on the overall tactical picture. Lieutenant Graff is unusually bright for a junior officer.

"Fleet is still go," I say. "Be a shame to waste all that ordnance just for a walk in the dirt. Let's go find us something to nuke."

Mission aborts are costly business. The Linebacker cruisers still have to clear a part of the minefield, which takes a hundred or so of very expensive ballistic interceptor missiles, but the rest of the fleet won't waste the even more expensive nuclear ordnance without precise targeting data. We would spend most of the missiles in the cruiser's magazines just to make a hole for the pickup drop ships. We don't abort drop-and-shop missions unless most of the team is dead and the survivors are bleeding from the eyeballs.

"Fabulous," the lieutenant replies. "Five more minutes for rest and water, and then let's go downtown."

With the new bug suits, avoiding the enemy is ludicrously easy. Our tactical computers do most of the brainwork. They scan the terrain, predict enemy movement vectors, and map out the safest and stealthiest route for us. We weave our way through settlement clusters of ever-increasing size and density as we get closer to the main Lanky city on this rock. My computer keeps count of all the individual Lankies we detect and projects the presence of several thousand of them in the area of the settlement. We're just five troopers, the only human beings on the entire planet, sneaking through what is alien suburbia like Jack tiptoeing through the giant's castle at the top of the beanstalk. Of course, we're not looking for treasure but for a target fix, so our warships can turn the giant's castle into rubble with a few dozen atomic warheads.

Back before I joined the service, I wanted nothing more than a chance to go into space. I had lots of romantic notions of the frontier life out on the colonies, but after half a decade of fighting on the settled planets, I've come to the conclusion that most of our terraformed real estate is hardly worth the effort. Two-thirds of our colony planets are just like New Wales—barren, rocky waste-lands that will take a few decades of backbreaking work to resemble even the least fertile patch of farmland back on our overtaxed Earth. To top off the futility, we're not even here to take the place back from the Lankies, because we can't. Instead, we're just going to ruin the place for both species, because showing the Lankies that we're willing to write off the planet altogether rather than letting them have it may discourage them from taking any more of our colonies. It's a desperate, insane, typically human strategy, but it's the only option we have right now other than rolling over. We've met our first competitors in the interstellar struggle for resources, and they are sweeping us out of the way without breaking a sweat.

The main Lanky settlement is fifty miles from the edge of the target zone. It's nestled into a curved valley between steep granite cliffs. We've climbed a tall hill to get a good look at the place, and my computer has already selected the optimal hypocenter and warhead yield to wipe the place out most efficiently.

"They're getting smart at this," Lieutenant Graff says. "I mean, look at where they put this town. Granite all around, like a bomb trench."

"Yeah, I noticed," I say. "Gotta score a bull's-eye right in the valley, or the blast wave'll go over their heads altogether. Pretty smart."

"Well, they're a spacefaring species," Sergeant Humphrey offers. "Dumb creatures don't build spaceships."

Lanky towns look a lot like underwater reefs. They don't build individual houses in tidy rows like we do. Instead, their housing clusters kind of flow together, like vast fields of interconnected starfish. The settlement covering the valley floor below us looks like it grew there naturally. In a way, I almost feel bad for showing the fleet how to destroy it, but then I recall the mission briefing, and remind myself that we lost twelve thousand colonists and a whole reinforced company of Spaceborne Infantry troops when the Lankies came and took the place away from us.

"All the markers are set," I tell the team. "Let's find a good spot to ride out the blast, and then I'll start the clock."

We study our topographical maps and settle on the reverse slope of a hill three miles to our rear, where the concentration of peripheral Lanky infrastructure is light. According to my computer, the distance will be sufficient to ride out anything less than a fifty-kiloton nuke going off in the valley below, and with the walls of the valley amplifying and reflecting the blast wave, a tenth of that yield will be enough to turn the place into a radioactive rubble field. The nearest atmo exchanger is the one next to our landing site, and that one is more than twenty miles away, more than enough to stay clear of the fifteen kilotons the fleet usually assigns to a Lanky terraformer.

"*Intrepid*, Combat Control," I send on my fleet C3 radio.

"Combat Control, *Intrepid*," the response comes, weakly. The signal is traveling a quarter million kilometers to the waiting *Intrepid*, and there's a lot of nasty weather between here and there.

"Flares are lit. We are heading for a safe spot now. Start the clock."

"Affirmative, Combat. We copy final targeting data. Good luck, and keep your heads down."

"Will do, *Intrepid*. Combat out."

I cut the transmission and switch to the team channel.

"Okay, people. Clock's ticking. Let's get to cover and put on those sunglasses."

The worst part of an atomic explosion is the blast. Unlike normal explosives, the pressure wave of a nuke goes back and forth, squeezing solid objects like a giant fist. There's the fireball, of course, which will vaporize anything in its radius at the moment of detonation, but that is a mathematical constant, easily predicted from the yield of the warhead, and short-lived. The shock wave radiates out from the hypocenter of the explosion, bouncing off mountainsides and flattening everything in its way, squeezing structures into piles of rubble and then blowing them apart. It's the most violent force we can generate at will, but it's unpredictable, indiscriminate, and easily deflected by a few hundred feet of hillside.

That doesn't mean, however, that riding out a nuclear blast behind a hill just five miles from its hypocenter is a fun event.

When the nuke goes off in the valley three miles away, my suit turns all sensor input off to keep me from going blind and deaf. I can still feel the force of the blast, however. The shock wave radiates out from the explosion at the speed of sound, shaking the ground beneath our position a few seconds later. Just like at the beginning of each mission, I always expect a miscalculation at the end, some fleet tech punching in the wrong number after a decimal point, and a ten-kiloton warhead dropping directly in front of my feet instead of the proper aiming point a few klicks away. In that case, I'd die just as quickly as if my pod hit a mine on the way in. I'd simply vaporize before the pain impulse from my suddenly superheated skin reached my already gone brain to inform me of my death.

My dad would get a kick out of the fact that my job involves fleet warships firing atomic warheads at a spot in my general vicinity. He'd say that I finally found a line of work that suits my intelligence level.

We wait out the explosion in our own private armor cocoons, with no sight or sound, until our suits have decided that it's safe to turn on the sensors again. When my vision returns, the first thing I see is the debris raining down all over the place, irradiated dust and dirt and fragments of Lanky buildings. Without my sensors, I'd be blind in this hurricane of dirt and rocks, and even with all the technology in my suit, I can only see a few hundred meters ahead.

Eventually, the fallout decreases in intensity, and we climb to the top of the hill to observe the target area. As we reach the crest, I see the mushroom cloud of the nuclear detonation rising into the sky just a few kilometers in front of us. It billows and roils like the skin of a living, breathing thing.

"I never get tired of seeing those," Sergeant Keller says.

"What are you, some sort of adrenaline junkie?" I reply.

"Not really," he says. "My folks got killed on Willoughby a few years back. Mom, Dad, both my sisters. I'd just joined up, or I woulda been there, too. Far as I'm concerned, every nuke dropped on these things is money well spent. Wish I could unzip this suit and piss on the ashes, too."

The valley is wiped clean. Just as I expected, the force of the surface blast has been amplified by the steep granite walls of the canyon, and the shock wave has bounced through the valley several times. Right in the center of the mile-wide rift, there's a new crater, a hundred feet deep. We can't see anything through our optical sensors—the billowing debris cloud making up the base of the atomic mushroom will linger for a while longer yet—but our radar, laser, and ultrasound imagers work in concert to give us a good idea of the devastation we visited on the Lanky settlement.

"*Whoo-ee,*" the lieutenant chirps. "Don't nobody pop off their helmet to scratch a nose. Radiation level is 'extra crispy.'"

With all the electromagnetic noise in the neighborhood of a nuclear explosion, voice comms with the fleet are out of the question. I do, however, have a redundant data link with the *Intrepid*, and I use it to send up another encrypted burst transmission, this one with a sensor-data upload and a status code for our team: mission accomplished, no casualties, ready for pickup. I repeat the transmission a few times on several sub-channels until my screen flashes with a reply code from Fleet.

"Taxi is on the way, friends and neighbors. ETA is two-five minutes."

"Fabulous," Lieutenant Graff says. "Another good day at the office."

The team sets up a perimeter while we're waiting for the arrival of the recovery ship. The security measure is largely ceremonial at this point because any Lanky alive within ten kilometers will be moving away from the unfriendly mushroom cloud, but training is hard to overcome.

I spend a few solitary minutes on top of the hill, surveying the destruction I've called down upon the unsuspecting Lankies in that settlement.

I'm not religious, and I doubt I ever was, despite my mom's efforts to get me into the embrace of the Mother Church back in Boston when I was young. I do know my Bible, however. I recall the Book of Exodus, the verses telling of the angel of death passing through Egypt at night and killing all the firstborn children, sparing only the houses with the mark of lamb's blood on the doorposts. In a way, I am an angel of death as well, but the power I serve is even more vengeful and merciless than the god of Israel. I'm the one who marks the doorposts in the night, and we pass over none.

CHAPTER 4

REASSIGNMENT

Time spent planetside: just a little under eight hours. Time spent in decontamination, medical post-mission checkup, debriefing, weapon return, and equipment inventory check: just a little under eight hours. When I finally fall into my bunk after grabbing some sandwiches from the NCO mess, I've been awake for close to twenty-four hours. Even without the no-go pills they offer to us after missions, I fall asleep almost instantly, dreaming dark dreams of ash and fire.

———

In the morning—or what passes for it on a windowless starship in deep space—I go over to the ops center to check on the results of our mission.

Our team wasn't the only one to go planetside. Two more teams hit the dirt just after we did, to locate and mark two smaller Lanky settlements on the same continent. Both teams dropped with a combat controller. The other missions were less eventful than ours, and both teams made it back to the *Intrepid* without any casualties. Overall, the mission was an unqualified success—fifteen troopers on the planet tagged three major settlements and twelve atmospheric processors for bombardment, and the fleet dropped fifteen warheads, totaling a quarter megaton of yield. The fleet uses the lowest yields needed to get the job done, to keep the eventual cleanup to a minimum if we ever get to reclaim the place. In terms of personnel and material, we came out way ahead. We spent about a hundred Linebacker missiles to make a hole in the minefield, and fifteen nukes to wipe out the ground targets. With that material outlay, we caused a few thousand Lanky casualties and wiped out 15 percent of their terraforming capacity. But when it comes down to scale, I'm not sure our efforts made much of a dent. The Lankies will grow new terraformers in less than a month in non-radiated alternate locations, and our Linebacker has fired a quarter of its missile stores for just three artillery strikes. It would take a task force ten times the size of ours to scrape all the Lanky structures off New Wales.

Almost five years of getting our omelets folded by the Lankies, and we've just now graduated to light harassment. Five more years of this asymmetrical exchange, and there'll be nothing left to defend.

We transition back into the solar system a day later.

"All hands, stand down from combat stations," the CIC announces on the overhead as we decelerate into the empty space between Earth and Mars where the Alcubierre chute from Theta Persei terminates. The ride back to Gateway will take another seven days.

I'm about to grab some more rack time in my berth when my PDP vibrates with a noncritical message alert. I pull the data pad out of my pocket and turn it on to find that my nominal department head, Major Gomez, is summoning me to his office "as soon as convenient."

"Staff Sergeant Grayson, reporting as ordered, sir," I say as I knock on the bulkhead beside Major Gomez's open office door.

The major looks up from the screen of his MilNet terminal and waves me into the room.

"Come in, Sergeant. Take a chair."

I can't exactly take one, since all the furniture is bolted to the deck, but I do as I'm told, and wedge myself into the space between the visitors' chair and the major's desk.

"What's the story, sir? My promotion to sergeant first class come through already?"

"You just made staff sergeant—what, nine months ago?"

"Eight," I say. I'd like to think that the major knows this fact off the top of his head, but he probably has my personnel file on the screen of his terminal right now, opened to the section with my promotion schedule on it.

"Well, then you get to wait another sixteen months in rank for the next chevron, just like all the other boys and girls on the promotion list. We just synced up with the Mars node. You have new deployment orders."

"I heard she's going in for a refit," I say, and glance at the computer printout the major has picked up from his desk. "What's it going to be this time?"

"You'll report to NACS *Manitoba* when we get back to Gateway."

"Huh," I say. "How about that?"

"How about what?"

"Oh, I've been on the *Manitoba* before. That was the ship that saved our asses back on Willoughby when we bumped into the Lankies for the first time."

"It's a small fleet," the major says, "and getting smaller all the time."

He hands me the printout. I glance at it to verify the name of the ship in the field marked "DUTY STATION: NACS *Manitoba* CV-1034."

"Trouble is, the *Manitoba*'s under way right now. They're coming back from Lambda Serpentis, and they're due back at Gateway fifteen days after we get there."

"Well, shit," I say.

With the *Intrepid* headed for the refit dock, I'll have to spend two weeks in the Transient Personnel Unit, the purgatory on Gateway where people spend their time with busywork while they wait for their assigned ships to return from deployment. I'd almost rather do combat drops against the Lankies instead.

"Why don't you burn up some of your leave, hop down to the old homestead?"

"I've used up all my leave for the year, Major," I say.

"It's January," the major says. "You signed up in a January, didn't you? Your next annual leave allowance comes available on February first. We won't be at Gateway until February third. You need some downtime between drops, just like the machines."

I was going to save up some leave time to spend with Halley, for whenever Fleet lets her take some time off, but then I remember that my girlfriend is stationed at Fleet School on Luna right now. Even if she can't take any leave, I'll at least be able to go up there on a personnel shuttle run to drop by for a visit.

"In that case, I guess I'll put in for leave, sir. If I have to spend another day in the TPU counting towels, I'll airlock myself."

I'd love to share the news with Halley face-to-face, but vidcomms have to be scheduled ahead of time to conserve bandwidth, and she's right in the middle of her workday at Fleet School. Instead, I dash off a message to her PDP across MilNet.

Do you have any downtime coming up? I'm coming back to Gateway for some enforced leave. I can come over to Luna for a visit if you want.

I send the message off to Halley and head back to my berth for some sleep.

When I wake up at the next watch change, I check the time on my PDP to find a new message on the screen.

>*I have a full roster during the day, but I'm free in the evenings, and I get Sundays off. Hope you didn't get any essential equipment damaged on that last mission of yours. Send me a message when you get to Gateway, and I'll pick up my berth a bit and tell the CQ to expect you. —H.*

I close the message and turn off my PDP with a smile.

Here we are, on the losing end of an interstellar war, with our world slowly falling apart around us, and I'm excited about going to see my girlfriend for a day or two. We may have gone from oar-powered galleys to half-kilometer starships in the span of two thousand years, but some things about humanity seem to be a universal constant, no matter the era.

It's almost impossible for soldiers to have contact with anyone on Earth because the military's network doesn't talk to the civilian world for security reasons. They do let us send messages to direct relatives, though. My mother has a mailbox on the system as a "Privileged Dependent/Relative," and she gets an hour or two of heavily restricted MilNet access per month. I know she treks down to the civil center every third Sunday of the month to collect her mail. Especially since during my first year of service, after Halley and I almost got killed on Willoughby when the Lankies made their first appearance, I started sending messages to my mother after a long dry spell of no communication.

At first I didn't have all that much to say to her, so I used the mail system as a journal of sorts. After a while, she started sending entries of her own, telling me what was happening in her world. Mom is actually a good writer—she's thoughtful and perceptive, and her updates let me see life in our old PRC in a whole new light. It's a shame that I had to go into space and light years away from home to find out that my mother actually has opinions worth reading.

I compose a message on my PDP and tell my mother that I have leave coming up, and that I finally want to stop by for a visit Earthside. When I send the message out to Mom's mailbox, I have the sudden urge to look for some sort of souvenir, something to bring back home for my mother as evidence of my activities, but when I look around in my berth, I realize that I don't own a single thing that wasn't issued to me by the military. Five years of sweating, fighting, and bleeding, with billions of kilometers traveled and over a hundred colony planets visited, and the only thing I have to show for it is a collection of colorful ribbons on my Class A smock and an abstract number in a bank account somewhere in a government computer. If I die in battle next month, there will be no evidence that I ever existed.

On the plus side, when everything you own can fit into a small locker, packing for a move is easy.

CHAPTER 5

—GOING DOWN TO EARTH—

I have two bags for clothing and equipment in my issued inventory. The larger one is a huge duffel bag with sewn-in polymer stiffeners. It's big enough to hold most of the contents of my shipboard locker. The duffel is mostly used to haul gear around between duty stations. Mine is worn and frayed after five years of skipping from post to post, ship to ship. The smaller one is called the furlough bag, and it's just big enough to hold enough clothes and a personal kit for a few days. The furlough bag is mostly used for going on leave, and mine is virtually pristine.

Since our trip back home takes a week, I have plenty of time to square away my gear and say my good-byes to my friends on the ship. By the time the *Intrepid* engages the docking collar at Gateway, I am ready to step off the ship and move on. I leave my heavy duffel on my rack for transfer pickup, and take my furlough bag to start my two weeks of leave. Against all my pessimistic expectations, CIC does not announce combat stations, and nobody whistles me back when I step past the security detachment at the main docking hatch to leave the ship for good. As I walk out into the hallway of Gateway Station beyond, I pat the last bulkhead frame of the ship in passing.

Farewell, NACS Intrepid CV-1941. May you die of old age in the decommissioning docks thirty years from now.

Gateway Station is the main hub for all military traffic from and to Earth and Luna. It's an orbital base and spaceport rolled into one huge, hulking structure, perpetually suspended in high orbit. There's a constant stream of people and material passing through this station, and it has been in need of an overhaul since well before I even joined the service.

It's a long hike from the outer ring where the carriers dock to the main concourse where I can claim a seat on a Luna-bound personnel shuttle. I walk through the familiar narrow corridors toward the central part of the station, swimming with the crowds of people going in the same direction. Whenever a carrier docks, hundreds of people end up clogging the same narrow intersections on Gateway at the same time, and it takes forever to get anywhere.

The main concourse is as crowded as I've ever seen it. There are fleet crews and Spaceborne Infantry troopers everywhere, most of them in the Class A smocks that are required wear for transfers to a new duty station. I take a quick visual survey and notice that most of them are junior enlisted personnel, likely fresh out of Basic and heading for Fleet School or SI's Infantry School. Many of them are wearing the same unsure expression I undoubtedly had on my face when I stepped off the shuttle and onto Gateway for the first time. As I pass through the crowd, I notice some of the new privates glancing at the modest collection of ribbons and badges on my Fleet Arm Class A smock and the scarlet beret on my head.

I elbow my way to the main row of Transportation Coordinator booths on the main concourse, where I stand in line behind half a platoon of SI troopers. When my turn comes, I step up to the booth and hand over my military ID for the desk specialist to scan.

"Where to, Sergeant?" the specialist asks, his gaze flicking from the screen of his terminal to the scarlet beret I have now stuffed underneath the left shoulder board of my uniform. The color is an ancient privilege—combat controllers are one of the few occupational specialties allowed a beret color other than the standard Homeworld Defense green, Fleet Arm black, or Spaceborne Infantry maroon. It's a hard-earned badge of office, but it does tend to make one stick out in a crowd.

"I need to hop up to Luna for a few days," I say. "Visiting an old friend in Fleet School."

"Shuttles to Luna are fleet priority until Saturday," the specialist says, not the least bit apologetic. "You want to go up there before then, you need to have valid orders for Luna."

"Well, crap. That's five days from now. Don't make me waste half my leave in the TPU."

"Sorry, Sarge. You can see that the place is popping at the rivets right now. All three recruit depots just let out a new batch of trainees this morning, and we're hauling them up to Luna as fast as we can. Come back Saturday and I'll get you on a shuttle, but right now every seat is fleet priority."

"Can you get me down Earthside at least?"

"Down to Earth? Sure. I have twenty empty shuttles going back every hour to haul up new people. Where do you want to go?"

"Closest spaceport to Greater Boston, I guess."

"That would be Cape Cod HDAS. Hang on, let me check what's going down that way."

He taps the screen of his terminal a few times while I swallow my disappointment at the delay of my reunion with Halley. I had planned to go up to Luna before visiting Mom, but now it looks like I have to flip my schedule around if I don't want to be stuck here on Gateway for a few days.

"Ah, here we go. Shuttle FA-2992, 1700 hours. Check with the loadmaster at lock Alpha Three-Niner."

"Thank you, Specialist."

I step away from the counter and shoulder my furlough bag again. It's 1540 hours right now, which gives me over an hour to fight my way across Gateway to personnel lock A39. Mom's scheduled MilNet access day is not until the weekend, and I have no other way to get in touch with her to let her know I'm coming down to Earth early, but I have her new address, and I can use all transportation networks free of charge. It's been five years since I last set foot on my homeworld, but I very much doubt that it has changed so much that I can't find my way around without an escort.

Between the time I step off the shuttle at Cape Cod HDAS and the time I arrive at South Station in the middle of the Boston metroplex, I get stopped four times by various military police patrols. Every time, they scan my ID to verify my "ON LEAVE" status. The military presence is dense, even in the civvie section of the transit system. There are armed MPs at just about every entrance and intersection, and in every train along the way. Five years ago, the MP venturing out into the civilian world carried electric crowd-control sticks and nanoflex handcuffs. Now they carry those *and* sidearms and submachine guns besides. The magazines of the submachine guns are made of translucent plastic, and the rounds stacked up inside of them are standard infantry issue: armor-piercing, dual-purpose antipersonnel rounds.

"You guys expecting Chinese infiltrators?" I ask of the leader of the fourth patrol to stop me for my ID, and nod at the PDW slung across his chest. He's a stocky staff sergeant whose buzz cut is turning gray at the roots. He opens his mouth for what I can already tell will be a humor-free reply. Then he looks at the unit flashes on the upper arms of my smock, and exchanges a look with the corporal next to him.

"Fleet Arm, huh? Been a while since you've been Earthside?"

"Five years," I say.

"Place ain't what it was five years ago," he says. "Not even close. Where you headed, anyway?"

"PRC Boston-Seven. Going to visit my mother."

"You're going to walk into a PRC in a Class A uniform?"

"Don't have any civvie threads left. Why?"

"Oh, boy." He exchanges another look with his corporal and scratches the back of his head, pushing up his green HD beret.

"Tell you what, Sergeant. You're just twenty minutes from the Cape. If I were you, I'd head back to the base and see if they can dig you up some civvie clothes. Uniforms aren't too popular in the PRC right now."

"I grew up in there. I know where the bad spots are. I'll be fine."

He snorts a humorless little chuckle.

"It's all bad spots now."

Mom's new address is in a pretty good spot, as far as desirable real estate in a tenement cluster goes. She's only two blocks away from the civil administration center, which is surrounded by the safest and cleanest section of the neighborhood.

I've been through this station many times when I still lived here, but when I walk up to the surface from the underground platform, my first impulse is to turn around and get back on the train, because it feels like I've gotten off at the wrong stop. The transit station looks completely unfamiliar to me. The Columbia Station I knew was a dingy 150-year-old building with water spots on the walls and paint flaking off exposed ceiling beams. The Columbia Station I step into is a new structure, stark-naked concrete everywhere. There are no water stains or flaking paint, but somehow the old, dilapidated structure looked more inviting. The new station looks like a concrete bunker, and that impression is enhanced by the scores of armed police I see all over the place. When I left this place five years ago, city cops didn't even wear helmets; now their outfits aren't much less advanced than the battle armor I wore in the Territorial Army. The cops are standing around in clusters of three and four in the entrance hall of the station, not bothering to move for the civilians that are streaming around them. I notice that the people walking past the cops keep a healthy distance. As I walk past a group of police officers, one of them glances at my uniform and gives me a semicourteous nod. I take the opportunity to stop for some information.

"Whatever happened to the old station?"

"Burned to the ground two years ago," the cop who nodded at me replies. "They torched it. Killed twenty-six officers that night, too."

"Welfare riot?"

"No, they were just *peacefully assembling*," the cop says, with ironic weight on the last two words. "I'm sure those flaming bottles were just an accident."

"Sorry," I say. "Haven't been able to stay on top of things up there. They don't let us watch the Networks much, and the news is always a month out of date at least."

"They censor all the juicy bits anyway. What are you doing here on the ground? Come to Boston for a vacation or something? Space not dangerous enough?"

The other cops laugh. They're all in a weird mood—most of them haven't stopped fingering the handles of their crowd-control zappers since I spotted their group, and I decide to be jovial.

"No, just visiting my mom. Got two weeks of leave, but I don't think I'm going to spend it all down here."

"I don't blame ya. Well, take care, and stay off the street at night. Nothing good ever happens out there after sunset."

"Will do. You guys be safe."

I adjust the strap of my furlough bag, give the group a friendly nod, and walk on.

"Sergeant," the first cop calls after me, and I turn around again.

"Yes, sir?"

He motions for me to come back, and I return to the group. When I'm standing in front of him again, he lowers his voice.

"How's it going up there? How are we doing?"

I look at the anxious expressions on the faces of the cops gathered around me. I want to say something upbeat, give them some inside scoop that will cheer them up a bit, but I know how badly we are getting mauled, and I can't bring myself to make up a cheery pep talk.

"Well," I say, and shrug. "We're trying to hold the line, you know? Just digging in, and holding the line."

I can sense their disappointment, but I can tell that they're happier with honesty than obvious *rah-rah* bullshit.

"Yeah, I hear you," the first cop says. "It's the same down here."

The streets outside are littered with garbage. In front of the transit station, I see the scorched husk of a hydrobus, pushed against the curb and stripped of everything usable. Near the station, there's a little concrete booth where they used to hold the monthly commissary voucher lottery, but the polyplast windows are shattered, and there are long streak marks of soot on the concrete above them. It looks like nobody has bothered to pick up garbage or issue vouchers here in a good while. The sun has already started to set, and the shadows of the gray and worn-down buildings are turning the street in front of me into a maze of dark and dangerous spots. I walk the two blocks to Mom's new tenement building as quickly as I can without breaking into a run. Soon, darkness will fall, and then the rats will come out in packs.

Mom has moved up a little in the world since I moved out. Her new apartment is on the second floor of a tenement building that looks roughly half as old and twice as clean as the one where we both lived for over ten years. I don't have an ID card to scan at the front door's access panel, so I ring the buzzer labeled with her name: GRAYSON P.

The access panel has a little vid screen, for the mutual verification of identities. The one in our old building was broken or coated with crap most of the time, but this one is working fine. When Mom answers the buzzer, her face shows up on the little armored display, and even on the low-resolution screen, I can tell that she has aged ten years in the last five. She squints at the camera mounted above her own little screen, and her eyes widen in surprise.

"Andrew!"

"Hi, Mom. I got in early. Let me in before they mug me out here."

Mom presses the button for the door opener in lieu of a reply, and I step into the building, mindful to check over my shoulder for anyone trying to follow me in to rob me in privacy.

I take the stairs instead of the elevator. Our old staircase smelled like stale vomit and fresh piss most of the time, but this one only smells like floor cleaner.

When I reach the second floor, Mom is waiting in front of the elevator door. She turns around when she hears the staircase door, and I give her a little wave.

"You know I always take the stairs, Mom."

"Andrew!" she says again. Then she rushes to meet me and gives me a fierce hug. "What are you doing here already? You said you were going to be here on Monday. I haven't even cleaned the place up yet."

"Don't worry about it, Mom. I had something on my schedule that fell through."

"Well, you shouldn't have walked here. It's too dangerous. I would have met you over at the civil center."

She stops her attempt to crush my rib cage and holds me at arm's length to examine my uniform.

"That looks pretty good on you. My, you've filled out, haven't you?"

"Lots of running and lifting. We don't exactly sit around all day."

My mother seems smaller than I remember her, more slight and insubstantial. She has lost the extra few pounds she had been carrying around for years, but instead of looking fit and lean, she just looks thin and used up. Her mousy brown hair has many gray streaks, and there are deep wrinkles at the corners of her eyes and mouth that weren't there before.

"You got a nicer unit, I see."

"They had me move out of our two-bedroom when you left for the military. They bumped me up a little, though. The old neighborhood is falling apart, you know. Every time there's a riot, they turn off the power and stop giving out rations—every single time. I got so sick of sitting in the dark without food for days on end."

She pats the chest of my uniform tunic and runs a finger across the ribbons above the breast pocket.

"I'm so glad you don't have to worry about any of this anymore, Andrew. All people ever do around here is watch the Networks and bitch about all the stuff they don't have. Now come inside, will you? Just don't mind the mess. I gave the help a month off."

Mom's new apartment is neater and more modern than the old one, but less than half the size. It's still palatial compared to my berth on the *Intrepid*. There's a living room with kitchen corner, a separate bedroom, a bathroom, and a large hallway closet. Not even the commanding officer of a supercarrier has this much personal space. I look through the rooms briefly, and see that Mom has put up a little collage of pictures on her living room wall, mostly low-res prints of photographs I sent her through MilNet. There's even a shot of me and Halley, taken two years ago on our joint leave back on the fleet rec facility on Mars.

"I don't have much in the way of food," Mom says from the kitchen nook, where she's filling two glasses of water from the tap. "They cut the rations by another thousand calories two months ago. Now I can't even put away anything for the riot outages. Not that I can heat anything when they cut the power."

"Don't worry about food, Mom. They said I can bring a dependent to the government canteens. We can take the train up to South Station. Their canteen's pretty decent."

"You think? Oh, that would be fabulous."

"Yeah. Shouldn't be a problem. Want to go right now? I'm sure they're serving dinner. The day shift is about to clock out. It'll be pretty crowded, though."

Mom looks out of the windows to gauge the level of remaining daylight.

"Oh, let's go, then," she says after a brief moment of contemplation. "Before it gets too dark out there."

After five years of hopping around from colony to colony, wide-open skies and empty landscapes, being back in the concrete warrens of my old hometown feels claustrophobically confining. There's a sense of danger and casual malevolence to the dirty cookie-cutter architecture of the Public Residence towers and the unkempt streets and sidewalks now. Outside, the shadows have grown long.

Mom and I step out of her residence tower, and I check my surroundings the way I used to do back when I grew up here. There's a group of kids sitting on the curb in front of the residence tower across the street, swigging some orange concoction from a clear jug they are passing around. There's a demarcation in age and demeanor when the young hood rats graduate from hit-and-run vandalism and blowing off steam to actively prowling for stuff to steal and people to harm, and from what I know about my youth days here, these kids are right on that cusp.

For a moment, I consider heading back into the residence tower behind me. Then I think about the fact that I've spent the last five years shooting at people and fighting Lankies in much worse spots than PRC Boston-7. The public-transit station is only two blocks away, and there are cops nearby.

"Let's go," I tell Mom, and steer her up the road. I glance over to the group of kids as we walk off briskly, and I can see one of them looking over to us and staring.

"You don't have your gun on you, do you?" I ask Mom.

"Of course not. It's in the kitchen, on top of the food warmer."

I glance over my shoulder and see that the group of apprentice hoodlums is now looking over at us, and there's an animated but hushed discussion going on between them.

"Walk faster," I tell Mom.

We're halfway down the block before I hear them trotting up behind us.

"Yo, soldier boy, wait up, man."

Mom looks around and opens her mouth to reply, but I shake my head.

"Keep walking," I tell her. They're younger and scrawnier than I am, but there's five of them and just one of me, and I'm unarmed.

A block and a half away, the public-transit station's bunker-like new architecture looks more inviting than it did earlier. There are cops milling around in front of a hydrocruiser by the entrance, but they're out of shouting range. We pass the mouth of an alley to our left, and as we do, the five hood rats rush up on the sidewalk next to us and nudge us into the alley, out of the view of the few people who are walking around on the street this evening.

"Got no dope or vouchers," I say to them, much more calmly than I feel. "Just going down to the station with my mother. Want to let us pass?"

"The fuck are you doing, coming down here in that?" one of them says, and points to my uniform jacket. He's a lean kid—all of them are—and his teeth are in bad shape even for a PRC resident.

"Don't have any other clothes right now," I tell him. I'm trying to gauge the right moment to go from appeasement to sudden violence as he steps closer. He's half a head shorter than I am, but he has four of his friends behind him. I've been killing SRA marines and Lankies for five years now, but out here, in my going-out dress blues and without any weapons, I'm vulnerable. I find that I don't like the feeling of powerlessness at all.

"What's in the bag?" he asks my mom. She takes it off her shoulder with a resigned expression, as if she has gone through this particular routine many times.

"Nothing you want," she says. She hands it to him, and he takes it as casually as if he's helping her out with her groceries. His four friends have fanned out in a semicircle around us. I don't see any weapons yet, and I resolve to deck the first of these kids who produces one.

The kid with the bad teeth opens Mom's bag and pulls out a rolled-up rain cloak. He drops it on the ground, rummages around in the bag, and makes a disappointed noise when nothing in there is to his liking.

"Hey," I say, anger welling up inside me. He looks up at me. There's neither concern nor curiosity in that gaze, just boredom and dull hostility.

"You may want to pick that up and hand it back," I say.

"Oh?" He looks at his friends and smiles thinly. The way they are standing, I can probably take down two or three of them if they don't pull out any weapons.

"Let's say I really don't wanna," he says. Then he lifts the bottom of his ratty shirt and flashes the taped-up handle of what looks like a homemade pistol.

"Don't," Mom says behind me. "Just don't."

There's a popping sound, and the kid with the bad teeth jerks convulsively. Then he drops to the ground. Behind him, on the sidewalk by the mouth of the alley, stand three cops in full riot gear. One of them has his stun stick aimed over his forearm. The other four hoodlum apprentices turn around. Two of them freeze in place. The other two take off down the alley like panicked rabbits.

"Dumbasses," one of the cops says, and takes off after them, barreling past us in his riot armor like a fleet frigate at full speed. The other two cops walk into the alley, stun sticks aimed at the hood rats who just tried to rob us. In front of me, the kid who took Mom's bag lies twitching, the electrical probes from the cop's stun stick right between his shoulder blades.

"Oh, look," the cop says. "Gun."

The homemade pistol has slipped out of the kid's waistband and onto the dirty asphalt. In a very casual motion, the other cop aims his stun stick as well, and shoots another pair of probes into the back of the prone hood rat, who convulses again.

"Look, he's down already," Mom says.

"He's lucky I didn't shoot him in the back of the head," the cop says. Their appearance has saved us from a mugging or worse, but for some reason I feel more of a threat from their casual use of force than I did from the blustering of the hood rats.

The cop stoops down and picks up Mom's bag. Then he hands it to her.

"Thank you," she says.

He turns to the other two kids, who are standing very still with their arms raised and their hands on their heads.

"That guy's in the *fleet,*" the cop says, and nods in my direction. "He keeps those giant ugly aliens from coming here and gassing us all to death. He's worth a *hundred* of you shit-eating wastes of calories."

They don't respond, just stare ahead, as if they don't want to give the cop the slightest excuse to use that stun stick on them. They're shitheads, but not terribly dangerous. The cops standing around us, on the other hand, radiate danger.

"Now get out of here," the first cop says to me. He raises the visor of his riot helmet, and I see that he's the sergeant I talked to earlier, back in the transit station. "Told you nothing good ever happens here after sunset. You're lucky we spotted you."

"Thanks," I say, but I'm not sure that I mean it.

"Let's go," Mom says, and we walk out of the alley quickly, as much to leave the cops behind as the kids who just tried to casually mug us.

From the looks of it, I'm not the only government employee to bring a dependent to dinner. The government canteen at South Station is packed from wall to wall, but only half the people in the room are wearing uniforms or government ID badges around their necks. Despite the crowd, the food issue counter works almost as efficiently as an enlisted mess at watch change on a warship. Mom and I only stand in line for five minutes before we both take possession of our food trays. There's no buffet option like in the service—everyone gets the same tray, with the same items, in equal amounts.

The food is lousy. It's merely a slightly more flavorful version of the processed soy crap in the BNA rations. Compared to military food, it's barely edible, but Mom tucks in like it's a gourmet meal. I eat a little bit to give my stomach something to work with, and then mostly push the food around on my tray while I watch Mom eat.

"Do they feed you like this every day?" she asks between two big bites of soy chicken. I haven't eaten a piece of processed soy since I joined the service, but I don't want to remind my mom that we get to eat actual food while she has to live on this recycled and reconstituted garbage.

"Yeah, kind of," I tell her. "We burn a few more calories than civvies, 'cause we run around with guns and armor a lot."

"Last time I got a commissary voucher, beef was up to five hundred dollars a pound," she says. "That was over a year ago. God knows what it's up to by now."

"I saw what they did to the voucher booth. So what, they just don't issue vouchers anymore?"

"They don't do anything anymore," Mom says. "Trash only gets picked up once or twice a month now, and they skip it altogether when there's a riot. You hardly ever see a cop anymore, either, *except* when there is a riot. Then they show up by the hundreds. It's like war every month. People get shot on the street corner, and nobody picks up the bodies for days."

"They don't do safety sweeps in the tenements anymore?"

Mom shakes her head.

"They're afraid to walk the streets. It was pretty bad for a while with the hoodlums, but it's a little better now. You can buy security escorts now, you know. A thousand calories for a day, you get a guy with a gun to walk around with you. The cops don't care anymore."

"Jeez, Mom. Who's keeping the peace now?"

"Nobody," she shrugs. "Everybody, I guess. Everyone's got guns now. Hell, I got one. I keep it in the apartment, though. It's not like I get to go out much anyway, except over to the civil center to read your mail, and they still have gun detectors at the door there."

When I still lived at home with her, Mom hated guns. I suspect that if she had ever caught me with one, she would have turned me over to the public-housing police herself. If Mom is keeping a gun in the apartment in violation of the law and her old philosophies, things must have become very grim indeed.

We finish our meal and clear the table for the people waiting in line for seats. As we walk out past the two security guards checking ID cards at the door, Mom looks around in wonder.

"You know, I've never been up here. Above the public platforms, I mean."

"Really?"

"Really. I've lived here for almost twenty years now, and I've never had a reason to come up these stairs."

"You've never been out of Boston, Mom?"

"Oh, sure," she shrugs. "When I first met your dad. Before you. We went down to the Cape for the day a few times. He took me to New Hampshire once. But we took the hydrobus back then. The one that used to leave from North Station."

I turn around and go back to the security guards at the entrance to the canteen.

"Excuse me, sir," I address the higher-ranking one, a thin, sour-faced guy with a sergeant's shoulder boards. I outrank him, but this is his turf, and he wields more clout down here than I do. The HD sergeant raises an eyebrow.

"What can I do for you, Staff Sergeant?"

"I've been off-world for too long," I say. "Could you tell me what the rules are these days for taking relatives with you on private transportation?"

"That your mom over there?"

"Yeah, she is."

"Dependents can ride along for free, up to five thousand kilometers per year. She's gotta be on your card, though."

"What does that mean?"

"That means," he says, in a tone that reminds me of a drill sergeant explaining something obvious to a slow recruit, "that she has to be in the files as your official dependent. No pals, no girlfriends, no other relatives."

"She's on my card," I say. "Thank you, Sergeant."

I walk back to where Mom is standing.

"What was that all about?" she asks.

"You want to go up one more level to where the private trains are? If you're not in a hurry to go back home, we can go for a little ride."

CHAPTER 6

–LIBERTY FALLS, VERMONT–

Mom studies the train schedule like someone perusing the menu at a fine restaurant. Up here, where the private rail network trains are, the security is even tighter than down in the public station. The public trains are free, but the private regional trains cost real money, and there's no way for a welfare rat to sneak a ride on one. There are guards checking boarding slips and ID cards, and the private security goons look even more cantankerous than the public transit cops and HD troopers in the station below.

The Regional Express station is the only part of South Station that gets to see any sunlight. It's perched on top of the many subterranean layers of the public-transportation system. Above ground, everything is a little cleaner, brighter, and less noisy than below. Technically speaking, the regional maglev network is public as well, since it's subsidized by the Commonwealth, but the trains bear private corporate logos. Riding the maglev out of the city costs money—real currency, not public-assistance credits on government cash cards. Back when I was a civilian, I never really thought about the reason for that, but now I know it's a way to keep the welfare rats from spilling out of their habitat.

"Where should we go?" Mom asks. The options before her seem to have stunned her into paralysis. The regional maglevs go all the way up to Halifax and down to the old capital, DC, and there are dozens of ways for paying customers to get out of Boston.

"What do you want to see, Mom? Mountains, ocean, big metroplex, or what? Sky's the limit."

"No big city," Mom says. "Somewhere where they have some trees left, maybe."

She studies the pictogram for the different regional routes again for a few moments, and jabs the screen with her finger.

"There. Let's go there."

She points at one of the northern stops of the Green Mountain transit line—a place called Liberty Falls, Vermont, right between Montpelier and Burlington.

"You sure?"

"Yeah. I'd like to go see some mountains and trees."

"Okay, then. I'll get us some tickets."

The departure hall is palatial compared to the cramped and perennially crowded underground platforms of the public system. The ceiling up here is thirty feet high, and there are tall picture windows lining the walls that are obvious projections, because they show a lightly clouded blue sky above Boston, instead of the shroud of smog and dirt that has been covering the city for as long as I've been alive. The back wall of the departure hall is taken up by a huge display listing destinations, departure times, and platform numbers. Underneath the display, there are rows of automatic ticket dispensers and a pair of information booths. We walk over to the info booths, and I speak our destination.

"Liberty Falls, Vermont."

A moment later, the screen in front of me displays an itinerary and a direction diagram. A pleasant female voice speaks out the text on the screen.

"I suggest the Green Mountain Line to Burlington, with stops in Nashua, the Concord-Manchester metroplex, Hartland-Lebanon, and Montpelier."

I select the "ACCEPT/PAY" button on the screen. The display flips to show me a variety of payment options: "CREDIT CARD," "GOVERNMENT ID," "FOREIGN CREDIT (EUROS, ANZAC DOLLARS, AND NEW YEN ONLY)," "OTHER." I choose the second option, scan my military ID, and enter "2" in the field labeled "NUMBER OF PASSENGERS." The terminal spits out our plastic boarding slips, and I snatch them out of the dispenser and hand them to Mom.

"Courtesy of the Commonwealth. Tomorrow morning, you'll be breathing some clean mountain air."

The maglev system was built long before I was born, back when the Commonwealth didn't yet spend every available dollar on colonization. That makes the newest trains in the system forty or fifty years old, but they're in much better shape than the ones used in the public system. The maglev train cars have compartments, each with seating for six or eight people, and there's a small restroom at the head of each car. The public trains smell of burnt rubber and piss, the seats are nearly indestructible polymer shells, and their ride is bumpy enough to shake loose ceramic tooth fillings. The maglev train cars merely smell like aging fabric, the seats are comfortably upholstered with antiseptic nanofiber, and the ride is so smooth that I can barely tell we're in motion. We claim one of the empty compartments, and have it entirely to ourselves.

The Boston metroplex stretches all the way to the New Hampshire border. For the first thirty minutes of our ride, all we see outside is a dark landscape of concrete, row after row of tenement high-rises, broken up in regular intervals by the dimly lit intersections of the planned street grids, like clearings in an urban forest. The maglev rides on titanium arches that rise thirty feet above the forest of concrete. As we get closer to the outer suburbs and away from the tenements, the buildings get smaller, and the streets wider and better lit. It's not until we've crossed the state line into New Hampshire that we see the first large patches of green between all the urban sprawl.

"So many people," Mom muses. She has been studying the world outside of the double-layer polycarb windows since we left South Station. "Think about all the people living on this patch of ground."

"Sixty million," I say. "And that's just Boston and Providence. New York's up to over a hundred million now."

"Oh, I know the numbers," Mom says. "It's just one thing to read them on a screen, and another to actually see it with your own eyes."

"The whole Eastern Seaboard is like that," I say. "One metroplex blending into another. We got too many for little old Earth. The colonies are mostly empty, still."

"What's it like up there? Do you ever get to spend any time on those planets?"

"I've been to most of ours, and a lot of the Chinese and Russian ones. It's different. Wild, barren. Harsh places to live."

"I used to put our names in the hat for the colony lottery every year, you know," Mom says. "Until they shut it down. I can't believe they stopped the colony flights."

"We've lost more than half of our colonies to the Lankies, Mom. I think Team Red didn't fare much better. You don't want to be a colonist right now. Those things show up in orbit, everyone on the planet is dead four weeks later. You can't fight back, and running and hiding won't do you any good. They just gas every city, like a bunch of rat nests."

"Maybe we deserve it," Mom says darkly, and looks out of the window again, where the city of Nashua is sleeping a restless slumber. Even little Nashua, with its million and a half residents, has a sizable public tenement on its outskirts, unmistakable clusters of tall, starkly utilitarian residence towers bunched together on the shittiest real estate in town. "Maybe we should all be gassed like rats. I mean, look at what we've done to this world, and now we're spreading out to others."

"Everyone wants to live, Mom. They're just a little better at spreading out than we are."

"You think they'll come all the way to Earth?" she asks. Her expression tells me that she's not particularly afraid of that prospect.

I consider her question, and shrug. "Probably. I don't see why they'd stop, now that they're on a roll."

I gaze back out at nocturnal Nashua, one ant hive among tens of thousands on this continent alone, stuffed to capacity with human beings who are just barely clawing out an existence. I imagine a Lanky seed ship in the sky above, raining down pods of nerve gas onto the city streets below. The Lanky nerve gas acts so quickly that people fall over dead just a few seconds after inhaling a milligram or two, or getting just a microscopic droplet onto their skin.

I want to disagree with Mom, but part of me concurs that a Lanky invasion of Earth would be a mercy killing of our species. We've spent most of our history trying to exterminate each other anyway. This way, we'll at least have some dispassionate outside referee settling all of humanity's old scores permanently. No more generational feuds, no more ancient grudges, no more pointless revenge carried out against people who inherited some old guilt from their great-grandparents. We will all just go down the path on which we've sent so many species ourselves, and we'll just be a note in someone else's xenobiology textbooks, listed under the header "EXTINCT."

It's not the first time I've wondered if there's a point to our struggle against the Lankies, but as we glide through the night above the sea of barely fed, discontented humans in the city spread out underneath the maglev track, I conclude for the first time that there probably isn't.

We both fall asleep in our comfortable seats before the maglev reaches the Concord-Manchester station. When I wake up again, the world outside is a tapestry of green and white, and the sun is just peeking over the horizon. I check the moving map display on the wall of the compartment. It's almost seven o'clock in the morning, and we're on the last leg of our trip, fifteen minutes from the stop at Liberty Falls. We've slept through Concord-Manchester, Hartland-Lebanon, and Montpelier.

Mom is still asleep in the seat across from mine. Her head is on the padded headrest, and she looks peaceful and relaxed. There are more lines in her face than I remembered, and her hair has gray streaks in it now. Mom's only forty-five years old, but she looks like she's pushing sixty. When you have access to private hospitals, your life expectancy is over a hundred years, but welfare rats tend to die at younger ages, due to the cumulative effects of bad nutrition and the stress of day-to-day life in the tenements. The public hospitals have long waiting lists for anything more serious than a nosebleed. When Dad died of cancer, they just gave him a bunch of DNA-coded painkillers to make his transition to recyclable biomass easier.

I reach out and touch Mom on the shoulder to wake her up. She opens her eyes slowly, and looks around.

"Are we there already?"

"Almost, Mom. Fifteen minutes to go. Check it out—it's snowing out there."

I point out of the window, where the wind is making bands of fine snowflakes dance among the trees as we're passing through rural Vermont at two hundred kilometers per hour. The train could cover the distance from Boston to the fringes of Vermont in less than two hours at full throttle, but they have to go slowly through all the urban centers, and New England is all urban centers until you're right on the edges.

"Well, will you look at that. I haven't seen this much snow on the ground in ages."

The snow that falls in a PRC is already dirty before it hits the ground because of the perpetual layer of smog and dirt in the atmosphere above the big cities. Out here, the snow looks pure and white—clean, untouched, inviting. The world outside looks like a snapshot from a long-forgotten past: untidy rows of trees covered in white, and only the very occasional wireless power transmitter spoiling the scenery.

"Beautiful," Mom says. "Like an old oil painting. I had almost forgotten that the world isn't all covered in concrete."

"Most of them aren't, up there," I reply.

Liberty Falls is so small that we pass through the outskirts only a few minutes before we reach the station. There are no tenement high-rises here, just neat rows of single-family houses lined up on tidy streets.

The train glides into a clean and well-lit station that has a transparent roof. I see patches of snow on the polycarb dome above us, and a blue and gray sky beyond. The sun is mostly above the horizon now, and the clouds are painted from below in a pale shade of pink.

The transit station is an airy structure, widely spaced support struts with large windows in between. There is plenty of daylight, and unlike the windows at South Station, these aren't projection screens that give people the illusion of a clear sky outside. We step out of the train and into the station. There's no heavy security out there, just a bored-looking civilian guard loitering on the platform and a pair of smartly dressed city cops standing at the entrance to the station. They give us friendly nods as we walk past them into the street.

When we walk out of the station, the air is so clean and cold that it hurts my nose. I had only been back in Boston for a few hours, but my nose had gotten used to the bad air in the metroplex again. Out here, it smells as clean as it did out at NACRD Orem, my Basic Training depot in the middle of the Utah desert.

Liberty Falls is a mix of old and new architecture. Out on the street in front of the transit station, the buildings are a blend of brick houses from the last century or the one before it, and modern poly-carb-and-alloy structures. The older houses are well kept, renovated and restored, not crumbling and covered in spray paint like their counterparts in Boston. There's a snow-covered green in front of the station, and it has real trees on it. The streets here are lined with little stores—books, groceries, auto-serve restaurants—and few of those stores have a security guard at the door. There's no litter on the sidewalks, and the people walking around look better fed than the government employees at South Station. We're only two hundred miles from the Boston metroplex, but this place feels like a different world altogether. Now that we're out here, I'm once again glad to be wearing my fleet uniform, because my old civvie clothes would have me sticking out like a dirty rag on a dinner table.

Mom wanders over to the little green in front of the transit station and walks across it, ignoring the cleared sidewalks that line the green. The snow on the green is knee-deep in spots, but Mom plows through it, undeterred. I join her as she makes her way across the green, leaving a narrow rut in the clean snow. When we reach the other side of the green, she stops and leans against one of the trees that stand around the edges of the green like an orderly row of fence posts. She bends over, scoops up a handful of the pristine snow, and holds it out for me to see.

"I haven't seen snow this clean since before you were born."

She raises her hand to her mouth and touches the snow on her palm with the tip of her tongue.

"Tastes like nothing," she proclaims.

"Colony planet I was on last year, their planetary winter lasts three years," I say. "All rocks and dust in the summer years, and forty below in the winter. Lousiest place I've ever been. Your suit malfunctioned, you'd be dead of exposure in a few hours."

"We went up to central New Hampshire the year before you were born," Mom says, as if she hasn't heard my little anecdote. "We went up Mount Washington. There was snow up there, in early October. Most beautiful place I've ever been. No cities for miles, just mountains and trees as far as the eye could see. Just this big blanket of orange and red and green, stretching all the way to the horizon."

"Was that your honeymoon with Dad?"

"Uh-huh. The month after, we moved out to PRC Seven, because they had a two-bedroom unit available. And then everything started turning to crap."

Mom has changed a lot since I left. I'm not used to her introspective side. Before I joined the military, I was convinced that my mother was just like all the other welfare drones in our PRC— glued to the Network screen all day and not giving much of a shit about anything but show schedules and ration day. Part of the reason why I didn't try harder to get some leave time down on Earth was my conviction that my mother wouldn't have anything interesting to say anyway.

"Did I mess things up for you? I mean, when I was born?"

She looks at me and shakes her head with a sad little smile.

"Oh, no, honey. I messed things up for myself. Your father helped a lot, too. But it was mostly me. Marrying your dad was just the wrong thing to do. But I was nineteen, and I didn't know anything about anything."

She drops her handful of snow and wipes her wet hand on the outside of her jacket. It's cold out here in northern Vermont, and

Mom's jacket doesn't look like it's adequate for the climate, but she doesn't seem to mind the cold.

"He said he was going to get into the service. Said he'd muster out after five or ten years, and we could take the money and buy a little house in the outskirts, away from the tenements. 'Just a few years,' he said."

She shakes her head with a chuckle that doesn't sound the least bit amused.

"Instead, he came home after two years. Kicked out for failure to follow orders. Not a dollar to his name. So he moved back into our unit, and the five or ten years in the tenement ended up twenty-five. I'm pretty sure I'll live in that place until I die, just like your dad."

"I'm sorry, Mom," I say, and I mean it. I've never felt so much sorrow for my mother in my life, and I'm ashamed when I realize it's because I've never seen her as deserving of empathy. I simply never considered that my mother had a story of her own, and that she wasn't an apathetic welfare rat just like all the rest of them.

"Don't be," Mom says. She reaches out and touches my cheek with her snow-cold hand. "At least you won't be stuck here doing the same thing we did. And don't think for a second that I've ever thought you were 'messing things up for me.' You're the only good thing that came out of that marriage. You're the best thing I've ever done in my life. Without you, I would have gone up on the roof of our old high-rise and jumped off it fifteen years ago."

I remember all the times when I sent out my weekly messages to Mom a few days late, and the times when I skipped them altogether, and I feel a burning shame that makes the tears well up in my eyes. I take Mom's hand off my cheek and place it between my own hands, to rub away the cold of the snow she was holding earlier.

"I'm sorry for being such a self-centered little shit all those years," I say. "I guess I wasn't much of a help to you."

Mom smiles at me, and shrugs.

"Andrew, you were just a kid. That's what teenagers *are*, don't you know?"

We stand together like this for a little while, Mom with her hand between my hands, both of us enjoying the sedate sounds of Liberty Falls waking up all around us—hydrocars gliding past, soft music coming from a few of the shops opening, people talking to each other in low voices as they walk past the little green and into the transit station. It's as if we have stepped off the train and into a different time and place altogether.

"You want to go and see if there's a place that'll feed us some breakfast on my fancy government ID?" I ask Mom, and she nods.

"I'm starving. This clean air is making me hungrier than I've been in forever."

———

We walk down the sidewalk of Main Street in search of a government canteen, or at least an automated eatery that has the government logo among the accepted payment methods stickered to the front door.

As we walk down the street, a man steps out of a door twenty yards ahead of us. He's wearing a white chef's uniform, and he carries an old-fashioned blackboard and easel, which he sets up on the sidewalk in front of his door. We watch as he sits on his heels in front of the blackboard to write on it with a piece of green chalk. As we get closer, I can make out the first few lines he has written:

Eggs Benedict—CD150
Frittata—CD125
Lumberjack Hash Browns—CD175

By now, I have roughly a million Commonwealth dollars in my government account, but I can't access any of it, and I don't have a single dollar of hard currency on me. I scan the line of payment symbols on the door, but "FED ID" is not among them.

The man in the chef's uniform notices us and gets up from his crouch. When he turns to face us, I can tell that he's doing just a little bit of a double-take at the sight of my dark-blue fleet uniform. From the way his gaze shifts to the beret on my head and then the ribbon salad above my breast pocket, I suspect that he knows what he's looking at. I nod at him in greeting, and he returns the nod with narrowed eyes.

"Combat controller," he says, a statement rather than a question. He's a tall, lean guy, and he looks like he's in very good shape. His hair is a closely cropped buzz cut that is streaked with gray.

"Correct," I say.

He looks at my shoulder boards and raises an eyebrow. "I'm not too good with the new ranks they came up with. You a sergeant?"

"Staff Sergeant," I correct. "E-6."

"Doesn't seem right, fleet NCOs going by those army ranks now," he says. "When I left, you would have been a petty officer first class."

"You a navy vet?"

"Damn straight. Twenty years in the fleet. Took my retirement just before the Lanky business started. Back when they still called it the navy."

"That was about the time I joined up," I say. "Got into the fleet a year before they unified the services and gave everyone army ranks. I was a petty officer third class for about two months, before they took away the chevron and called me a corporal."

"Well, how about that," he smiles. Then he wipes his right hand on the apron he's wearing and holds it out to me. "Steve

Kopka, Master Chief Petty Officer. *Retired*," he adds, with a hint of regret in his voice.

"Andrew Grayson," I reply, and take the offered hand. His handshake is firm and businesslike. "This is my mom."

"Ma'am," he says to her with a nod.

"Pleased to meet you," Mom replies.

"So," he says, eyeing Mom's clean, but obviously welfare-sourced clothes. "Out for a stroll this morning? You on leave?"

"Yeah, my tub's in for a refit, and I took some time off between assignments."

"I worked with you combat controllers a bunch when I was in. Only my beret was maroon back then, not scarlet."

"You were Spaceborne Rescue?" I ask, and he nods.

"God knows what color their beanies are these days."

"Still maroon," I say. "They took away all the fleet ranks and gave everyone new shoulder boards, but they didn't mess with the podheads' beret colors. Guess they were afraid of the riot that would have followed."

"Damn straight," Master Chief Kopka says. "You of all people know how much fucking sweat goes into earning one of those. Pardon my language, ma'am," he adds in Mom's direction.

"Not at all," Mom says. I can tell that she has no idea what we're talking about, but I also know she's pleased to witness our exchange.

"Master Chief Kopka here is a former Spaceborne Rescue man," I explain to Mom. "They have the only job in the fleet that's more dangerous than calling nukes down on your own head. They're the guys who launch in ballistic drop pods to rescue crashed pilots."

"Oh, my," Mom says with a smile. "And you made it all the way through your service doing that? You must have been good at it."

"That was before the Lankies," Chief Kopka tells her. "We just tussled with the Russians and the Chinese every once in a while. Your son here has a tougher job than I ever had."

"So what are you doing now, Master Chief?" I ask him. "You trade in your beanie for a chef's hat?"

"Yeah," he says. "Took my retirement money and went in with a friend to open this place. He died last year, so it's all mine now." He looks at the old but clean brick building with obvious pride of ownership.

"Good for you, Master Chief. Pleasure to run into you."

"Are you two in a hurry? I'd like to make you some breakfast, if you'll let me. Don't run into a fellow podhead too often, and I have a 'free meal' policy for the old brotherhood."

"Oh, no, we *couldn't*—" Mom says.

"*Absolutely*," I say at the same time.

"What's a podhead?" Mom asks in a low voice as Master Chief Kopka leads us into his little restaurant.

"Fleet special ops," I tell her. "Spaceborne Rescue, combat controllers, Space-Air-Land teams. The rest of the fleet calls us that because we use the ballistic drop pods a lot."

"That's what you do?" Mom asks, disturbed. "I thought you were sitting at a network console somewhere in a starship. You never told me about drop pods and nuclear weapons."

"That's 'need to know,' Mom. And you didn't need to know."

In front of us, Master Chief Kopka lets out a low chuckle.

We walk into a cozy little dining room. There are maybe a dozen tables in the room, all decked with the same kind of cream-colored tablecloths, and each adorned with little flower vases. Mom looks around with an expression that couldn't be more bewildered if she had just stepped off the Gateway shuttle and onto the big spaceport on Luna.

"We're not open until eight," Chief Kopka says over his shoulder. "My waitress won't be in until quarter 'til, but I have the kitchen fired up already."

He leads us to a corner table that's right by one of the streetside windows and pulls out a chair for Mom.

"You folks sit down, and I'll bring you some menus. What would you like to drink?"

Mom takes her seat and looks up at the chief.

"Gosh, I have no idea. Coffee, maybe?"

"Good call. I got in some fresh beans the other day. One coffee, coming right up. What can I get you, Sergeant?"

"I'll have one, too," I say. "Don't waste the top-shelf stuff on us, Master Chief."

"You leave that up to me," Chief Kopka says.

He walks off toward the kitchen, and Mom gives me a look that is equal parts bewilderment, excitement, and amusement.

"Does that happen to you a lot?"

"This is the first time. I've never gotten anything from anyone for wearing this outfit."

The chief returns a few minutes later. He's carrying a little serving tray with two coffee cups on it. Mom watches in wide-eyed wonder as he puts the cups down in front of us. He takes a small creamer off the tray and places it on the table in front of us.

"That's some local cream, from actual Vermont cows. I have an arrangement with a dairy farm just down the road."

He adds a little bowl of granulated sugar to what is already a hundred-dollar breakfast without any food in the mix, and puts down two leather-bound menus. Then he winks at Mom and points to her coffee cup.

"You go ahead and enjoy that coffee while you pick out something to eat. Disregard the headers that say 'Lunch' or 'Dinner.' I can make you anything you see on that menu. I'll be back in a few to take your order."

With that, he walks off, leaving Mom sitting in slack-jawed amazement.

The coffee is much better than the powdered stuff we get to drink in the fleet, and it bears very little resemblance to the atrocious instant-coffee-flavored soy powder they include in the BNA rations. Mom carefully assembles her cup by adding two spoonfuls of the sugar and a small splash of cream. She handles the creamer like the ChemWar guys would handle vials of nerve gas, as if one spilled drop would be a catastrophe. When her coffee has reached the right color and sweetness, she dips a finger into the milk container and sticks the fingertip into her mouth to taste the pure cream.

"Oh my God," she says after a moment of closed-eyed bliss. "That stuff is so rich. You could stand a spoon up in it. This is incredible."

"Easy with the dairy, Mom," I warn her. "If you're not used to it, too much will screw up your plumbing. And don't ask me how I know this."

"It would be worth it," Mom says. She takes a sip of her coffee and lets out a sound of utter contentment.

I add some cream and sugar to my own coffee and take a sip. It's so rich and flavorful that it makes the fleet coffee seem like bilge water.

"So what are you going to eat?"

"Oh, I don't know," Mom says. She opens the menu in front of her carefully and picks up the corner of the first page with her fingertips. "I'm sure everything is very good, and that whatever I order will be the best thing I've eaten in five years."

Five minutes into our breakfast, Mom revises her opinion, and lets me know that Chief Kopka's food is the best thing she's ever eaten in her *life*. The menu has meal options and price tags that seem like a cruel prank to a welfare rat from the tenements. The dinner menu has steak and shellfish dishes listed, and the price tags next to them have four digits before the decimal point. Not wanting to take shameless advantage of the chief's generosity by ordering a $1,500 cut of meat, we pick some moderately priced items from the brunch menu. I order the lumberjack hash browns, which are a glorious mess of real potato cubes mixed with bits of corned beef, and topped with a fried egg. Mom picks the eggs Benedict, which have a heart-shaped poached egg artfully stacked on a muffin, along with a thick slice of bacon, and a piece of avocado underneath. As far as I can tell, there's not a single bit of soy in either meal.

When our plates are nearly clean, Chief Kopka comes out of the kitchen and walks over to our table. He is clutching a leather-bound book.

"May I join you for a few minutes?" he asks. "I have something I'd like to show you, Sergeant."

"Sure thing, Master Chief. Pull up a chair. It's your place."

The chief sits down at our table and puts the book on the linen tablecloth between us. I open it to the first page and see that it's a collection of photo printouts and mementos from the chief's time in the fleet. As I leaf through the album, I see that a lot of the pictures seem to be from the chief's senior NCO days, as if he had only started the whole collection once he got close to retirement. A few pages in the book are dedicated to unit patches from ships Chief Kopka has served on: NACS *Independence* CV-606, NACS *Nassau* FF-476, NACS *Wainwright* CA-41, and a half dozen others. There are pictures of the chief hanging out in the mess or rec room with his petty-officer buddies, and some shots of scenery from colony planets, with unmistakable prefabricated colony housing units in the background.

"Let me ask you a question, Sarge," the chief says after a while. "You're up there all year long, and you're on the ground, not flying a console. How bad is it?"

"You know I can't tell you details, Chief."

"I'm not asking you to violate OpSec. Just give me a quick sketch. Whatever news we get on the Lankies, they've put it through so many cleanup cycles that it's as bland as that shit they feed people in the welfare cities." He looks at Mom and gives her a sheepish smile. "Pardon my French, ma'am."

"Not at all," Mom says, smiling back. "It *is* pretty bland shit, after all."

"I don't think I'm giving anything away," I say, "but we're getting our asses kicked. There's nothing left to defend past the Thirty. They've taken it all away from us."

"Holy crap." The chief sits back in his chair and exhales sharply. "They keep saying we're 'engaged' past the Thirty."

"Well, they're not lying. We're doing what we can to be a pain in their asses, but it's all hit-and-run raids and nuclear bombardment. Even if we could kick them off our colonies again, it wouldn't do us any good in the long run. First thing they do, they wreck our terraformers and set up their own. If they ever restart the colony program, we'll have to do all the work from scratch again."

"Figures." Master Chief Kopka shakes his head in disgust. "Twenty years in the fleet, and I go into retirement just before the real fight starts. I picked one hell of a time to get out."

"I'd say you picked the perfect time, Master Chief," I say. "We struggle on the ground, but at least we get our licks in. Those ugly things are tough as shit, but you can kill 'em. Their spaceships? Forget about it. We've *never* won a ship-to-ship engagement with a Lanky seed ship. Every time we've stood and fought instead of running away, they've hammered our cap ships to scrap. Being in the fleet, flying a console—that's almost as dangerous as ground combat now."

"Yeah, well, I'd rather be manning my post up there. All I got down here's a wall rack full of kitchen knives, and a stun gun in my desk back in the office. Kind of hard to go on with life as usual when you know what's out there and you know that you won't be able to do a damn thing but kiss your ass good-bye if they show up."

I want to tell the chief that those are pretty much our options out on the colonies as well, but I understand his point. One of the reasons why I signed the reenlistment form was the dread I felt at the thought of not being able to control my own fate anymore, not even in whatever small measure afforded to me by my armor, weapon, and tactical radio sets. As things stand right now, I have at least some influence on events, and some purpose in life. If I had to sit down here on Earth, knowing how bad things look at the moment, and condemned to spend my days with mundane tasks, I'd probably feel exactly the same way.

"Well," the chief says. "You two enjoy the rest of your meal. Thanks for the heads-up, Sergeant. I have to get the place ready for the rest of my crew."

"No problem, Master Chief," I reply. "And thank you for the food. It beats the living hell out of anything I've had since day one in Basic."

"You're welcome. Do you think you could pass on a message or two once you get back to the fleet? They won't let civvies onto MilNet, except direct dependents. I'd like to let my old crew know that the old master chief is still kicking."

"Sure thing. Give me a few names, and I'll send it on. I won't be able to pass on any replies, though."

"Oh, that's okay," the chief says. "I'd just get depressed anyway if I knew what fun they're having without me."

"I'll do it," Mom offers, and the chief looks at her in surprise.

"What's that, Mom?"

"I'll pass on whatever it is you want to send back. Just send it to my mailbox with your weekly mail, and I'll send it on to the chief."

"They won't let you copy anything off the MilNet terminals," I remind her. "And the automatic censor will strip out all the last names and ship names."

"So you'll keep the messages short," Mom says. "I'll go straight home, type them into my public net terminal, and send them on to the chief here. No big deal. Least I can do for all this fantastic food he's been feeding us."

I exchange glances with the master chief, and we both smile at Mom's eagerness to skirt regulations.

"Well, I'd sure appreciate that, ma'am," the chief tells her. He pulls a menu out of his apron, opens it to the last page, and puts it in front of Mom.

"Hope you saved some room for dessert."

When we leave Chief Kopka's little restaurant half an hour later, Mom walks out of the place with a slight stagger, like someone who has had just that one drink too many.

"I think I just had more calories for breakfast than I've eaten all week," she says to me, glancing over her shoulder at the restaurant we just left. "I can't believe he fed us all that food for *free*."

"I can't believe we ran into a fellow podhead," I say. "Aren't too many of those around, in the service or out of it."

While we were eating our opulent breakfast inside, the sky above Liberty Falls had turned from mostly blue to mostly gray, and as we walk down Main Street again, snow starts falling in thick, white flakes that swirl around us silently in the morning breeze. Mom squints up into the sky, a serene smile on her face.

"I wish I could just drop dead on the spot, right here and now," she says.

Five years ago, I would have been appalled at that sentiment, but now I know exactly what she means.

CHAPTER 7
HALLEY

When I was still a civilian, the moon was a mythical destination. Our first permanent base in space, yet still in view of Earth—with a decent telescope and a clear sky, you can see most of the structures on the Earth-facing side of Luna. When I was a kid, I used to dream up all kinds of imaginative and wildly impractical ways to get up there without the money for a ticket to Luna City.

After five years of service in the fleet, I've been on Luna dozens of times. I've been back for Fleet School, tech school, and half a dozen specialty courses for the combat controller career track. By now, any mystique the location once held for me has long since evaporated. Part of the reason may be that the military buildings on the moon are generally windowless, so being in a building on Luna feels just like being in a starship that's under way. We did get to do a lot of vacuum excursions during combat controller training, but I was usually too busy filling my battle armor with sweat to stop and admire the view. Most of the military installations are on the dark side of Luna anyway, so there's nothing to see overhead but empty space and distant stars.

Nobody comes up to Luna for fun. On my shuttle ride over from Gateway on Saturday morning, I'm the only one in the passenger compartment who isn't obviously on the way to a new duty station. On a normal weekend day, transit shuttles to and from

Luna are usually half empty, but this one is full almost to the last seat, evidence of the accelerated training schedule adopted by the fleet. We're losing more and more ground to the Lankies, but we're stuffing more and more garrison troops onto the worlds we have left, and the fights with the SRA over the remaining real estate out there are getting more vicious and costly.

Halley is an instructor at the Combat Flight School. CFS takes up a fair chunk of lunar real estate on the fringes of the huge Fleet School complex. I ride the lunar transit tube out to the CFS stop, and by the time the doors of the tube pod open, I am the last passenger on the train.

Halley is already waiting for me when I walk through the double airlock that separates the transit platform from the main hub of the fleet's Combat Flight School. She's standing in front of the CQ station, bouncing up and down lightly on the toes of her flight boots. She's wearing an olive-green flight suit and her usual short and shaggy helmet-friendly haircut.

"Sorry I'm late," I say as I walk up to the CQ station to sign myself in. "They wouldn't let me catch a shuttle from Gateway earlier."

There's a corporal staffing the CQ post, and I step in front of Halley to render a formal salute to an officer in the presence of junior ranks. Before I can bring my hand up to the headband of my beret, Halley grabs me by the lapel of my Class A smock and pulls me toward her. The corporal behind the CQ desk looks away as she plants a firm kiss on my lips.

"Welcome to Drop Ship Elementary, Sergeant," Halley says when she releases me again. "Now let's get up to my berth, so I can peel off this monkey suit and have my way with you."

I'm not used to Halley's unabashed display of affection in front of junior personnel, but I don't object to the proposed course of action, so I follow her as she takes me by the hand and pulls me into the corridor beyond the CQ booth. Behind us, I can hear the corporal on duty chuckling softly.

Halley doesn't seem to be in the mood for preliminary chit-chat. As soon as the hatch of her berth locks behind us, she makes good on her declared intent and undoes the buttons of my uniform with impatient urgency. Her one-piece flight suit is more convenient to unseal, and I tug on the zipper to peel off the baggy green outfit the pilots call a bone bag.

My formerly neat Class A outfit joins the flight suit on the floor of Halley's berth. Her cabin is cluttered with books, manuals, printouts, and other school-related debris, a disorderly state that is highly unusual for my overachieving by-the-book girlfriend. As long as I have known her, Halley has always been a hundred-percenter on every test, and by every military standard. The Halley I knew in Basic wouldn't have left so much as a dirty sock on the floor of her berth. This Halley has three different uniforms spread out on her bed and the little foldout table next to it, and a full laundry bag in the corner of the room. She pulls me over to the bed and sweeps all the clothing laid out on it onto the floor. Then she takes me by the shoulders, tosses me onto the bed, and climbs on top of me.

Our coupling is fast, furious, and urgent. Halley is a lot more rough and aggressive than I remember her. By the time we have spent ourselves on each other, I have gouges on my back and blood on my lower lip.

"Whoa," I say, still out of breath and slightly dazed from the experience. "Don't use me up all at once. I have a few days left on this leave."

"If you think that's all you have left, then get your ass out of my bunk." Halley grins. "Go find me the young studly private who could go three times in a row back in Boot."

"He's right here," I protest. "He's just a little tired from heroically trying to save the Commonwealth."

"Don't worry so much about the Commonwealth," she says, and kisses me on the corner of the mouth. Then she gets out of the bunk and walks over to the bathroom, kicking discarded clothes and paper manuals out of the way. "Just worry about staying alive. I'd hate to have to look for a new boyfriend at this point."

"Like you'd have a hard time finding a replacement," I say. "Fleet's lousy with studs in tight flight suits who would love to, uh, fly close formation with you."

"And that's the problem," she says from the bathroom. "Pilots are all overconfident, self-centered adrenaline junkies. I want one of those, I can just date myself. Less hassle that way."

I look around in Halley's messy little officer berth while I listen to the sounds of water splashing in the shower. In the last five years, she has lost her by-the-book valedictorian uptightness when it comes to rules and regulations. What she hasn't lost is her hypercompetence. She doesn't keep her medals and commendations on the walls of her berth, but I know the abilities of the average junior officer, and Halley is one of the best drop-ship jocks in the fleet. I know there's a Distinguished Flying Cross tucked away in her locker somewhere, and she made the jump to first lieutenant after the absolute minimum required time in service. I have no doubt she'll be a twenty-star general someday, if she decides to become a lifer and the Lankies let us all live that long.

In the bathroom, the two-minute timer shuts off the shower. A few moments later, Halley comes out drying herself with one of the scratchy standard-issue fleet towels. Her dog tags jingle softly on their chain as she starts drying her short dark hair.

"You hungry?" she asks.

"Somewhat," I say.

"Drop Ship U has a pretty good rec facility. Class One galley. Come on, get dressed and let's get some chow. I want to talk to you about something."

The dining room of the Fleet School's rec facility has a real viewport, a huge slab of triple-layer polyplast that takes up a ten-meter section of one of the walls. When Halley and I sit down at an empty table with our meal trays, we can see Earth—one of its hemispheres, anyway—rising above the built-up lunar horizon in the distance. The fleet complex on Luna was built before they deemed the inclusion of complex exterior viewports an unnecessary expense and just went to camera-fed screens instead. It seems slightly obscene to be eating what must be a two-thousand-calorie meal in view of the North American continent, where two-thirds of the population have to make that many calories stretch all day.

Halley pulls two bottles of soy beer from the leg pockets of her flight suit. She pops the caps off both, then pushes one toward me.

"Officer privilege," she says. "You're on leave, and I am off duty until tomorrow morning. Drink up."

"Yes, ma'am." I sketch a salute and take the bottle from her. I don't particularly like soy beer—it tastes like fermented tofu with a bit of a fizz—but it's one of the few alcoholic drinks we can get through the official supply chain.

"So what do you want to talk about?" I ask.

"Us," she says. "I mean, where we are and where all this is going. This is, what, the sixth time we've actually gotten together since Basic?"

"Seven," I say. "Eight if you count the *Versailles*." I have a slightly sinking feeling that I'm about to hear a Dear John speech. "Considering our occupational specialties, that's actually not bad for five years."

"No, it isn't. But it's not great, either. I don't want to keep having to wait nine months between leaves to get enough of you to last me for the next nine. It's not ideal, you know?"

"No," I say. "It's not. But unless we manage to get assigned to the same ship again, it's what it is."

"We already used up that particular golden ticket," Halley says. "So we need to figure out some alternative. Because this super long-distance boyfriend thing isn't enough for me anymore."

I take a bite of my food. Today's galley special is beef over egg noodles. The sauce has a vague soy tang to it, but the beef is real, not some soy imitate like the civilians in the PRCs get.

"We're in the military," I say. "In the middle of a shooting war. Two of them, really. I don't think the fleet is going to make it a priority to accommodate some random couple in the ranks so they can spend a little more bunk time together."

"No," Halley says. "Of course not." She stabs the beef with her fork and shovels a healthy amount into her mouth. Halley is smart and pretty and the most capable junior officer I know, but ever since I met her in boot camp, she has eaten with all the speed and grace of a calorie-starved space dockworker.

"But we can use the system to make them give us more of what we want," she continues.

"Oh? How so?"

She studies me for a moment as if she's trying to decide whether to go through with letting me in on her plan. Then she puts more food into her mouth and chews before answering.

"What do you know about my family, Andrew?"

"Not a lot," I shrug. "You don't talk about your folks a lot. I know you're from the 'burbs, and that your parents weren't happy when you joined up."

"Not quite true," Halley says. "They all but disowned me. Ever wonder why I never ask you to come home with me on leave?"

"I figured it was because we decided that we didn't want to burn up most of our leave time in transit."

"There's that," she says. "But mostly it's because I didn't want to kick off World War IV at home by showing up in uniform and with what they'd consider a sexual lunch bag."

I chuckle around a mouthful of beef and noodles.

"But," she says, and waves a beef-tipped fork at me, "if I brought home a respectable prospect for future grandkids, I'm pretty sure it would take the sting out of the whole military enlistment thing. For my mom anyway. And she's the one we really have to worry about."

"Wait," I say. "You mean getting *hitched*? Are you *proposing* right now, First Lieutenant Halley?"

Halley is a pragmatist, not the romantic type at all. Hearing her talk about marriage, however oblique, is about as surprising as hearing a Lanky recite Shakespeare in flawless English. I look at her with an incredulous grin.

"Well, here's the thing," she says. "I looked up the regs. Married couples get extra family leave. We could see each other twice as often. And if one of us buys the farm, the other inherits eighty percent of the end-of-term bonus."

In the five years we've been together, I never considered marriage, and if I had, I wouldn't have suggested it to Halley. I always had the feeling that she was happier with our loose commitment, but part of me is immensely pleased by her implied proposal, even if it's wrapped in Halley-esque pragmatism.

"My parents aren't just middle-class," she says. "Mom's the chief surgeon at a private hospital, and Dad designs ballistic-delivery systems for the Colonial Administration. I'm their only kid. I come home with a presentable husband and dangle that grandchild carrot in front of them, we could have a pretty good life back home. A place to take our retirement bonus."

"Too bad we just re-upped," I say. I remember Liberty Falls, that pristine upper-middle-class enclave in the mountains of Vermont, and the thought of getting to live in such a place seems almost surreal. Fresh air, clean streets, dairy farms. No weekly BNA rations. No need to check your back every time you walk down the street.

"Look, you know I'm not the sappy type," Halley says. "And I don't give a shit about engagement rings or anything like that. But I don't want you to think I'm just making a business proposal here."

She takes a slow breath and looks over to the viewport, where Earth hangs low in the sky, blue and gray against the all-absorbing black of space.

"We *match*," she continues. "We laugh about the same stuff, I don't have to explain much to you, we have a good time when we're on leave, and we've seen some pretty hair-raising shit together. You're a good boyfriend, and you'd make a good husband. I've met enough guys in the fleet to know that I'd have to look long and hard for someone that fits me as well as you. We've been the closest thing to family for each other since we met. Let's make that status official."

She shrugs and gives me a lopsided little smile. If I didn't know better, I would say she's nervous.

"Might as well get the monetary benefits, too, you know?" she says.

I laugh, the tension in me releasing like a decompressing airlock.

"Holy shit," I say. "That's the most romantic thing you've ever said to me."

I reach across the table and take her left hand in mine, touching my thumb to the area on her finger where an engagement ring would go.

"I do," I say, and she laughs.

"Come on. Let's see what it takes to get hitched in the fleet."

We're in the Armed Forces of the North American Common-wealth, and the NAC military doesn't ever let you do anything in one step when they can make you do it in ten. We head over to the base's personnel clerk to check on the procedure for a marriage between service members, and it's like a cold shower after the rush of excitement from earlier.

"You file your intent today, and you get your marriage license in six months," the clerk tells us.

"That's one hell of a wait for two frontline troops," I tell him. "I don't know if you've noticed, but there's a war on."

"I don't make the regs," he says. "Fleet rule. So people don't get hitched just before a drop to make sure their folks get the bonus."

"Wouldn't want to fuck the government out of money by leaving a grieving spouse too soon," Halley says. She chucks her military ID card onto the counter in front of the clerk. "Go ahead and file it, Corporal."

I get out my own ID and put it next to Halley's. Then she looks at me, and her expression softens a little.

"I'm not going to let it ruin my mood," she says. "Let's grab some more of that beer and head back to the berth. I want to fool around with my fiancé."

The personnel clerk takes our IDs and scans them into the admin console in front of him. A few moments later, we are officially engaged in the eyes of the fleet.

"Clock's ticking," I say to Halley when we take our ID cards back from the clerk. "Now we just have to stay alive for another six months."

"Easier for me than you," Halley says. "But I want you back here in six months. Whatever you have to do."

"I'll do my best," I say.

"Whatever you have to do," she repeats.

"I promise I'll be back in one hundred eighty days sharp."

"*Better*," Halley says.

CHAPTER 8

——— MISSION BRIEFING ———

The leaves I spend with Halley are always too short, but this one's even shorter than usual, and by the time she has to go back to teaching young pilots how to stay alive, I report to the Transient Personnel Unit with great reluctance to wait for the arrival of my new ship.

Once upon a time, when the fleet was water bound, a ship would return to its homeport after a deployment and stay in port for a while, to give the crews some downtime. The modern, space-borne fleet doesn't have enough hulls to allow such indulgences. Instead, every ship in the fleet has two full crews, called Gold and Blue, and switching them out is a swift and well-practiced process. The *Manitoba* is cleaned up, restocked, and ready for a new deployment only six days after I step aboard to report to my new command.

"Our target," Major Gould announces, "is Sirius Ad."

The briefing room erupts into a cacophony of murmurs as we process this information. The Sirius A system has been solidly Sino-Russian territory since shortly after the colonization waves started in earnest. It's almost as much established enemy soil as St. Petersburg or Dalian.

"The name of this operation is Hammerfall. For the last few years, we've been defending our own turf against their raids.

Command figured that the time has come to let them have a taste of their own medicine."

"They'll need to send along an empty fleet tender just for all the body bags," my seat neighbor, a fellow combat controller sergeant named Macfee, says to me in a low voice, and I nod in agreement. The Sino-Russians are paranoid when it comes to planetary defenses. They set up fully integrated air- and space-defense networks before the first wave of civvie construction ships even touches down on a new colony. A place that's been in their possession for eighty years is likely to be carpeted with defensive structures. There's a reason why we mostly fight over the new real estate—the old colonies are tough nuts to crack, and they're hardly ever worth the attendant butcher's bill.

"I know what you're thinking," Major Gould says. "You're thinking that this will be another Barnard's Star. You're also thinking that Command has lost the plot completely, and that the old man can afford to be all gung-ho because he won't be bleeding down in the dirt with the rest of you."

There's some chuckling from the SI troops in the front rows, but Macfee and I don't join in, because Major Gould is pretty much right on the money. Barnard's Star was a failed offensive three years ago. The NAC tried to take an ore-rich mining colony away from the SRA, and we got a severe mauling in the process. The attacking force expected a Russian regiment in garrison; they ran into a full Chinese combined arms brigade instead. Our forces attacked with force parity and suffered a three-to-one casualty rate.

"Well, this won't be another Barnard's Star, and I'll tell you why."

The major toggles the holographic display on the wall behind him, and it comes to life with a three-dimensional tactical display of our target planet.

"First off, we have perfect intel this time. Fleet let us have three of those superexpensive new stealth recon drones, and they've been collecting data in-system for the last seventeen days. We also have a SigInt boat on station out there. We know the size of the planetary garrison, and their exact disposition on the surface. We know they have a visiting task force in orbit—a supply ship and the space control cruiser *Kiev*. We know the commanding officer's name, how many times per week he hits the head for a shit, and what kind of reading material he takes along. Hell, I bet the SigInt guys can even tell you the enemy's mess hall menu for the next two weeks."

He toggles a switch on his remote, and the display zooms out until Sirius Ad is just a speck in the center of the screen, and we see a general overview of the inner system.

"Secondly—and this is kind of the big deal—we have figured out where their Alcubierre transit zones are located. That's both inbound *and* outbound chutes."

Some of the troops present actually shout out in surprise at this revelation, and the room is once more abuzz with barely suppressed conversations. Major Gould smiles, clearly pleased with the reactions. Finding the enemy's transit zones, the areas where their Alcubierre travel chutes enter and exit the system, is a major intelligence coup. The locations of a system's transit zones are tightly guarded secrets, because an opposing force armed with that information can ambush a transiting fleet, or simply mine the transit zone to cut off a system from reinforcements. Getting bushwhacked while popping out of Alcubierre is a warship commander's greatest fear.

"Holy hell," Sergeant Macfee says next to me. "If that's true, we may actually clean their clocks for a change. I'm impressed."

"Military intelligence usually ain't," I remind him. "What do you want to bet they thought they had 'perfect intel' at Barnard's Star, too?"

"Here's the rough sketch," Major Gould continues. "We're going to punch them in the nose, hard. For this one, we'll be Carrier Task Force Seventy-Two. We're going in with two Linebackers, two destroyers, a frigate, a minelayer, and one of the new Hammerhead space control cruisers. We're also taking along the entire Second Regiment, Fifth SI Division. That's in addition to our own Fourth Regiment."

I can't remember when we last hit a target with half a brigade of troops dropping from space. Two full regiments of Spaceborne Infantry represent a fearsome amount of combat power: four thousand fighting troops in advanced battle armor, two wings of drop ships, four batteries of mobile field artillery, and two reinforced armor companies.

"At this point, our Russian and Chinese friends are spread a little thin. They've been steadily shuffling troops from the established colonies to those mobile task forces they've been annoying us with. Right now, Intel says that the garrison down on Sirius Ad consists of a single understrength regiment, the Chinese 544th Combined Arms. They're also dispersed all over that rock, so we can first hammer them from orbit, and then hit them with both our regiments in turn. With any luck, we'll be facing an understrength *company* once the Shrikes are done with them."

Staff officers are notoriously overoptimistic in mission briefings, but I can't help feeling just a little flare of hope that this mission won't be quite the epic body-bag filler it had appeared to be at first. If our intel is good, and we can sew the system shut while we're hammering the garrison, there's even a chance Major Gould's optimism is justified.

"Once we transition in, the minelayer and a frigate escort are going to peel off and make straight for the enemy's transition zones. Once there, they'll salt the place with nuclear mines, and Sirius A will be 'No Exit/No Entry' for a while. The bulk of CTF Seventy-Two is going to continue to Sirius Ad, where we are going to engage and destroy the ships in orbit. After that, we hit the garrison from above, land the troops, and mop up whatever the Shrikes have left for us."

"And the other team is just going to lie down and take it," I say to Macfee.

"Soon as they figure out what's happening, they'll shove a whole fucking division through the chute to take the place back," he replies. "Hell, *we* would."

"Be nice to pull one over on them for a change, though," I say. "I'm getting sick of this chickenshit hit-and-run business."

"Mission briefings will commence soon," Major Gould says. "We're five days out from the chute to Sirius A, and ordnance will start flying as soon as we're out of Alcubierre, so use the time wisely. Operation Hammerfall commences in one hundred and twenty hours. Get your gear ready for business, and check your PDPs for briefing schedules. *Dismissed.*"

We spend the time to Alcubierre transition with maintenance, training, and the kind of recreational pursuits common among those about to go into battle. During the days, we're at the firing range, in the shipboard gyms, or in our unit briefing rooms. In the evenings, we're in the mess hall, the NCO club, and the makeshift gambling parlor some of the grease monkeys have set up clandestinely in a quiet corner of the storage hangar.

Joining a new unit means being the new guy all over again, and having to earn everyone's respect once more. I only have a few days to get to know the troops that will soon rely on me in battle. I suppose some people would keep their distance, knowing that five days aren't enough to really bond with anyone, and that some of them most likely won't come back from that mission anyway. I don't keep to myself because I want to know as much as I can about people whose hide I may have to save, or who may have to save mine. We're not motivated by money, and only the most naive or optimistic among us are convinced we're on the winning side, sandwiched as we are between the Lankies and the Sino-Russians.

I don't believe the patriotic agitprop anymore—if I ever did—and I'm disgusted at the stupidity and shortsighted aggression on both sides, wasting lives and material by squabbling over whatever the Lankies haven't taken away from us yet. I don't think we're any better than the SRA. Our motives aren't any more noble than theirs, and our methods are the same. At the rate things are going, we have a few more years, a decade at the most, before all our colonies are swallowed by the Lankies, and we have nothing better to do with that borrowed time than to kill each other, like two spoiled kids fighting over how to divide their room while the house is burning down around them.

Still, I drink and joke around with my new comrades, and I know that when the time comes, I will suit up with them, and drop into battle alongside them. I will do so terrified, but on my own free will, and maybe even with a measure of gladness.

CHAPTER 9

COMBAT DROP

"Combat stations, combat stations. All hands, combat stations. This is not a drill. I repeat . . ."

I'm already suited up and fully armed, and the announcement holds no added urgency to me, or to the rest of the regiment lined up on the hangar deck. We have been gearing up for our drop for the last two hours, and we're ready for combat. In front of us, flight deck techs swarm all over the drop ships lined up to ferry us into battle, removing safety caps from ordnance fuses and autocannon muzzles. I check my kit for the thirtieth time—armor integrity, weapon status, comms gear function, oxygen levels, filter condition.

The flight deck is a cavernous hall that takes up the entire bottom half of the ship almost from bow to stern, and it's packed end to end with drop ships and troops. Each drop ship can ferry a platoon, and we're dropping with a full regiment today. Twenty-four drop ships are running up their engines on the other side of the flight deck, the most I've ever seen parked wingtip to wingtip in one spot. As scary as it is to be part of an operation that actually requires the deployment of this much brute force, it's also sort of exhilarating. I'm a cog in a machine, but on days like this, I'm reminded just how large and powerful a machine it is.

"First Platoon, *on your feet!*"

The platoon sergeant, SFC Ferguson, walks down the line of battle-ready SI troopers, patting the polymer shell of his M-66 rifle for emphasis.

"Time to earn this month's paychecks, boys and girls. I see any bolts cycling before I give the go-ahead, we *will* have the first casualties of the day."

I'm embedded with the First Platoon of Alpha Company, Fourth Spaceborne Infantry Regiment. We're in the first attack wave, and Alpha Company is tasked with pinning down and destroying the garrison company entrenched in the third-largest settlement on Sirius Ad. Alpha Company is the sharp point of the spear, and that's why they get one of the fleet's three combat controllers along for the drop. Macfee is going in with a company of the Forty-Second Regiment, and the third combat controller assigned to the *Manitoba* is dropping with the command element of the Forty-Fourth. The grunts carry rifles, rocket launchers, and antiarmor missiles. We combat controllers carry radio suites and integrated TacLink computers that can practically remote-control Shrike attack birds and orbital ordnance. On the whole, the grunts are almost as protective of their embedded combat controllers as they are of their medics.

The tail ramp of our drop ship opens with a soft hydraulic whine, and the ship's crew chief steps out onto the ramp. He uses both his arms like signal sticks for taxiing aircraft, and waves us into the cargo hold of the waiting ship.

"Double-line, double-time. Take your seats, buckle in, and stop the yapping," Sergeant Ferguson shouts over the din of the dozens of engines warming up on the flight deck.

We trot up the ramp and file into the cargo hold of the Wasp. There are two rows of seats, one on each side of the hold, so half the platoon sits facing the other half across the cargo bay. At this point, everyone's helmet visors are lowered, in case the ship suffers a sudden hull breach. With the polarized filters of the visors, our faces are invisible to the others, and nobody has to pretend not to be nervous.

When I drop out of a ship in a bio-pod, I shut down my sensor input and go completely dark until I hit atmo. On drop-ship ingress, I do the opposite. As our ship gets picked up by the docking clamps to be lowered into the drop bay, I turn on my tactical network computer and tap into the *Manitoba*'s TacLink. By the time we have settled in the bay to wait for the drop signal, my three-dimensional display shows me exactly what the main tactical plot in CIC is projecting. A warship's battle plot looks like a tapestry of abstract symbols and vector lines to the uninitiated, but I've worked with tactical plots for so long that I can interpret the data while half asleep or fully drunk. It's a completely alien way to see the world, but once you know how to read it, you become almost omniscient.

When I bring up the main tactical plot on my helmet's display, the attack is already under way. We are half a million kilometers from Sirius Ad, and the distance to the planet is shrinking rapidly as the *Manitoba* and her task force rush into drop position at top speed. In front of our force, the display shows only two enemy fleet units—one moving our way on an intercept course, the other running in the opposite direction. The Chinese supply ship is running for the Alcubierre chute, and the space control cruiser is going on the offensive to cover the retreat. It's a valiant move, but one aging Chinese cruiser fighting it out with our supercarrier task force is merely a noble form of suicide. My fellow drop-ship passengers are unaware of the short and sharp clash of arms that is about to commence. Their world is limited to the windowless hull into which we are neatly packed like meal trays in a box of rations.

When the Chinese cruiser reaches the outer edge of our anti-ship weapons envelope, our own cruiser, the NACS *Alaska*, starts launching her missiles. I see first eight, then sixteen, then thirty-two blue missile symbols emerging from the *Alaska* and rushing toward the enemy ship. One or two of them would be enough to put the Chinese cruiser out of commission, but the SRA have pretty good point-defense systems on their ships, so fleet doctrine calls for saturating their defenses with the first strike. It's a costly way of doing business, but even three dozen antiship missiles are a good trade for a space control cruiser.

The Chinese don't intend to roll over without putting up a fight. When our missiles have covered half the distance to the lone Chinese ship, a swarm of missile symbols emerge from the enemy unit, crimson vees to meet our blue ones. They fan out from the *Shenzhen* and rush toward our incoming barrage. Then the *Shenzhen* fires her own antiship missiles, her commander's attempt to make sure he won't show up in Valhalla alone today. Our two Linebacker ships take up the challenge, and start pumping their interceptor missiles into the intervening space, until the tactical plot is littered with red and blue vee symbols rushing to annihilate each other.

The outcome of the battle is never in doubt. There are two or three blue missile symbols to every red one, and the Chinese cruiser has emptied her magazines, while our Linebackers are just getting warmed up. One by one, the red missile icons on the plot converge with blue ones and disappear along with them, until there are only blue vee shapes left. The *Shenzhen* dies silently and without drama on the sterile plot display. Six or eight of our cruiser's volleyed antiship missiles converge on the red "CRUISER/HOSTILE" icon, and snuff it out of existence. Just like that, we have turned thirty thousand tons of starship and five hundred people into a cloud of orbital debris.

"The Chinese cruiser just bit the dust," I inform the platoon in my drop ship.

There's whooping and hollering, as if they have just heard the score in a sports event and their favored team is in the lead.

With the cruiser out of the way, the task force moves in to begin the ground bombardment. Sirius Ad is a small planet, but it's still two-thirds the size of Earth, and even with all the ordnance we've brought along on half a dozen warships, we wouldn't be able to subdue the entire planet from orbit, unless we used a whole mess of hundred-megaton metroplex busters. Since we want to seize the place, not turn it into a radioactive wasteland, we need to apply our firepower more judiciously. The size of the planet works against the defenders as well—they can't put a missile battery on every square kilometer of ground down there, and our recon drones have had three weeks to map out the defensive grid on the surface.

The second stage of the assault commences as we coast into orbit above our landing zones. All the ships in the task force start unloading their space-to-ground missile silos, to hit the hundreds of priority targets designated by the SigInt drones. All we can hear in the drop ship is the muffled roar of the igniting missile motors in their silos well above our heads as the *Manitoba* disgorges her land-attack ordnance. After a few minutes, the tactical display looks like an air defense commander's worst nightmare— swarms of missiles that streak into the atmosphere at thirty times the speed of sound, and then multiply their number twentyfold when the missiles release their nose cones and launch their independent warheads. All those MIRVs carry half-ton conventional explosives or high-density bunker busters instead of nuclear payloads, but with the sheer number of warheads raining down into Sirius Ad's atmosphere, I imagine that this will be a small consolation to the troops we are targeting down there.

The first barrage is followed by a second, then a third, a steady rain of missiles that will multiply into hundred- and thousandfold death on the ground. And then it's our turn to be launched at the enemy.

I don't see the drop hatch opening below the ship, but I know the little jolt that goes through the hull when the automated docking clamp drops us the last few meters into launch position. All along the bottom of the hull, two dozen drop hatches have just opened, leaving nothing between our bodies and open space but the armored bottom hulls of our battle taxis.

Some drop-ship commanders use the intercom to ease the troops' tension and their own with jokes, or they keep the mudlegs in the back apprised of what's happening outside the overstuffed troop compartment, but our ship's pilot isn't the talkative type. Just before the docking clamp releases our ship, the status light on the forward bulkhead changes from green to red, and then my stomach lurches upward as our Wasp falls through the open hatch and out of the *Manitoba's* artificial gravity field.

I've done these drops a hundred times or more, but every one of them feels a bit like what I imagine an execution must feel like to the condemned. You know you have time for a few more breaths before the switch is thrown, but you don't know how many, and then the event takes you by surprise anyway.

Then we're weightless in our seats as the drop ship races toward the atmosphere of Sirius Ad. On my tactical screen, we are one little blue inverted vee in a long chain of them, moving away from the safety of our host ship and into the teeth of the waiting defenses.

"*SAM launch, SAM launch!* Banshee Two-Eight, countermeasures."

The Wasp has no windows back in the cargo hold, but with my TacLink display, I have a front row seat anyway. My comms set is dialed into the drop-ship flight's channel, and my tactical display shows the plot from all the computers in the flight put together.

We're thirty klicks from our drop zone, and we just managed to fly past an enemy missile battery that survived our initial orbital bombardment. Thankfully, we're at the very edge of the battery's detection range, so we have plenty of warning about the eight supersonic surface-to-air missiles that just left the racks of the launcher to catch up with our four-ship flight.

"*Rog.*" Banshee Two-Eight's pilot sounds almost bored as he turns on his active jamming pod and puts his bird into a series of jinks to shake off the missile's lock. One by one, the Russian missiles go dumb, chasing imaginary electronic shadows. Only one of them stays on Two-Eight's tail, and her pilot kicks out decoy drones and dives for the deck. Both red missile icon and blue drop-ship icon disappear from my plot. For a moment, I'm convinced that Two-Eight and the forty troops riding in her are now finely dispersed organic fertilizer, but then Two-Eight reappears from the shadow of a valley a few klicks off to our right.

"That one scraped off some paint," Two-Eight's pilot sends, and he doesn't sound bored anymore.

I mark the location of the enemy battery on the tactical plot, and toggle my radio to the TacAir channel to contact the flight of Shrike attack craft patrolling nearby.

"Hammer flight, you have an enemy SAM battery at nav grid Alpha One-Four. Looks like an SA-255."

"Hammer Two-Three, copy that. Y'all tell your bus driver to back off on the throttle, so we can clean up in front of you."

"Three minutes to drop zone," the pilot of our ship announces, and the status light on the forward bulkhead goes from a steady to a blinking red. A few moments later, the Shrikes pass our dropship flight, and even though they are a few thousand feet above us, their supersonic pass makes the hull of our Wasp vibrate. I watch the tactical plot as the Shrikes go into attack formation and streak ahead to sanitize the landing zone.

For once, our intel data seems to be spot-on. The landing zone is quiet as we swoop in. No hidden gun batteries, no missile launchers, and no entrenched troops are waiting to receive our company. The landing zone is a small plateau on a low mountain ridge ten miles from the target settlement. As far as combat landings go, this one is a walk in the park on a sunny day. We file out of the drop ships at a trot, assemble in battle marching order, and head out to pick a fight with the defenders of Sirius Ad, entrenched just a few miles away.

"Looks like they got one right," Sergeant Ferguson says to me when we march off the little plateau and down into the valley leading east. "This is some real recruiting-vid shit right here."

Behind us, the drop ships take off to clear the LZ and take up stations overhead. Whatever we tossed at the defending garrison from orbit, it wasn't enough to take the fight out of them, because a few moments after the Wasps thunder off into the clear blue sky, I see the red vector lines of incoming artillery fire coming from the outskirts of the SRA town.

"*Incoming arty, vector nine-two!*" I shout into the all-company channel, and the troops dash for cover in the rocky landscape. My threat display isn't picking up any targeting radar sweeps, but the plateau is a likely landing zone, and the enemy arty probably had the place dialed in as a target reference point. I hunker down beside a large boulder, mark the incoming fire for the Wasps, and wait for the enemy shells. Once more, our luck holds—the Chinese are firing blind, cranking out shells at preset coordinates, and their fire soars over our heads and lands on the plateau we have just vacated moments ago.

Some real recruiting-vid shit, I think to myself as the Chinese artillery shells shake the earth and rain dirt and rocks down on us.

CHAPTER 10

—THE BATTLE OF SIRIUS AD—

The Chinese marines are understrength, outnumbered, cut off from the rest of their regiment, and without air support, but they put up a good fight anyway. We push into town slowly and carefully, but the Chinese troops are well entrenched, and they've had years to prepare for this defense. By the time we have most of the town under control, my platoon has suffered eight casualties, a fifth of our combat strength. Chinese marines don't surrender, and they rarely retreat.

"If I ever find the bastard who designed those new autonomous cannons, I'll skin him with a salted pocketknife," our platoon sergeant says. Ahead of us, the civil administration building has been turned into a strongpoint by the Chinese, and every other window on the top floor seems to have a crew-served weapon behind it.

"Alpha One-Niner, watch the emplacement on the top floor, northwest corner. They got one of them new cannons, the ones that fire duplex ammo," the platoon sergeant warns.

"Alpha One-Niner, copy. I'm all out of MARS rockets. Send Third Squad around to that—what is that thing at Bravo Seven, a water tank? They should be able to get a clear shot at that corner from there," First Squad's leader replies.

"Charlie One-Niner, you listening in?" the platoon leader sends.

"Affirmative," Third Squad's leader sends. "I got two thermo-barics left. We're on our way."

The Chinese civil administration building doesn't look very civil at all. It's a reinforced three-story structure that looks like it could survive a near miss from a five-kiloton nuke. I'm hunkered down with the platoon's command section in an alley a few hundred meters away. The Chinese autocannons fire sporadic bursts at build-ings and intersections in our vicinity. The defenders don't know where we are precisely, but they have a good idea, and trying to leapfrog across the intervening distance would get us killed. Their autocannons are remote-controlled via a data link that's impossible to hack and very difficult to jam. The Chinese gunners can sit any-where within a quarter mile of their gun, and hammer us from the air-conditioned safety of a command bunker. The new models can be switched to fully autonomous firing mode, where the gun's com-puter selects its own targets. The Commonwealth Defense Corps had its own version, but erased the autonomous capabilities from the software after combat use showed that the computer had a 1.3 percent error rate when telling hostiles from friendlies. The Sino-Russians have a more lenient acceptable-friendly-fire ratio, so they left their guns capable of running themselves without humans behind the trigger.

I watch Third Squad's little cluster of blue icons make its way to the water tank at nav grid B-7. They leapfrog across intersec-tions and hug the walls of the modular Chinese colony housing. The heavy automatic cannon on the top floor of the admin build-ing keeps hammering out short bursts of fire, but the gunners are not tracking the progress of our squad. Finally, Third Squad is in position to get a clear shot at the gun emplacement with their MARS launchers.

"Fire in the hole," their MARS gunner calls. In the distance, I hear the muffled pop of a launching missile, and a second later we see the white-hot exhaust of a MARS rocket streaking over the low rooftops toward its target. Then there's an earthshaking boom, the familiar low thunderclap of a thermobaric warhead explosion, and the enemy gun stops firing.

"Bull's-eye," Third Squad's leader says. "Put in another one for good measure."

"First and Second Squads, up and at 'em," Lieutenant Benning orders. "First Squad on the northwest corner, Fourth on the southeast one. Third Squad, move up for overwatch. Let's get this shit over with."

Back in NCO school, I had to read a ton of papers by mostly clueless theoreticians, prattling on about the "changing nature of modern warfare," and the need for the modern, post–Terran Commonwealth Defense Corps to be tooled and trained for "low-intensity colonial actions." In truth, warfare has changed very little since our great-great-grandfathers killed each other at places like Gettysburg, the Somme, Normandy, or Baghdad. It's still mostly about scared men with rifles charging into places defended by other scared men with rifles.

There's nothing "low-intensity" about our final assault on the Chinese admin building in this colony town on Sirius Ad. We pop smoke and charge in, and the remaining Chinese marines open up with everything they have left. We dash from cover to cover, and plaster the building ahead with rifle grenades and MARS rockets as we advance across the last few hundred meters of narrow streets and uniform colonial box architecture. I summon down Third Platoon's drop ship for close air support, and the Wasp comes shrieking out of the blue sky a minute or two later, gun pods blazing. The north face of the building ahead erupts in a shower of sparks and concrete dust as the Wasp rakes the structure with a stream of armor-piercing thirty-millimeter cannon shells. The Chinese admin building is designed to be an emergency shelter, and it has thick walls and a nearly bombproof structure, but the drop ship's cannons pour out two thousand rounds per minute each, and most of the windows on the north side end up taking a cannon shell or two. When we make our final dash across the road right in front of the building, the fire from the defenders has stopped.

Even with their defeat obvious, the Chinese marines don't hand over the keys to the place voluntarily.

"Holy shit," Lieutenant Benning remarks. "Take us three weeks to patch the place up again."

The interior of the admin building is a mess. The thick walls kept out most of our ordnance, but most of the windows on the north-facing side ate a MARS or a cannon shell, and the interior walls didn't do much to stop those. We're in the middle of what looks like a squad berth, and the rubble in here is almost knee-deep. Near the windows, we see what's left of three Chinese marines who probably stood in the way of a few thirty-millimeter rounds.

"You think we'll be here that long, LT?" I ask. "They'll send half their fleet through the chute once they get the word that we're here."

"Fucked if I know, Sarge. That's above my pay grade." He toggles his radio switch to check on the squad leaders.

"Third Squad, move up. Fourth Squad, keep up the perimeter. Stay sharp, people."

We're on the ground floor of the admin building. Above us, we hear an irregular staccato of rifle fire and grenade explosions, progress markers of the First and Second Squads sanitizing the upper floors. There isn't a room on the ground floor that doesn't have a dead Chinese marine or two in it, and our TacLink sensors show maybe fifteen defenders left in the building. Our suit sensors employ a complex voodoo of low-powered millimeter-wave radar, infrared, and half a dozen other technologies to spot enemy troops through walls and ceilings. It's not infallible tech, especially not against opponents in battle armor of their own, but it's accurate enough to keep our casualty count low. Our troops aren't taking any chances. They shoot through walls with buckshot shells, and toss grenades through doorways in pairs and threes. However long the Chinese had to fortify this place, they weren't expecting our attack when it came, and the defenders are disorganized and off their guard.

Room by room, we claw the admin building away from its own-ers, who die one by one in its defense. They must know that the battle is lost, but they fight us anyway, because that is what combat grunts do, and that's what we would do in their place as well.

Finally, the gunfire ebbs, and our two squads meet up in the middle of the top floor, with no defender left between them.

"Building secure," Lieutenant Benning calls out over the pla-toon channel. "Check for intel and enemy WIA, and watch your steps. Those little fuckers love their booby traps."

Down in the basement, we walk into what must have been the command post for the Chinese garrison company. There are five or six dead SRA marines on the floor, plucked apart by shrapnel and fléchette bursts. Only two of them are in full battle rattle. The others are in various states of combat readiness, with partially donned armor. The highest-ranking dead SRA marine, a Chinese major, is dressed merely in battle dress fatigues, and armed only with a pistol. Lieutenant Benning walks over to the dead major, pulls the pistol from his grasp, clears the chamber, and sticks the gun into the webbing of his battle armor. The Commonwealth Defense Corps stopped issuing pistols to frontline infantry a while ago—even with fléchette ammo, a handgun is virtually useless against an opponent in battle armor—but the SRA officers wear them as badges of rank, and some of our guys collect them, a less messy form of taking scalps.

I pick up a mangled chair and sit down on the padded seat that has stuffing spilling through shrapnel wounds. On my tactical screen, I can see that our mission is a planetwide success. The second wave of NAC troops has landed, and the few remaining SRA defenders on Sirius Ad are fighting with their backs against the wall.

"Looks like something went according to plan for a change," I say to Lieutenant Benning, who is sifting through the rubble on the floor with the toes of his armored boots.

"Don't call it a win just yet," he says. "Party ain't over until our boots are back on that carrier deck."

As if to make his point, the thunderclap of heavy ordnance exploding shakes the walls of the basement and almost tips me out of my chair.

"Enemy air," Third Squad's leader shouts into the platoon channel a few moments later. "Pair of attack birds, coming in from zero-zero-nine!"

"Warm up the missiles. First and Second Squads, get your heads down."

"Incoming ordnance!" someone from Third Squad yells. On my tactical display, the red aircraft symbols have just cleared the edge of my current map overlay when four small inverted vees separate from the enemy attack birds and rush toward our position.

"Hit the deck," I shout, and dive for the floor. Next to me, Lieutenant Benning and the platoon sergeant follow suit.

The four rockets hit our building simultaneously, with a cataclysmic bang that sounds like the *Manitoba* fell out of orbit and crashed onto the roof. My suit shuts down all sensor feeds automatically, turning me blind and deaf to protect me. When the video feed returns, it's in the green-tinged shade of low-light magnification. All the lights in the basement have gone out, and the air is thick with concrete dust. My tactical screen comes to life again, just in time for me to see the symbols for the two enemy attack craft passing overhead. From Third Squad's position, two MANPAD missiles rise in the wake of the SRA aircraft. One of the missiles catches up with its quarry and blots one of the red plane icons from my data screen. The other aircraft rushes out of range, its pursuing missile deflected by decoys.

"One down," Third Squad's leader announces over some general utterances of triumph. "Other one's gonna come back around—you can bet your asses on that."

"Get me some counter-air down here," Lieutenant Benning tells me. "Whatever's close by. I'm not picky right now."

"Already on it, boss," I say.

I check my airspace for the nearest fleet air units. Our platoon's drop ship is nearby, but a Wasp doesn't have the armament or speed to take on a fast mover. The next closest fleet units are two Shrikes, circling in a CAP pattern thirty miles away and twenty thousand feet high. I check their ordnance racks remotely and see an air-to-ground mix supplemented by four air-to-air missiles each on the outer wing pylons of the Shrikes.

"Raptor flight, this is Tailpipe Five. Counter-air," I call out on the tactical air channel.

"Tailpipe Five, Raptor One-Three. Go ahead." The voice on the TacAir channel is chopped, curt, and professional, just the way I remember Halley's voice on our squad channel in Basic.

"Data uplink commencing. Fast mover right above the deck near our datum. You are cleared to engage. Get him off our asses."

"Copy that, Tailpipe Five. On the way."

"Cavalry's coming," I tell the lieutenant. "Two Shrikes."

"If they shoot that bastard down and he bails out, I'll chase him down and string him up by his balls," the platoon sergeant says darkly. "I'm not getting shit for vitals from First and Second Squads upstairs."

"Third Squad, sitrep," Lieutenant Benning sends on the platoon channel. "What's the picture out there?"

"LT, where the fuck are you?"

"In the building, Sarge. Down in the basement."

"Ain't no building left, sir. Top floors are gone. So's the south half of the first floor."

"We're coming out. Check on the ground level on the north side, see if it's full of rubble. And see if you can raise anyone from First and Second Squads. We're not getting zip down here."

There's a brief pause before the sergeant replies.

"They're gone, LT. Building's gone. Their vitals are off the network."

"Goddammit," our platoon sergeant curses next to me in the darkness. "And just when we had this son of a bitch in the bag."

I just grunt my agreement, and follow the platoon's two-man command section out of the tomb that used to be the SRA company headquarters.

Some troops have a thing about not wanting to be that last unlucky bastard to buy it in a battle, the one who catches a stray fléchette or laser tripwire when everyone else is already breaking out the beer, but that thought never bothered me in the least. Whether you're the first one to die on the drop, or you stumble over something and break your neck just as you're stepping back onto the carrier deck after the battle, you end up in the same body bag, active antiseptic green polymer, impervious to pathogens and body fluids. If they recover your meat, that is, and you didn't get blown to bits by a Chinese fuel-air warhead, like the troopers from First and Second Squads who, to a man and woman, just died a few dozen feet above us. None of the dead are any less lucky than the others.

The staircases are all filled with rubble from the collapsed floors above us. The basement has two exits to the surface, so we pick the one that has less debris in front of it and start digging ourselves out. Outside, Third Squad tries to work their way inside. Finally, we emerge from the acrid darkness of the basement back into the sunlight of Sirius Ad.

"What now, Skipper?" Third Squad's leader asks the lieutenant.

"Keep up the perimeter, call down the bird for evac, and let's see if we can find our guys in that shit. Check for suit transponders."

In the blink of an eye, our combat strength has been cut by half. We have the remaining eight troopers of Third Squad, and the seven members of Fourth Squad a few hundred yards away. We landed on Sirius Ad with thirty-nine troops, and we're down to eighteen. We took our objective and accomplished our task, and we traded twenty-one lives for a smoldering pile of rubble and an understrength platoon's worth of SRA corpses.

There's a sudden cacophony of small-arms fire from the area where Fourth Squad has taken up covering positions by the main road through town. I only realize that some Chinese civvies had started to venture out into the open to observe the aftermath of the battle when they all dash away again, back to the dubious safety of their thin-walled houses. At the same moment, the platoon channel comes alive with frantic status reports from Fourth Squad.

"Where the fuck did *they* come from?"

"Incoming!"

"Street corner, one hundred, three guys with a rocket launcher!"

"Alpha One-Niner, we have a shitload of SRA coming in from the direction of the airfield. Make it fifteen, twenty—shit, looks like half a freakin' company out there."

"Copy that," the lieutenant sends back. "Fall back and draw them our way. We'll come up the road and set up a blocking position by that second intersection down from you, at Charlie Two."

"Affirmative. Fall back and draw the enemy to blocking position at second intersection. Bugging out."

We check our weapons on the run. With most of a company bearing down on us, only some air support is going to keep us from ending up in a Chinese POW camp or a mass grave. I fire up my TacAir screen as I'm dashing from corner to corner, and once more check for air assets.

"Banshee Two-Five, this is Tailpipe Five. We have a counter-attack coming our way, one platoon plus. Dust off and cover us from above, if you can."

"Tailpipe Five, that's a roger. We're on the way. ETA two minutes."

Our drop ship has used up most of its air-to-ground ordnance in the initial assault, and strafing runs with the guns are dangerous business, but without Banshee Two-Five's automatic cannons, there may not be anyone left for them to ferry back to the carrier. On my helmet display, red "HOSTILE" symbols are popping up with increasing frequency as the troopers from Fourth Squad are spotting enemy troops, and the red symbols outnumber our blue ones at least four to one.

Fourth Squad is doing an orderly retreat, leapfrogging across intersections ahead of us. The main street going through the settlement is barely twenty yards wide and flanked by tight rows of prefabricated one- and two-story structures. We reach our target intersection just ahead of Fourth Squad and hastily set up firing positions to cover their retreat.

"Make 'em count," the platoon sergeant says. "We cover Fourth Squad, let them pass through us, and leapfrog back to the town center if we have to."

I check the seals of my armor, make sure for the twentieth time that my rifle has a round chambered, and kneel down behind a climate unit parked in front of what looks like a tea joint. The buildings out here are thin-walled, standard colonial living modules, just like our own colony settlements. The walls don't stop fléchette rounds or shrapnel, but using them as cover is mentally more satisfying than duking it out in the open.

"Here they come. Watch your sectors," the platoon sergeant says.

In front of us, three troopers from Fourth Squad come dashing around a corner not fifty yards away. I can't see the squad of Chinese marines in pursuit, but my helmet display continuously updates with enemies spotted by other troops in my platoon, and the alley around that corner is lousy with red symbols. I switch the fire mode selector of my rifle to computer-controlled mode, and draw a bead on the intersection ahead.

"Grenades," the lieutenant orders. "Air burst, twenty meters. Give me a volley over those rooftops to the right."

With my extra comms gear, I don't carry rifle grenades on my harness, but most of the platoon's regular members do. Behind me, half a dozen grenade launchers belch out computer-fused forty-millimeter grenades that arc over the rooftops to our right. They explode above the adjacent alley in a series of low, muffled cracks. We hear shouts and screams as the Chinese marines fifty yards away get peppered with high-velocity shrapnel. In front of us, the second half of Fourth Squad comes sprinting around the corner, legs pumping to a soundtrack of automatic rifle fire from the unseen SRA marines. With our presence announced, only an idiot or a green recruit would come around the corner to shoot after our retreating squad, but a pair of Chinese marines does just that, and promptly gets drilled by fléchette bursts from ten different rifles. To our right, there's a sound like someone throwing a bucket of nails onto a metal roof, as the remaining Chinese marines start firing at us through the thin walls of the houses.

"Fall back, in order," the platoon sergeant shouts.

Half our number leave cover and follow the Fourth Squad troopers back up the road to take up new firing positions, away from our now compromised position. The rest of us stay put to cover their movement. In the alley just to my right, a door opens, and the muzzle of a rifle pokes out. The SRA marine fires a burst in my direction, and I duck behind my cover as the fléchettes scream past my corner and through the walls of the house across the alley. At the ranges dictated by these narrow streets, infantry combat turns into a shoot-out in a toilet stall.

"They're cutting through the back walls," I shout into the platoon channel, and return fire. My tactical computer switches the rifle to fully automatic suppression fire, and my ammo count is revised downward rapidly as my M-66 burps out twelve hundred fléchettes per minute, spraying the doorway and adjacent walls with tungsten penetrators.

"First section, haul ass," the call comes over the radio. "Watch the side alleys!"

Behind me, the second section has taken up position to cover our retreat. A bounding overwatch movement is always a leap of faith—you trust your squad mates not to shoot you by accident, and to keep the enemy from shooting you in the back while you're running away. I raise my rifle, rake the alley with another burst for good measure, and get up from my crouch to beat a retreat. All around me, dozens of rifles are chattering their reports—ours high-pitched and hoarse, theirs low and slow, like hydraulic hammers. As we pull back from the contested intersection, the Chinese marines return our earlier favor—behind me, half a dozen grenades go off in the road, a chain of large and angry firecrackers.

"Tailpipe Five, this is Banshee Two-Five. I got line of sight, but you're awfully close together down there."

I dash into a doorway where a tall garbage recycler is offering some minimal shelter, and toggle into the TacAir channel. "Banshee Two-Five, hit that corner I'm designating, and walk your fire down the alley that goes north from there. Hurry up, they're getting pissed down here."

"Tailpipe Five, copy that. Hit the designated corner and work north from there. Starting our gun run now."

The rounds from the drop ship's autocannons smack into the intersection before I can hear the guns rattling in the distance. Large-caliber autocannon fire is shockingly sudden and violent when you're only seventy yards from the spot where the shells hit. The building I just raked with rifle fire simply blows apart. Pieces of laminate rain down onto the surrounding buildings. Then Banshee Two-Five's pilot shifts his fire as instructed, and the alley beyond turns into noise, fire, and smoke.

"Banshee Two-Five, that's a bull's-eye. We have bad guys swarming all over those alleys to the left of your TRP. Bring it down close."

"Shifting fire. Y'all keep your heads low."

With the SRA marines dodging cannon fire, our half-strength platoon disengages and leapfrogs back toward the center of town. Overhead, no more than a hundred feet above the deck, Banshee Two-Five closes in, cannons hammering out a steady stream of noise and death. The roar from the Wasp's multibarreled chin turret mixes with the dull claps of the exploding shells. If there are any civvies hiding in the buildings around us, they are now in a very bad spot, but their plight is nobody's concern right now—not ours, and not that of the Chinese marines that are supposed to be their defenders. All that matters right now is that only one group is going to walk off this rock in their own boots, and both teams are doing their level best to be it.

"Tailpipe Five, you have some hostiles advancing on you through the alleys on your left. I'll make another pass, but it's getting awfully tight down there."

"Copy that, Two-Five," I reply. "Do what you can. We're hauling ass back to the admin center at Bravo Three. Anything to my east and west is hostile."

Two-Five's cannons bellow again, much closer than before. It sounds like our drop ship is almost directly overhead. This time, the cannon rounds rake a stretch of alley no more than twenty yards to my right, just on the other side of the squat, ugly building container I'm passing at a run. I hear the shouts and screams from the SRA marines and the rattling of their rifles as they return fire at the Wasp.

"Tailpipe Five, this is Hammer Seven-Six. We are overhead with air-to-ground. Got a use for us?"

In all the excitement, I haven't checked my TacAir screen in a while. Hammer flight, our two-ship escort of Shrike attack craft, is circling high above the battle, far removed from the noise and chaos, but aware of our status through the integrated tactical network we all feed.

"Hammer Seven-Six, you bet. We have a company of infantry on our asses. Use Banshee Two-Five's TRP, and drop all the anti-personnel stuff you have left on your racks. Danger close, you are cleared hot."

"Tailpipe Five, copy that. Take over TRP from Banshee Two-Five, and clear the grid. Rolling in hot. Cover your ears, gentlemen."

"Banshee Two-Five, break off CAS and return to station. Thanks for the assist."

"Copy that," Two-Five's pilot replies. "Hauling ass."

Overhead, the noise from the drop ship's engines increases as Two-Five's pilot gooses the throttles to gain altitude. Behind us, the cacophony of small-arms fire and grenade explosions swells as the Chinese recover from the strafing run and give chase once more. They're mistaking our sudden desire to clear the area for all-out flight, or maybe they know exactly what's about to happen and they want to get under our belts to make life hard for our air support.

We're almost back at the ruined admin center when Hammer flight's ordnance hits the ground just a few hundred meters behind us. I'm in the middle of a sprint between covering positions when my audio feed cuts out, and the shock wave of the explosion kicks me in the back and sends me sprawling face-first into the dirt. When my hearing returns, the firing behind us has ceased completely. For a few moments, there is no sound except for the reverberating rumble of the detonations rolling over the town, as if the blasts have stunned everyone into silence.

I get back on my feet and turn around to the familiar sight of a huge smoke pillar rising into the sky. There's debris raining down all around—bits of buildings, pavement, and people, all intermixed with the dusty red soil of the planet. Without my enhanced helmet sensors, I wouldn't be able to see my hand in front of my face. Ten or fifteen blocks of the Chinese town have ceased to exist, and with them all the people within, civilians and SRA marines alike. There's nothing left of the light colonial architecture but a burning field of strewn rubble and the occasional mangled wreckage of a light vehicle.

"Holy shit," someone chimes in nearby. "Flyboys don't fuck around, do they?"

"Hammer flight, this is Tailpipe Five," I send to the pilot. "That's a *shack*. I'd say you can paint about a hundred hash marks on your bird for that strike."

"Tailpipe Five, copy that. We aim to please."

We spread out and keep our guard up while the dust from the bombardment settles, but it's clear that if there are any SRA marines still alive, they've vacated the area wisely. The ordnance from Hammer flight has cleared a quarter square kilometer of densely packed modular housing.

"Fall back to the admin center," the lieutenant says. "Let's dig out our guys and call down the bird."

We head back to the center of town, where sixteen of our troopers are buried in the rubble of our target building. The Chinese civvies are once again coming out of their homes, but they quickly move out of the way when they see us, and none of them challenge our newly won ownership of the place. It feels like I've been dodging rifle fire and calling down airstrikes all day, but my suit's computer shows that not even three hours have passed since we boarded our drop ship.

The Chinese town isn't much of a prize. It's just a square kilometer of basic housing modules, and it was unimportant even before we scraped a quarter of it off the map with high explosives. If we were to garrison this shithole, the locals would shoot us in the back at the earliest opportunity, and the SRA will be more than willing to blow up the rest of the town trying to reclaim it. We're not going to garrison the place, of course. We lost twenty—almost two squads of our own—and killed hundreds of SRA marines and civvies, just to poke a sharp stick into the eye of the SRA high command—a job we could have completed just as well with a dozen warheads fired from orbit.

"What a pile of shit," the platoon sergeant mutters next to me, and kicks a piece of debris out of his path. "Can't afford too many more victories like this one."

We dig through the rubble of the collapsed admin center carefully, but without heavy equipment it's like trying to empty a bathtub with a spoon. All around us, the Chinese residents of the town are filling up the streets again. Now that the shooting has stopped, and we have shown that we won't gun them down in the street on sight, the locals are getting bolder by the minute, yelling at us from an ever-shrinking distance.

"You see weapons pointing our way, you shoot," the lieutenant tells us. "We're not here to make friends. I've collected enough fucking dog tags for one day."

I'm standing off to the side, eyeing the crowd milling around in the street near the admin building, when the tactical network comes alive with a burst of priority transmissions. I toggle into the fleet's TacLink screen, but before I can make heads or tails of the incoming transmission codes, the network goes dark altogether.

"What the fuck?"

"Problem, Sarge?" Lieutenant Benning asks.

"Fleet started broadcasting priority code, and then I lost my uplink."

The lieutenant walks over to where I'm standing and cycles through his own command links.

"I got a link to our ground units back to Company level, but that's it," he says. "Battalion HQ dropped off."

Some of the Chinese civvies shout in surprise, and look up into the darkening sky. I look up and follow their gaze. Up in the purplish blue of the late afternoon sky, there's a rapidly expanding sphere of brilliant white—the signature of a nuclear explosion in high orbit. Lieutenant Benning looks up as well, just in time to see a second fireball flash up some distance from the first one. Even at this range, our helmet visors kick in the polarizing filters to protect our retinas from the blinding pinprick flares of the nuclear fireballs. I feel a sudden and overwhelming weakness in my knees.

"Oh, *shit*," the lieutenant says.

I scroll through the incoming messages my tactical computer buffered before the link went down. It's a mess of burst transmissions on the priority fleet channel, encrypted ship-to-ship comms that are illegible to my tactical computer and its limited access level.

"Try to raise Company," I tell the lieutenant. "I'll check in with Fleet over voice."

I open a channel on the fleet emergency band, override the EMCON protocols of my comms suite, and crank my transmitter up to full power.

"*Manitoba*, this is Tailpipe Five. Do you read, over?"

For a moment, all I get in return is static. Then the reply comes down from the *Manitoba*, and going by the barely restrained panic in the voice of the comms operator in CIC, things have gone very wrong indeed.

"Tailpipe Five, kindly keep out of the ship-to-ship emergency comms. We are under attack. *Manitoba* out."

I hear a crescendo of overlapping alarm klaxons in the background before the transmission ends.

"The fleet is under attack, sir," I tell the lieutenant. "I have no clue what's going on up there, but it sounds like they're in deep shit."

Then the fleet TacLink comes back to life, and another burst transmission scrolls across my screen, colored in the crimson red of high-priority TacLink updates.

"ALL GROUND UNITS ABORT CURRENT OBJECTIVES AND ASSUME DEFENSIVE POSTURES. TASK FORCE IS ENGAGED. ABORT RPT. ABORT ALL INBOUND TRAFFIC TO MANITOBA."

I tap into the newly established link to our carrier and call up the CIC's situation display. It takes much longer than usual—all the data nodes between the task force units are exchanging massive bursts of data, and there's no bandwidth left for non-priority data traffic. Fifteen seconds after I send my request, the tactical plot on the *Manitoba*'s main CIC screen unfolds on my helmet display, and I feel myself getting nauseous with fear.

The task force is scattering before a new arrival in orbit, but the newcomer's tactical icon is not the red symbol of an SRA capital ship. Instead, it's blaze orange.

High up in the sky, more nuclear explosions are blooming, like short-lived new suns. By now, NAC troopers and Chinese civvies alike are looking up at the fireworks, none of them aware of the magnitude of the new threat.

Finally, I find my voice again.

"Lankies," I say over the platoon channel. "It's a fucking Lanky seed ship."

CHAPTER 11

———— THE FATE OF THE ———— TASK FORCE

"Well, *that's* a shitty end to this day," the platoon sergeant says.

I can't help but chuckle at what has to be the understatement of the decade. Everyone is cross-talking on the platoon channel, so I open a private channel to the lieutenant.

"LT, we need to call the drop ship down and get the fuck off this rock, right now."

"Orders say to sit tight and go defensive," the lieutenant replies. "If that's a Lanky ship up there, we'd climb right up into the middle of a shootout."

"Look." I splice off the feed from the *Manitoba's* CIC and send it through the private data link. Our fleet units are splitting two ways, like the small SRA task force we engaged earlier. The carrier and one of the destroyer escorts are moving out of orbit, away from the Lanky ship, and the Hammerheads and the space control cruiser are shielding the *Manitoba's* retreat. The space between our ships and the advancing Lanky seed ship is a sea of missile icons—the three cruisers are emptying their magazines at the new arrival. Together, they carry a few dozen megatons of nukes, enough fire-power to turn a small moon into an irradiated wasteland, but Lanky seed ships are incredibly tough, and nukes aren't a quarter as effective in hard vacuum as they are in a planetary atmosphere.

121

"They're trying to make the chute, and the cruisers are going to buy them time. If we're still dirtside in another five minutes, they'll be out of reach, and we'll be breathing CO_2 in another month. They won't come back, sir. They won't risk another task force for a lousy regiment or two. You know it."

"They get blown out of space, we die with them, Sarge."

"They make Alcubierre, we're safe. Otherwise, we're dead, one way or the other. It'll just take a few days longer, that's all."

"Fuck." The lieutenant doesn't deliberate for long before he cuts the private link and speaks up in the platoon channel.

"All right, cut the yapping. We are bugging out. Mark a spot for the bird. We're getting out of here while we can. Banshee Two-Five, come on down for evac."

"Copy that. ETA thirty seconds."

We mark a clear spot for the drop ship and wait for our taxi, mindful of the Chinese civilians who are still loitering on the perimeter, unsure of the sudden burst of activity on our side. With my TacLink, I have a real-time picture of the battle overhead, and knowing the extent of our troubles, the thirty seconds until the arrival of our drop ship feel like three weeks. Then Banshee Two-Five comes descending out of the darkening blue sky, makes one low pass overhead to eyeball the landing spot, and sets down gracefully right on top of our markers.

I'm part of the rear guard, and I keep my weapon trained on the Chinese civvies as the first half of our decimated contingent runs over to board the Wasp. In front of me, I see forty or fifty locals in the narrow streets beyond the ruined admin building. Most of them are just watching us, but some of them have worked up the courage to yell insults or throw debris in our direction.

You poor bastards, I think. *Survived our guns and our bombs, and now you're all going to die anyway, either by Lanky nerve-gas pods or by choking like fish on dry land.*

I don't speak enough Chinese to inform them of their fate, but even if I knew more than the few phrases we learned in fleet training—stuff like *stop, surrender, go fuck yourself*—I wouldn't take the time to tell them. They'll know soon enough, if the nukes going off in high orbit didn't already make things clear. We don't use atomic arms against the SRA, and they don't use them against us, because it's bad policy to start irradiating the very same resources you're fighting over. The only time we use nuclear warheads is when we go up against the Lankies.

"Second element, *move, move, move!*" the platoon sergeant calls out. I trust the other half of the platoon to watch my rear, and turn around to run for the tail ramp of the drop ship idling a hundred meters away. In the pile of rubble to my right, the bodies of our platoon mates still lie buried and unclaimed, in the spots that will have to serve as their graves until we can come back to reclaim Sirius Ad from the Lankies, who will own the place completely in another month.

I run up the ramp, strap into a seat in the cargo hold, and look out of the back of the Wasp. As the tail ramp rises up, my last view of Sirius Ad is that of a gaggle of Chinese civvies swarming over the rubble that was their government's local outpost, and it feels like I'm leaving a prison full of death row inmates, with the executioner striding into the place just as I'm walking out.

While we're climbing back into orbit, I have nothing to look at except for gray-painted bulkhead, and nothing to do but to tighten my seat straps, so I stay glued to the tactical screen. The battle overhead is a shootout between profoundly unequal adversaries, our best technology employed against an enemy so advanced that we might as well be hurling rocks and sticks instead of twenty-megaton warheads for all the damage we're failing to do. Our cruisers are between the Lanky ship and the retreating carrier, pumping out salvo after salvo of antiship missiles, but the trajectory of the seed ship isn't changing as it shrugs off our warheads. The *Manitoba* and her two escorts are leaving the neighborhood at maximum acceleration, but the Lanky ship has a lot of momentum, and the cruisers aren't even slowing it down.

We climb into low orbit at full throttle, but our progress feels agonizingly slow. With every minute our ship is clawing for more altitude, the carrier and her bodyguards are increasing the distance. When I finally feel the weightlessness of orbital flight lifting me out of my seat and into the harness straps, the *Manitoba* is almost a quarter million kilometers away. The Lanky seed ship is much closer.

"Ain't no way we're going to catch up," the crew chief says to us from his jump seat by the forward bulkhead. "Not unless they slow down a bit and let us close the gap."

"If we don't, we'll just go back dirtside," Lieutenant Benning replies. "Can't get fucked much worse than we are right now anyway."

As if on cue, the pilot chimes in on the intercom.

"Brace for evasive."

The ship pitches and rolls in the low gravity. We're blind and deaf in the cargo hold, unaware of the threat that made the pilot put the craft into an evasive pattern, and the lack of control and awareness is almost worse than being stuck in a bad firefight. I scan the shipboard data nodes, and tap into the Wasp's external video feed. For a few moments, I see nothing but distant stars careening across the dorsal camera's field of view, but then the pilot straightens out our trajectory, and the feed of the wide-angle lens shows a piece of the battle in progress nearby.

Off our starboard bow, one of the Hammerhead cruisers is in a spin, bleeding air and frozen fluids out of hundreds of holes in its outer hull. Just beyond the cruiser, the massive bulk of the Lanky seed ship pushes its way through the hastily erected blocking position. The Lanky ship is enormous, a glistening oblong shape that looks like a cross between a seedpod and a rifle bullet. It dwarfs our cruisers, which look like sparrows trying to attack an eagle. I know that a Hammerhead is almost four hundred meters long, and the seed ship looks to be at least five times that size. I've seen drone shots of the seed ships in many intel briefings, but this is the first time I am looking at one through a direct camera feed, and the sight of it makes me want to crawl into my armored boots. All three of our cruisers are tattered, with hull damage I can spot even through the fish-eye lens of the dorsal camera from hundreds of klicks away, but the Lanky ship has no visible scars on its seamless black flanks. The Hammerheads are our newest capital ships, supermodern fleet defense cruisers that can hold their own against an entire SRA task force, but the Lanky seed ship just brushed two of them aside without even putting on the brakes.

The pilot changes our trajectory to catch up with our fleeing carrier, and the new camera angle points away from the Lankies and into the space between Sirius Ad and our clandestine Alcubierre transition point. I'm not an astrogator, but I can read movement vectors and do some relative speed calculations in my head, and it's pretty clear that the crew chief is right—there's no way we'll catch up with the *Manitoba* and her escorts, and our pilot is pushing the Wasp as fast as it will go already. Our carrier is running away at full acceleration, trying to make Alcubierre before the Lanky seed ship catches up and hammers our hundred-thousand-ton flagship into scrap.

"What a fucked-up day," the platoon sergeant says to no one in particular.

Without the hint of a warning, the rear cargo door of the drop ship disintegrates. The concussion of an impact slaps through the ship like the shock wave of a grenade. Something fast and super-heated tears through the troop compartment from back to front and then bores through the bulkhead on my right. There's violent decompression in the cargo hold as all the air gets vented through the wound in the drop ship's outer hull. My suit automatically seals itself and turns on its own oxygen feed as I get whipped around in the straps of my seat. The back of my head makes contact with the hull behind me, and even with the padding of my helmet, the impact is enough to make me see red stars in front of my eyes. The sudden chaos in the cargo hold is complete—everything that wasn't strapped down is getting blown around. With the air gone, there's no sound coming from my external audio feed, and the silence lends a surreal quality to the event. When my vision returns and my world slows its spin, I reach for the rifle next to my seat out of pure habit, only to find that my M-66 has disappeared, torn from its storage bracket.

The cargo hold is a scene of utter carnage. Whatever blew through the rear hatch tore through the ship from tail to nose at a slight angle from right to left of our centerline. Bits and pieces of bulkhead armor, seats, webbing, and people are rushing past my eyes on their way out of the rear of the ship. I look to my left to see that we are trailing a comet tail of debris and frozen oxygen. The row of seats across the aisle from me is no longer there, and nei-ther are the people who were strapped into them just a few moments ago. Half the cockpit bulkhead to my right is torn away, and instead of seeing into the drop ship's galley and head that should be beyond the shattered bulkhead, I look into empty space. The armored door to the cockpit is gone, and the area in front of it looks like we ran nose-first into the *Manitoba*'s armor belt at top speed. From the movement of the stars beyond the massive holes in our hull, I can tell we're in a spin.

Some of the troopers are calling for help on the comms now, but everyone's cross-talking, yelling and shouting in shock and fear. The cargo bay has two rows of seats, one on each side, and I'm near the front of the starboard side. The entire rear half of the starboard-side seat row has been torn out of the ship, with nothing but mangled metal and shredded hull lining remaining where the Lanky projectile plowed through the Wasp. Half the port-side seats are gone as well, everything from the wing roots in the middle of the ship all the way to the cockpit bulkhead. Sheer luck of the draw has placed me in one of the spots that didn't get pulverized by millions of foot-pounds of kinetic energy. In the long run, it won't matter— the ship is destroyed, and we're in a very high orbit over Sirius Ad. All our fleet units are either engaged in battle, destroyed, or running away from the Lankies, and there's nobody out there to stop and pluck me out of the wreckage.

Against my better knowledge, I toggle into the pilots' intercom channel.

"Banshee Two-Five, you copy?"

There's no answer, of course. I strain forward in my seat straps, unwilling to release the harness lock and risk getting flung out of the back of the ship, and peer around the corner of the doorway in the cockpit bulkhead. The armory nook is still there, and the right side of the cockpit looks relatively undamaged, but the left side has been hammered into a pulp. The left seat is missing altogether, and the right seat is occupied by a pilot who is slumped over sideways in his seat. His head is gone, along with most of his neck, and little frozen blood bubbles are drifting out of the smashed cockpit and into space like a cloud of tiny pink balloons.

"Headcount," one of the squad leaders says on the platoon channel. "Sound off if you're still alive."

I check my tactical screen for suit telemetrics and find that I'm one of four people still alive in the cargo hold. There are two more still strapped into their seats, but their vitals are flat—a suit that didn't seal in time, a piece of high-velocity shrapnel through the helmet. Half a dozen live troopers are floating in space outside the hull, getting left behind like dumped cap-ship garbage as the Wasp's inertia carries it further out of orbit.

"Grayson here," I reply. "Check your oxygen levels and hang on to something solid. I'll try to get Fleet on emergency comms."

"For what it's worth," the squad sergeant sends back. "Hope they hear you. I got two hours of air in my suit."

I check my own oxygen supply, and it's not much better. Three hours and thirteen minutes at present rate of consumption, the suit's computer informs me in unnecessarily precise fashion. The tanks in our suits are low-capacity reserves designed for emergencies in hard vacuum, like a drop-ship hull breach on descent, but the designers assumed that rescue units would be close by. Battle armor makes lousy extra-vehicular activity gear—the joint seals aren't the sturdiest, and a nick from an enemy fléchette means that your three-hour supply of air becomes a five-minute supply. The bug suits have much bigger oxygen systems because they're designed for fighting on high-CO_2 Lanky worlds, but my own bug suit is in a locker in my berth on the *Manitoba*, which is now almost half a million kilometers away.

I fire up my comms suite again, turn the transmitter to full power, and start broadcasting the news of our impending death.

"All fleet units, all fleet units. This is Tailpipe Five on Banshee Two-Five, type Wasp. We have suffered a catastrophic hull breach and are coasting ballistic. Both pilots are casualties. We have four survivors in the hull, and six more outside. Declaring an emergency."

I listen for a reply, but all I hear is the hiss of an unused carrier wave. I repeat the broadcast three more times, but nobody out there is willing or able to respond.

"Well," the squad sergeant says. "That's that, then."

"Anyone have any weapons left?" one of the other survivors asks.

"Yeah, Goodwin. I got my rifle," the sergeant replies. "Why, what are you going to do with that fucking pellet gun out here?"

"I got two and a half hours of air left," Goodwin says. "Two hours and twenty-nine minutes comes around, I'm gonna borrow your rifle for a second if you don't mind, Sarge."

"I'll be dead by then, girl. You're welcome to it at that point."

"'Preciate it, Sarge," Goodwin says with lighthearted politeness, as if the sergeant had just agreed to trade z-ration desserts with her.

"What a fucked-up day," the sergeant says, echoing the words of the platoon sergeant who was sitting across the aisle from me, and who probably died in a millisecond when the Lanky penetrator rod tore through the ship.

We drift in the darkness in silence, reflecting on that epitaph. I conclude that as far as last words go, the platoon sergeant did pretty well.

Floating in the dark, silent hull of our wrecked drop ship, there is no up or down. Without the chronometer of my helmet display, I wouldn't be able to gauge the passage of time at all. I send out the same emergency broadcast every five minutes, but half an hour after the death of Banshee Two-Five, nobody has acknowledged our calls for help. My suit's low-frequency data link to the fleet has stopped real-time updates, and my tactical display is showing only best-guess positions. Both our Linebackers are flashing emergency beacons, and the Hammerhead space control cruiser has disappeared from the plot entirely. The *Manitoba* has traveled beyond the range of my tactical map, along with the Lanky seed ship. We are alone in space above Sirius Ad.

The cooling elements in my suit are working overtime to keep my body heat from boiling me in my armor. My air is good for another two and a half hours, and the battery pack will run the suit for another day or two before everything shuts down. I wonder if I should leave a last message in the memory banks of my armor's tactical computer, one final good-bye to Mom and Halley maybe, but then I decide it would be pointless. Sirius Ad's gravity will snare the wrecked drop ship sooner or later, and then we'll burn up in the atmosphere. Some bits and pieces of us might survive, but even if we ever retake the Sirius A system, nobody's going to mount a search for a few dog tags and some charred memory chips.

Forty-five minutes after my initial call for help, another emergency beacon pops up on my screen, with a vector marking indicating that the ship in distress is far outside my display's scope. Then the TacLink network connection drops altogether.

"Well, *shit.*"

"What's the matter, Grayson?" the other sergeant wants to know.

"We lost the *Manitoba*. Her crash buoy just popped up."

There are groans of despair from the other troops. The *Manitoba* didn't make the Alcubierre chute in time. Nobody will know about our fate until our task force is overdue at Gateway and they send someone to look for us. Between the carrier and the three cruisers alone, we lost ten thousand people today, and another five thousand infantry grunts are trapped down in the dirt on Sirius Ad, waiting for their inevitable extermination by the new masters of the system. I have no idea how many civilians will be added to the total by the time the Lankies have finished the takeover, but it's an old colony, settled half a century ago—a million or more settlers, third-generation off-Earthers at least.

I'm twenty-six years old. For the last five years of my life, I have served the Commonwealth wherever they sent me. I have lost count of the number of people I've killed—directly, with my rifle, or indirectly, by calling down air strikes and close air support on them. I've ordered nuclear strikes on Lanky towns, and I've shot our own citizens, in the welfare riots back in my TA days. All of it has steered me toward this fate—to suffocate in the wrecked hull of a drop ship, high above a second-rate colony we never planned to keep anyway, or to end it all with a quick rifle shot.

I think of Halley—the first time we met, on the first day of Basic, bunkmates by the luck of the alphabet—and I feel a profound gratitude for the interrupted, hectic, and strange relationship we've had, intense and exciting despite all the obstacles thrown into our path by an uncaring military. I think of Mom, and about the sadness she will feel at the loss of her only child, but I'm glad that we got to spend some time together just before I shipped out on this particular goat rope.

I conclude that I have no regrets, and that I'd do it all again, in exactly the same fashion, if I had the choice. If my life was short, at least I managed to live the last part of it on my own terms.

At the hour mark, when my air supply is down to a little over two hours, I turn up the transmitter again.

"All fleet units, all fleet units. This is Tailpipe Five, on Banshee Two-Five. We are dead in space, and running out of oxygen. Anyone left out there, please acknowledge."

I don't expect a reply, and when I hear a static-speckled voice responding to my distress call, I flinch so hard with excitement that I hit the back of my head on the hull behind my seat.

"Tailpipe Five . . . *Nassau*. Copy one by five. Say position."

"*Nassau*, we are above Sirius Ad in a wrecked Wasp, and our suits are running dry. Sending nav data right now. Got anything you can send our way?"

"Tailpipe Five, that's a negative," the reply comes after I have sent the burst transmission with our coordinates. "We are forty-five minutes from Alcubierre, and there's a Lanky between us and you. Sorry," the comms operator adds.

The *Nassau* is the frigate escort of the minelayer that peeled off the task force right after our arrival in-system. She has her own drop ships, but if they're less than an hour from the transition point, they are over four hours from our position. Even if they came about and headed our way at full acceleration, we'd be dead by the time they got here, and their captain is not going to go back where a carrier and three cruisers just met their end. I swallow my disappointment at having this new spark of hope extinguished.

Then there's a new voice on the emergency channel, clear and loud and impatient.

"*Nassau*, belay that. Come about and prepare the flight deck for inbound traffic. This is the CAG, *Manitoba*."

I check my tactical display for the source of the new transmission, and see a formation of four drop ships climbing out of Sirius Ad's atmosphere. The lead ship bears the designations *CAG* and *CO 4/5 RGT*—Commander Air Group and Commanding Officer, Fourth Regiment. The first boat in the formation has both the *Manitoba*'s air group commander and our infantry regiment's commanding officer on board, two of the highest-ranking people in our task force. I want to hold my breath to stop any extraneous sounds, so I won't miss a word of the new message traffic.

"CAG *Manitoba*, *Nassau*. We are unable to reverse course. We're forty-five minutes from transition."

"*Nassau*, CAG *Manitoba*. I see you on the plot, fella. Decelerate and loiter by the transition point. I have a four-ship flight stuffed with troops here. We can pick up Tailpipe Five and his entourage on the way, and catch up with you in four hours."

"Sir, there's a Lanky seed ship on our tail, in case you aren't up on current events."

"I can read a plot. The Lanky isn't accelerating anymore. We can dogleg it around their position. Why am I even talking to *you*? Get me *Nassau* Actual, right fucking now."

There's a ten-second silence in the channel, and a new voice comes on.

"CAG, this is *Nassau* Actual."

"Lieutenant Colonel Carignan, I'd very much appreciate it if you'd decelerate and give us time to catch up."

"Pete, you're asking me to risk my ship here. Did you see what happened to the *Manitoba*? I have no desire to add us to the casualty list."

"The Lanky is on a reverse course, and nowhere near you. Wait near the transition point, and if that seed ship moves in against you, get out and leave. Otherwise, let us try and sneak around the Lankies and over to you. I have a hundred people on these ships, and you're the only unit left that can make Alcubierre."

The *Nassau*'s captain lets another ten seconds elapse before he responds to the request.

"Colonel, I can't do that. My first responsibility is my crew."

"Okay, then," the CAG says, and his voice is flat with anger. "Let me rephrase that request. We have four Dragonflies here, and a total of sixteen standoff nukes between us. Do as I suggest and decelerate to wait for us, or I'll launch every last fucking missile I have. They may not catch up with you in time, but that's your bet to lose, mister. Those nukes do fifty gees sustained acceleration, and that old bucket of yours makes a fat target."

I can barely suppress a laugh into the shocked silence that follows the CAG's threat. Colonel Barrett, the commander of the

Manitoba's air group, has a reputation for abrasiveness, and it seems that the prospect of being abandoned in a Lanky-controlled system has excised whatever sense of diplomacy he had. I have no idea if the CAG is merely bluffing, but I sincerely hope that he isn't. The long-range standoff nukes on the Dragonflies are not really meant for antiship use, and the point defenses of a carrier would intercept them long before they got into range to do harm, but the *Nassau* is just an old frigate, and sixteen half-megaton warheads would saturate her point-defense system.

"You're threatening to shoot *nukes* at my ship? Are you out of your fucking *mind*? You know I'll have you locked up and court-martialed," the *Nassau's* captain finally replies. He sounds every bit as pissed as the CAG now.

"Yeah, we'll worry about that shit later," Colonel Barrett sends back.

"You have four hours," *Nassau* Actual says. "We're decelerating. If you're not in the docking clamp by then, we transition out. If the Lanky starts moving our way, we transition out without you. *Understood?*"

"Good enough. CAG out."

Nassau's captain does not bother to send a final end-of-transmission phrase.

In the darkness of our shattered drop-ship hull, I let out an exuberant cheer.

The flight of Dragonflies homes in on our dead Wasp, and the ten minutes of orbital maneuvering feel like ten hours to us. The Dragonfly drop ships have EVA airlocks for special ops, so we have a way into the ships without forcing their passengers to de-atmo the hulls. Still, without proper EVA suits, and with the last zero-gravity training session a few months behind me, changing ships in high orbit is a thrill I could do without. Under normal circumstances, the scene outside would be a breathtaking sight— the streamlined and lethal Dragonfly attack drop ship, position lights blinking, matching trajectories with our wreckage with the red and brown expanse of Sirius Ad below us as a backdrop. I mostly have eyes for the EVA hatch on the Dragonfly, a small target twenty yards beyond the destroyed tail ramp of our Wasp. When I push off, I miscalculate my trajectory and tumble toward the hatch too high, but the Dragonfly's pilot fires his thrusters for a fraction of a second and expertly catches me with the hatch like a catcher plucking a ball out of the air with his mitt. A few moments later, the EVA hatch closes again, and I hear the rush of ingressing air as the crew pressurizes the hatch compartment again. The drop ships don't have artificial-gravity gear like the big starships, so I have to hold on to the webbing that covers the inside of the hatch compartment to keep from careening around in the interior like a pea in a can.

"Hang on for about twenty seconds, trooper," someone says over the intercom. "I'll open the troop hatch as soon as the pressure is back to normal."

"You got it," I reply. "No rush."

In the weightlessness of high orbit, I can't feel the acceleration of the ship directly, but when the pilot revs the engines again, the increased vibrations transmit from the hull right into the webbing I am grasping. On my tactical screen, I can see our four-ship diamond formation detaching from the symbol that marks the dead Banshee Two-Five, and then heading away from Sirius Ad at maximum acceleration. With nothing left between us and the distant *Nassau* but a four-hour flight and a Lanky seed ship to avoid along the way, I shut down my tactical screen. If we make our escape, I'll owe my life to a drop-ship pilot for what seems like the fiftieth time, and if the Lankies intercept us, I don't want to have a count-down to my impending death again.

When we dock with the *Nassau* a few hours later, I expect to see a security detachment on the flight deck to escort us straight to the brig, but the *Nassau's* captain seems to have decided to save the court-martial business for later. When we file out of the troop bay, our only welcoming committee is the chief of the deck, who waves us on impatiently. The *Nassau's* little hangar is made to hold two combat-ready drop ships and two standby spares, and with four of the huge new Dragonflies cluttering up the deck, the ships are now parked wingtip to wingtip.

"All hands, prepare for Alcubierre transition. I repeat, all hands prepare for Alcubierre transition. Countdown one-five min-utes."

With almost a hundred new arrivals on the tiny frigate, the ship is now overstuffed with people and gear, and there are no seats for us to strap into. We sit down wherever we can claim a few square feet out of the way. I find a corner in a storage room, peel off my helmet, and sit down on the oil-stained floor to await our transition into the Alcubierre chute.

When we transition for the trip back to our own solar system, we leave behind a carrier, a destroyer, and three cruisers, lost with all hands. On Sirius Ad, we abandon the better part of two full Spaceborne Infantry regiments, thousands of fellow troopers who aren't geared to fight the Lankies that are about to descend upon them. Even if they evade the Lankies on the ground, every human being on that planet will succumb to the newly unbreathable atmosphere in another two months at the most. We pulled off a textbook planetary assault, won all our battles on the ground, and

suffered the worst military defeat of NAC forces in half a decade—
ten thousand dead in thirty minutes, another five thousand about
to die, and the Lankies in possession of a system that is just seven
light years and a single transition away from our homeworld.

I have talked to hundreds of fleet Medical Corps shrinks after
combat missions. We get a psych eval every time we come back
from a drop with casualties, to make sure nobody's going to snap
and shoot up a mess hall or eat a rifle round. The psych hacks
always ask the same questions, so they can get the answers that
will let them make check marks in the right places on their eval
forms. A lot of them are concerned about survivor guilt—the
notion that we combat grunts beat ourselves up mentally for having survived battles that claimed our friends and comrades by the
job lot. It's all a bunch of horseshit, as far as I'm concerned.

As we enter the chute, and the Alcubierre field around the ship
makes every molecule in my body develop a low-level ache, the
only guilt I feel is for being relieved at not being among the poor
bastards on the ground, my comrades in arms who are now facing
certain death at the hands of the Lankies. But I don't feel any guilt
for having escaped that fate, and I know that most of the troops
we are leaving behind wouldn't feel any guilt for surviving in my
stead, either.

CHAPTER 12

———— ON THE ROPES ————

If we were half as good at fighting Lankies as we are at wiping out each other, the fleet would assemble a huge task force and transition en masse to the Sirius A system, to kick the shit out of the Lankies and rescue all the troops we left behind. Instead, the only people jumping into instant action are the fleet's pencil pushers.

All through our transition from the Alcubierre chute back to Earth, the fleet brass tie up all our comms bandwidth to hold video debriefings with the survivors of Task Force Seventy-Two. I talk to an endless procession of majors, colonels, and generals, with a smattering of NAC and DOD officials in civilian garb thrown into the mix for good measure, and I repeat the same narrative dozens of times. Since I am the only surviving combat controller of the entire two-regiment force on the ground, the data storage modules in my battle armor are of particular interest to the brass, and they send a fleet Intel captain with an MP escort to collect my armor for data retrieval, as if I'm dumb enough to accidentally overwrite my computer's memory with streamed Network news, or broadcast all the recorded plot data to everyone on the *Nassau*.

After the third straight day of video debriefings, I do something I've never done before in my career—I duck out of duty by going to sick bay. It doesn't take much to make the shrink put me on sedatives and sleeping pills, and I spend the last three days of our trip back to Earth pleasantly doped up on a semiprivate folding cot in Storage Locker 2204L.

"Now hear this: All hands, prepare for arrival at Independence Station. ETA one hundred and twenty minutes."

"*Independence* Station?" Staff Sergeant West repeats. He looks at me with a raised eyebrow. "That's the corporate civvie station. Wonder what's wrong with old Gateway."

"Beats me," I say, and take another sip of my coffee. "Maybe it finally fell into the North Atlantic. Every time we get back there, it looks more run down."

"You know the fleet. They'll run it 'til it breaks, and then they put it back together with polyglue and run it some more."

Sergeant West is one of the troopers who survived the demise of Banshee Two-Five with me. Over the last few days, we have spent a lot of time in the NCO galley, working through the events in the Sirius A system by talking about different things entirely, the roundabout combat-grunt way of dealing with mental trauma.

The change in routine, combined with the fact that our in-system comms have been restricted ever since we popped out of Alcubierre a week ago, seems like a harbinger of bad things to come. When I share that concern with Sergeant West, he just shrugs.

"You've been in long enough, Grayson. Never assume malice if you can explain it with lack of planning."

When we finally dock with Independence Station, we are greeted by a welcoming committee of what looks like a company or two of Intel officers and military police. More ominously, there are also people in civilian garb among them, and I don't have to look at them twice to know they're NAC domestic security agents. We're funneled into separate rooms and split up into ever-smaller groups, until I find myself sitting in a small fabric-walled office unit with a dour-looking Intel captain.

"Staff Sergeant Grayson," he says, reading off the data pad in his hands. "Sorry about the *Manitoba*. I'm sure you've lost a lot of friends on that ship."

I didn't really have a lot of friends on the *Manitoba* yet, since I had just transferred onto her, but I nod anyway.

"That wasn't the first ship you lost, I see. There was the *Versailles* back in 2113. Can't get away from the Lankies, can you?"

"Not my doing, Captain. I'd gladly stay away from them if they'd let me."

"Yeah, they're getting annoying." He flicks through the screen on his data pad with his forefinger. "You were on the surface when the seed ship arrived. Did you get the flash message traffic that ordered all ground units to stay put and go defensive?"

"I don't recall that one, sir. Things were a bit hectic, you know, what with the nukes going off in high orbit."

"Your suit's computer says you did. You then advised the platoon leader to call down the unit's drop ship and head back to the carrier, against orders."

"See those?" I point at the rank sleeves on my uniform, a chevron in a U-shaped border on each shoulder. "That means 'staff sergeant.' The platoon leaders had a star on each one. That means 'second lieutenant.' Those don't take orders from staff sergeants."

The Intel captain looks at me impassively for a moment, like a biologist watching a strange specimen twitch at the end of a needle. Then he puts his data pad onto the desk in front of him, and leans back in his chair.

"You're a *combat controller*. You're the fleet liaison on the ground. Any platoon leader with half a brain will follow your advice. The only reason you're alive is because you acted against orders, and because your ship's CAG threatened to shoot nukes at a task force ship. That's good enough for a court-martial for everyone above the rank of corporal on those four drop ships, as far as I'm concerned."

I look at the captain in disbelief for a moment. Then some gasket in my brain gives way.

"Are you seriously taking us to task for getting off that rock alive? You have *got* to be joking."

"That's absolutely not the case, Sergeant. I don't have an issue with the fact that you survived. I just have an issue with the fact that you acted against orders."

"*Fuck you,*" I say, and fold my arms across my chest. "I'm done talking to you. Get me JAG counsel in here or get out of my face."

"You don't need legal counsel. You're not charged with anything yet."

"Then either charge me and have the MP haul me off to the brig, or stop wasting my fucking time."

The captain picks up his data pad again and taps the screen studiously. I have to suppress the urge to reach across the desk and rip the damn thing from his hands. Right now, they're looking for a way to pin the tail on the donkey, to find someone to take the heat, to make it look like the brass aren't the collection of ticket-punching career desk pilots they've always been. We're losing the war for the survival of our species, and the people in charge are still willing to throw the grunts out of the airlock to save their own careers.

"You're a fleet asset, Staff Sergeant Grayson. We don't have enough combat controllers to let you spend a month or two in Leavenworth while the corps decides whether to throw the book at you. Rest assured, however, that the incident will go on your record, and that we'll revisit the issue once things have settled a bit."

I shake my head and chuckle.

"We just got our asses kicked by the Lankies, *seven light years* from this place. The way things are going for the home team, I'm not too worried about a fucking court-martial right now, Captain."

The fleet has an informal term for sailors who survive the destruction of their ship: HLOs, hull-loss orphans. "Halos" usually get shifted from one Transient Personnel Unit to another as the fleet tries to find a new home for them. Those of us who survived the disaster of Sirius Ad aren't treated like halos, even though we are. Instead, they treat us with a combination of movement restrictions and benign neglect that makes us feel only marginally more welcome than SRA prisoners of war. We're not allowed onto MilNet, and we're berthed in a restricted area of Independence Station, with a screen of military police guards keeping us away from the other troopers and sailors passing through the place. The week after our arrival sees an ever-increasing stream of personnel and gear, until Independence looks like a slightly cleaner and newer version of the perennially overcrowded Gateway Station. I've been in the fleet long enough to know that our comms blackout means that the brass don't want the news of our ass-kicking to get out among the rank and file just yet. The meaning of the swelling troop buildup in one of the NAC's three major orbital hubs is pretty clear—we're gearing up for a major operation, and Command is throwing everything but the kitchen sink at the Lankies this time.

Finally, after a week and a half of more debriefings, extended naps, medical checkups, and long stretches of mind-numbing boredom, the fleet has figured out what to do with me.

"Staff Sergeant Grayson," the lieutenant says as he walks into the storage room that serves as our temporary mess hall. I put down my ham-and-cheese sandwich and get up to render a salute.

"As you were, Sergeant," he says, and sits down across the table from me. He is wearing the standard black fleet beret, and his specialty badge marks him as a Logistics & Personnel pencil pusher, not an Intel officer like all the other brass I've seen this week.

"Yes, sir," I say, and push aside my sandwich. "What's the word?"

"Vacation's over. The fleet needs you to jump back in, if you're ready."

"Of course, sir."

He produces a data pad, taps around on the screen, and then turns it so I can see the display.

"You'll be reporting to NACS *Midway* at 1300 Zulu tomorrow. She's on her way to Independence Station right now."

"The *Midway*?" I search my mental data bank for information. "Didn't they decommission her a few years back?"

"She was put in reserve. They bumped her back into the active fleet last week. The maintenance crew is ferrying her over from strategic-reserve fleetyard."

"Wow," I say. "Fleet's scraping the bottom of the barrel. The Pacific-class ships are *eighty fucking years old* by now. I thought they were all scrapped already."

"All but *Midway* and *Iwo Jima*," the lieutenant says. He puts away his data pad and gets up from his chair. "Fleet's short on hulls, Sarge. The Pacifics are old, but they're big hulls. Good luck in your new assignment."

"What about my gear? My bug suit burned up with the *Manitoba*, along with all my other stuff."

"Ask the supply guy in charge on the *Midway*. They'll reissue everything, I'm sure."

When they fitted me for my bug suit, I had to come to the fleet's Special Warfare Center on Luna to get fitted, and the process took three days of adjustments and a week of field testing. I know without the trace of a doubt that the supply monkeys on that scrapyard candidate won't have a new bug suit in storage. I know I'll be sent into battle against the Lankies without proper armor, on a ship that got a last-minute reprieve from its date with the scrapyard's plasma torches. But the personnel clerk in front of me doesn't care about any of that, nor would he have the clout to do anything about it if he did, so I just salute and watch him walk out of the storage room.

As a civvie station, Independence has some luxuries that austere Gateway can't match. Many of the public areas have viewports that offer a good vista of Earth through multiple layers of inch-thick polycarb panes. On Gateway, you can look at Earth through external camera feeds, but nothing can match seeing the planet with your own eyes. There's a small lounge in our restricted area, and I spend much of my remaining idle time until *Midway*'s arrival sitting there, watching the orbital traffic and the swirling weather patterns in the atmosphere below. Somewhere down there, beneath the cloud cover, Mom is going about her business in PRC Boston-7, warming up her BNA ration while watching Network shows. Luna is on the far side of the station, out of my field of view, but I know that Halley is in a classroom or a drop-ship cockpit right now, teaching the next batch of space bus drivers how to fly a Wasp. The only two people I care about are closer to me than they've been for most of my half-decade career, and my travel and comms restrictions mean that they might as well be sixty light years and half a dozen Alcubierre hops away.

For the first time in my life in the service, I don't want to leave Earth.

CHAPTER 13

── *MIDWAY*, DEPARTING ──

The *Midway* is a relic, a loose confederation of parts flying in vaguely carrier-shaped formation. When I arrive at my new duty station, there are still swarms of civilian fleet yard techs everywhere, hammering the ancient carrier back into fighting condition. Everywhere I look, there's evidence that the *Midway* had a long and rough life in the fleet, and that she didn't get the benefit of a final overhaul before being mothballed. The lining on the deck floors is shot, the paint on the bulkheads is old and faded, and the whole ship smells like a long-disused storage locker. I look around for some redeeming feature, but after a few hours on board, the best thing I can say about the old warhorse is that her hull still seems to be mostly airtight.

"I know what you're thinking," my new commanding officer says. His name tag says MICHAELSON. He's a captain, not a major like all my other COs. The special-operations company on a carrier is usually headed by a staff-officer rank, but the fleet seems to be running out of even those.

"I'm not getting paid to think, sir," I tell him. "That's for the ranks with the stars on the shoulder boards."

I take stock of the cloth badges on the captain's fatigues. I've never met him in the fleet, but he looks vaguely familiar, and he has the proper credentials—SEAL badge, drop wings in gold, all the right specialty tabs, and a SpecWar badge on the black beret tucked underneath his shoulder board. The fact that he's in battle dress instead of Class A rags is somehow comforting.

"Yes, I'm active duty," he says when he notices my glance at his patches. "I'm the new CO of the SpecWar company on the *Midway*. Such as it is."

"If you don't mind me saying, sir, I'm surprised they assigned a full company of podheads to this tub."

He gives me a curt smile and folds his hands across his chest.

"Me, too, Sergeant. In any case, we're only a full company on paper right now. You and I are it at the moment, until the rest trickles in. I'm supposed to get two SI recon platoons, two Spaceborne Rescue guys, and a team of SEALs."

"How many more combat controllers, sir?"

"They promised me two more, but so far, you're your own team."

"I'll need all new gear, sir. My junk burned up with the carrier we lost at Sirius Ad. Bug suit, uniforms, everything."

"Sirius Ad?" the captain repeats, and leans forward with sudden interest in his eyes. "Holy shit. You were one of the ones who got out of there?"

"Yes, sir. Me and about a hundred mudlegs from SI. Four drop ships' full."

"They just put the news on MilNet three days ago, just before all the movement orders got canceled. It seems they're reshuffling the whole damn fleet. I was Earthside for an instructor tour at Coronado. Hadn't even sorted my shit into the locker when my new orders came through. So much for six months on Earth." He leans back in his chair and puts his feet on the desk. His boots are well worn, but spotless. "You are one lucky son of a bitch, Sergeant. If I end up going dirtside on this deployment, I'm going to stay close to you."

"I wouldn't, sir," I reply with a smile. "I've used up all my luck last week. Things go to shit, I'll probably be the first to buy it."

He rasps a laugh.

"Go find your berth and get settled, Sergeant. We'll have a company powwow once the rest of the crew gets in. I'd direct you to the supply group, but I just got here myself, and I've never been on a Pacific-class before. Just ask one of the yard monkeys."

The *Midway* is a relic, but her berthing spaces are roomy. I have nothing to put away, since all I have with me is the uniform set I borrowed from the supply sergeant on the *Nassau*, so claiming my berth is just a matter of walking in and punching my name and rank into the security panel at the hatch.

When I finally locate the *Midway's* supply-and-logistics group, the sergeant sitting behind the clothes- and kit-issue counter looks familiar. We both look at each other in dawning recognition, and then the supply sergeant snaps his fingers and points at me.

"Fleet School," he says. "You were in my platoon. Grayson, right?"

I read his name tag, and my brain finally sorts him into the right spot.

"Simer. You were at the other end of the platoon bay. How have you been?"

"Oh, you know," he says, and shakes my hand. He looks a bit soft around the edges, evidence of a career mostly spent sitting at a desk or folding laundry. "Ship-hopping every six months, just like everyone else. Although I have no clue what I fucked up to get posted to this bucket. What can I do for you?"

"I lost all my kit when my last ship went down," I say. "I need the basic set again, the whole sheet."

"I'll see what we have in the back. What's your MOS?"

"One Charlie Two Five One."

"Combat controller? Holy crap. I thought you were off to Neural Networks School after Great Lakes."

"I was. It's a long story. I sort of switched tracks along the way."

"Yeah, I guess you did." He picks up a data pad and consults the screen. "Truth be told, I don't know half the shit I have right now. Things have been a bit nuts. They're all trying to do three weeks of pre-deployment work in three days."

He flicks through a few screens on his pad.

"You guys have a ton of specialized shit I've never even *seen*. I have all the standard gear for sure, but I don't have any HEBAs. They don't issue those in the regular supply chain."

"Yeah, they fit those at the issue point."

"I'll put a request into the system anyway. Maybe they'll get one ready for you Earthside before we leave Gateway."

"Any idea where we're going? I haven't heard anything from the brass yet."

"They're all mum about it. But I will tell you one thing." Sergeant Simer looks around, and then leans toward me and lowers his voice. "There's some weird shit going on. I see the stuff popping up in the supply logs, and I've never seen that kind of pre-dep loadout."

"Like what?"

"Well, for starters, we got three times as much food as we need for a six-month cruise. And they're filling all the missile tubes with nukes. I've never seen so many nuke supply codes come through the system at once. Someone upstairs must have cracked open a big-ass warehouse full of megatons."

I grimace at this revelation. The fleet only goes heavy on nukes when we go up against the Lankies, and just a week after Sirius Ad, I don't want to go near Lanky-controlled space again already, especially not with all my good gear missing.

"Food stockpiles, nukes in the tubes . . . sounds like we're in for a shit sandwich."

"Maybe we've found the Lanky homeworld," Sergeant Simer offers. "Maybe we're headed downtown into Lanky Central."

"You better hope we're not," I say, and shudder at the thought of transitioning into a system crawling with Lanky ships. I remember the sight of the solitary seed ship, taking on our entire carrier task force without getting its hull scratched. Just one of their ships wiped out 5 percent of our entire fleet in less than forty-five minutes, including three of our biggest and newest warships. A dozen of them could probably go through our whole fleet like a fléchette through a block of soy chicken.

We're about to run our heads against the same unyielding barrier, and once again, the brass seem to have concluded that our approach isn't working because we're not running at the wall fast enough

---

As big as the *Midway* is, the fleet manages to fill it up with people and gear quickly. Two days after my arrival, the supply crews have filled every storage room on the ship to the ceiling, and navigating the fore-and-aft gangways and corridors becomes an exercise in weaving between pallets and gear pods stacked along the walls. Even the carrier's flight deck, the only open space on the ship big enough for running, resembles an overstuffed storage shed at a maintenance depot.

"They'll turn this boat into a supercarrier by weight if they don't stop stacking shit on every flat surface," Captain Michaelson says as we observe the hustle and bustle on the flight deck on the third morning of the *Midway*'s hurried deployment preparation. We came down to the flight deck to get in a few miles before breakfast, but I doubt that even the most efficient ballistics computer in the fleet could plot a clean course through the mess in front of us. There's a flight of drop ships parked over to one side of the deck, like a quartet of barely tolerated guests, and the rest of the flight deck is a sea of cargo containers, munitions pallets, and fuel bladders.

"Those drop ships are ancient," I say, and point at the cluster of olive-green spacecraft. "Wasp-A. You don't even see those in the fleet anymore. I thought they had all been upgraded or junked by now."

"I'll bet you anything all this gear is from the strategic-reserve stockpile. Looks like it's all or nothing."

At the far end of the flight deck, some supply crews are erecting what look like SI field tents. Several neat rows of them are already standing, and from the number of tents laid out on the deck beyond, it looks like the supply guys are putting together a tent village big enough to quarter an entire regiment of Spaceborne Infantry in full kit.

When I see Sergeant Simer walking nearby, a data pad in his hand and a harried look on his face, I wave at him to flag him down.

"Hey, Simer," I say. "What's up with Tent City back there? Are we picking up refugees?"

"Fucked if I know," Simer shrugs. "They said to get 'em up before we deploy. Rumor has it we'll get a bunch more passengers along for the ride. As if we don't have this thing loaded up to the gunwales already."

"Any guess on where?" the captain asks me when Simer walks off again.

"Nukes in the tubes, enough tents for a regiment on the deck, and everyone's in a rush," I say. "I hope the brass have their priorities straight, and we're going back to Sirius Ad to kick some Lanky ass."

"That would be good and proper," Captain Michaelson agrees.

And that's how I know we're going somewhere else, I think.

If we launch in the next few days and haul ass back to the Sirius A chute at maximum acceleration, we can make it back just in time to get our people out before the Lanky terraforming turns the place into a toxic pressure cooker. If we would only join forces with the SRA for once instead of fighting over the leftovers, we could even kick the Lankies off that rock and save what's left of the civvie population.

I remember the faces of the podheads that dropped with me on that mission. I wonder if Macfee, my fellow combat controller, survived the initial Lanky onslaught, and if he's hiding out with an SI squad somewhere on Sirius Ad, waiting for the rescue ships he already knows won't come in time.

"If that's not where we're going, I'm going to look at alternative employment," I say.

Captain Michaelson looks out over the mess that is the hangar deck, his expression unreadable. "If that's not where we're going, we should start loading flag officers into those missile tubes," he replies.

He looks at me and smiles curtly, as if he had just realized that he shouldn't have voiced that thought in the presence of a noncom.

"God knows they're dense enough. Shoot a pod full of generals into a Lanky ship, you might actually do some decent damage. Sure as shit won't be a loss to us either way."

We get our first look at the tenants of Tent City at lunch, when we sit in the crowded NCO mess near the flight deck. I'm sitting with my back to the hatch, and when I hear a sudden increase in conversation buzz behind me, I turn around to see a group of troopers stepping into the room. They're all wearing standard NAC camo fatigues, but the berets tucked underneath their shoulder boards aren't fleet black or SI maroon. Instead, they're a subdued shade of green.

"Homeworld Defense? What the fuck are *they* doing here?"

The new arrivals look around with that particular expression of subdued anxiety that's exclusive to grunts in a new and unknown environment. They spot the back of the chow line and walk over to claim their spots. Except for the color of their berets, they are every bit as hard-edged and lean as our SI troopers.

"You have got to be kidding me," Sergeant Simer says next to me. "I've never seen any HD on a fleet ship, not in five years of service."

"I haven't, either."

"Looks like we're really down to the dregs this time, eh?"

"Hey." I shoot him an unfriendly look, and Simer raises an eyebrow. "Can the shit talk, Simer. I was HD before I joined the fleet."

"No kidding?"

"No kidding. Back when it was still the Territorial Army, before all the unified service bullshit."

The newcomers are keenly aware of the fact that most of the people in the room are staring at them, but they ignore the attention. After a minute or so, the novelty has worn off, and the noise level in the room returns to its regular mealtime volume.

I eat my lunch while half-listening to the conversations around me, and keep an eye on the HD troopers that end up clustering at a table near the hatch. When they get up to stow their meal trays, I do the same and head for the hatch at the same time.

I loiter in the hallway outside until the HD sergeants come out of the mess room. They walk down the corridor in small groups, still looking out of place and unsure, like kids in a new school on the first day. The last HD trooper out of the hatch is a sergeant, one rank below me, but close enough to negate rank etiquette. I fall in beside him as he walks off to follow his comrades.

"Sergeant, wait up."

He gives me a reserved smile.

"Staff Sergeant."

"What's Homeworld Defense doing up here in space? I thought you guys don't do hard vacuum."

"I guess we do now," he shrugs.

"Andrew Grayson," I say, and offer my hand. "I was TA for a few months, back when I joined. 365th AIB, out of Dayton."

"No shit?" He shakes my hand. "John Murphy. I've never heard of a TA grunt going fleet."

"Yeah, it hardly ever happens. I was lucky. Or unlucky, depending on your point of view."

He looks at my chest pockets, the cursory glance of the military man checking out someone else's cloth patch credentials, and his gaze lingers for just a moment on my Master-level combat-drop badge, identical to the one he's wearing.

"365th, huh? They're still around. We did a drop with them a few months back. We're the 309th, out of Nashville."

"You guys run out of shit to do down there?"

"Hardly." Sergeant Murphy lets out a brief snort. "We do three drops a week inside the periphery these days. You wouldn't think those welfare shits had anything left to burn in there, but it's a fucking war zone every ration day."

"I dropped into Detroit with the 365th once. Five years of combat drops on the colonies since then, Lankies and all, and I've never been as scared as I was that night. Almost had my tag punched, too."

"Detroit," he says. "Boy, that's the master shithole right there. What happened?"

"Squad got chewed up bad. I got stitched with an M-66, two of our guys bought it, and the sarge lost her leg."

"Who was your squad sergeant?"

"Staff Sergeant Fallon. She made SFC just after. She's probably a twenty-chevron sergeant major by now. Do you know her?"

He chuckles in reply. "Everybody knows Master Sergeant Fallon. She's a freakin' legend."

He taps the unit patch on his sleeve with his index finger.

"We're the advance logistics team for the 309th. The other battalion shipping out with us is the 330th, out of Knoxville. Master Sergeant Fallon is the main ass-kicker in the 330th."

I don't have much to do except to stow my kit and exercise, so I spend most of my time on the flight deck, working out while keeping an eye on the shuttles that are delivering personnel and gear every few minutes.

The HD troops start arriving in force in the afternoon. The docking clamps haul up shuttle after shuttle loaded with troopers in battle armor, hauling gear bags. From the other side of the hangar deck, I can't make out individual faces, and all the HD grunts look alike in their bulky armor suits, but when Sergeant Fallon's shuttle arrives, I have no trouble making her out in the crowd. Shortly before the late afternoon watch change, the docking arm deposits a weather-beaten fleet shuttle on the deck, the main hatch opens, and a group of HD troopers step out on the flight deck as if they are deploying in the middle of a hostile city. They have their rifles slung across their chests, and there are no magazines in their weapons, but the disembarking HD troopers still radiate a tense readiness.

I recognize Sergeant Fallon instantly. She walks down the ramp with the efficiency of movement I remember well. There's nothing casual about her stride. She walks onto the *Midway*'s flight deck like a predator checking out a new environment. I know that her left leg underneath the battle armor is titanium alloy and nanocarbon fibers instead of flesh and bone, but there's no way to deduce it from her gait. As she steps off the ramp and toward her unit's assembly area on the other side of the black-and-yellow safety line, there's a phalanx of her troopers around her—not bodyguards, but limbs of the same belligerent organism, ready to strike out in any direction if needed.

I watch as her group gathers in a circle for a quick briefing and then moves over to their assigned area, where they start to make this unfamiliar territory their own, safety and comfort in numbers.

I haven't seen Sergeant Fallon since I left the TA four and a half years ago, and we have only exchanged a few dozen Milnet messages since then. Still, the knowledge of her presence on board puts my mind at ease a little. As we prepare to leave Gateway for God knows where, doing God knows what, it's comforting to know at least one other person on this ship. Having my old squad leader nearby makes me feel a little less alone in the universe right now.

CHAPTER 14

——— A BRIEF REUNION ———

"Now hear this: All hands, prepare for departure. Repeat, all hands prepare for departure. Secure all docking collars."

I'm back in the supply group picking up my new-issue gear when the departure alert comes over the 1MC. With all the activity everywhere on the ship, it seems impossible that the *Midway* is already stocked and crewed for combat operations, but it looks like we're off to war anyway.

"Already?" Sergeant Simer says, echoing my own thoughts. "Jeez. It's like they're pushing us out the door with our shoes untied."

"And in our underwear," I add. "No way this bucket is already in fighting shape."

"You got quarters yet, Grayson?"

"Yeah, I grabbed a berth in NCO country. Weird—they're stacking the grunts three high on the flight deck, and half the permanent berths on my deck are empty. I got a two-man berth all to myself. It's like we're running on a skeleton crew."

"We are," Simer says. "Sixty percent of normal, at best."

"But we have three times as many grunts as a supercarrier. And most of them are garrison troops who have never been in space before."

"We gotta feed all those mudlegs for a month, we'll get to wherever we're headed with empty food stores," Simer says. "Hope it's a fast trip to the chute."

By now, everyone but the most oblivious private straight out of tech school has figured out that our upcoming deployment is going to be anything but a bread-and-butter task force cruise or planetary assault. They never inform the rank and file of the mission specifics until we are out of the Alcubierre chute in the destination system, so all we can do is speculate. Since we have three times our normal contingent of infantry, and not enough drop ships to land them all at once, the general consensus in the NCO mess is a garrison deployment, reinforcing some SI detachment on a backwater colony planet close to the Thirty. The presence of Homeworld Defense troops and the aged equipment of our hastily assembled battle group spawn other rumors, magnitudes wilder than the usual pre-deployment scuttlebutt: *We're evacuating Earth. We're assaulting the Lanky homeworld with everything that can ride an Alcubierre chute. We secretly made peace with the SRA, and we're going to help them fight off the Lankies on Novaya Kiev. We secretly surrendered to the SRA, and we're delivering half the fleet's tonnage for disarmament.* Enlisted soldiers have active imaginations, unlike the brass at Joint Command, or the bureaucrats holding the reins back on Earth.

Whatever the rumors, however, the conclusions are similar in every mess hall and crew berth on the ship. This deployment will be a hasty clusterfuck of epic proportions, and at the end of the day, the grunts and pilots and wrench spinners will be left holding the bag.

I finally run into my old squad leader in the most fitting of all places on the *Midway*—the shooting range over in SI country.

Since I lost all my kit with the *Manitoba*, the armorer on the *Midway* had to scrounge up a pair of armament sets for me. Ever since they gave us new gear for use against the Lankies, every spaceborne grunt has two sets of weapons, called Alpha and Bravo kit. The Alpha kit consists of a modular fléchette rifle with a grenade launcher, for use against other humans. The Bravo kit is centered on the M-80, a giant jackhammer of a rifle that fires a twenty-five millimeter round with the destructive power of a light-vehicle cannon.

The Alpha and Bravo kits I get from the armorer are from the tail end of the supply chain, just like everything else on this ship. The M-66 looks like it has been cleaned to death by fifty cycles of recruits, and the M-80 is so loose and rattly that I suspect it was used for stress-testing experimental loads at Aberdeen Proving Grounds. Still, I want to be sure that my new rifles actually hit roughly where I point them, so I haul the entire kit down to the range on a slow morning.

When I check in with the range master, I can see through the armored windows that all eight of the computerized shooting stations are taken up by HD troopers, and more grunts are lined up and waiting behind each station. The troopers in the firing lanes are putting their fléchette rifles through their paces, shooting bursts at computer-generated targets. All the HD troopers on the range carry their standard M-66s, which are almost useless against thousand-ton Lankies that can cover forty klicks in an hour at a leisurely gait.

It's strange to see the Homeworld Defense troops in their unfamiliar battle armor on fleet turf. The HD armor suits are subtly different from those worn by our Spaceborne Infantry grunts. Their shoulder pauldrons are bigger, the chest and back plates are more faceted, and the sensor bulbs on the helmets are in slightly different spots. I notice that most of the grunts on the firing line have battle scars on their armor plating, shrapnel gouges and pockmarks from bullet impacts. Whatever the HD battalions riding along with us have done Earthside lately, it looks like they were no less busy than our frontline assault regiments.

The HD troops use helmet-mounted sights, just like we do, so all the troopers on the firing line are in full battle rattle. They wear name tags across the backs of their helmets, but I don't need to read the one labeled FALLON to recognize my old squad sergeant. She's in the last lane on the far right of the line, standing half a head shorter than the next smallest of her troopers. The rifle in her hands burps out a steady stream of short bursts. There's something about her bearing and economy of movement that would make her stand out in a parade ground among a whole regiment of troopers. I watch as she works through her magazine, putting simulated tungsten fléchettes into imaginary holographic enemies until the bolt of her rifle locks back on an empty feedway. She raises the muzzle, yanks the disposable magazine block out of the rifle, and checks the chamber before vacating her spot in the booth for the next trooper in line. Then she walks up the firing line to the exit hatch where I am standing, and I give her a curt wave when she raises the visor of her battle helmet. Her purposeful stride falters just for a fraction of a second, and I see a hint of surprise on the part of her face I can see through the visor slot of her helmet. Then she walks over to where I'm standing and motions for me to follow her out through the armored hatch of the firing range, away from the hoarse staccato of the fléchette rifles.

Outside, in the range master's vestibule, she removes her helmet and turns around to face me.

"Andrew Grayson," she says, and pulls me into a firm one-armed hug. Nearby, two of the HD troopers about to walk onto the range exchange looks of surprised amusement at the sight of their senior sergeant hugging some fleet puke. "What the fuck are you doing on this rusty piece of shit?"

"Good to see you again, Sarge," I say. "This rusty piece of shit is my new duty station as of last week."

"You must have pissed off the brass something fierce again."

"No, my shiny new ship got shot to shit by the Lankies a few weeks ago. But what the hell are *you* doing here? I thought you didn't *do* space."

"Yeah, well, so did I. Division says we're on loan, so we pack our shit and go. Trust me, I'm not ecstatic about it."

I haven't seen Sergeant Fallon in person since my last day with the Territorial Army, half a lifetime ago. She hasn't changed much at all. Her hair is neatly gathered into the same tight ponytail I remember, and her features are still hard and sharp. From her service history, I know Briana Fallon is about ten years older than I am, but I never asked her exact age, and she never volunteered it. I could no more guess her year of birth than estimate the manufacturing date of a well-serviced drop ship. A weapon maintained at peak efficiency is all but ageless. The only obvious difference between this Sergeant Fallon and the one who led my squad into Detroit five years ago is the rank device on the chest of her battle armor. She has gained two ranks since then, and now wears the triple chevrons of a master sergeant.

She taps the single chevron of my staff sergeant rank sigil with the finger of her armored glove.

"Climbed the ladder a bit, huh?"

"Yeah. You know the fleet. They give those things to everyone."

"You did good," she says, and nods at the combat controller flash on my helmet. "I'm glad you didn't stick with that console jockey job Unwerth shoved you into."

"They never have enough nutcases for the suicide track. Whatever happened to Major Unwerth?"

Sergeant Fallon shakes her head with a disgusted snort.

"Major Unwerth is now *Lieutenant Colonel* Unwerth. He's the new XO of the 365th. Place ain't what it used to be, I tell you that."

"How come you switched units, Sarge?"

"Had no choice, Grayson." She lowers her voice a little. "The 330th is a penal battalion of sorts. It took a mauling in the New Madrid riots last year, so they dissolved it and rebuilt it with all the misfits and malcontents the brigade wanted to dump. Keeps us all in one place, you see."

She looks around to check if anyone is close enough to listen in, but the range master is on the other side of the range door, and we're alone in the vestibule.

"I have to get back to my troops, Grayson, but keep your schedule clear. Meet me after evening chow, at 1900. We have a bit of a club set up in one of the maintenance sheds. Foxtrot Deck, F2029. We have stuff to talk about."

I spend the rest of the day sighting in my rifles and running my new battle armor through all its self-test protocols. My specialized combat controller kit is two generations behind the stuff that burned up in my locker on the *Manitoba*, but all the comms and network modules work as they should, and my armor doesn't have any dents or leaks. Without a bug suit, my combat endurance on a Lanky world is measured in hours instead of days, but since none of the other grunts have been issued a HEBA kit, I consider it a fairly safe bet that we're not going head-on against an established Lanky colony.

Like a good soldier, I head down to Foxtrot Deck fifteen minutes early. Unit F2029 is a maintenance and storage cube in a corner of the grease monkey zone by the hangar, partitioned from the rest of the deck with plastalloy mesh wiring. Two HD troopers stand by the open entrance, but they don't do anything to keep me from entering. In the storage cube, someone has piled up stacks of modular equipment crates all along the mesh walls, forming a sight barrier eight feet high. Inside the makeshift privacy walls, more equipment crates have been requisitioned as furniture, serving as benches and tables. There are a dozen HD troopers lounging in the storage unit, and all of them turn their heads my way when I walk in.

"Get lost somewhere, Sergeant?" a first lieutenant asks me, with only the barest hint of cordiality in his voice.

"Looking for Master Sergeant Fallon," I say. The stares from the HD troopers aren't exactly hostile, but they're not welcoming, either. I'm suddenly keenly aware of the fact that I came down here unarmed, and that every one of the HD grunts in the room is wearing at least a combat knife.

"He's okay," Sergeant Fallon's voice comes from behind me. She steps past me into the room, still in battle armor. "Grayson was one of my guys in the 365th. He's been in the shit with me."

The suppressed hostility dissipates from the room. I notice that even the first lieutenant instantly defers to Sergeant Fallon. She walks over to one of the makeshift benches and drops down on it with a grunt.

"Come and have a seat, Grayson," she says. "The guys don't bite. We're all friends down here."

I do as directed and sit down across the makeshift table from Sergeant Fallon, who is opening the latches of her chest and back plates with practiced hands. She pulls off the hard shells of the outer armor and lets them drop to the deck.

"Long fucking day," she says to me, and puts her feet up on the crate that serves as a table. "I don't know how you fleet pukes can stand it, spending months in these coffins. I've only been walking around in here for a day and a half, and I'm already getting claustrophobic."

"It helps to remind yourself just how much room there is on the other side of that hull," I say. "Think of it as cozy. Just be glad you're on a carrier. Lots of legroom. Frigate's about a twentieth of the tonnage."

"This is what you've been doing the last five years? Sitting around in one of these tin cans?"

"Well, that, and taking it to the Lankies. Tell you what, those SRA marines aren't half bad when your other option is fighting something that's eighty feet tall and bulletproof."

"Did they tell you where we're going?"

I shake my head. "Not a clue. They dragged this old thing out of mothballs and rushed us out the door, and that's all I know. That was the fastest pre-deployment prep I've ever seen."

"You know how they got us ground pounders ready for this shit?" Sergeant Fallon asks. "Six days at Camp Jarhead, with a bunch of SI instructors. *Six* days! And half those space monkeys didn't know their ass from a hole in the ground. If those guys are supposed to be our first line of defense up here, we must be good and fucked."

"Six days," I repeat in disbelief. SI combat school for infantry soldiers takes three months, half of which are spent in zero-g and hostile environment training at Camp Gray on Luna. Six days are barely enough to get people used to moving in low gravity without killing themselves.

"Yeah," Sergeant Fallon says. "And no new gear, either. They showed us how to fire those M-80s and the crew-served autocannons, but they didn't *issue* us any. What the fuck are we going to do with our popguns up here?"

I don't have a good answer for her, so I just shake my head in commiseration. With two battalions of Earthside grunts lacking anti-Lanky weaponry, our still-secret destination has got to be an SRA colony planet; otherwise those fifteen hundred Homeworld Defense troopers are just very inefficient ballast.

"A squad *can* take a Lanky with those popguns," I say. "You just have to get the drop on it and blow your whole ammo load, and even then it's a shaky thing. Also, they run in groups, just like we do."

"Awesome," one of the other troopers says, and the others start an unhappy little chorus of murmurs.

"Doesn't matter," Sergeant Fallon says. "If we get to go up against those things, we're all fucked anyway, cruising around in this museum exhibit. But I doubt that's why we're up here."

She looks at me for a moment, biting on her lower lip slightly as if she's appraising me.

"You keeping up with the news from Earthside, Grayson?"

"Not really," I say. "Don't have much time to watch the Networks. Whatever we get is canned shit anyway. MilNet's just boring shit, unit news and feel-good crap."

"They're keeping the lid on tight," Sergeant Fallon says. "Color me shocked."

"You suggesting that Fleet Command sanitizes our news?" I ask with mock incredulity. Several of the troopers chuckle, but Sergeant Fallon does not even smile at my joke. Instead, she looks around again, and then leans across the table, propping her elbows on the scuffed olive-green polyplast of the crate.

"You remember Detroit, right? The night we lost two drop ships and a bunch of troops?"

I lightly touch the side of my tunic, placing two fingers onto the spot where some welfare rioter with a stolen rifle put two fléchette rounds into me, piercing one lung and a few yards of intestine.

"Yeah, I remember Detroit," I say. "Wish I didn't."

"Well, five years ago, that was an emergency. These days, it's the rule. The PRCs have their own *militias* now, and they own the ground. Most of the big cities, the cops don't even go in anymore, 'cause the welfare rats have better hardware. All our calls are 'weapons free' from the start now."

"You have got to be kidding."

"Wish I wasn't," she says, precisely aping the tone of my own remark. "You people up here, you're at war with the Sino-Russkies and the Lankies. Down Earthside, we're at war with our own people, Grayson."

"All the PRCs? That's, what, half a billion people? Shit, BosProv has twenty million all by itself. There's no way they can keep a lid on all of those."

"We're not," Sergeant Fallon says. "We're barely holding the line. We let them kill each other all they want, let them run their own shows in the PRCs. We only come out of our forts to break kneecaps whenever the sewage starts spilling out into the 'burbs, and they torch a few middle-class citizens in their hydrocars and their air-conditioned crackerbox houses. If it's just two groups of welfare rats shooting it out, nobody gives a shit anymore."

"And they can afford to send two full battalions up here to help *us* out?"

"*Ah.*" Sergeant Fallon smiles without humor. "And now we get to the heart of the matter."

She looks around at her troops, as if checking for consent. Nobody says anything.

"We're troublemakers, Grayson. Mutineers. The 330th is a penal battalion, like I told you. So's the 309th. Your SI troopies with their maroon beanies and the live ammo in their rifles, standing around the edge of the flight deck? They're not there to teach us the ropes or boost our combat power. They're there to keep us in check, in case we get silly ideas."

It's common knowledge that the fleet is taking advantage of the peculiar nature of message distribution across interstellar distances to present a selective and sanitized version of world news. As I listen to Sergeant Fallon's narrative of the NAC's recent trouble on its own soil, I am nonetheless amazed at how thoroughly they've kept us in the dark. I remember my trip to see Mom in Boston just a few weeks ago, and the omnipresent riot cops that all seemed to be on edge constantly. They had told me just how bad things had gotten in the old neighborhood, but according to Sergeant Fallon, Boston is a calm oasis of civil tranquility compared to almost every metroplex south of the Mason-Dixon line or west of the Rockies. The colony flights have stopped entirely, the Basic Nutritional Allowance rations are getting reduced by hundreds of calories every other month, and the pressure in the tenements has become too great without the few safety valves there used to be. Now the PRCs are lawless free-fire zones, and only the thin green line of Homeworld Defense troopers is keeping the place from unraveling completely. Once again, it seems that the Lankies aren't doing anything to our species that we can't do to each other all on our own.

"The first mutiny wasn't even one," Sergeant Fallon says. "It was just some company CO down in Atlanta-Macon, refused an order from the battalion CO to clean out a tenement high-rise with gunships. They didn't even get violent or anything. Company CO tells his unit to stand down, and they do. No bloodshed. Division takes the whole battalion off the line, and dissolves the company. One hundred and forty-eight discharges on the spot, all benefits and accrued paychecks forfeit."

"Holy crap," I say. "Kicked out the whole company?"

"Every last grunt, from the company commander down to the privates folding laundry back in the supply group."

"What a shit move."

"Now the second mutiny—that was a real one. This time, they had a captain who had taken Neo-Constitutional Law back at Officer U, and he decides in the middle of a drop that using remote sentry cannons on unarmed civvies is illegal. So he tells his people to stand down. Only this time, Battalion sends in another company to arrest them and secure their gear, and the captain with the law degree decides that *that's* an illegal order, too. So they don't come quietly, and start a two-company firefight in the middle of a busy PRC that's already in full riot anyway. The armed civvies jump into the fight on the side of the mutinous unit, and before you know it, there's a hundred dead grunts on the ground, the battalion's standby gunship wing making bombing runs with incendiaries, and ten square miles of SoTenn-Chattanooga are burning. That did *not* look too good on the Networks, I'll tell you that."

I should be astonished and angry, but I'm not really surprised, and I've long since lost the right to be outraged. Five years ago, I held the line on the ground against people who could have been my neighbors and schoolmates had we dropped into Boston instead of Detroit, and I ended up putting a bunker-buster missile into a building full of people. Part of my conscience tries to convince me to this day that there were no unarmed civvies in the high-rise by then, that anyone with half a brain would have gotten out of there when the shooting started, but my rational side knows better. I remember how we fought our way through the darkened city that night, scared shitless, standing on a carpet of discarded fléchette sabots, and mentally marking everything not in TA battle armor as a "kill on sight" target. Whether we were justified or not, whether it was legal at the time or not, morality left the equation the first time one of us pulled the trigger on a welfare citizen. If my oath of service commits me to the protection of the rights and freedoms of the Commonwealth's citizens, I've violated it dozens, hundreds, maybe thousands of times since I got out of boot camp.

"We have guys going home on leave all the time. Nobody's picked up any rumors about HD units in mutiny."

"There's nobody to talk to," Sergeant Fallon says. "Most HD units are confined to base between drops now, and when you get down there on leave, they won't let you anywhere near a hot PRC or an unstable unit. How many HD froggies did you bump into when you were last Earthside, Grayson?"

"None," I say. "Just cops and MPs."

Sergeant Fallon turns her palms up in a "there you have it" gesture, and I digest this information for a few moments.

"HD grunts are the main muscle on the ground. They get enough battalions just sitting down and saying no, they won't have any way to keep the welfare rats in the PRCs. Unless they start giving drop ships and infantry training to the city cops."

"Exactly," she says.

"So how did you end up on the shit list, Sarge?"

"Oh, hell, you know me," she says with a smile. "I don't think it was any particular thing, really. I've been a pain in Division's ass since before you joined us. They say I have a problem with authority. I say I have a low tolerance for *stupid*."

"What was the excuse?"

"Failure to comply with a direct order from a superior officer, conspiracy, blah blah blah. You know the mutinous company I told you about, the one that ended up shooting it out with another unit?"

"Yeah."

"That was Bravo Company, from the 300th. The 365th was the one they called up first to smoke 'em out. You remember your old pal, Major Unwerth? He was the head Indian in charge at Battalion that day. I told my company commander that my platoon wouldn't shoot at fellow HD grunts, and the captain came around to my viewpoint."

She smiles again, this time with a spark of genuine joy in her eyes.

"God, it was such a pleasure to tell that useless sack of shit to go fuck himself. I may have even used the all-battalion channel. Terrible abuse of non-commissioned-officer-in-charge privileges."

"Terrible," I concur, and we both grin.

"He got the last laugh, of course. I spent a month in the brig after that. They didn't want to give me a proper court-martial. Didn't want the pictures of the sergeant with the Medal of Honor on her Class A standing before a tribunal. Plus, some of the NCOs from the 300th used the unlawful-order defense, and the media got wind of the whole thing somehow. So they let me out of the brig a few weeks later and handed me my marching orders. Dissolved the platoon, and spread us out all over the 330th. The whole battalion is nothing but obedience-challenged grunts from all over the brigade."

"They're not helping us out," I conclude. "They're getting rid of you."

Sergeant Fallon shrugs.

"That way we're not a bad influence on the units that still do as they're told."

"And you don't cause the brass any sleepless nights, having to worry about a whole battalion turning on them and giving drop ships to the PRC militias."

"Better to just shunt us off into space, get ground up by the Lankies, or cool our jets on some deserted rock far away from Earth. You got it, Grayson."

"The question is—where the hell are they sending us? Where are they going to stick two battalions of combat troops they want to keep away from the rest of the corps?"

"Beats me," Sergeant Fallon says. "All I know is that the corps is at the end of its rope, and so's the entire Commonwealth. Things are going to come to a head pretty soon, and we're getting ringside seats to that particular show."

Overhead, the speakers of the shipboard announcement system pop to life with a brief squelch.

"Now hear this, now hear this. All hands, prepare for Alcubierre transition. Repeat, all hands prepare for Alcubierre transition. Infantry passengers, report to your assigned areas. Countdown twenty minutes."

All the HD troopers in the room look at me, eager for some explanation of the unfamiliar protocol.

"We're hitting the chute for FTL travel to wherever the hell we're going."

"How long is that going to take?" someone asks.

"No idea. Depends on the system. Could be two hours, could be twenty. They never tell you the destination ahead of time."

Beyond the wall of crates making up the walls of the makeshift lounge, there's the shuffling of many pairs of boots on the deck as the crewmembers of the *Midway* rush to their duty stations.

"Well, you heard the brass," Sergeant Fallon says, and stands up to collect her armor plates. "Let's go back to our little tent village and see where the rabbit hole pukes us out."

She claps me on the back as she walks by.

"Good to see you again, Andrew. Maybe we'll have some more time to catch up on things before the world completely goes to shit."

I spend the last twenty minutes before our Alcubierre transition composing two last messages to Mom and Halley. I know they'll most likely never leave the *Midway*'s neural-network data banks, but I send them anyway, just in case this is my last chance to say good-bye.

I will keep my promise. See you in six months. I love you.
—Andrew

When I hit the send button on the message to my fiancée, I realize that this is the first time I've said those three words to her.

Wherever we're going, I'm determined to come back from it, even if I have to shoulder aside every Lanky in the universe.

CHAPTER 15

—————— REVELATIONS ——————

Task Force 230.7 is barely deserving of its name. The small group of mostly tired old hulls that transitions through the chute with us could probably defeat a single new destroyer, but I wouldn't want to be part of the crew that tried it. There's the eighty-year-old *Midway*, escorted by a light cruiser that's almost as old, a frigate from another near-obsolete class, and a cargo ship from the auxiliary fleet. We have exactly one hull in our task force that's younger than I am. However, that hull is the *Indianapolis*, and she's just a lightly armed orbital-patrol craft barely big enough for a fusion plant and an Alcubierre drive. The only bright spot in the order of battle is the *Portsmouth*, one of the fleet's fast and well-armed resupply ships.

Our misfit assembly of ill-matched ships pops out of Alcubierre after seven hours of transition. I've ridden the interstellar pathways of the fleet's Alcubierre network hundreds of times, and while you can't ever deduce your destination before the transition—the fleet ships vary their speeds and never go a direct course to the outbound chutes—you can tell the distance traveled by the time spent in transition, because ships can't dogleg or vary their speed in the bubble. Seven hours puts us close to the Thirty, and I pull out my PDP to check the star charts for possible candidates at that distance, but the CIC saves me the work with an all-ship announcement.

172

"All hands, stand down from transition stations. Welcome to Fomalhaut."

Fomalhaut, I think. A huge system that's mostly hostile to human life. If they wanted to ship us off to an interstellar gulag, they picked just about the perfect spot.

Four hours after our transition into the Fomalhaut system, Captain Michaelson summons the SpecOps company for a briefing. When I walk into the makeshift ready room, there are maybe four squads' worth of troopers sitting on the hastily arranged folding chairs. Captain Michaelson is at the front of the room, leaning on the briefing lectern.

"This is not a mission briefing," he says when everyone has settled in. "It's just a status update from upstairs. Don't worry about taking notes."

I do a quick headcount and beret-color survey in the room. There are thirty SI troopers, most with recon patches on their sleeves. Three fleet guys are sitting in a group in the front row, and on the other side of the room, there's another trooper with the red beret of the combat controller fraternity. Captain Michaelson surveys the assembly and shakes his head, clearly irritated.

"I'm supposed to have a reinforced company sitting in front of me right now. Instead, I get one understrength recon platoon, three Spaceborne Rescue guys, and two combat controllers. I seem to be short my SEAL team and an entire recon platoon."

"What a shock," one of the recon guys in my row murmurs.

"But whatever," the captain continues. "I guess I should be glad I'm not standing here by myself and briefing the wall over there, the way things have been going."

He turns on the briefing screen on the wall behind him.

"Let's make this one quick and easy. Anyone in this room who hasn't been to lovely Fomalhaut yet?"

A few of the SI troopers raise their hands, rather sheepishly.

"Good. The rest of you are repeat customers, then."

He brings up a strategic chart of the system, a bright Type-A star with a massive debris disk around it, and three planets orbiting somewhat forlornly in the space between.

"Let me do the quick tour for you new people," Captain Michaelson says. "Fomalhaut is the low-rent district of the galaxy, as far as cosmic neighborhoods go. It's big and cold and empty, and there aren't a whole lot of decent places to pitch a tent out here."

He picks one of the orbiting planets and zooms in on it.

"None of the planets here are terraformable. Fomalhaut is too close to the parent star, and gets cooked with radiation. Fomalhaut b is a Jovian gas giant. Fomalhaut d is a frozen ball of gas way beyond the debris disk. The only real estate we could get livable in this system are two moons—one around Fomalhaut b, and one around Fomalhaut c. One belongs to us, and the other to the SRA. Guess who got the more hospitable patch of ground in this system."

As he talks, he isolates the planet's moon on the display and zooms the perspective until the dirty-looking little sphere takes up most of the screen.

"That would be New Svalbard. It's our watering hole here in Fomalhaut, but it ain't much else. Hope you all packed your warm undies, because we're going to beef up the garrison down there for a while."

There's an upswell of unhappy murmuring in the room. One of the Spaceborne Rescue sergeants raises his hand.

"Sir, where are we going to stick two battalions and a whole regiment down there? Camp Frostbite doesn't hold much more than two or three companies."

"We're not," Captain Michaelson replies. "We're splitting up our HD friends among all the terraforming bases. One platoon per station. Their HQ platoon stays with our guys at Frostbite. The SI regiment goes on rotation—one company dirtside, the other three up here on the *Midway* with the drop ships, as a mobile reaction force. I'm keeping the recon platoon and all three of you Spaceborne Rescue guys, too. The combat controllers will be embedded with HD, one of you per battalion. You'll be the fleet liaison, give the big guns something to shoot at if the shit hits the fan. Keep an eye on our HD friends while you're down there, too."

As the captain goes into details, I consider this new development, and can't help but feel a bit of grudging respect for the genius at Fleet Command who decided where to put those two shaky battalions without having to tie up three thousand bunks in military prison. It's too bad the only truly clever people upstairs use their smarts to screw over their own instead of coming up with better ways to kill Lankies.

According to my commanding officer, part of the reason for embedding me with the HD troops is to keep a dependable set of fleet eyes in their ranks, so I feel more than a little seditious when I seek out Sergeant Fallon right after our briefing to fill her in on the fleet's plans for her battalion.

"That's pretty devious," she says when I have sketched the big picture for her. "Splitting us into platoon-sized chunks, so we can't get too many rifles to bear all at once. Without our drop ships, we're stuck wherever they're putting us."

"And they can come down on uppity units with most of a regiment from orbit, since they have all the airmobile gear."

"But what's to keep our grunts from just wandering off and meeting up to re-form companies anyway?"

I shake my head. "This is New Svalbard, Sarge. Ever done any cold-weather training back on Earth?"

"Yeah," she says. "Tierra del Fuego and Antarctica."

"Well, picture Antarctica in the really shitty time of the year. Outside of the tundra belt around the equator, that would be called a heat wave on New Svalbard. Most of the moon is a sheet of ice, ten kilometers thick at the poles. We have one big town down there, and sixty-four terraformers. They're all along the equator, like a girdle. We got this strip of tundra worked out, but you're still talking three-hundred-kilometer winds in the cold season. Even the heaters in your armor won't keep you alive long enough to walk from one atmo exchanger to the next. You want to stay real close to that fusion plant at the terraformer."

"Well, isn't that special," Sergeant Fallon says, and exchanges glances with the other HD troopers sitting around the table. "That's one hell of a good way to keep us all holed up and in a predictable spot."

"We'll figure something out," one of the troopers says with conviction. All around the table, HD grunts nod in agreement.

"Of course we will," Sergeant Fallon says. "That's what we do. Improvise, adapt, overcome. I'll be damned if I let myself get out-foxed by some fleet pukes."

She gives me a curt nod, and raps the surface of the makeshift table with the knuckles of both fists.

"Thanks for keeping us in the loop, Andrew. I owe you one."

"Not at all, Sarge," I say. "Just starting to pay back everything I owe you. Plus five years of interest."

I head up to Captain Michaelson's office nook. He's looking at a tactical map of New Svalbard when I knock on the frame of the open hatch, and he waves me in without turning off his screen.

"You been down there before, Grayson?"

"Yes, sir. Bunch of times, for water stops. Never had to set foot outside Camp Frostbite, though."

"I haven't been down there in three years, since I was a second lieutenant," he says. "I'm sure it hasn't turned into a tropical paradise since then."

"Have you decided where to embed me, sir?"

"No, I haven't. Why, you got a preference?"

"I know someone in the 330th, sir."

He looks at me with an unreadable expression for a moment, and I'm just about convinced he'll assign me to the 309th instead, when he shrugs and returns his attention to the screen of his data terminal.

"Sure, go with the 330th. Might as well make our stay as pleasant as we can. Go check in with their CO, and get your stuff ready for the ferry drop. We'll be in orbit in six hours, give or take."

It feels strange to board a drop ship at a stroll, without the haste and urgency of an impending combat drop. When the call to board craft comes, I line up on the flight deck with the headquarters platoon of the 330th, and trudge aboard the assigned Wasp. We're all in combat armor, and everyone is loaded down with weapons and personal gear units, all our issued kit in a tough, wheeled polyplast container with a DNA lock.

I claim a seat and buckle in. As I fumble with the lock on the old-style seat harness, someone else drops into the seat next to mine with a grunt. I look over and see Sergeant Fallon's face.

"Ready for a dirtside vacation, Andrew?"

"Hey, Sarge. I didn't know you were in the HQ platoon."

"I'm not." She winks at me. "Actually, I'm the NCOIC for Delta Company. Don't tell anyone, though."

She puts her rifle into the storage bracket next to her seat, and engages the lock.

"We did a little rearranging, you see. The staff platoon is going to Camp Frostbite, not the terraforming stations. We stacked the deck a little bit, to make sure all the aces end up in the right spot. You never know what's going to happen, right?"

"That's the damn truth," I say.

———————————

Camp Frostbite is a cluster of ferroconcrete domes hugging a hillside. It's next to the main terraforming hub on New Svalbard, right in the center of the habitable tundra belt carved out along the equator by a few decades of relentless terraforming. Of course, "habitable" on New Svalbard only means "not instantly fatal to exposed personnel." When the ramp of our drop ship lowers onto the flight pad of Camp Frostbite's airfield, a polar gale sweeps through the cargo hold instantly, a chilly welcome to one of the most inhospitable places humanity has ever settled. To a man and woman, all the troopers in the hold lower the visors on their helmets.

There's no welcoming committee on the windswept landing pad. I step out onto the concrete, which to my surprise is not covered in snow like on my previous visits to New Svalbard. Behind me, Sergeant Fallon stops at the bottom of the ramp, and then takes a slow and deliberate step onto the tarmac. She scrapes the surface of the concrete with the toe of her boot a few times and walks over to where I'm standing.

"First steps on a different world," she says to me over private suit-to-suit comms. "Doesn't really feel any different from Earth. I'm a little underwhelmed."

"We pick them for easy access to minerals or water," I say. "*Pretty* isn't very high up on the list. Most of the colonies are pretty rough."

"Well, at least the air's clean. Great view, too."

Sergeant Fallon turns in a circle to take in the scenery all around the base. The town in the valley below is the only evidence of a human presence in sight. Behind us, there's a chain of snow-covered mountains rising into the steel-gray sky, and beyond the town there's a vast expanse of tundra and glaciers, devoid of any trace of life.

"Hardly any people," Sergeant Fallon says. "Beats a metroplex all to hell, it does. Crank up the thermostat a couple dozen degrees, and it'd be damn near paradise."

Camp Frostbite has expanded since I was last down here for a water stop. Before, there were enough buildings to house a reinforced company and a platoon or two of vehicles. Now the number of structures has more than doubled. There are four company buildings, a new mess hall and rec facility, and a much bigger vehicle hangar. As we walk through the flight facility on our way to the company quarters, I notice that the local garrison now has its own flight of drop ships. Four brand-new Dragonflies are neatly parked inside the heated and spotless aircraft hangar. What used to be a grungy little outpost with the barest set of amenities has grown into a proper military base.

"We're in Building Two, along with the 309th's staff platoon. Enlisted on the second and third floors, noncoms on the fourth floor," the platoon sergeant says when we file into the central courtyard with all our gear. "The fleet guys are already here, so don't be stepping on any toes. They're over in Building Three."

The new company buildings are squat, loaf-shaped structures with rounded corners and thick walls, looking more like bunkers than living quarters. The four of them are all lined up in a row on one side of the main road that bisects Camp Frostbite. With the garrison company in Building One, and a company of the *Midway*'s SI regiment in Building Three, the two staff platoons of the

Homeworld Defense battalions are neatly corralled between superior numbers of Spaceborne Infantry troops.

We drag our gear up to Building Two, find some rooms, and stash our stuff in the new berth lockers we find. Once again, I get to claim a room of my own, continuing a chain of luck unbroken since I got back into the fleet after Combat Controller School. I transfer my gear and battle armor into the locker, take out my PDP, and check for local network access. Whoever did the upgrades to Camp Frostbite didn't forget the data infrastructure, because I'm on the local MilNet node instantly, without the transmission lag typical to most backwater colonies.

I check my message inbox for incoming traffic, hoping against my better knowledge that Halley managed to dash out a reply before the *Midway* did her last pre-transition database synchronization. All the new messages I've received are just administrative garbage from the fleet, of course. If I left the solar system for the last time when we transitioned out, then the common history I share with Halley will have no final period, no formal epilogue.

I don't want to dwell on things that are outside of my control, so I stow my PDP and leave the room to do the sensible and soldierly thing—I head for the chow hall to check the quality of the local food.

The day on New Svalbard is over a hundred hours long, but most of us have lived in windowless tubes on six-hour watch cycles for so long that we don't need a daylight transition to be able to sleep. I spend the next two watch cycles sleeping, eating, and getting settled in my new environment. It's the middle of summer on New Svalbard right now, which means that we can walk around outside in our regular fatigues without turning into expressionist ice sculptures within a few minutes. The road from the main gate of the base down to the town has been upgraded from dirt to a high-traction hardpack mix, and the town itself has grown so much closer to the base that walking down to the base seems feasible now.

"You can walk it," the gate guard says, guessing my thoughts as I stand and survey the tundra. "It's a kilometer and a half. We do it all the time when the weather's good. Just don't try it when we have winter gales blowing, 'less you're in heated armor."

"Anything down there worth the hike?"

"They got some bars in town. The new rec building here on base is nicer than anything the civvies have, but sometimes you want to see people who aren't wearing uniforms, you know?"

"Yeah," I say. The gate guard nods and returns to his duties, scanning the screens in the gate booth for sensor alarms.

I walk past the gate and down the hardpack surface of the road for a little while, until I'm out of earshot of the gate booth. There's a breeze coming from the north, where snowcapped mountains form a ragged wall on the horizon. It's cold enough that I wouldn't want to spend an hour out here in just my battle dress, but for the moment, I don't mind the cold. Most of the time, I breathe the scrubbed air on spaceships, and whenever I drop onto the surface of a colony planet, I'm usually too busy with staying alive and killing things to stop and appreciate the clean planetary atmosphere. New Svalbard is harsh, cold, and barren, but there's a clean purity about it that is breathtaking to someone who grew up in a Public Residence Cluster, where a single tenement building has more people in it than the entire population of the little town in the valley below the base. I wish I could record some vid footage for Mom. In all my years on Earth, I've never been anywhere you can see for twenty miles in any direction and not spot another human being.

Ten more years of terraforming, and this place will be pretty, I think. *And then the SRA will try to take it from us, once we've done all the hard work for them, and we'll turn this little moon into a battlefield. If the Lankies don't come in and grab it for themselves long before then.*

Overhead, two drop ships come swooping out of the overcast sky. They keep their tight formation as they make a pass over Camp Frostbite, navigation lights blinking. Their wing pylons are crammed with cargo pods. The *Midway*'s drop-ship wing has been shuttling people and gear from ship to surface for the last two watch cycles, a steady flow of traffic between the carrier and the outposts. In less than twelve hours, the number of Commonwealth troops on the ground has increased tenfold. The two HD battalions spread out among the terraforming stations don't have any organic air support or heavy armor, but even so, the SRA would find this place a tough nut to crack for anything less than a brigade. To the Lankies, our presence wouldn't matter—just a few more anthills to kick over.

I want to walk around on the cold tundra some more, enjoy this rare solitude and the wide-open spaces around Camp Frostbite, but then the speakers of the base announcement system come to life and disturb the tranquility of the scene.

"All off-duty personnel, report to mess hall at 1600 hours for a briefing. Repeat, all off-duty personnel report to the mess hall at 1600."

I check my watch to find that I have fifteen minutes left, so I make my way back to the gate reluctantly.

———

The new mess hall on the base is barely big enough to hold all the troops now present on base. When I walk in, almost all the tables are occupied. Sergeant Fallon and her HD entourage are seated near the back of the room by one of the exit hatches, and she waves me over. I make my way through the crowd and sit down with the HD grunts.

"Wonder what they have to say to us that requires every pair of boots in the same room," Sergeant Fallon says.

"Beats me," I say. "This is a first."

The brass don't make us wait too long. We hop to attention when the garrison company's CO and the battalion commanders walk into the room. Both the HD officers are lieutenant colonels and outrank the SI officer who is merely a major, but the SI major is clearly in charge.

"Listen up, people," he says. "The task force commander wants to address all units."

"Attention, all hands," a voice comes out of the address system. "This is General Pearce, Commanding Officer, Task Force 230.7.

"I'll cut right to the chase, gentlemen. We have arrived in the Fomalhaut system, and here we will stay. We are reinforcing the garrison here on New Svalbard. The reason for all those extra supplies is this: Our stay here is open-ended.

"The good news, if you can call it that, is that fleet Intel finally figured out how the Lankies move around, and how they find our colonies. The bad news is that the ugly bastards use our own Alcubierre networks against us."

At this revelation, not even military discipline and briefing protocol can stop the assembled troops from voicing their surprise. All at once, a few hundred conversations break out in the room. I look at the SI major, and notice with some satisfaction that he seems just as surprised as we are. Fleet Command played their cards closely on this one, and even though I had guessed that the grunts were going to get the short end of the stick again, the magnitude of the news leaves me momentarily gut-punched.

"We don't know how they pull it off exactly, but we do know that the Lankies use our transition nodes—ours and the SRA's—to pinpoint our colonies. We've basically set up a bunch of blinking road signs for them. Therefore, Fleet has decided to shut the whole network down until we figure out how to counter those seed ships. Our transition to Fomalhaut was the last one before

Fleet turned off the transit node on the solar system side. The beacons are deactivated, and the transition points are being mined with nukes right now."

"Shut it!" the major at the front of the room shouts when the swelling din of exclamations from the assembled garrison threatens to overwhelm the audio from the overhead address system, where the general is undoubtedly on a one-way feed. The noise level in the room decreases, but not by much.

". . . can't tell you how long this task force will be on station in this system. I can tell you, however, that we will fly the flag of the Commonwealth on New Svalbard for however long it takes—a month, a year, or more. We *will* defend this moon against any threat, whether Russian, Chinese, or Lanky, until Command reopens the Alcubierre network and relieves us.

"Until that happens, nothing will change. Promotion schedules are still in effect. Anyone whose term of enlistment expires during our stay will be able to reenlist for another regular term, or have their original term extended until we get back to Earth. Those of you who choose to serve another full enlistment will be eligible for an additional discharge bonus."

Some of the troopers at the table let out suppressed laughs at this. The HD soldiers are mostly either shell-shocked or talking amongst themselves. The commotion in the room is at an entirely unacceptable level for an address by a general officer, but the brass at the front of the room don't make much of an effort to suppress the noise.

"I expect every one of you to keep doing your duty until we are relieved and called home. The ships of the task force will set up a picket and assume orbital-patrol duties.

"We're in a good position, tactically speaking. We have enough ordnance to hold off a superior force, and enough supplies to stay on independent duty out here for many months. We have two battalions plus on the ground, with combat teams of at least platoon strength at every terraforming station. We have an embarked regiment on the *Midway* that can drop onto any trouble spot on the moon within an hour. We have all the gear and troops we need to give a bloody nose to half a brigade of SRA marines. And if the Lankies find this rock before the fleet calls us back, we'll throw everything we have at them the second the first of them puts a toe on this moon."

Every Spaceborne Infantry grunt in the room knows that if the Lankies want the place, they'll take it, regardless of the number of rifles we point at them. The general's little pep talk is probably designed to make the HD contingent less anxious about getting dumped on a backwoods moon to mount a hopeless defense, but I can see on the faces all around me that the bullshit detectors of the Home World Defense troopers are just as finely calibrated as ours.

"Say, Staff Sergeant Grayson," Master Sergeant Fallon addresses me, loud enough for the rest of the table to hear. "How many colony planets and moons have the Lankies contested so far?"

"Forty-four at last count, Master Sergeant Fallon," I reply in the same volume.

"And how many did we successfully defend, Sergeant Grayson?"

"Zero at last count, Master Sergeant Fallon."

There are nervous chuckles all around us. At the head of the room, the SI major launches another appeal to keep the noise level down. Overhead, the general continues his little speech over the one-way circuit, unaware of the sudden unrest among the ranks.

"We will dig in, and we *will* hold the line until we are relieved. The Lankies have never shown any interest in the Fomalhaut system, and the Sino-Russians have other problems, so I predict we will have a nice, quiet stay on New Svalbard."

Sergeant Fallon leans back in her chair and folds her arms across her chest. Unlike most of her HD troopers, she doesn't look shocked or dismayed. Instead, there's a knowing sort of smile on her face, as if she just heard the punch line to a good, but familiar joke.

"Now, see," she says in my direction, "I wouldn't bet any money on that."

CHAPTER 16

——— A CONFLICT OF ——— AUTHORITY

We waltz into town like the command section of a conquering army.

I'm in the back of one of Camp Frostbite's armored cargo mules, eight-wheeled transport tanks shaped like giant doorstops made out of composite armor. The troop compartment is big enough for a ten-man squad in full kit. I'm the only fleet puke in the vehicle. The other seats in the troop bay are occupied by the COs of the two Homeworld Defense battalions, the major in charge of the Spaceborne Infantry garrison company, and all three of their senior sergeants. In the bucket seat next to mine, Sergeant Fallon is napping, or pretending to, with her arms folded across her chest. By orders from upstairs, we're all wearing full combat armor minus our helmets, and we're carrying sidearms and rifles. The general in charge of the task force is a reservist who hasn't seen any combat since the tussle with the Lankies started, and he's utterly afraid we'll all be caught with our pants down if the Lankies suddenly show up in orbit. Those of us who have been fighting them for the last five years know that it won't make a bit of a difference if we're in armor or not when they show up, and that our little oxygen tanks will merely give us a few hours to contemplate our impending deaths. But orders are orders, so we look like a bunch of heavily armed football players spoiling for a fight with the locals.

When we roll past the first buildings of New Longyearbyen, the HD troopers turn in their seats to peer out of the small armored windows in curiosity. I follow suit, even though I've seen plenty of colonial architecture in the last few years. Only the major in command of the garrison company doesn't bother craning his neck, and Sergeant Fallon is still snoozing with her head on her chest.

New Longyearbyen is like no other colony settlement I've ever seen. Every single building is overengineered, almost bunker-like, to withstand the harsh winter climate that locks the moon down for half the planetary year. Where the housing and facilities on a warm colony world are mostly the same standard squares of prefabricated modular housing, the structures here on New Svalbard are custom-made domes with meter-thick ferroconcrete walls. The buildings are laid out not on straight and even street grids, but in loops and irregular patterns designed by computers to minimize the effects of the hundred-klick-per-hour winds that blow even in the temperate tundra belt in the middle of the winter season.

Our driver snakes the huge armored mule along roads that are mostly turns.

When we pull up in front of the civilian admin building, and the mule comes to a gentle stop with a snort of its hydropneumatic suspension, Sergeant Fallon's eyes pop open, and she looks around in the crew compartment with an exaggerated yawn.

"We there yet?"

"Yeah," I say. "Welcome to the booming metropolis of New Longyearbyen, population ten K."

We climb out of the armored troop hatch, battle armor scraping against polysteel laminate plating as seven of us in full kit squeeze out of a hatch no designer ever tried to negotiate while wearing hardshell battle rattle and carrying rifles with twenty-inch barrels and clunky attachments.

The admin building here in town is even more solid looking than the bunker-like one the Chinese had on Sirius Ad before their own attack craft blew it into rubble. The whole thing looks like a huge loaf of bread. It's windowless, and judging from the visible wall thickness by the regularly spaced entrance alcoves, the concrete is at least two meters thick. All along the top of the building, there are sensor domes and retractable comms antennas that make the building look like the top half of a fleet frigate buried in the permafrost.

The four HD troopers look around with interest, while the SI major and his company sergeant look pointedly casual, old hands at the planetary excursion business. There are snowcapped mountains in the distance, much higher than anything the Eastern Seaboard back home has to offer, and I have to concede that as far as first visits to another world go, New Svalbard is one of the more scenic ones.

As we stand and gawk, the closest door of the nearby admin building opens, and a uniformed civvie steps out. He's very tall, and his blue-shirted chest has a circumference that would give any fleet armorer sweats if he had to be issued off-the-rack battle armor. His uniform is a dark-blue set of fatigues with white arm patches, and there's a shield-shaped badge over his left breast pocket that identifies him as a colonial constable, a civilian peace officer. He's wearing glasses with small, circular lenses. As he walks out of the entrance vestibule and over to where we're stretching our legs, I notice that he has a five o'clock shadow at nine in the morning. There's a sidearm in a well-worn Durathread holster on his thigh, an older model large-bore metallic cartridge autoloader. The military stopped issuing those a hundred years ago because they're useless against battle armor, but run-of-the-mill civilian criminals don't routinely wear ballistic hardshell.

"Hey, Matt," the SI major greets the constable. "How's it going?"

"Not too bad," the cop says. He eyes the armored eight-wheeler behind us. "What's with the hardware? You expecting trouble?"

"What do you mean?"

The constable nods at the thirty-five-millimeter autocannon on the roof of the mule. The weapons mount is modular, and the crews usually run the local mules without heavy armament, but our task force commander's new orders regarding battle readiness aren't limited to trooper armament.

"Yeah, that," the major says, almost sheepishly. "New management. Some Earthside one-star reservist who hasn't been in a tussle with the Lankies yet. I think he's expecting them to drop out of the sky any second."

"Well, I'm glad you folks have some sensible leadership now," the constable says with a dry smirk. "That peashooter's going to make all the difference if we get a seed ship dropping on our heads this afternoon. I'll tell the rest of the colony we're invasion-proof now."

Everyone has a good, borderline insubordinate chuckle at this. I decide that I like the tall constable already.

"Introductions," the major says. He points to each of us in turn. "Lieutenant Colonel Kemp, Lieutenant Colonel Decker, Master Sergeant Fallon, Sergeant Major Dalton, Sergeant Major Zelnick, Staff Sergeant Grayson. This is Constable Guest, the senior law-enforcement official here on New Svalbard."

"Head of a vast army of minions," Constable Guest adds. "Twenty-one sworn officers, and four part-timers." He looks at the assembled interservice mix of troops. "Lot of brass here for one little moon. I heard about all the new Earthside soldiers you dropped at the terraformers. Two battalions' worth? Don't tell me we're getting ready to fight someone for this place."

"Not as far as we know," the major says. "We got something else going on, though. Is the administrator in?"

"When isn't he?" Constable Guest says. "The science crew is here, too. They're doing their weekly admin devotional."

"Without you?"

"Stepped out for some fresh air," he shrugs. "Go on in. Second floor, the big conference room next to the kitchen. You know the place."

"Yeah, I do." The major turns to the rest of us. "If you want to follow me, I'll show you around and introduce you to the administrator and his crew. Staff Sergeant Grayson, you may want to head over to the airfield, meet up with the ATC on duty, and familiarize yourself with the facilities, in case we need your services later on."

"Roger that, sir," I reply. "Never was much of a meeting type anyway."

I watch as the other troops file into the building behind the major. Behind me, the driver of the mule gingerly maneuvers his oversized vehicle into a clear spot next to the building across the narrow street to free up the path for other vehicles. Some colonists are milling around at a safe distance to watch the camouflaged steel monster with its out-of-place cannon armament try to fit into spaces never designed for Spaceborne Infantry fighting vehicles. We probably could have taken one of the light, unarmored mini-mules or walked the mile and a half outright, but the new brass elected to take the steel beast, and I just tagged along for the ride as the junior member of the entourage.

I've been to New Svalbard a few times, but always as a passenger on a ship stopping for water. I've never been down to the civvie airfield. When I ask Constable Guest if he can give me directions, he shrugs with a smile.

"Sure thing, but it's a bit of a hike. You can hoof it across town, or I can give you a ride, if you don't mind being the passenger on a dinky ATV."

"I'd appreciate that," I say. "And you can be sure that any dignity I may have retained after Basic is long gone by now."

The airfield is much more sophisticated than I expected. I had pictured a gravel landing pad and a few fuel tanks, like the ones that seem to be standard on every minor colonial outpost. Instead, the constable's ATV rolls onto a facility that looks more advanced than the drop-ship landing pad up at Camp Frostbite. There are half a dozen hangar buildings with abnormally thick concrete domes, and as we drive up the central alley formed by the hangars, I can see thick hydraulic blast doors that look like they'd stop a MARS warhead cold.

"They built it to handle all the planetary freight traffic and then some," Constable Guest says over the low hum of the ATV's electric drive. "We don't have an orbital replenishing facility yet, but the crew at the water storage depot can refill the tanks on a tanker shuttle in twenty minutes flat."

The tarmac here is smooth concrete. There's a landing area for VTOL traffic that has a dozen individual landing zones stenciled onto it, and the facility has an actual runway, thousands of meters of smooth blacktop stretching into the distance.

"Dual redundant AILS, for the frequent shit weather, full civil and military refueling capacity, and all the latest in weather systems and navigational aids. We even have a satellite network now for comms and nav fixes. The place may not look like much, but we have pretty shiny gear down here. All we're missing is an orbital service facility, so the big guys don't have to send the tanker shuttles down here to top off their drinking water or reactor-fuel mass. 'Course, the way things are going, we won't be getting any upgrades any time soon. Not with the colony flights at an end."

The constable lets the ATV roll to a stop in front of a building that looks like a small-scale copy of the massive admin facility in town. The only difference is the obvious air-traffic-control tower grafted onto the short side of the building that faces the runway and the VTOL landing pads.

"It's not just the colony flights," I say into the silence following the shutdown of the ATV's power train. Constable Guest looks at me with a raised eyebrow. "You're missing a peach of a briefing up there in Admin Central," I tell him. "You want to tag along while I bring the local ATC crew up to speed?"

It takes me all of two minutes to introduce myself and share the news with the half dozen air-traffic controllers and pilots on duty this morning. By the time I finish, there is utter silence in the flight-ops control room for a few moments, and the expressions of polite interest have given way to unconcealed shock and dismay.

"You can't be serious," the flight-ops supervisor says. He's a stocky and hard-looking man who wouldn't look out of place in a master sergeant's uniform. His name tag says BARNETT, and even though the civvie overalls don't have rank insignia, his demeanor marks him as the guy in charge. "Shut down all of it? The whole thing?"

"Yes, the whole thing. No traffic into or out of the solar system, or between the extrasolar transit hubs. They pushed out a bunch of ships with supplies for the colonies, and pulled the plug. We're on our own."

"For how long? We got all the water we'll ever need, but we do need food deliveries. This place isn't exactly popping with agriculture, you know."

"I have no idea," I say. "I'm a staff sergeant. They don't usually invite me to staff officer briefings. The general says they'll keep it locked until they've figured out how to stop the Lanky expansion."

Chief Barnett chuckles without humor.

"If the people at Defense are as dim as the ones running the Colonial Administration, that could take a few decades."

"I guess we better figure out how to grow lettuce and potatoes in permafrost," Constable Guest says.

The local airfield's control center has better gear than any military facility I've ever seen. I'm in the middle of updating my tactical computer with the civilian frequencies when the earbud of my comms unit chirps with incoming traffic.

"Sergeant Grayson, Major Vandenberg. What's your status over there?"

"Updating my tac kit, sir. Another ten minutes, and I'm good."

"You may want to expedite. We're heading back to the ranch, RFN."

"Copy that. I'm on my way. Grayson out."

I shut down the data link to my portable tactical unit in mid-update reluctantly, and gather my kit.

Constable Guest and his ATV are gone when I get downstairs, so I walk back the way we came. When I'm about a quarter mile from the admin center, the mule comes rolling around a corner in front of me, much more quickly than safety regs proscribe for driving through a civvie town. I jog toward them, and the mule stops in front of me, suspension snorting air.

"Hop in," the company sergeant says through the open hatch.

"Something wrong?" I ask as I climb into the mule and reclaim my seat.

"Just a bunch of civvies throwing a tantrum," the major answers for him. "We're used to it. Hard batch of people down here."

We drive back to the base, but instead of going back the way we came, our driver goes straight to the outskirts of town and then drives around the settlement across rough terrain. We have to buckle in as the mule heaves and bounces on the rocky, uneven ground like a ship in stormy seas. Finally, he picks up the hardpack road well outside of town, and the ride becomes smooth once more.

I know better than to prod the brass for more information. Instead, I give Sergeant Fallon a questioning look. She smiles a brief and clandestine smile, and very briefly forms a letter T with her hands, the signal for "time."

"It was a dipshit idea to go down there in an armored vehicle, anyway," Lieutenant Colonel Kemp says. He's the CO of Sergeant Fallon's HD battalion, and right now his mood seems to be somewhere between amusement and exasperation.

"Not my orders," Major Vandenberg says. "You may take that one up with your task force CO upstairs. I could have told him that the civvies around here don't take kindly to the military putting their hands on civilian assets on the best of days. Rolling in with a tank and wearing body armor, well . . ."

We're back in the ops center on the base. I still don't know exactly what transpired at the meeting with the civilian administrator, but from the comments between the brass, I have a pretty good idea.

"Well," Lieutenant Colonel Kemp says. "I'm not going to make *that* call, that's for sure. Let me get on the comms with the old man, and see what kind of flag-officer wisdom he can dispense." He sneaks just the slightest amount of sarcasm into his inflections. I decide that the mood among all the ranks—enlisted, NCOs, and officers alike—is unusually weird. Under normal circumstances, a staff officer rank openly criticizing the flag officer in charge would be tantamount to insubordination, especially in front of junior personnel.

Sergeant Fallon, who has been leaning against the wall near the window, shoots me a glance and nods toward the door. I return a nod of confirmation and walk over to the hatch, to leave the officers and senior NCOs to have their little command powwow among themselves.

I leave the room and head down the corridor toward the chow hall. A few moments later Sergeant Fallon hails me from behind.

"Wait up, Andrew," she says. I stop to let her catch up.

"Let's find a quiet corner somewhere, shall we?" Sergeant Fallon suggests.

We grab some coffee at the chow counter and sit down at a table by the windows. The local chow hall is much nicer than anything in the fleet, a compensation for being stationed on a frigid wasteland where you can't even step outside without heated armor half the planetary year.

"Here's the deal," Sergeant Fallon says. "Fleet said we are to take charge of all the civvie resources on this rock. Food storage, water reserves, everything."

"Looks like our general doesn't want to go beg the civvies for food and water once we run out of what we brought."

"Well, their head guy told our brass to go piss up a rope. His exact words, too. He also invited them to convey that message to the general. Said he'd post his cops by all the storage facilities, and that he'd have anyone arrested who sets foot on them without permission."

"With civilian cops? He's nuts. No way his guys can keep us out. They have freakin' *pistols*. Might as well throw rocks at someone in battle rattle, for all the damage you'll do."

"That's not the point, Andrew. You think we can just walk in and start popping civvie police? The locals outnumber us twenty to one. We piss 'em off enough, we're in deep shit. I doubt that one-star reservist who thinks he's running the show from up there has the stomach to tell us to start shooting civvies."

"And what if he does?" I ask.

Sergeant Fallon takes a sip of her coffee and looks out of the window, where the planetary sunset paints the snowy mountain chain on the horizon in muted shades of ochre and purple.

"I'm done shooting at civilians," she says quietly. "If we get deployed, and they order us to open fire on those barely armed cops, I'll order my troops to stand down, and fuck orders. I doubt the brig here on base is big enough to hold a company's worth of troops. Assuming we'd go quietly," she adds.

She looks at me expectantly, as if she wants me to argue the point with her. I don't have to think about it very long.

"Shit," I say. "Remember Detroit? If I have nightmares these days, they're not about the Sino-Russians or the fucking Lankies. They're about that clusterfuck."

I ponder the swirl pattern of the creamer in my coffee.

"I was done shooting at civvies the moment they medevaced me out of that shithole. I'm not too keen on starting again."

Sergeant Fallon nods with satisfaction and looks out onto the landscape of our temporary homeworld again.

"I don't know about you, but I'm done shoveling shit for these people. If the Lankies show up, I'll gladly shoot every round in our supply chain at them. But if that idiot general tells me to point my rifle at civilians without danger, I'll turn in my rank sleeves and tell them to stick my retirement money up their asses. Along with that Medal of goddamn Honor."

CHAPTER 17
———— BASTILLE DAY ————

We spend the next few days squaring away our new quarters, unloading cargo from the orbital shuttles, and eating way too many meals in the fancy chow hall. After a week has passed since our ill-advised sojourn into town, I allow myself some hope that the task force commander isn't completely off his rocker.

On day eight of our stay, that little kernel of hope is squashed, not exactly to my surprise.

Whoever is in charge of the whole thing has either a flair for drama or a sadistic streak. We're all barely out of our bunks when the combat-stations alarm in our building starts blaring. I'm brushing my teeth in the head when the lights switch to the ominous red-tinted combat illumination. All around me, the noncoms of the HD staff platoon drop their morning kit and rush out of the room.

"That better be a Lanky invasion," Sergeant Fallon says from behind one of the stall doors near me.

"Well, whoever it is, you better cut things short in there," I reply.

"Grayson, if this is a bullshit alert, there's no reason for me to rush. And if it's the end of this place, it won't make a difference whether I finish taking a dump, will it?"

"See you at weapons issue," I say, and leave the room with a grin.

The HD grunts are every bit as squared away as the Space-borne Infantry. Every single member of the platoon is in full battle rattle and standard combat loadout less than five minutes after the first sound of the combat-stations alarm. We don't have designated posts, so we fall out in front of the building and trot over to the ops center, heavy with weapons and ammunition.

"HD platoon, briefing room Charlie," one of the senior SI sergeants greets us at the main entrance. He's in his battle dress fatigues, not in armor, so I deduce that we don't, in fact, have a Lanky seed ship or Russian invasion fleet headed for Camp Frostbite at the moment. We file into the building and sit down in briefing room Charlie as directed. The SI troopers on duty in the ops center move around without great urgency.

"That's just fucking mean-spirited," one of the HD sergeants mutters as we claim our seats, cramming our armor-clad bodies into chairs too small by half for troopers in battle gear. "Coulda waited until after breakfast with this shit."

Nobody disagrees. There's an unwritten protocol to the alert system, and it's considered harsh to summon a whole platoon or company with a combat-stations alert without emergency while the unit is in the middle of personal maintenance or chow.

"Ten-*hut!*"

The HD platoon's lieutenant jumps to his feet when the SI major and his company sergeant enter the room. We all follow suit.

"As you were," the major says.

Forty grunts in armor lower themselves into their too-small chairs again.

"Apologies for the alert before morning chow," the major continues. "The old man upstairs called that one. I'm guessing he's not keeping track of the local time."

"That's not the only thing he isn't keeping track of," someone behind me murmurs.

"I realize this is going to go down without rehearsal," the major says. He steps up to the briefing lectern at the front of the room and picks up the remote for the holographic screen on the wall behind him. "The word just came down an hour ago. This one's called Operation Winter Stash."

He turns on the holoscreen, which instantly shows a 3-D image of New Longyearbyen. Several spots on the map are marked with drop-zone icons.

"This should be a quick thing, since we're only facing mostly unarmed civilians. We're going to seize control of the civilian storage facilities under emergency regulations."

The drop-zone markers on the map flash in turn as the major points at them.

"Objective A is the main food storage. Objective B is the water farm. Objective C is the control center for the hydroponic greenhouses, and Objective D is the fuel storage at the civvie airfield. We're sending your platoon in, one squad per objective."

Members of the platoon are silently absorbing this information. I look at Sergeant Fallon across the room, and her face is impassive and unreadable. Finally, the platoon lieutenant raises a hand.

"Sir, you're going to send four squads into a town of over *ten thousand* to take their most important resources?"

"You'll be in battle armor, and you'll have all four Dragonflies supporting you from above. The most dangerous stuff they have down there are sidearms and maybe some stun sticks."

"Why isn't the SI company going in?" Sergeant Fallon asks. "Sir," she adds, with a bit of acid in her voice.

"The general feels that the HD platoon is better suited for this task. You folks are trained and geared for exactly this kind of mission profile, and you have a lot more experience handling belligerent civvies than we do."

I have an unpleasant flashback to a drop into Detroit almost five years ago: our squad holed up against the side of a building, and a surge of angry civilians coming toward us like a natural disaster. Then the hoarse chattering of our rifles, and our fléchettes cutting through bodies, mowing down rows of people in a bloody harvest. I don't believe in souls, but if I have one, a big chunk of it died that night in Detroit.

"We do a quick vertical assault with the drop ships. One Dragonfly per squad, so we can get you all on the ground in the same second. Secure the facilities, establish your perimeters, and call in the cavalry once you've seized the objectives. If the civvies get cranky, use nonlethal deterrents. Once you give the all-clear, the Dragonflies are going to RTB and pick up one platoon of SI each, to reinforce the objectives. Should be a cakewalk."

"Spoken like a man who ain't gonna be there," the SI sergeant next to me mutters under his breath, and I nod in agreement.

I want to talk to Sergeant Fallon before we board the ships for our little cakewalk, but on the way to the flight area, she's in a walking huddle with the rest of the platoon's NCOs. With my fleet-pattern armor and my fleet weaponry, I already feel like a bit of an interloper among the HD troops, and walking to the flight line by myself only reinforces the feeling. Just before we get to the flight-ops area, the wandering HD powwow breaks up, and I notice some of the NCOs shooting me sideways glances.

We walk up to the ramp of our waiting Dragonflies without much enthusiasm. The troop bay is designed to hold a full platoon, and our little squad has lots of legroom. I sit by the tail ramp for faster egress, but Sergeant Fallon and two of her noncoms sit by the forward bulkhead, right by the crew chief's jump seat and the passageway to the cockpit.

As our Dragonfly lifts off into the cold morning sky, I have a very strange feeling about the upcoming drop.

Our four-ship flight takes a course away from the settlement, to gain altitude out of sight and earshot. When we are high enough to be inaudible from the ground, we swing around and head straight for our targets.

"Prepare for combat descent," the pilot says over the shipboard intercom.

When we're directly above the town, twenty thousand feet above the hard deck, our drop ship banks sharply, cuts its engines, and drops out of the sky. The pilots are either adrenaline junkies or they don't get very many opportunities to do combat descents. We're all grunting in our seats as the drop-ship jock at the stick holds a three g turn for what seems like minutes. Then the engines rev up again, and gravity pushes us back into our seats. The Dragonfly slows its rapid descent, and a few moments later, the skids hit the ground roughly.

"All squads," Sergeant Fallon's voice comes over the platoon channel. "*Bastille, Bastille, Bastille.*"

"Up and at 'em," the crew chief calls out. We unbuckle and grab our weapons from the storage brackets.

Most of the squad exits the ship at a run, but Sergeant Fallon and the two NCOs with her don't follow them. I stop at the bottom of the ramp and look back to see that one of the HD sergeants has his rifle aimed at the crew chief, who looks utterly perplexed. Sergeant Fallon rushes up the passageway to the drop ship's cockpit, with her remaining NCO at her heels.

I jog back up the ramp, careful to keep my hands away from the carbine slung across my chest, lest the HD trooper holding the crew chief at gunpoint thinks I'm about to intervene in whatever crazy-ass plan Sergeant Fallon is executing.

"Hands off the comms gear," the HD trooper instructs the

crew chief, and emphasizes the command with a wave of his rifle muzzle. I walk past them to follow Sergeant Fallon into the cockpit, and the HD trooper gives me a curt nod.

When I step into the open cockpit hatch, I see Sergeant Fallon and her NCO holding sidearms against the helmets of the pilots.

"Listen up, flyboy," Sergeant Fallon tells the pilot, who looks every bit as stunned as his crew chief. "Your ride is now HD property. Unplug your helmet, get out of your seat, and walk off the ship."

"Are you out of your fucking mind, Sergeant?" the pilot says.

"Not half as nuts as I was the day I signed up for this bullshit," Sergeant Fallon replies. "Now make your call. Your fingers touch any buttons, I'll put a round right through your hand, sport."

She reaches across his chest and removes his sidearm from its holster. The muzzle of the pistol in her other hand never wavers. The pilot carefully unbuckles his harness and starts to get out of his seat.

"No need for violence, Sarge. It's not like you can do a damn thing with this bird anyway."

"Whatever you say," Sergeant Fallon says.

When both pilots are out of their seats, Sergeant Fallon marches them out of the cockpit at gunpoint. I retreat into the armory nook behind the cockpit to let them pass.

"Cameron, she's all yours. Andrew, you may want to come with me."

In the cockpit, the HD sergeant picks up the pilot's helmet and wedges himself into the right-hand seat.

"Uh, Sarge?" I ask. "You sure you want him to fly this thing?"

"Why the fuck not?" she says. "That's what he does for a living back home. He's one of our Hornet pilots."

I remember her comment about reshuffling the HD battalion's personnel roster, about making sure the right people are in the right places. The HD "sergeant" behind the stick raises two fingers to the brow ridge of his helmet in a casual salute, and I grin.

You can't land something as big and noisy as a Dragonfly in the middle of a colony settlement without drawing instant attention. Whatever element of surprise the combat descent may have bought us, the HD troopers let it evaporate by not charging into the storage bunker that was our squad's objective. A few minutes after our arrival, the place is lousy with curious civilians. The HD troopers merely stand in a group near the entrance of the bunker, helmet visors raised and weapons slung.

"All squads, objectives secure. The birds are in the nest."

Sergeant Fallon sends out a curt acknowledgment in reply. Then she takes off the helmet and walks up to the nearest gaggle of civilians.

"Go fetch the administrator and the chief constable, please. And be quick about it. We don't have much time."

The colony administrator shows up a few minutes later on an ATV, accompanied by Chief Constable Guest and two of his officers. They climb off their vehicle and approach Sergeant Fallon, who is the only one of us without a full-coverage helmet on her head. The administrator looks livid, and the cops don't seem to be in a friendly mood, either.

"The hell are you people doing at the food bunker, geared up for a fucking war?" he shouts at Sergeant Fallon. "Pack up your troops and go back to base. You have no business claiming civilian assets."

"Shut up and listen," Sergeant Fallon replies. "We didn't come to seize your shit. But the people they'll send after us are going to."

The administrator looks from Sergeant Fallon to her combat-ready troops.

"So what are you here for, dressed up like that?"

"They told us to seize your food and fuel," she explains. "But I have no interest in following illegal orders today."

Constable Guest folds his arms in front of his barrel chest and looks at me with a raised eyebrow and the faintest of smiles.

"You guys staging a mutiny, or what?"

"Looks like we are," I reply.

"I don't suppose that fleet in orbit is going to share your legal interpretation?" Constable Guest asks Sergeant Fallon.

"No, I don't suppose they will," she says. "Mainly because the guy who gave the order is in charge of that fleet, too."

"That could be a problem," the administrator says. "You guys are just a squad. They can come down here and haul you off to the brig any time they want, and then take our stuff anyway."

"We're a platoon," Sergeant Fallon says. "The rest of my people are over at the airfield, your hydroponic farm, and the water facility. They're digging in to defend."

"How many troops they got up there, in orbit?"

"Most of a regiment of Spaceborne Infantry. Plus the two SI companies up at Camp Frosthite," I say. "But the fleet isn't going to be keen on shooting anything into the middle of civvie towns. They'll have to come and pry us out the hard way."

"I'm not wild about the idea of a shootout right here in the middle of town," the administrator says. "There's over ten thousand people down here, you know. Not a lot of clear space for stray bullets."

"Yes, but they know that, too," Sergeant Fallon says.

The administrator looks over to the handful of troops by the entrance to the food storage bunker again.

"You guys are nuts. Not that I don't appreciate your offer, but what can you do with a platoon against a whole regiment? That's what, forty against a thousand?"

"Two thousand," I say.

"Well," Sergeant Fallon says, and smiles a lopsided little smirk. "We also have two full battalions of my own Homeworld Defense guys sitting all over this rock already. You have a bunch of those atmospheric puddle jumpers at the airfield, don't you?"

The administrator and the constables stand off to the side for a few minutes, debating the situation in hushed, but animated talk. Then they walk back to where Sergeant Fallon and I are standing.

"Look," the administrator says. "I don't relish the thought of you grunts shooting it out with each other right in the middle of my town."

He looks at the food storage bunker and chews on his lower lip for a moment.

"But I sure as hell didn't sign up for a military occupation by my own people. Commonwealth Constitution says you serve us, not the other way around."

"You're the ranking civilian down here," Sergeant Fallon says. "Until they open that chute again and send us orders to the contrary, that makes you my boss, not that one-star pencil pusher up there on the carrier."

She nods at the troops by the bunker entrance.

"You want to keep all that stuff in civilian hands, you say the word. If you want them, I'm putting my whole outfit under your authority. Chances are they won't want to try and root out fifteen hundred of us. And if they do, they'll find out that Homeworld Defense is better at this game than they are."

"How you going to handle those drop ships?" Constable Guest asks. "They can drop on top of us any time they want. You got something here that'll scare off a flight of those?"

Sergeant Fallon smiles.

"We sort of, ah, borrowed the garrison's brand-new drop ships. All four of 'em."

Constable Guest shakes his head with a smile.

"Do it," the administrator says. "Before they get wind of what you guys are doing down here. I'll get on the radio with the fleet boss upstairs once you're set up. See if I can talk some sense into him."

Constable Guest turns to his fellow cops.

"We're going to need a shitload of badges. I want to deputize every last one of these guys."

"Time to pick a side," Sergeant Fallon says to me a little while later, when the squad is setting up defensive positions at the food bunker. "I could use your help. You're a pro running the tactical network. I need someone to coordinate the puddle jumpers and drop ships. Let us know when they send us company from orbit. But I'm not going to hold a gun to your head to keep you here. You want no part of this, you can go back to Frostbite, and no hard feelings. We're probably all going to end up at a court-martial, best-case scenario. I'm not asking you to flush your career down the toilet."

I don't like the idea of taking sides against my fellow soldiers and fleet sailors. If I throw in my lot with Sergeant Fallon and her HD battalions, I will be forever persona non grata in any fleet chow hall and ship berth, even if I don't spend the next twenty years in a military prison for mutiny. Since we're at war, they probably wouldn't leave it at that. What we're doing here could get us all in front of a firing squad.

But to what end are we here? If we exist to defend the colonies, how can siding with the civvies down here be treason?

I remember the oath of service I took at my reenlistment ceremony just a few weeks ago. *To bravely defend the laws of the Commonwealth and the freedom of its citizens.*

Do we honor our oaths if we try to defend the Commonwealth's laws by letting our commanders ignore them? Do we defend the freedom of its citizens by taking it away at gunpoint?

I don't want to shoot at my fellow soldiers. But the thought of shooting at civilians is even more upsetting. I don't want to pick a side, but now that I am forced to choose, I know which one I have to join.

"Maybe they'll put us in neighboring cells at Leavenworth," I say, and Sergeant Fallon smiles.

She pats me on the shoulder, and turns around to address the civvies standing around the ATV. "Can one of you folks give Sergeant Grayson here a ride to the airfield?"

By the time I get to the civilian airfield on the outskirts of the town, the administrator has passed the word down to all the colony facilities already. I pair my control deck with the main console of the local ATC system, and do a quick scan of the air and orbital space above New Longyearbyen.

"Sarge, this is Grayson," I send to Sergeant Fallon. She has turned the platoon channel into our new top-level command circuit. The encryption isn't completely bulletproof, especially not against our own people, but even with the hardware they have on the *Midway*, it will take the fleet a while to break into our renegade comms network.

"Go ahead," she replies.

"I'm plugged in. Nothing at all in the air between us and the task force. Looks like they haven't caught on yet."

"Oh, they're getting a good idea. The base has been pinging me with comms for the last fifteen minutes. Something about the whole drop-ship flight being off the air."

I grin and look outside. On the drop-ship pad below the ATC tower, all four of Camp Frostbite's Dragonflies are lined up on the concrete, with running engines and hot-refueling probes in their fuel ports. Without any air mobility, the two SI companies back at Frostbite don't have a prayer at getting their main airborne firepower back, and if the task force in orbit sends a strike team down to the airfield, the Dragonflies can be in the air and on the move before the carrier's Wasps are within five hundred miles.

"See if you can get me a comlink to the fleet units upstairs. I want to have a private tight-beam chat with those ship captains individually without any noise from our esteemed leadership."

"I'll see what I can do with the local gear," I say.

"Good enough. Let me know right away if we get any visitors, air or ground. Fallon out."

The hardware in the civvie ATC center is so good that keeping tabs on everything is ludicrously easy. The main ATC console is a three-dimensional projection that makes the holotables in our warships look like outdated junk. It presents unified sensor data from dozens of different sources—ground, air, and weather radar, environmental data from all the terraforming stations, satellite sensors. Everything is cross-linked with the comms network. It takes me just a few moments to tie the Dragonflies outside into my list of available assets, check the status of the airfield's puddle jumpers, and assign them into separate flights to start ferrying HD troops from the terraforming stations. I assign the Dragonflies their own encrypted data and comlinks, and upload the mission data to their onboard computers.

"Gentlemen, this is Tailpipe One. I will be your combat controller today. Comms check, please."

"Copy, Tailpipe One," one of the pilots sends back. "Are we recycling call signs, or what?"

"Check your TacLink screens. You gentlemen are henceforth Rogue One through Four."

"Copy that," another pilot says with an audible chuckle. "Rogue Two copies five by five."

"TacLink complete. So far, the coast is clear. I'll call out inbound traffic once we get company from above, so keep your birds ready for immediate dustoff."

"Understood," Rogue One sends. The other pilots append their acknowledgments.

If the units up in orbit were Chinese or Russian, we'd be in a lousy tactical position. The civvie sensor network covers the entire moon, so sneak attacks with drop ships won't be easy to pull off against us, but all that shiny sensor gear sits right out in the open, vulnerable to kinetic or guided munitions attack from orbit. Still, we're holed up in a settlement of ten thousand, and even the clueless reservist at the stick up there probably won't be eager to order an orbital bombardment of one of our own colony towns. If they decide to squash our little mutiny with a regiment-strength assault from orbit, we'll see them coming from a long way out.

"Grayson, this is Fallon."

"Go ahead, Sarge."

"The civvie admin is gathering all the pilots for those puddle jumpers. Send them out as they get ready, please, and have them start picking up our guys. I want to have as many troops as I can back here before I get on the comms with the fleet."

"Understood. I'll send them out to the closest terraformers first."

"You do that. Also, the constable is sending a bunch of his guys over to the airfield. I want you to have someone issue them some guns from the drop-ship armories. None of the heavy weapons, but something with a little more pop than those antiques they carry around right now."

"Copy that. I'll let them draw some rifles and armor."

The idea of arming civilian cops with military-grade weapons makes me feel like we're crossing a line, but we're preparing to defend this place against battle-tested soldiers. With our limited strength, I have to admit that it makes sense to upgrade the capabilities of the cops that are responsible for the town's safety in the first place. It's not like we're opening the armories and throwing missile launchers out for the farmers and ice miners to use. When we all end up at a court-martial, I doubt that violating weapons regulations will make our trouble any deeper in the end.

On the tarmac in front of the tower, the four Dragonflies are sitting with idling engines. They're the entire armed component of our rebellious little air-and-space force, waiting for my word to intercept whatever the fleet will send our way to yank us back to the doghouse by our collars. We're outnumbered in the air, vastly outgunned, and in a ludicrously exposed and predictable position. For some reason, however, I'm more at ease than I have been in months—or perhaps years.

CHAPTER 18

—HE WHO BLINKS FIRST—

For the next two hours, I coordinate the shuttle flights between the base and the atmospheric-processor stations. The civvie shuttles are slow and ponderous compared to our stolen drop ships, but we can't spare any of our sparse airmobile firepower for taxi duties. The civvie shuttles start bringing back the exiled HD battalions, one platoon at a time. On my fleet comms, the urgent traffic from our old command goes unanswered. Sergeant Fallon has instructed us to ignore fleet messages until she can make her broadcast to the rest of the NAC units on New Svalbard. Outside, the new Dragonfly jocks are killing time by practicing dry attack runs at the end of the runway between puddle-jumper arrivals.

Finally, the people in charge over at Camp Frostbite are tired of leaving messages. One of the ground sensors at the outskirts of town picks up vehicle traffic coming down the road from the camp. I paint it with active ground radar, and use the optical sensors on the array to get a fix on what's coming our way. A pair of the camp's armored personnel carriers come down the gravel road at a cautious pace. Their modular weapon mounts are fitted with autocannons.

"Fallon, this is Grayson," I send on our encrypted command circuit.

"Go ahead."

"We have incoming, ground. Two mules with cannons. They're coming down the road from Frostbite. Figure ten minutes to contact at their current pace."

"Understood." She pauses for a few moments. "Send one of the Dragonflies to intercept. Shots across the bow first. Give 'em fair warning."

"Copy that. Grayson out."

I relay Sergeant Fallon's instructions to the flight of Dragonflies currently swarming the far end of the airfield.

"Rogue One, move to grid Delta Seven and play goalie. When they get in range, sweep them with the fire-control radar. Let's hope they get the message before we have to trade shots."

"Rogue One copies," the pilot sends back. "We're on our way."

The Dragonfly breaks off its mock attack run, pulls up, and accelerates across the airfield at full throttle. When the seventy-ton war machine passes overhead, the sealed windows of the control tower rattle in their reinforced frames.

"Time to go public, I suppose," Sergeant Fallon says. "Andrew, patch me into the fleet channel. Make sure they can pick me up down at Frostbite, too."

I fire up the civvie comms, which have about a hundred times more output than the radio suite in my armor. Then I open a link to the fleet emergency channel, and route Sergeant Fallon's comlink through it.

"You're on," I tell her. "Until they jam us."

There's a moment of static on the channel, and then Sergeant Fallon's voice comes on again, this time in her Squad Leader Lecture cadence.

"All Commonwealth units, all Commonwealth units. This is Master Sergeant Briana Fallon, 330th Autonomous Infantry Battalion, Homeworld Defense.

"I have taken charge of all Commonwealth units in the city of New Longyearbyen. Three hours ago, we received an order to seize the civilian food storage and production facilities in the city. I refuse to execute that order. I will not be part of a military dictatorship on this moon. The troops under my command are now under control of the civilian administration.

"All Commonwealth units outside of the city: Do not approach the town under arms, or you will be fired upon. We may be outgunned, but we are not defenseless. Any assault on the civilian assets we're defending will be considered a military coup attempt, and answered accordingly.

"All fleet units in orbit: We're sitting on most of the food, fuel, and water in the system. If you attempt an orbital assault or bombardment, you will endanger thousands of civilians and destroy vital supplies. All you grunts and space jockeys: The choice is yours now. You can choose to follow orders without question, or you can choose to follow the law. Keep in mind that without the law, we're not a military, just an armed gang that dresses alike.

"Make your choice wisely, but don't think for a *second* that we won't shoot back. Fallon *out*."

There's a brief and total silence on the emergency channel. Then my comms suite starts lighting up with dozens of incoming comms requests from all levels of our command hierarchy. I block all requests for now and shut down the open link.

"Well, I'd say that got their attention," I tell Sergeant Fallon.

"They think we're bluffing," Rogue One says on the combat-control channel. "Dumb SI fucks."

I check the display to see that the two armored personnel carriers from Frostbite have resumed their slow and cautious course toward New Longyearbyen. I tap into the ground comms, but they have switched to their own encrypted private network, taking a page out of our playbook.

"Rogue One, they're not talking. Paint 'em with the fire-control radar. See if they get the message."

Rogue One fires up his radar dome and zaps the two mules coming down the road with short sweeps of focused millimeter-wave radar. If their threat detectors are working, the tactical consoles of those vehicle commanders are lighting up like pachinko parlors right about now. I check the video feed from the Dragonfly's forward sensor array to get a view of the drop ship's quarry.

The two mules stop by the side of the road, halfway between Camp Frostbite and New Longyearbyen. Then one of them activates its remote weapons mount. The autocannon on top of the mule turns toward the drop ship's targeting camera. I see the muzzle flashes before I can hear the rumbling staccato of the cannon all the way from the other side of town. The targeting image skews as the pilot takes evasive action.

"I'd say they got the message loud and clear," the pilot sends.

"Weapons free," I reply. "Try for mobility kills. Don't want to shed blood unless we have to."

"Copy that."

The view from the targeting camera flashes, and the bottom of the display shows "MANUAL OVERRIDE." Then the reticle slews to cover the ground just in front of the belligerent mule.

The drop ship's nose turret hammers out a short, rasping burst. A second later, the view from the targeting camera is obscured as the chin cannon's high-velocity rounds kick up the frozen dirt and gravel in front of the mule. From half a mile away, the cannon sounds like the distant thunder of a far-off summer storm. I watch the camera feed from the drop ship's turret as the two mules come to a stop. The lead mule swivels its weapons mount as the gunner looks for a target. Over the audio feed, I can hear the threat detectors in the cockpit of our drop ship warbling a harsh alert.

"*What* a dipshit," the pilot says almost conversationally. The chin turret thunders again. This time, the grenades hit even closer to the mule. The pilot walks his reticle from the front of the vehicle over to a corner. One shell strikes the bow armor at a sharp angle and glances off in a shower of sparks and laminate armor shards. Another hits the front-left road wheel of the mule dead-on and blows it into tiny little pieces. The mule heaves to one side as the combined force of the grenade and the exploding tire rock the vehicle.

"Slave your cannon to the rear and turn off your targeting radar, or I'll put the next burst right down your centerline," the pilot instructs the mule's crew over the emergency channel. "I'm not in the mood to play tag here."

The chirping from the threat receiver stops as the gunner in the mule turns off the active targeting aids for the autocannon. Then the weapons mount swivels backwards until the gun is pointed away from the drop ship. The other mule has popped a burst of polychromatic smoke, and the Dragonfly's radar says he's retreating at a fair clip.

"The other one's pulling out. Let him go. This turkey makes a shifty move, blow off the other tires, too," I tell the Dragonfly crew.

"No worries," the pilot says. "They try to use that gun again, I'll shoot it right off their ride."

Well, at least they fired the first shot, I think.

The main situational display on the holotable next to me chimes to announce new data. I shift my attention in time to see four red inverted vee symbols enter the sensor sphere from above, almost five hundred miles from the airfield. They drop down into the atmosphere at high speed, drop ships or ground-attack birds on a tactical mission profile. Their course is away from New Longyearbyen, but I don't take any solace in that information. I know the tactical handbook for this type of scenario, and I know exactly what I'm looking at.

"Raid warning, raid warning," I announce over the tactical channel. "Two flights of two entering atmo from orbit. They're going to hit the weeds outside of sensor range and come in as close to the deck as they can. Likely approach vectors are two-twenty through two-forty degrees. I repeat, raid warning, air threat red."

The Dragonflies break off their practice runs and take up their designated patrol patterns overhead. Being armed for light air-to-ground action, they aren't terribly useful for fending off an air assault, especially if the strike package contains Shrikes. But I want our valuable Dragonflies in the air and moving around, not sitting ducks on the landing pads.

"All shuttle flights, stay out of the weeds and watch your EMCON. Snowbird One-Four, expedite your approach and descend to four thousand as soon as practical. You want to get out of that airspace pronto."

Snowbird One-Four is one of the colonial puddle jumpers, slow and unarmed cargo aircraft. We still have half of our HD troopers in transit or awaiting pickup from their terraforming stations. If only one of the fleet jocks has an itchy trigger finger, we have the setup for a quick and thorough bloodbath.

"I'm stretching us thin everywhere else, but I'm sending most of a company over to you," Sergeant Fallon sends. "They'll hit you first—bet on it."

"I know. I'd do the same. They don't need to get the drop ships back if they can park a squad or two on the refueling station."

"So keep your head low. And don't let them have that airfield, or our little mutiny is over."

"I'll do my best, Sarge."

"If they blow you up, I want you to know that I think you're a pretty able grunt for a fleet puke. Must be that superior TA influence you got before you had to get all snobby and run off into space."

I smile at the holographic display in front of me. "Too bad we didn't get to spend more time catching up and drinking without getting shot at."

"Stare down the fleet and get rid of that SI regiment for me, and I'll take you out for all the fucking coffee you can drink, Andrew."

"Piece of cake," I laugh. "Be easier if we had some nukes of our own to aim skyward, though."

On my holotable, the display shows a brief red blip at a bearing of 230 degrees. Somewhere out there, one of the land-based sensor arrays picked up a brief return from a drop ship or Shrike that popped up out of the mountain valleys for just a moment too long.

"Incoming, vector two-three-zero, distance one five-zero."

If that raid package includes Shrikes, we're completely outmatched. With our heaviest antiair ordnance being the shoulder-launched MANPADs from the drop-ship armories, there's not much we can do if there's a pair of ground-attack craft out there intent on blowing our infrastructure into rubble. The best defense we have is the fact that we're embedded among ten thousand civilians.

At the front of the holotable, there's a console with a set of red hardware buttons. I smack one of them with my palm, and a moment later the harsh trill of air-raid sirens comes from every corner of New Longyearbyen.

"Air raid, air raid. All personnel, seek shelter."

As new and sophisticated as the civvie air-traffic control system is, it has a major shortcoming. On a military system, I would be able to let the network tie together all the assets and control every last bit of hardware automatically. The grunts on the ground would just have to aim their missile launchers in the general direction of the threat, switch their fire control to TacLink, and the computer would scan for threats and fire whatever missile is within intercept range. The civilian system has no such amenities. All I can do is to direct all my assets manually and hope I make the right calls.

"Rogue Three, Tailpipe One. Reverse course, point yourself to two-three-zero, and take up station at Delta Two. Keep EMCON, but I may need you to play radar picket on short notice."

"Copy that, Tailpipe One. Wilco."

Rogue Three swings his ship around and moves up to cover the likely threat axis.

The plot chirps again as two contacts materialize on the plot, right along the bearing where I saw the echo a little while ago. They're rushing in at low altitude, six hundred knots, which means they're either drop ships at full throttle, or Shrikes on economy cruising speed. For our sakes, I am hoping for the former. Their transponders are turned off, their contact icons a hostile crimson. Then two more icons detach from each of the incoming craft and streak toward the center of my plot at hypersonic speed.

"Vampire, vampire. Incoming missiles," I call out on our emergency channel. "Threat axis two-three-zero. All units, defensive. Jammers hot."

My plot projects the course of the incoming missiles, and the time to impact. The first pair is aimed right at the center of my holographic hemisphere, where the radar and lidar transmitters of the main sensor station pump out energy and radiation.

"Rogue Three, drop down to one hundred and go goalkeeper on your turret. They're shooting HARMs at the radar."

"Copy, wilco."

Rogue Three's millimeter-wave radar takes command of the gun turret on the Dragonfly's chin. The fire-control system can shoot down missile threats all by itself if the missile crosses its engagement range. On the holotable, the missile icons streak in toward the center of the display. The numbers next to them rapidly count down: twelve, ten, eight, six. The turret gun of the Dragonfly hovering above the far end of the airfield rasps three short and exact bursts with the precision of a computer pulling the trigger. Just beyond the runway, there's a flash and a rather unspectacular crack as one of the anti-radar missiles disintegrates at three times the speed of sound. My heart pounds as I see one of the icons on my display snuffed out just before it reaches the center of the hologram. The drop ship's turret gun barks again, but the other missile is only a blink away from the radome now. A moment later, there's a sharp, tinny-sounding explosion over at the sensor array, and my holotable blinks. When the hologram returns, it's devoid of missile icons.

Where did the other pair go? I think.

There's a blinding flash of light outside, and then I'm on the floor on the other side of the control room, ears ringing and breath squeezed from my lungs. The tower heaves like a welfare tenement in an earthquake. When I sit up, half the windows in the control tower are blown out, and the smell of burning fuel fills the room. There's squawking on my earpiece, but I can't make sense of it. The lights in the control tower are all out, and the holographic display has died.

By the time I make it to my feet, acrid smoke is wafting in through the broken windows. I stagger across the debris-strewn floor of the control room to take a look outside. Below, on the other side of the drop-ship landing pad, the refueling station is a mess of twisted, burning debris. The concrete walls of the hangar behind the refueler are charred and pockmarked by shrapnel. Whatever hit the refueling point was just big enough to blow the surface structure to bits without so much as cracking the concrete below.

My armor's tactical computer didn't even miss a beat. I put my helmet back on my head and turn on the visor display.

"All units, this is Tailpipe One. They took out the main radar and blew the refueling probes at the airfield all to shit. Control tower took a beating, too."

"You okay, Andrew?" Sergeant Fallon asks.

"Yeah. Just a bit rattled. Those fuel pumps blew up fifty yards from me."

"I heard it. That was kind of rude, wasn't it?"

"At least now we know they're doing this the hard way. Watch for incoming. There are two pairs of drop ships out there, and my radar's holed."

"Don't you worry," she says. "They want to play rough, we'll play rough."

With the radar gone and the holotable offline, there's no reason for me to stay up in the control tower. I pick up my carbine and make my way down the stairs to the bottom level of the control center. The two civvies who had been on duty when I walked in a while ago have disappeared.

Outside, the smoke from the burning fuel bites my throat, so I seal my helmet and check the tactical display again. Rogue Three is hovering nearby, scanning the area beyond the airfield for more incoming threats.

"Get the hell out of there!" a voice behind me calls. I turn around to see one of the civvie air-traffic controllers waving me over from behind the corner of a hangar fifty meters away. "There's a hundred thousand liters of fuel under that landing pad, fella."

I run over to the hangar to join the civilian tech, who has a thirty-meter head start by the time I round the corner.

"Fucking assholes," he pants when we come to a stop between two hangars. "The fuel tanks have safety seals, but if those fail, half the airfield's history."

"They just blew up the refueling probes," I say. "Keep us from juicing up our birds. Any way we can repair those?"

"Probably. We got spare parts. Ask the boss about that. I'm just one of the peons."

"Incoming," Rogue Three's pilot calls out on comms. "Drop ship, two-three-zero degrees, five klicks out. Coming in at full throttle, headed right for the airfield."

"They're going to drop a platoon right on top of us," I say. "Where's that short company, Sarge? Things are about to get interesting over here."

"They'll be there any minute," Sergeant Fallon replies.

I check my TacLink screen for data. The drop ship spotted by Rogue Three is already entering my short-range tactical map, barreling toward the airfield at top speed. On the other side of my map, the symbols for friendly infantry start populating the display. It doesn't take a tactical wizard to realize that the red and blue icons are about to converge in the middle of the map, right at my current position.

"Get out of here," I tell the civilian next to me. "There's going to be gunfire in about thirty seconds."

The civvie tech scurries off to safer parts. For a moment, I have to fight the urge to follow him. Then I check the loading status of my carbine and run to the edge of the hangar, for a clear view of the runway.

The fleet assault comes in right above the deck. When I see the drop ship, an old Wasp, it's so low that it drags a rooster tail of ice and frozen dirt. When the ship is over the runway, the pilot pulls up the nose and fires the engines downward to scrub off speed. The second ship is nowhere in sight.

"Don't let him open that tail ramp," I tell Rogue Three. "He gets those grunts on the ground, we'll have to pry 'em out from between the hangars."

Rogue Three clicks his transmit button in acknowledgment, and paints the incoming Wasp with every active targeting system on his Dragonfly. For emphasis, he fires a burst of tracers that just barely miss the armored belly of the Wasp. The pilot of the other drop ship pulls away from the incoming fire and whips his bird around. When the nose of the Wasp points toward the hangars again, I can see the chin turret swiveling in search of a target.

"I have you locked up," Rogue Three warns the pilot of the Wasp. "Turn off your radar, put her down, and keep that tail ramp *closed*."

The Wasp's pilot replies with a burst of fire from his ship's chin turret. Rogue Three replies with his own gun—not the high-cadence chainsaw sound of his own chin turret, but the low, rolling *boom-boom-boom* of the large-caliber ground-attack cannon mounted on the underside of his hull. The Wasp's starboard engine blows apart under the hammer blows of the autocannon, followed by the starboard ordnance pylon. Then another shell tears off the tail rudder assembly. I hear the engines of the Wasp howling as the pilot tries to compensate and get his bird on the ground in one piece, but his altitude is too low already. The Wasp banks sharply to port and rapidly plummets to the deck. At the last moment, the pilot manages to right his ship, and it almost looks like he'll be able to pull off a hard emergency landing, but then one of his landing skids catches on the ground, and the ship flips over onto its side with a resounding crash.

Before I even have time to be horrified, there's a loud boom coming from the other side of the airfield, followed by the thunderous roar of a Shrike's multibarreled assault cannon. A hundred feet above and behind me, Rogue Three takes the burst of armor-piercing cannon shells head-on and falls out of the sky. When the Dragonfly hits the ground nearby, the explosion sends burning parts and aviation fuel everywhere. The attacking Shrike passes over the airfield at supersonic speed, trailing noise and destruction in its wake.

I sealed my helmet against the smoke of the refueling station fire a few moments ago, so the burning fuel showering me is merely alarming, not fatal. The battle armor, imbued with much faster reflexes than its owner, has already sealed itself tightly and activated my emergency oxygen supply. Out on the edge of the runway, a hundred meters from my position, the fleet's Wasp is shuddering on its side with the engines at full thrust, digging a furrow into the concrete with the broken wing root of its portside pylon. I look on in horror as smoke starts rising from underneath the ship. Then the Wasp is on fire, smoldering in the middle of a small lake of burning fuel.

Somewhere over New Longyearbyen, I hear missile launches. On my TacLink screen, I see that the remaining Dragonflies have networked their fire-control systems and launched their antiair ordnance after the Shrike that just took out a quarter of our offen sive air power. The computers ripple-fire all the missiles on the Dragonflies' wingtips—one, two, four, eight, twelve. The Shrike is fleeing the area at full throttle, but the missiles can pull much higher acceleration. The attack ship's automatic countermeasures lead some of them astray, but half a dozen missiles hurl themselves right up the Shrike's engine nozzles, and the ship is swatted out of the sky. It careens to the frozen ground like a clumsily thrown piece of sheetrock, and plows into some civilian housing on the far side of town. A moment later I see the icon of the pilot's eject capsule pop into existence on the TacLink screen. The remaining half dozen air-to-air missiles have nothing to spend themselves against, so their computers detonate them in midair.

I run to the cover of a nearby hangar and roll on the frozen ground to put out the burning fuel sticking to my battle armor. After the cacophony of heavy gunfire, supersonic booms, and explosions, the silence is surreal. I want to call for support, but find that my mouth is too dry to talk into the helmet mike. Instead, I smother the flames on my armor and lie on the ground to catch my breath.

After a while, a group of civvie techs in firefighting suits run toward me, and I sit up to show them that I'm not a corpse.

"You okay, soldier?" one of them asks, and stops in front of me. The others continue to the burning wreckage of the fleet Wasp, fire suppressant hoses and tanks in hand.

I raise my visor and wave him off.

"Yeah, I'm fine. Got a little singed, that's all."

"What the hell didn't," he says. "Half the airfield's on fire. What the fuck happened?"

"They thought we'd blink first, and we thought they would," I say. "Looks like we were all wrong."

CHAPTER 19

———— BLUE ON BLUE ————

"Well, that didn't go so great," Sergeant Fallon says.

We're in the hardened shelter underneath the massive civilian admin building. In the room with us are the battalion commanders of both mutinous HD battalions, their senior sergeants, and a half dozen civil administration people.

"That's an understatement," Lieutenant Colonel Kemp says. He's the CO of the 330th, and nominally Sergeant Fallon's superior, but even the brass clearly defer to her at the moment.

"We lost one drop ship and the refueling station," she concedes. "They lost a drop ship, plus a Shrike and two dozen grunts. They got hurt worse, but they can replace their losses. We'll miss that Dragonfly when they send the next raid in. Tactically, it was a draw. Strategically, we're still holding the short end of the stick."

"That's an awfully clinical way to write off almost thirty lives," the administrator says.

"That's *war*," Sergeant Fallon says flatly. When the civilian gives her an appalled glare, she snorts. "Look, what did you think was going to happen once they decided to fight us for your stuff, and we decided to fight back? Did you think they were going to pull up their drop ships, say 'Well, *darn*,' and head back to the carrier?"

The administrator shakes his head. "No, I guess not. But I'm not used to the military way of dealing with casualties. It's not a mathematical equation."

Sergeant Fallon takes her rifle off her shoulder and slams it onto the table in front of her. The administrator takes a step back.

"Last riot drop I did back on Earth, I lost twenty-seven of my troopers in fifteen minutes. I damn sure know the names of every single one of my troops who bought it that day. And the pilot of the Dragonfly we just lost? His name was Chief Warrant Officer Beckett Cunningham. Three Silver Stars, five Bronze Stars, three Distinguished Flying Crosses. We've been friends for eight years, he saved my life a few dozen times, and now he's a smoking lump of carbon and jet fuel on your fucking airfield. You don't have a clue about how I deal with that. So don't run your mouth about our way of dealing with casualties."

The administrator glances over to the rest of us and chews on his lower lip. Then he shrugs and turns to Sergeant Fallon again.

"Sorry. I guess it was a little presumptuous. I'm just a little shaken, that's all. I'm new to this warfare business."

"They'll try again," I say. "They won't back down now. And without that radar, we won't see them until they're close enough for the Dragonflies to pick them up. Not a whole lot of warning for a raid."

"We have a company at each of the critical sites," Sergeant Fallon says. "Once the rest of the 309th gets in, we'll have another three companies in reserve. They have the mobility, though. If they hit us hard enough at each site in turn they can defeat us in detail."

The flight-ops supervisor, Chief Barnett, clears his throat. "Radar's a bit chewed up, but that's a big array, and those were small missiles. I have a bunch of guys working on it right now. We should be back online within an hour or two. Looks like they only took out one of the four transmitters."

"That's good news," I say. "Still leaves us pretty myopic for a few hours, though. They could be dropping out of orbit with most of the regiment right now, and we wouldn't know it until we saw the drop ships doing a combat descent."

"What about the fuel pumps?" Sergeant Fallon asks.

"They shredded the refueling probes, and I don't want to start putting up new ones until we've had time to check the tanks underneath," Chief Barnett says. "There's other fuel tanks on the airfield, but those don't have the right probes for your military birds. We could rig up a manual transfer with the handheld pumps for the time being. Take a while to fill up one of those monsters, though."

"Let's get something set up, then, before our birds fall out of the sky for lack of fuel."

One of the civvie radio techs walks into the conference room and looks around, clearly unsure of the military hierarchy. Then he turns to Sergeant Fallon, who looks like she's in charge wherever she goes.

"There's an encrypted tight-beam comms request from orbit. They want to talk to Sergeant Fallon."

"That would be me." She picks up her rifle and gestures for me to follow her.

"You might as well tag along, sirs," she says to the two light colonels in the room, and they do.

"Put it on speaker, please," Sergeant Fallon instructs the comms tech when we walk out of the conference room and into the operations center.

"This is Master Sergeant Fallon, New Svalbard Territorial Army," she says. "Go ahead."

"This is *Indianapolis* Actual, Colonel Campbell," a familiar voice says. "I also have the skipper of the *Gordon* in the circuit with us."

Sergeant Fallon looks at me and raises an eyebrow.

"The *Indy* is the orbital combat ship," I tell her. "Little escort tin can. The *Gary I. Gordon* is the auxiliary freighter." Then I address *Indy* Actual directly. "Colonel Campbell, this is Staff Sergeant Andrew Grayson. I was your Neural Networks admin on *Versailles*."

There's a surprised laugh at the other end of the tight-beam connection. "Well, I'll be damned. How are you doing these days, Mr. Grayson?"

"Doing fine, sir, all things considered. Glad to see they gave you a command after Willoughby."

"Yeah, they did," he says. "They gave me an OCS that's a fifth the size of the *Versailles*. Some promotion." He pauses for a moment. "But she's a fine little ship, with a crack crew."

"We were expecting to hear from the *Midway* first, sir," I say. "Did they bump the *Indy* to task force flagship, or is this a private call?"

"We have, *ah*, parted ways with TF 230.7. My XO and the skipper of the *Gordon* agreed with your sergeant's interpretation of Commonwealth law. We left the task force two hours ago, and I've escorted the *Gordon* into a different orbit."

There's a moment of stunned silence in the room as we all process this new development.

"I guess we're now the space component of the New Svalbard Territorial Army. But please go ahead and pick an official acronym, because that's a mouthful to transmit."

"Understood, sir," I chuckle.

Across the room, Sergeant Fallon gives the tech the signal to mute the line. Then she looks at me. "Is he for real, or is this a setup?"

"He was my XO when my first ship got shot down by the Lankies," I say. "He's a good guy. I don't know what they'd gain from playing tricks with us at this point. They're holding all the cards up there."

"Well, let's play ours close, just in case."

"Understood," I say. Sergeant Fallon nods at the comms tech.

"Be advised that the *Midway* is dropping a bunch of boats right now," the colonel continues. "As far as I can see, they're all drop ships, not attack birds. Can't tell you for sure, though. They locked my ship out of the task force TacLink when we announced our intentions."

"Sir, I'm a combat controller, and I have a data suite in my armor. Would you let me get an uplink to *Indy*'s TacLink? That way, I could get a better picture of the situation."

"I don't see why not," Colonel Campbell replies. "I'll let the tech do the voodoo. Who's in charge down there?"

"The ranking officers on the ground are Lieutenant Colonels Kemp and Decker, but Sergeant Fallon's running ops right now, sir. I guess that makes you the highest-ranking officer in this outfit."

"Super. I'll have the supply group make me a uniform with lots of stars."

Lieutenant Colonel Decker and his sergeant major laugh at this, and even Sergeant Fallon cracks a smile.

"Well, don't expect any sage advice," Colonel Campbell continues. "I don't know shit about ground combat. I'm just a tin can skipper. If Sergeant Fallon and Colonel Decker want to take point on this, they're welcome to the job. Not that the chain of command is still relevant at this point."

"The way things are going right now, they'll need to reserve an entire wing for us at Leavenworth," Lieutenant Colonel Decker says.

With the help of the Neural Networks tech on the *Indianapolis*, I reconnect to the ship's TacLink and look at the sensor feed. The

Indy and her charge are in their orbit by themselves, well away from the rest of the task force. I've never been on one of the brand-new orbital combat ships, but I've heard rumors about their capabilities, and now that I'm tied into the nerve center of one, I see that even the sensationalist rumor mill was short of the mark. She's less than half the size of a fleet frigate, but her sensors and neural-networks suite are better than anything I've ever seen. When I check the sensor data from the networked auxiliary freighter that's flying formation with her, I see that the *Indy*'s radar return is only a little bigger than that of a drop ship, even without any stealth measures enabled. Her armor is light, but her eyes and ears are fantastically acute. I do a quick check of her armament and weapons stores. She doesn't have much in the way of ship-to-ship armament, but her air/space-defense missile system could give headaches to an entire carrier full of Shrikes, and there are four tubes of surface-attack nukes parked amidships, each missile armed with twenty-four MIRVs. For such a small ship, *Indy* packs quite a wallop against ground targets. Our defecting skipper has command of the smallest warship of the task force, but she's the most modern by a huge margin—the only hull in TF 230.7 that wasn't a scrapyard candidate from the reserve fleet.

"Incoming," Rogue One announces. The Dragonflies are serving as a makeshift radar picket, flying overlapping figure-eight patrols above New Longyearbyen. "Four contacts, bearing three-ten, distance ninety, altitude forty thousand. Looks like a ferry drop, not a combat descent."

I look at the contact information on my screen and gauge the flight pattern of the incoming formation.

"*Indy* says they're Wasps, not Shrikes. We have eyes and ears in orbit now, by the way."

"Looks like they're shuttling stuff into Frostbite," Rogue One says. "Bet you anything they picked that northerly bearing to avoid overflying the town."

"I'd call that a fair assumption," I say. "Sarge, we have a drop-ship flight inbound from the north. They're coming in slow on a regular descent into Frostbite. Could be they're trying to pull a fast one on us, though."

"Pass the data to the grunts," Sergeant Fallon says. "We have Delta Company playing goalkeeper on the northern approach. Tell them to warm up the MANPADs just in case."

A drop-ship flight of four can ferry an entire battle-ready infantry company minus their heavy weapons. With our deployment pattern, we can meet them at company strength on equal terms anywhere they choose to land in the city, but the thought of two infantry companies duking it out in the middle of a populated civvie town makes me feel more than just a little queasy.

"Copy that," I say, and pass the data on to Delta Company's CO and platoon leaders. "Let's hope they're not feeling sneaky."

"Of course, if they're hauling troops into Frostbite, we'll have a whole different set of problems soon," Sergeant Fallon says.

"I don't think they're dumb enough to try a land assault with their light armor," I say, but as I voice the thought, I feel some uncomfortable doubt. An hour and a half ago, I wouldn't have thought the SI brass would try a vertical assault on the airfield with a single drop ship and a Shrike in attendance.

"Last of the birds will be in the barn in thirty minutes," Chief Barnett says. "Not a minute too soon, either. We have some bad weather coming in from the north."

"Bad how?" Sergeant Fallon wants to know.

"New Svalbard bad. You got here just at the tail end of what passes for summer. You have no idea how lucky we were to be able to run flight ops for a week straight. Those puddle jumpers don't do so well when it gets cold outside, so they stay in the hangars in the winter."

"This isn't cold?" Sergeant Fallon eyes the temperature readout on the big status screen at the front of the operations center. It shows "–18C/25knNNE/VIS15Km."

"That?" the chief chuckles. "That's what we call T-shirt weather down here. Ever seen a temperature readout of triple-digit negatives? There's a reason why we build the way we do."

"Minus one hundred Celsius?" Sergeant Fallon says in disbelief, and Chief Barnett nods.

"And hundred-klick winds on a calm winter day. We basically go underground for three or four months."

Sergeant Fallon looks over at me and smirks. "Andrew, forget what I said when we got here, about this place being damn near paradise."

"Yeah, well," the chief says. "If it was perfect real estate, everyone would want it. We're just a frozen little moon at the ass end of the Thirty. I doubt even the Lankies would be interested in this place. The Chinese or the Russians sure haven't bothered us any."

"Good thing, too," Colonel Decker says, looking up from the stack of printouts he has been studying for the past fifteen minutes. "'Cause your planetary defense network is a pile of shit. I've seen welfare clusters that were better defended than this moon. Whoever designed this defense grid needs to be fired for gross incompetence, or shot for treason. Maybe both."

"In all fairness, we're not a settled planet," Chief Barnett says. "This is just a scientific research station and a water stop. We won't be ready for full colonization until those atmo processors have done their thing for another ten years."

"Still," Colonel Decker says. "No orbital defenses. No nuclear stockpile. Not a scrap of long-range artillery. One airfield big enough to support fleet ops, and that one's right next to the only settlement on the moon. No combat armor except for a half dozen mules at Frostbite. Absolutely no integrated air defenses. A pack of Cub Scouts with pocketknives could take this moon."

"I don't know, Colonel," Sergeant Fallon says. "All things considered, I'm kind of glad the space monkeys over at Frostbite don't have any tanks or artillery at their disposal right now."

"That's one way to look at it. Glad you haven't lost your ability to see the silver lining, Sergeant."

"Yes, I have," she says. "Back on Earth. Right around the time I had to shoot my first welfare rat out rioting for something to eat other than recycled shit."

"You know we're fucked one way or the other, right?" Sergeant Fallon says to me a little while later when we step outside for some fresh air. The temperature has dropped so much in the last few hours that I'm very grateful for the heating elements in my battle armor.

"Yeah," I say. "Fleet wins, we end up in the brig, and then it's off to military prison for the next twenty years. We win, we get to hang on to this frozen wasteland only until they turn the network back on, and more fleet shows up. Network stays down, we have to worry about the Lankies finding us. No happy endings either way."

"So why'd you switch sides? You know I wouldn't have kept you from going back to Frostbite with those drop-ship jocks, right?"

"I know that." I peel my unit patch off the pauldron of my battle armor and look at it. "Bunch of reasons, really."

"Like what?"

"Because I didn't like the stuff we had to do back in the TA. All those riot drops we did. I mean, they were shooting at us in those welfare clusters, but only because we dropped into their living rooms ready to kick their asses, you know? I don't hold a grudge. Not even over the two rounds I took in Detroit."

Sergeant Fallon looks at me with an unreadable expression.

"And then I get the fleet billet," I continue. "The whole shit with the Lankies started, and I actually felt good about what I was doing. Saving humanity, and all that shit. Hell, even fighting the Russians and the Chinese. At least they were legit enemies. And they were just as well armed as we were. I don't hold grudges there, either. But it's like you told the fleet over comms. I'll be damned if I go back to that ghetto police shit. We turn against our own, we have no fucking reason for existing."

Sergeant Fallon smiles, something she does so rarely that she looks like a completely different person for a moment.

"We're supposed to be hard-asses, Andrew. That's why we get the guns, and the special chow, and the bank accounts at the end. So we stay on the leash and bite everyone they point us at."

"Point me at a Lanky colony, and I'll let you shoot me right into it with a bio-pod from orbit, and call in a nuclear strike on my own position. But if they want me to play prison guard again, they need to find someone else."

"That's what we were supposed to do," she says. "That's why we came along for the trip. Get us off Earth, make us keep the civvies in line like we do back home. You guys were supposed to hold our leashes."

"Not working out all that well so far, is it?"

"No, it isn't." She kicks a few pebbles with the toe of her boot. "Truth be told, I wouldn't mind being a fly on the wall back at Defense on Earth right now. If they can't count on their crack outfits to keep some HD reprobates under control out here away from the press, I doubt they're having better luck back home. Maybe there won't even be a North American Commonwealth by the time we get home. If we ever get home, that is."

"Could be worse," I say. "Could be they turn the network back on, and when we arrive back at Earth, there's a few hundred Lanky seed ships in orbit, and the atmosphere's twenty percent carbon dioxide."

Sergeant Fallon shrugs. "Then I'll fight the urge to eat my own rifle, and join whatever part of humanity wants to go look for a new place to live. Humans are hardy, Andrew. They'll do whatever they can to keep on living, no matter how shitty life gets. Just ask the poor bastards in the welfare clusters back home."

"And I thought I caught a huge break when they sent me the acceptance letter," I say. "One out of a hundred applicants, and all that."

"Well, you're here, aren't you? Could be worse. At least you have a rifle and some skills. Enough anyway to be able to tell our esteemed leadership you're not playing anymore."

The chirp of a priority comms signal interrupts our conversation.

"Tailpipe One, *Indianapolis*."

"Go ahead, *Indy*," I say.

"Be advised that *Midway* is launching Shrikes, without any drop ships to escort. Looks like half their wing. We can't verify their exact loadouts, but it looks like they're carrying external ordnance."

"Copy that, *Indy*. Feed me the CIC plot, please."

The tactical display shows the sensor feed from the *Indianapolis*'s ridiculously advanced main array. The Shrikes are pairing up and entering the atmosphere in short intervals, at a speed that suggests heavy loadouts.

"Got 'em. I don't think that's just a ferry flight, and they're sure not escorting shit. I'd bet some non-soy steak that we're looking at a strike package."

"I wouldn't take that bet, Tailpipe. You guys keep your heads low down there. We'll track and update as far as our radar can follow."

"Copy that, *Indy*. Tailpipe One out."

I switch my comms suite to our local guard channel.

"All units, raid warning. Raid Two is three pairs of Shrikes entering atmo above the northern hemisphere. Warm up MAN-PAD seekers and stand by for threat vectors. Sound the civvie air-raid alert. Repeat: raid warning, raid warning."

All around us, the air-raid sirens of the civilian warning system start sounding their harsh warble.

"Air raid, air raid. This is not a drill. All personnel, seek shelter."

Next to me, Sergeant Fallon checks her rifle with the casual thoroughness of someone who has performed the action a million times before.

"Well, it was nice being all introspective, Andrew. Now let's get back to shooting people."

CHAPTER 20
THE BATTLE OF NEW SVALBARD

The first pair of Shrikes come thundering in with no subtlety whatsoever. They overfly the town at high altitude, five thousand feet above the deck at full throttle. The lead ship has all its active transmitters turned off, but the trailing ship is putting out enough radio energy with its jamming pods to cook a soy patty from a klick away.

"Rogue flight and all ground units, hold your missile fire," I warn over the guard channel. "It's a Wild Weasel combo. They're trying to get us to commit our MANPADs."

The Shrikes stay at full throttle as they fly overhead. The booms from their supersonic pass roll through the streets and alleys like not-so-distant cannon fire. Both attack birds are spewing out ECM decoys, but no missiles rise in response. One of our Dragonflies raps out a burst of cannon fire as a statement, but the autocannon's grenades can't reach that high, and the tracers fall way short.

"I'm lodging a complaint with the fleet," someone sends from the civilian ops center, and I recognize Chief Barnett's voice. "Flagrant breach of air-traffic regs, going supersonic above the city like that."

Someone else in the circuit laughs. "No kidding. That shit can cause hearing damage."

"We have activity at Frostbite," Rogue One warns. "Six—make that eight—Wasps, heading this way."

I watch the plot as the gaggle of drop ships from Camp Frostbite splits up into four pairs. The Wild Weasel flight has disappeared to the south, but the other Shrikes from the *Midway* swoop down from the steel-gray clouds and take up escort positions beside the drop ships.

"Here we go. Four assault elements, two Wasps and a Shrike each. Designating Raid One through Four."

"At least they're not half-assing it this time," Sergeant Fallon says. "Airfield team, they'll hit you again. Don't give 'em space for a foothold."

"Copy that." The commander of the TA company at the airfield sounds much more relaxed than I feel at the prospect of two SI assault platoons dropping on our heads in the next few minutes.

"Rogue flight, do not engage the drop ships yet. Use whatever missiles you have left on the Shrikes. You light up one of those drop ships, the Shrikes are going to tear you up."

The remaining Dragonflies send their acknowledgments. All the assets are on the board, and now it's a matter of playing out the first moves to see who had the better hand at planning the match.

"Get your ass into the ops center," Sergeant Fallon sends from around the corner, where she is checking the deployment of the platoon tasked with defense of the building. "You're our whole C3 section now. Nobody else can use that slick computer of yours."

"I'm touched by your concern, Master Sergeant," I reply.

"Just trying to preserve our limited stock of knuckleheads."

I watch the red icons on the plot. They're steadily advancing toward the town. Each of those icons represents thirty or more troops, people I've shared a mess hall with, men and women who wear the same flag we do. The universe is falling apart around us, and we still have nothing smarter to do than to try and kill each other. I don't have any love for the Lankies, those strange, planet-stealing, casually genocidal creatures, but in four years of constant combat against them, I've never seen two of their kind fight each other.

Overhead, the formation of drop ships and attack craft splits into two groups. One turns to the east and stays at altitude. The other turns to the east and rapidly descends toward the expanse of the airfield and its acres of open space.

"Airfield, incoming," I announce. "Four Wasps, two Shrikes, heading right for you."

The Shrikes zoom ahead and take up stations on both ends of the airfield as the drop ships do a textbook combat descent, a high-speed corkscrew maneuver to deny enemy antiaircraft gunners a predictable trajectory for their cannons. The air is practically crackling with radio energy as the Shrikes support their charges with electronic jamming to mess with the targeting radars we don't have.

The Wasps descending on the airfield have barely leveled out just above the ground when two blue inverted vee shapes pop up on my tactical display right in the center of the airfield.

"Goalkeeper, *execute*," Rogue One sends.

The two Dragonflies that just popped into existence on the plot do a synchronized turn to the south and ripple-fire three short-range air-to-air missiles at the Shrike that took up station at the south end of the airfield. At such a short distance, the pilot doesn't even have time for any evasive action. He has barely begun to pull his bird up and goose his engines when all three missiles hit him amidships, and his red icon disappears from my display in a blink. I can feel the shock of the resulting explosion through the soles of my boots from over half a klick away.

"Rogue flight, splash one," I narrate automatically. "Second Shrike is breaking off toward zero-two-zero."

The other Shrike goes supersonic and rapidly zooms skyward to get out of MANPAD range. Then he does a wing-over and comes barreling back toward the airfield on a reciprocal heading. At this distance, the multibarreled heavy assault cannon of the Shrike sounds like a Lanky with flatulence, if the Lankies had digestive systems like we do. Over by the airfield, the heavy armor-piercing grenades from the Shrike's big gun carve a hundred-foot trench into the runway concrete.

As soon as the Shrike pulls up from its strafing run, half a dozen handheld MANPAD launchers disgorge their missiles after it. The pilot kicks out countermeasure pods like parade confetti and once again pushes his bird through the sound barrier. Then I hear more cannon fire even before I see the two blue aircraft icons for the pair of Dragonflies popping up on my display again. The drop ships have linked their fire-control computers to use their radars and gun turrets as a makeshift antiaircraft cannon battery, and their bursts perfectly anticipate the turn rate and vector of the fleeing Shrike. I bring up the video feed from their targeting cameras just in time to see a cannon shell chew into the left engine pylon of the Shrike, sending bits of armor flying. For a moment it looks like the Dragonflies just scored another air-to-air kill, but then the pilot of the Shrike rights his wounded craft and runs away at full throttle, trailing smoke.

"*Fuck*, those things are tough," Rogue Two says. "Can't believe the son of a bitch is still flying."

"I've seen one make it back to the carrier with half its port wing gone and one engine shot off the airframe," I say. "They're built to take a beating. You guys did good."

There are four hostile red carets left on my tactical screen. The image from the Dragonflies' targeting cameras slews to show the quartet of Wasp drop ships disgorging troops by the side of the runway, only a few hundred feet from the control tower.

"Hate it for ya," Rogue One says, with what sounds like genuine regret in his voice. Then the chin turrets and hull-mounted heavy autocannons of the Dragonflies open up at the same time. The Wasps and their infantry passengers are sitting ducks, caught in the most vulnerable phase of an assault landing. My stomach clenches as I watch.

The Wasps are armored against small arms and light cannon fire, but even their laminate hull plating isn't designed to withstand the beating of large-caliber heavy antiarmor cannons at point-blank range. The first bursts from the Dragonflies tear into the flanks of the fleet drop ships like sledgehammers into sheetrock. The Wasps are in the middle of troop deployment, and the soldiers rushing to get clear are caught in a storm of exploding grenades and flying armor shards. Even though Rogue flight is selectively targeting control surfaces and engines, the carnage on the screen is shocking. In less than ten seconds of short cannon bursts, all four fleet Wasps are smoking wrecks, their vital parts blown to bits all over the runway. Around the immobilized gaggle of drop ships, there are at least a dozen fallen SI troopers who didn't get out of the line of fire fast enough. The rest are rushing the hangars and heading for cover, but they're clearly shell-shocked.

When our HD troopers open fire from their positions between the hangars, a short and violent firefight erupts. The SI troopers are caught out in the open, trapped between their burning drop ships and prepared defensive positions, and it doesn't take long for them to realize the hopelessness of their situation. Then our Dragonflies move in behind them. As quickly as it started, the shootout ends, and the remaining SI troops put their weapons on the ground and raise their hands.

"Cease fire," someone orders. "They're packing it in."

"First smart thing they've done today," Rogue One replies. He has steered his ship away from whatever shelter he had used to hide from the Shrikes, and moves over to the burning Wasps, chin turret trained on the surrendering troops. "You know, these new fleet birds are all right. I think I'm gonna keep this one."

"Casualties at the airfield," I tell Sergeant Fallon. "Theirs, not ours."

"Send some medics over there ASAP," she tells the platoon leaders. "And for fuck's sake, disarm those jarheads first. I don't want them to change their minds about their winning odds."

"We'll find a quiet corner for them somewhere," the airfield company's CO replies.

"Andrew, where's the other flight?"

I check the tactical display.

"Coming around and back in from the east. They're still at five thousand. Hard to tell what they have in mind, but they sure as shit blew their chance for a surprise attack."

"I'm tracking them optically," Rogue Four says.

"Keep your active sensors cold," I tell him, and tap into his camera feed.

"Yeah, roger that. I'm not interested in getting a HARM up my ass today."

"They really ought to either piss or get off the damn pot," Rogue One says.

When they're right above the center of town, still high up and out of range of our infantry's shoulder-launched MANPADs, Raid Two finally breaks cruise formation. The Shrikes take up close air support positions overhead, and the Wasps start their combat descents, spiraling groundward like a handful of overeager autumn leaves hurling themselves off a tree branch. My tactical computer shows their projected trajectory, and the dotted red line of their predicted flight path ends right on top of the spot where Sergeant Fallon and I are standing.

"Raid Two is dropping on the admin center," I announce, much more calmly than I feel.

The Wasps swarm in from all cardinal directions of the compass rose. They pull up into position on all four of the intersections around the admin center, each only two blocks from where I am. They put their craft into a hover above the intersections and deploy assault lines out of their open tail ramps. A moment later, SI infantry start rappelling down the lines from fifty feet up. This time, there are no surprise Dragonflies breaking up the deployment with point-blank cannon fire, and the HD troops on the ground hold their missiles, for fear of sending a Wasp crashing down into the densely packed civilian housing. Then all four of their platoons are on the ground, and the Wasps streak skyward again with screaming engines, ejecting clouds of countermeasures along the way.

"We have a company on the dirt at the admin center," I announce, even though my tactical computer has already shared the data with every battle armor and vehicle on our TacLink network.

"Admin center platoon, heads up," Sergeant Fallon says. "We'll hold 'em by the nose for the ass-kicking."

The SI platoons break up into squads and start their rush toward the admin center. I run around the corner and join Sergeant Fallon and the squad that's dug in by the corner of the building. There's no actual digging on the permanently frozen ground, so the fighting positions are made from intermeshing parts of modular ferroconcrete barriers.

"About time," Sergeant Fallon says when I leap over the low barrier and land next to her. "I was wondering if you were planning to take on those jarheads all by yourself."

"Right," I say. "And get two to the spleen again."

The deployment pattern of our HD platoon fully anticipated a textbook four-pronged airborne assault from precisely those intersections. When the SI troops round the corners of the last block across the intersection, they're faced with mutually supporting firing positions, and autocannons sheltered by concrete. On all four corners, fléchette rifles start chattering as the SI troops start a leapfrogging assault. On all four corners, the rifle fire is instantly answered by much more authoritative autocannon reports. The SI assault elements abandon their mad dash for the admin building and seek cover in doorways and behind garbage containers. Smoke rolls across the street as the SI troopers deploy smoke grenades, even though they have to be aware that our own helmet sensors can see right through most of it.

"Side alley, eleven o'clock, fifty," Sergeant Fallon calls out over the din. I adjust my aim and see four SI troopers taking up firing positions in the mouth of a narrow alley between two housing units. The lead trooper is readying his rifle's grenade launcher. It's impossible to tell whether he's preparing a smoke grenade or a proximity-fused frag grenade. Sergeant Fallon rasps out a burst with her rifle. The fléchettes tear the weapon from the SI trooper's hands and send him sprawling backwards. His comrades drag him out of sight, firing at us as they do.

"Keep an eye on those drop ships," Sergeant Fallon shouts.

My tactical plot is a mess of blue and red icons, five platoons of fighting troops duking it out in a four-block area around the admin center. The fleet Wasps are circling high above the fray, out of missile range, waiting for the close air support calls from their charges on the ground. All around me, I hear the din of rifle fire and the chest-pounding low staccato of the autocannons firing sporadic bursts.

More blue icons show up on the plot as one of our HD companies moves in and engages the SI troops from the rear. Now the attackers are sandwiched between two groups of defenders, caught between a hammer and anvil. I only have to look at my plot to know that the SI troops alone won't be able to take the admin center away from us, not while having to defend 360 degrees just a few minutes into the assault. Without our auto-cannons, it would be a close call. With each of the building's corners defended by a pair of them, the SI troops are in a very bad spot.

"Fast mover, bearing in from two-eight-zero true," Rogue Four warns. "He's making a gun run, the nutcase."

In the distance, I hear the familiar banshee wail of a Shrike at full throttle. Then the first high-velocity cannon shells pepper the area around the squad fortification to our left. The small-arms fire all around us is drowned out by the thunderclaps of exploding dual-purpose shells. In just a second or two, the squad position on the southwest corner of the admin center is obscured by a cloud of frozen soil and pulverized concrete. Then the Shrike thunders past overhead, low enough for me to make out the markings on the armored fuselage. For a moment, there's a lull in the shooting on the ground. When the smoke clears, half the concrete barriers on that corner of the building are gone, and there are a dozen impact craters the size of mule wheels in the thick concrete of the admin center's wall.

"Those damn things are murder," Sergeant Fallon says. "Another run like that, and we can pack it in."

The SI troops at that end of the building pop smoke in front of the ruined position and come charging across the street. There's return fire from the squad position, but it's from just a rifle or two at the most. I slap down the face shield of my helmet, switch sensor mode to multispectral, and dump a whole magazine in fully automatic mode at the outlines of SI troops rushing through the smoke. Next to me, some of the HD troopers shift their fire as well, and the SI assault falters halfway across the intersection. Several of the SI troops go down, and the rest retreat to the cover of the buildings behind them.

"They're not going anywhere," one of the HD troopers says.

"If that Shrike makes a few more passes, they won't have to," I reply. "They can just wait and then stroll in to mop up our bits and pieces."

"Keep that attack bird off our asses," Sergeant Fallon tells the Rogue Dragonflies. "We just lost most of a squad. Don't let him get in another one of those gun runs."

"We'll do what we can," Rogue One says. "Fucker's too fast for our cannons unless he's close, and we're Winchester on air-to-air."

I hear more heavy gunfire in the distance—not the Devil's Zipper sound of the Shrike's massive antiarmor cannon, but the slower staccato of drop-ship autocannons. Somewhere in the alleys beyond the contested intersection, MANPAD launchers send their ordnance skyward. I can't tell who launched them, or whether they're aimed at our drop ships or theirs. My plot is a mess of red and blue icons in close proximity, the battle rapidly escalating into an unwise clusterfuck of epic proportions. One of the fleet Shrikes makes a low pass at full throttle, gun blazing at a target over by the airfield half a klick away. I shoot a hundred-round burst of fléchettes after it in frustration, even though I know that the little three-millimeter tungsten needles from my rifle won't do much more than scratch the paint. The Shrike banks sharply to the left and roars away, dumping clouds of countermeasures in its wake.

The shock wave of an explosion shakes the earth under my feet so hard that I have to take a step back from the concrete barrier for balance. When the sound of the detonation rolls across the city, I know right away that whatever just went off was way too big for a conventional warhead. All around me, the shooting ebbs. I turn toward the source of the sound and see a massive plume of frozen earth and ice reach a thousand feet or more into the sky to the north. Some of the troopers next to me shout in surprise and confusion. Then the ground shakes again, another titanic thunderclap bounces the dust on the street in front of us, and a second plume of frozen ground and dust rises near the first one. Now all the shooting near the admin building has ceased, friendly and hostile fire alike. There are only two kinds of weapons in the task force arsenal that can throw frozen dirt half a klick high on impact like that, and I've had enough nukes lobbed into my vicinity to know that these are not nuclear warheads.

"What the fuck was that?" Sergeant Fallon asks in an almost comically quizzical tone.

"Kinetic strike," I answer. "Someone sent down a little notice from orbit."

"Now hear this," Colonel Campbell's voice comes over the fleet emergency channel. "All fleet units, listen up. This is *Indianapolis* Actual.

"I just fired two kinetic warheads at the ground between Camp Frostbite and New Longyearbyen. There are ninety-eight more of those in my magazine. All combat action against colonial units or civilian assets on New Longyearbyen will stop as of this moment, or I will launch the next pair right into the middle of Camp Frostbite. If you're still shooting at your own people after that, I will shoot the rest of my kinetic warheads at every piece of fleet equipment down there that's bigger than a belt buckle."

In the brief pause that follows, some of the HD troopers nearby look at each other and laugh in disbelief.

"I also have all four of my nuclear launch tubes warmed up and dialed in on the *Midway* and her escorts. Rest assured that I *will* get my nukes off if you shoot missiles at me. I've also released both my stealth interceptors with nuclear ordnance, and those things are so sneaky that even *I* couldn't find them.

"The fleet will cease all offensive ops on the moon, and recall all its birds to the *Midway*. Take any offensive action against *Indianapolis* or any of the civvie installations on the surface, and I will launch every nuke in my tubes at *Midway*. Then you can test if your point-defense systems from two modernization cycles ago can handle two dozen half-megaton warheads from short range."

Sergeant Fallon shakes her head with a disbelieving grin and looks at me. "Did he just threaten to shoot nukes at one of our own ships?"

"He did," I confirm. "But he does have a history of that."

"I think I love that man. I want to meet him."

"What you're doing on that moon down there is reckless idiocy that's costing lives," Colonel Campbell continues on the emergency channel. "Consider putting someone in charge on that flag bridge who isn't a clueless part-time warrior. Now recall those birds and cease fire, or the next brace of kinetic warheads goes out into Camp Frostbite in sixty seconds. *Indianapolis* Actual *out.*"

Nearby, some of the HD troopers clap and cheer.

"You think he'll do it?" Sergeant Fallon asks.

"I wouldn't doubt it for a second."

"Gee, too bad they shuttled their entire space ape regiment into Camp Frostbite just a little while ago," she says wryly. "I'd hate to be back there right now. Those kinetic rounds hit pretty hard. I bet they make big holes."

All around us, dust and dirt from the massive impact plumes to the north of town have started to fall like dirty rain.

"Yes, they do," I say. "All the punch of a low-yield nuke, without that nasty radiation."

The terse reply from the fleet comes over the emergency channel well before the minute is up.

"Hold your fire, *Indianapolis*. All fleet units, stand down. I repeat, all fleet units, stand down. Airborne units, disengage, disengage."

Within moments, all gunfire in the city ebbs. Across the intersection, the SI troopers withdraw into the warren of residential domes and narrow alleyways behind a rapidly thinning smoke screen. We track them with our rifle sights until they are gone from view. Someone turns off the fire-control system on the autocannon, and its electric servos stop humming. The sudden silence feels a bit surreal after the din of battle.

Sergeant Fallon slaps my shoulder pauldron and leaps over the concrete barrier into the road.

"The day's looking up, Andrew. Let's get some medics out to First Squad. Keep a watch, in case they change their minds."

CHAPTER 21

—A LOGISTICAL CONUNDRUM—

"I want that general in the brig. Then I want him in front of a court-martial. And if they have the good sense to put him up against a wall, I want to stand behind the firing squad and wave good-bye."

Sergeant Fallon isn't speaking with a raised voice, but I know her well enough to tell that she's implacably angry.

"That might be a bit difficult," Colonel Campbell says over the vid link from *Indianapolis*. "He's the ranking officer in this boondoggle of a task force. And if you come down on him, we also have to come down on the button pushers who executed his orders."

"You say that like it's unreasonable," Sergeant Fallon replies. "We have thirty-nine dead and seventy wounded down here. We're down a Dragonfly, a Shrike, and four Wasps, and those hothead attack jocks put a thousand rounds of cannon shells into a civvie settlement. If the houses down here weren't built like fucking bunkers, we could probably add fifty or a hundred civilians to that tally. The idiot who ordered that strike mission needs to walk the plank, Colonel."

"Look, Sarge, I'm not greatly troubled by the prospect, but it's not like I can send my sergeant-at-arms over there to put cuffs on the general," Colonel Campbell says. "What do you suggest?"

"Tell them that there will be no food or water replenishment from the colony unless they relieve the general of command and put him in the brig pending a court-martial."

"I'm not sure they'll respond well to that, Sarge."

"They'll come around when their water recyclers run dry," Sergeant Fallon says flatly.

"Your show down there. I'll send it on to the task force."

"Have they been poking around for you at all, Colonel?" I ask.

"Oh, yeah. Nothing aggressive, but the whole task force is running with their active sensors cranked all the way up. Even with this stealth boat, I have to keep my distance."

"How's your supply situation?"

"Well, this is an orbital combat ship, not a deep-space combatant. We have enough water and food for a few more weeks. But I want to work out a schedule for water replenishment and crew rotation as soon as practical. This thing isn't really built for month-long deployments, and I don't want my crew to go stir-crazy."

"Absolutely, Colonel," Sergeant Fallon says. "And if you can pencil yourself in some dirtside time, I'd love to sit down for a drink with you. The locals make a fierce moonshine, and there's plenty of ice around all over the place."

"That sounds pretty good, Sarge," Colonel Campbell says. "I'll take you up on that offer as soon as we have the situation here in orbit unfucked and I can put the safeties back on my nuclear launch tubes. *Indy* Actual out."

The briefing room on the bottom floor of the admin center has all the charm of a military mess hall, albeit with nicer furniture. A large holographic panel takes up the wall behind the head of the conference table. The colony is new, so all the communications gear is state of the art, more advanced than even the stuff in the CIC of the brand-new *Indianapolis*. Sergeant Fallon has been using the room for a while now to talk to the captains of *Indianapolis* and the *Gary I. Gordon* without fear of eavesdropping.

"Not exactly an impressive navy," I say. "One orbital combat ship and an ancient freighter. Those fleet units still outgun us fifty to one in ordnance."

"Yeah, but thank the gods for the nukes on that ship," she says. "That's the only thing keeping the fleet off our asses right now. That and the fact that the one captain defecting to our side has the stealthiest ship of the bunch."

There's a knock on the door, and one of the colony's administrators sticks his head into the briefing room.

"Sergeant Fallon, there's someone here to see you."

"Military or civilian?"

"Uh, civilian, ma'am. She's the head of our science mission."

"Well, by all means, send her in."

The woman who walks into the room is dark haired, slender, and almost as tall as I am. She is wearing an irritated expression on her face. She strides toward the conference table where Sergeant Fallon and I are sitting next to each other, and sits down in the chair directly across the table from us.

"Don't expect me to ask permission to sit down," she says. "I'm not used to asking the military for the use of our own facilities, and I don't think I'm going to start any time soon."

Sergeant Fallon raises an eyebrow and smiles the tiniest of smiles.

"And you are?"

"Dr. Stewart," the woman says. "I'm the head of the scientific detachment here on the colony."

"I'm Briana Fallon. Do you have a conventional first name, too, or did your parents anticipate your future academic achievements when they picked your name?"

Dr. Stewart replicates Sergeant Fallon's tiny almost-smile.

"My first name is Janet," she says. "You have to forgive me for not addressing you by your proper rank. I'm not fluent when it comes to military rank insignia."

"I don't think it matters much at this point," Sergeant Fallon says. "Our new chain of command down here is a bit unorthodox. Bur for what it's worth, I'm a master sergeant. And this fellow next to me is Staff Sergeant Grayson."

"Andrew," I offer. Dr. Stewart nods at me.

"How can we help you?" Sergeant Fallon asks.

"Well." Dr. Stewart folds her hands on the tabletop and smiles curtly. "You certainly get down to business promptly. I appreciate that in people."

She looks at the big holoscreen on the other side of the room, but it only shows the gray standby screen.

"You could help me and yourselves a great deal by packing up all those extra troops you crammed into this settlement and taking them back home as soon as you can. Preferably before the start of the winter."

Sergeant Fallon snorts and shakes her head.

"I would like to do nothing better right now. But just in case they left you science folks out of the loop, the fleet turned off the Alcubierre network and mined all the off-ramps. I'm afraid we're stuck with each other for the foreseeable future."

"Then I hope you brought enough sandwiches for a few years. I know the pencil pushers in the administration office aren't all that great at math, so they probably haven't pointed this out yet, but we don't have nearly enough food on this moon to feed ourselves and a few thousand dinner guests."

"I thought you grow your own," I say.

"Mostly. We're still dependent on shipments from home for quite a few things. With our normal population, we could probably run things lean for a long time, but not with the current headcount.

Simply put, we have food capacity for x people, and right now we have x times two people on this moon."

"Can we increase capacity? Put up a bunch more greenhouses?" I ask.

"Wish it were that easy," Dr. Stewart says. "But we don't have the local facilities to make those prefab greenhouse modules. And even if we did, the growing season down here is really short, and we're almost at the end of it."

"The carrier has a lot of food and supplies in its stores, but we're not exactly on lunch-line terms with the rest of the fleet right now."

"Once we get the fleet units to stop shooting and start talking, we can pool our supplies," Sergeant Fallon says. "With the stuff from your food stores and the task force reserves, I think we can make it through to the next growing season. And that's about all I can put on the table right now, because I can't just tell a thousand of my troops to commit suicide for the sake of the headcount."

"No, of course not." Dr. Stewart smiles curtly.

"That's assuming we make it all the way to the next season without the Lankies paying us a visit," I say. "Because if they show up, the supply problem is the least of our worries."

"They've never shown any interest in this system," Dr. Stewart says. "There isn't much here, you know. Two little moons, one too hot and one too cold for proper colonization. If it wasn't for the ice on this moon, we wouldn't even have a presence here. Too desolate and too far from home."

"Let's hope they share your views on the value of this property," I say. "Because if they show up in orbit one morning, we're all compost a few weeks later."

"You mean all those extra troops won't make a difference?"

"Not in the long run, no."

"Then why are they here?"

"So they're off Earth and well away from anywhere they could be starting trouble," Sergeant Fallon answers for me. "We're mostly malcontents and troublemakers with a history of insubordination. Your little moon is now a penal colony, more or less."

Dr. Stewart smiles her wry little smile again.

"Lovely. Get killed by the Lankies, or starve to death eventually. I suppose there isn't much of a point for me to update my résumé."

"Welcome to the end of the species," I say. "At least we have ringside seats."

"Well." Dr. Stewart folds her hands in her lap and looks at the standby pattern of the holoscreen again. Then she looks at us and shrugs. "I'm not too good at sitting on my ass and waiting for the shot clock to run out. Now, I'm no good at shooting a gun or flying a drop ship, but I have a scientific research facility full of smart people. Is there anything we can do to improve our position? Do you have a plan of some kind?"

Sergeant Fallon smiles.

"That term implies a level of organization that I'm not willing to claim just yet. Right now, we're still in the 'winging it' stage."

CHAPTER 22

——UNEXPECTED GUESTS——

The fleet has a hard and not-very-generous weight limit for personal possessions. Shipping a kilogram of stuff over dozens of light years is insanely expensive, so each Fleet Arm member is entitled to just twenty kilos of nonissue items. We can send physical mail back home, but only a total of five hundred grams every six months, and we can only receive two hundred grams in return from Earth. The contents of the personal compartment of my locker weigh just under seven kilos, the less to haul around between deployments. I mailed my medal cases home to Mom over the years for safekeeping, and because I knew she would be pleased to have them. She never sent anything back until last year when I got a letter from her—not a MilNet e-mail, which we exchange every month or so, but an actual physical letter, written on sugarcane paper in her narrow old-fashioned cursive. It was just four pages long, and it contained nothing she couldn't have typed into the MilNet terminal at the civil administration building back home, but it was a physical object, something that she had held in her own hands.

Right now, that letter is the only possession I have left. It's tucked into the waterproof document pouch in my leg pocket, where it has been ever since I received it last year. All my other stuff is in a locker back at Camp Frostbite, unless the SI troops crammed into the place haven't already dumped or looted all our gear. All I have left now are those four sheets of sugarcane paper, so thin you can almost see through them. As a welfare rat, I've never owned much, but I've never been entirely without possessions until now.

I'm peeling unit patches off my battle dress smock when there's a knock on the door of the storage room that serves as my temporary berth.

"Come in."

The door opens on creaky hinges, and Sergeant Fallon sticks her head into the room. She looks at the small pile of cloth patches at my feet and raises an eyebrow.

"Might as well dispense with the notion that we're still members of an organized military," I say. "I have half a mind to throw out all the rank sleeves as well."

"Have the tailor make you some new ones," she says. "Nobody says you can't be a goddamn two-star general in this outfit."

She steps into the room, crouches in front of me, and picks up one of the unit patches I discarded.

"Weird, isn't it? We've spent so much time and sweat on these things, and in the end they're just cheap-ass fabric squares with some sticky thread backing. Not much to show for fifteen years and half a leg, is it?"

"Don't forget the bank account," I say. "A million worthless Commonwealth bucks."

"Almost *three* million worthless Commonwealth bucks," she says. "Three reenlistment bonuses, a hundred and fifty monthly deposits, and jack squat to spend it all on. Just a bunch of numbers in a database somewhere, that's all."

She knocks on her prosthetic lower leg.

"There's this little souvenir, of course, but I don't think it counts. I wouldn't have needed it if the military hadn't sent me to the place where they blew off the original one."

"What about the shiny medal on the blue ribbon?"

259

"The Medal of Honor?" She snorts a derisive little laugh. "*That* fucking thing. The moment they put that around my neck, I became a goddamn PR asset for the military. I had to practically blackmail them to stay in a combat billet. Although I will admit that it got me out of a court-martial or two. Doubt it'll get me out of this mess, though."

"They can't put two entire battalions up against the wall," I say.

"You haven't been Earthside the last few years, Andrew. I honestly can't say they wouldn't. The more their grip on the rabble slips, the tighter they wrap the leash on their guard dogs."

Outside in the corridor, an announcement sounds over invisible speakers. It's a pleasant female voice, so vaguely cheerful that it can only be a computer.

"Attention, all personnel. This is a Level Two weather alert. Winds from the north at sixty to eighty kilometers per hour, light to moderate snow, temperature negative two-zero degrees Celsius. All exposed personnel, seek shelter or don appropriate protective clothing. I repeat, this is a Level Two weather alert. Monitor the MetSat channel for updated conditions. Announcement ends."

"Minus twenty?" Sergeant Fallon says. "That's a bit chilly."

"And snow. Looks like winter's starting."

"Well, grab your armor, and let's go take a look. I haven't seen any clean white snow since that combat drop into Trondheim back in '99. 'Course, that snow didn't stay white long."

We've only been inside the admin center for two hours, but when we step outside again, the place looks like it has been transplanted onto a different planet. The sky is the color of dirty concrete, and the snow is blowing so densely that I can barely make out the lights on the buildings across the little civic plaza even though they are only fifty meters away. The arctic wind, sharp as a blade, turns the skin of my face numb in just a few moments, and I lower the face shield of my helmet and take a few steps outside. The snow on the ground reaches halfway up the armored shin guards of my battle armor.

"Damn," Sergeant Fallon says when we're back inside, ice and snow caking our armor plates despite our merely two-minute sojourn into the weather. "That is some nasty climate out there all of a sudden."

One of the civvie techs in the entrance vestibule, a burly fellow in smudged blue overalls and a thick thermal jacket, hears her comment and chuckles.

"That? We call that a light dusting. Typical late fall weather."

Behind us, the announcement system comes to life again. This time it's not the pleasant artificial female computer voice, but that of the comms tech down in the ops center.

"Sergeants Fallon and Grayson, please report to the OC. Priority tight-beam link from orbit."

I brush the snow off my armor and stomp my boots on the concrete a few times to knock off the slush.

"Back to work, I guess," Sergeant Fallon says. "That's why I hate positions of authority. Everyone always bugs the shit out of you."

"They popped up on our long-range gear a few minutes ago," Colonel Campbell says over the voice connection from the *Indianapolis*. "Three AUs out. They're right on the ecliptic, heading for us as straight as they can, as far as my sensor guys can tell."

"Lankies?" I say, dreading the reply.

"Doubtful. Unless they've learned to spoof emergency transponder signals bit for bit. Our bogey is squawking an SRA distress signal in sixty-second intervals."

Sergeant Fallon looks at me.

"I'm out of my field with this space warfare stuff," she says. "What do we have here? Are we humped?"

"He's coming our way and sending a distress signal from that far out, he's not spoiling for a fight, and he isn't a Lanky," I say.

"Unless it's a ruse of some kind," Colonel Campbell says.

"Has the task force picked him up yet?"

"Doubtful. Nobody there is stirring. Our sensor gear is better than theirs by a lot, and I have snooper buoys out away from the noise. But the way he's coming in, they'll hear him before too long. I give it a few hours, depending on how awake their sensor guys are."

"Any idea what he is?"

"He's still awfully far away, but from the ELINT signature and the optical profile, I'd say he's a large deep-space combatant. Heavy cruiser maybe, or one of their big-ass space control cans."

"Why would one of those come our way with the radio blaring?" Sergeant Fallon asks.

"Well, it's either a ruse to make us look one way while his buddies come from a different bearing, or—"

"He's really in trouble and looking for help," I finish.

"If he's running from something, it's not one of our guys on his ass," Colonel Campbell says. "Every fleet unit in this system is in orbit around this rock right now. And if he's not running from one of ours . . ."

Nobody finishes his sentence, but it feels like the temperature in the room just dropped by twenty degrees.

"Let's hope it's a ruse, and there's an SRA task force heading our way," Colonel Campbell concludes dryly. "At least that would give us a fighting chance."

I spend the next hour on one of the consoles in the ops center. The console is linked to the computer in my battle armor, which is tapping into the data feed from the *Indianapolis*'s CIC. Sergeant

Fallon knows tactical diagrams, but she's not familiar with translating them four-dimensionally to make sense of things scattered across light-hours of space, so I explain them to her as we look at the feed from *Indy*'s sensor suite.

"If he's sending a distress code, and he doesn't care if we see him coming, maybe he has a legit emergency," Sergeant Fallon suggests. "Stranger things have happened, right?"

"I don't think that's likely," I say, and point out some markers on the plot. "*Indy* is marking his position every time he broadcasts his signal. See here? That's Mark One. There's Two. Three, Four, and Five. You extend the line through these marks, and he's headed right for us. But if you follow it back and kind of eyeball the way he came . . ." I finish the arc with my index finger. "That's the moon with the only SRA colony in the system. Even now, he's a lot closer to *it* than he is to us. If it's just a shipboard emergency, why wouldn't he go to his own base instead of the enemy base on the other side of the system?"

"I don't like that line of thought," Sergeant Fallon says.

"Neither do I. The only thing that makes sense to me is that someone got the jump on the Russian base, and this cruiser got away. If that's the case, then whatever flushed him our way will follow right behind sooner or later. And with the Alcubierre network offline, our backs are against the wall."

"Alert the grunts?"

"Not yet. That SRA cruiser is still a long way out. And if he has a Lanky seed ship on his ass, it won't make a bit of a difference. Might as well die well rested."

"It's the *Arkhangelsk*," Colonel Campbell says over the encrypted downlink an hour later. "Fleet intel said she was in the system when we transitioned in, and the ELINT signature of the bogey matches. She's one of their old Kirov-class cans. A little behind on tech these days, but tough ships. Lots of firepower. If he's playing a trick and cruising for trouble, he's a pretty even match for the task force."

"I'd almost wish he's doing just that," I say.

"Something else—he's not moving like he's running from anything. He's pulling a quarter-g acceleration. That's less than what their slowest supply tin cans can make."

"How long until he gets here?"

"At his current acceleration, it'll take him eight days just to get to turnaround. Make it three weeks, give or take."

"Has the task force picked him up yet?"

"Doesn't look like it. Won't be long, though," Colonel Campbell says.

"What are they going to do when they spot him?" Sergeant Fallon asks. She has been following our tactical shoptalk quietly, clearly uncomfortable to be out of her area of expertise.

"Hard to say, with that desk pilot for a task force commander," Colonel Campbell says. "But seeing how he handled the little mutiny, I'd put some money on him storming off to meet the threat."

"It's not like we're going anywhere," I say.

"I'm not in charge of your grunts, and I don't want to be. It would be a little silly to pull rank at this point. But I suggest you get the shop down there prepared for action. SRA ruse or Lankies on that bogey's tail, chances are someone's about to disturb the peace pretty soon."

"Right." Sergeant Fallon sighs and looks at me. "Keep us posted on the bogey, Colonel. We'll see what we can come up with down here. In the meantime, let's hope that the Russian cruiser just had a fusion bottle fail or something. I'm not sure I'm prepared for the other scenarios yet."

"Will do. *Indianapolis* Actual out." The speaker in the comms console chirps the descending two-tone trill of a dropped tight-beam connection.

"Let's pretend there's a Lanky ship behind that cruiser coming our way," Sergeant Fallon says. "With all that combat experience against them, what would you do?"

"Tuck tail and run," I say. "Except there's no place to run in this system, and the transition point out of here is closed." I shrug. "Arm everyone to the teeth, issue every last rocket launcher and tactical nuke in the magazines. Hit 'em when they land and make them pay for the place. But if they want it, it's theirs already."

"Such defeatism. They teach you that in the fleet?"

She raps me on the back of my armor with her fist.

"Let's go see the science crew. I want to see if those smart people have any ideas for making the event memorable. If I'm going to die, I want to at least make it into one of those 'Epic Last Stands in History' books."

CHAPTER 23

— A SCIENTIFIC APPROACH —

"Run that by me again," Dr. Stewart says. "You want me to do *what* now?"

"We need you to help us figure out how to blow a Lanky seed ship out of space," Sergeant Fallon says. "It kind of goes without saying that you have a pretty good motivator to find a solution."

"Correct me if I'm wrong, but isn't that the kind of thing more in your ballpark? I thought you soldiers were in charge of coming up with new ways to break things."

"We've tried," I say. "Once they're on the ground, we can shoot them, but that's difficult. Or we can nuke them, which is easier, but we don't have the elbow room to fling around a lot of kiloton warheads on this moon. And nobody has ever cracked a seed ship."

"Your nukes don't work on them?"

"Not in space. Nukes aren't all that effective in a vacuum. And those seed ships have hard shells. I've never heard of anyone actually cracking the hull on one, and I've been in a battle where a whole task force chucked every nuke in the magazines at it. Dozens of megatons, and not a dent in the trim."

"I see." Dr. Stewart leans back in her chair and crosses her arms in front of her chest. I can't tell whether the expression on her face is amusement or incredulity.

We're in her office in the science department of the admin center. It's small and messy, just a desk with data tablets and printouts all over it, and a few office chairs that are weighed down with reference material. If a tidy office is a sign of a cluttered mind, then Dr. Stewart's mind is as squared away as a boot camp recruit's locker.

"Let me get this sorted out," she says. "You people have been trying to figure out this problem for over four years. None of your soldier toys do the job, and all those military scientists haven't come up with a solution in half a decade. And you're asking me to solve it for you in seven days?"

"Earlier if possible," Sergeant Fallon says. "So we can prepare the defense before the bad guys are overhead."

"Once they are, they'll start landing scouts, and every human settlement they find is going to get nerve-gassed from orbit. Then they'll tear down our terraformers and set up their own, and two months later the atmosphere's mostly carbon dioxide," I say.

"I've read all the intel," Dr. Stewart says. "At least the stuff they let us civvies read. And I have to admit it doesn't make me overly optimistic."

Sergeant Fallon smiles curtly. "That's the understatement of the month. Personally, I don't give a bucket of warm piss for this place if we have to go up against those things with what we have. My people are Homeworld Defense grunts. They don't have the training, don't have the right guns, don't have the experience. I have two battalions of glorified riot police with popguns."

"I have a pocketknife," Dr. Stewart says. "A few containers of hydrochloric acid down in the lab. Two cargo rail guns that can't be aimed at anything unless you coax someone into just the right spot in orbit. And our constables carry sidearms and stun sticks. Not exactly a mighty arsenal, I'm afraid."

"What about those rail guns?"

"Those are for lobbing freight containers into orbit. Ship comes with empty cargo pods, they drop them on the moon for recovery, we fill cargo pods up with water, and up into orbit they go with the rail guns. Saves on fuel for orbital lifts. We have two sites, but they're fixed. And they just generate enough juice to put things in a low orbit with the minimum amount of energy required."

"Can we juice them up a bit?" Sergeant Fallon asks.

"Some, but there's no point. They can't be *aimed*. They're just ramps in the ground. And even at full power, they won't launch things fast enough to give you more energy than fifty gigatons' worth of nukes. They were designed for putting payloads into orbit, not for use as planetary defense weapons."

"So there's not much we can do, and nothing we can do it with," Sergeant Fallon says.

"That sounds like an accurate assessment." Dr. Stewart leans back in her chair again and studies the computer screen that's shoved into a corner of her crowded desk. "I'm not an expert on weaponry. I'm an astrophysicist. But give me a list of your assets, and I'll see what we can think up down here in Science Country. I need to know what kind of ships we have, and their list of ordnance loadouts, especially anything with nuclear warheads. I also need to know the maximum power output of their fusion reactors, and their acceleration data."

"We'll get that to you," I say. "It'll be a short list. Right now we have two ships on our side, and one of them is a ratty old freighter."

Dr. Stewart lets out a little sigh.

"Not much we can do, and nothing to do it with," she echoes Sergeant Fallon. "Well, let me see if we can add something of value, Sergeant."

"Seven days," Sergeant Fallon muses as we walk back to the ops center. "If we don't come up with a way to knock your aliens out of space in seven days, we're fucked."

"Could be that Russian cruiser isn't running from a Lanky ship," I say, even though I can't even convince myself of the possibility.

"Could be that I'm not really on some forsaken ball of ice at the ass end of the settled galaxy," Sergeant Fallon says. "Could be that this is all a bad dream caused by too much shitty soy beer at the NCO club. What do *you* think?"

"I think if they don't come up with something really fucking clever in Science Country, we're fucked," I concur.

"Never thought I'd kick it out in space. Always figured I'd get my lights turned off in a PRC somewhere. Look around the wrong corner, *bam*. Not this alien invasion business."

I have a brief flashback to a hot night five years ago, memories of a rifle in my right hand and an injured Sergeant Fallon hanging off my left side. I still recall the feeling of absolute certainty that we were both just moments away from death as the fléchettes from rioters' guns whizzed past us with supersonic cracks. I can still feel the blood running down my side, and the way every breath hurt as if someone was driving a knife between my ribs. But the worst of it was the feeling of total abandonment, of being left to die in the middle of a filthy, squalid welfare city, surrounded by people who hated us so much for who we were and what we did that they would have torn us limb from limb with their bare hands.

"If our time is up, at least we'll be dying in fresh air," I say. "With rifles in our hands and a hearty 'fuck you' on our lips."

"There are worse ways to go," Sergeant Fallon agrees. "'Course, I want to explore every other option before we get to the 'dying in fresh air' part."

In the windowless admin building, with the wind blowing the snow around outside in fifty-knot gales, it's easy for us troopers to fall back into a watch-cycle routine. I spend my watches in the ops center in front of an admin deck, looking at the data from the orbital sensors and the packages the Neural Networks guy on the *Indy* sends down over encrypted half-millisecond bursts. The *Indianapolis* has the latest in computers and the very latest in stealth technology, which is the only thing that gives me even a glimmer of hope now. The battered SRA cruiser—if they are indeed damaged and not just pulling a ruse to get into missile range—is creeping closer to New Svalbard with every hour, but even the advanced ELINT gear on the *Indy* can't yet see what they're creeping away from. The fleet units are holding the truce, but their frigate is definitely running an independent search pattern, trying to sniff out the *Indy*. The *Midway* and her light cruiser escort are doing slow, predictable laps in orbit, active sensors sweeping the area in equally predictable patterns. In sheer combat power, the light cruiser alone outmatches *Indy*, but watching those two relics trying to nail down the location of that brand-new stealth ship is almost embarrassing.

At some point, I look up from the screen to see that I'm the only person left in the ops center. I check my computer's clock and find that it's 0230 local time, the middle of the night. I lean back and stretch with a yawn.

Behind me, the door to the ops center opens, and Dr. Stewart steps through it. She looks about as fresh as I feel, and there's a big, old-fashioned porcelain mug in one of her hands. She has a data pad under the other arm.

"Good evening," she says when she sees me sitting in the corner. "Or good morning, I guess."

"Everyone's gone," I say. "The ops guys turned in a while ago."

"Actually, I'm here to see you. Where's the other sergeant?"

"Master Sergeant Fallon? In her quarters, I guess. That mutiny business will wear you out," I add, and Dr. Stewart smiles wryly.

"For what it's worth, the civilian crew really appreciates that you decided to stand with us."

"It wasn't right for them to try and grab what they did," I say. "We're supposed to be a defense force, not an occupying army."

"I had my prejudices," she says. "But you've managed to put a dent into them. I'm not used to the idea of soldiers being reflective about the ethics of their jobs. I thought you do what they tell you to do."

"Generally. Not always. They don't surgically remove your sense of right and wrong when you show up for boot camp, you know."

"May I sit down?" she asks.

"Sure," I say. "Your place."

She pulls up one of the empty chairs from the console bank next to me and rolls it to where I'm sitting. I make her some room and move my rifle, which was leaning against the desk. She sits down with a sigh and puts coffee mug and data pad on the desk next to my loaner admin deck.

"Why aren't you in your bunk as well? You took part in that mutiny business, too, as far as I recall."

"I'll go when Sergeant Fallon is up," I say. "Somebody's gotta be down here keeping an eye on things, in case the *Indianapolis* up in orbit has news to share. They're sort of our eyes and ears right now." I point at the admin deck. "That thing is linked with my armor's computer so I can stay tapped into the telemetry."

"Is that your job? Communications? I thought you were, you know, a rifleman or something." She nods at the M-66 carbine leaning against the desk.

"That's for personal protection. *That*"—I point at the screen of the admin deck again—"is for calling in the real guns. I'm the guy on the ground who calls in airstrikes, coordinates attack runs, that sort of thing. I can do a lot more damage with the data deck there than with that rifle."

"I see." Dr. Stewart takes a sip from her mug and makes a face. "Lukewarm now," she says. "And too strong. It's been sitting out too long."

"So why aren't you sleeping at this hour?"

She puts down the mug and picks up her data pad.

"Your little science homework," she says. "I've been trying to think up a way to turn this dinky little water stop into a threat to Lanky ships, but so far I'm not coming up with anything. I guess I'm not used to thinking like a soldier."

"We could fight them on the ground if all those troops dirtside were in bug suits and had bug weapons," I say. "We have a lot of boots on the moon right now. The trouble is that they all have guns for shooting people, not Lankies."

"So we can't really take them on once they land," Dr. Stewart says. "What about before they get into orbit? I mean, you've said that nobody's ever destroyed one of their seed ships, but have they ever made one turn back, run away?"

I shake my head. "They're hard to kill on the ground, but impossible to kill in their ships. Those things are immune to anything we can throw at them."

"They're using organic weapons, right?"

"Yeah, some sort of penetrator. Get close enough to a Lanky ship, they launch a few thousand of 'em. Goes right through the laminate armor on our ships."

"Have we tried doing the same?"

"Our main ship-to-ship stuff is missiles. Nuke-tipped for the Lankies. I don't think they've ever made any difference in combat."

Dr. Stewart taps around on the screen of her data pad and furrows a brow.

"If the fleet would be a little more forthcoming with data on the Lankies instead of treating every little thing as a state secret, maybe we would have found a solution already. But I guess they don't want to upset the civilians."

She looks up at me with a frown.

"Anyone ever hit one of their ships with something really big?"

"Some cruiser skipper rammed one with his ship once. Didn't work. Our biggest ships are a hundred, a hundred and fifty thousand tons. Those seed ships are a few kilometers long. They probably weigh a few *million* tons. You drive a twenty-K cruiser against a seed ship, it won't even slow 'em down."

"That would depend on how fast you drive it," Dr. Stewart says. "Their hulls may be so tough you can't crack them with shipboard weapons, but those creatures are living, organic beings. They can't be immune to physics. I guarantee that if we hit one of those seed ships hard enough, it'll kill every living thing inside."

"We haven't made a *dent* with a few hundred megatons of nukes. You'd have to go pretty fast to hit them a lot harder than that."

Dr. Stewart smiles and slurps more of her cold coffee.

"See, I may have a hard time thinking like a soldier, but you think too much like one. Forget *gigatons*. Start thinking like a scientist. Think *exajoules. Petajoules.* We don't want a battle, we want to cause an astronomical event you'll be able to see on Earth with a telescope in twenty-five years."

I can't help but smile at the idea of turning a Lanky seed ship into a new star in the Fomalhaut system.

"I'm all on board with that," I say. "But how do we get there from here? All we have is that ancient unarmed freighter and a patrol ship. Like I said, not exactly a fearsome task force."

"Think physics, not guns. A fist-sized rock isn't so fearsome, right? But throw it at something at one-tenth the speed of light, and the impact energy would be enough to make life really interesting on this moon for a short time."

She picks up her data pad again and starts scribbling on the screen with her finger.

"Say, how much does that freighter weigh?"

"Five, six thousand tons maybe," I say. "Fully loaded, three or four times that. But you can't just ram the thing into a Lanky ship."

"Why not?"

"Well, you won't find a crew to man it. Not for a one-way trip."

Dr. Stewart shrugs. "Who says it needs to be manned? All we have to do is to point it the right way and open the throttle. And if your visitor—*our* visitor—is coming in on an unchanging trajectory, we won't even need to nudge the stick after launch. Those Lanky ships are huge, right? It's not hard to hit a five-hundred-meter bull's-eye even at high speed. Not for a computer."

"But someone needs to—"

I look at the admin deck next to me. It's showing tactical plots right now, but I went to Neural Networks School half a lifetime ago, and I know that only security firewalls keep me from controlling all the essential systems on the *Indianapolis* remotely. The old freighter with her has far less complicated systems. And it's a military freighter from the auxiliary fleet, so it has military network hardware, not civilian gear.

"Never mind," I say. "It's a super-long shot, but it may actually work."

"I do science all day," Dr. Stewart says. "*Astrophysics.* 'It's a super-long shot' is practically the motto of our profession."

CHAPTER 24

—— A SUPER-LONG SHOT ——

"Looks like somebody's finally awake over there," Colonel Campbell says over the tight-beam connection.

Sergeant Fallon and I are standing in front of the ops center's modest situational display. The Networks admin has routed the feed from my tactical computer onto the holographic display. The fleet units in orbit are still rendered in friendly blue instead of enemy red, despite our current less-than-cordial relationship. The icons representing the carrier and its two escorts are rapidly climbing out of the predictable orbital racetrack they've been on for the last day and a half. Their new bearing points them roughly toward the incoming Russian cruiser, still almost three AUs from New Svalbard.

"Either their sensors are shit or their tactical guys have their heads up their asses," I say. "They should have seen that boat twelve hours ago."

"Probably a combination of both," Colonel Campbell says. "Half of that crew is fleet reserve."

"At least you won't have to play hide-and-seek up there anymore," I say. "And we only have to worry about that SI regiment they've crammed into Camp Frostbite."

"I wouldn't worry about them too much right now. I count most of the drop ships back on the *Midway*. They've got a pair of Wasps on the ground right now, that's all."

275

"It's not exactly great flying weather out there anyway," Sergeant Fallon says while eyeing the weather status display on the wall.

We watch the display as the carrier group leaves orbit altogether and burns to accelerate away from the moon. They pull away at one-g—not a sprint, but certainly not wasting time, either. Fifteen minutes pass, then thirty. An hour after my comms alert roused me from the smelly little cot in the storage locker, it looks like the task force is well on the way to an intercept and not just playing a ruse to get back into New Longyearbyen.

"What's the plan?" I ask Sergeant Fallon.

She lets herself drop into one of the nearby chairs and exhales warily.

"I think we can stand down from full battle rattle a bit," she says. "Keep a watch toward the camp, make sure those SI grunts don't get any super-dumb ideas. But let's cycle the Dragonflies through a standby schedule for now. One bird on alert, one on Ready Five, one off for rest. Let those pilots get some rack time."

She looks up at me and nods over to the ops center's main hatch.

"Same goes for you. You've had three hours of sleep after standing the watch in here all night. Hit the rack and don't come back until 1800 at least. Anything major goes down before then, I'll ring you out of bed, don't worry."

I know better than to argue with my old squad leader. Instead, I take my carbine, check for safe, and head toward the ops center hatch on heavy feet.

When I wake up in my bunk a good nine hours later, it's because my body wants to, not because some alarm goes off or my comms kit intrudes with an urgent message.

I climb out of the folding cot and sniff my fatigues. I've been wearing the same set through the combat landing and the subsequent skirmish with the fleet, and not even the antibacterial fibers of the CDUs can mask the slightly rank smell of the body underneath. It gets hot under battle armor, and I've spent most of the time since leaving Frostbite in mine.

According to my computer, it's 2000 hours. I've slept soundly and without interruption for nine hours, and my brain is rested, but my body feels like it usually does after a hard battle, as if I had stacked heavy crates all day and run a five-thousand-meter race in full combat kit before bedtime. The hours I spent sitting in a chair in the ops center didn't help things, either.

I straighten out my wrinkly fatigues, put on my boots, and open the door of the storage room. I leave the combat armor in the corner by my cot, but I take the rifle and sling it over my shoulder before stepping out of the room.

I've been in my chair in the ops center for barely five minutes when my comms alarm chirps a sequence announcing an incoming priority tight-beam connection from the *Indianapolis*.

"Ops center, this is *Indy* Actual."

"*Indy* Actual, ops center. Go ahead," I reply. The feeling of dread in my stomach clashes with the coffee I've guzzled since walking into the ops center. *Indy* Actual is Colonel Campbell, and he doesn't make tight-beam priority calls without good cause.

"Approaching visitor has a tailing unit," Colonel Campbell says. "It's a Lanky. Ring the alarm downstairs. Get ready for incoming."

I summon Sergeant Fallon, the HD brass, and the civilian admin crew. Not ten minutes later, everyone is in the ops center to listen to the news coming down from the *Indy*.

"Are we one hundred percent positive it's a Lanky?" Lieutenant Colonel Kemp asks. He's the head of Sergeant Fallon's HD battalion, the 309th AIB, which is spread out over New Longyearbyen and about a dozen of the terraforming stations.

"Yes," Colonel Campbell says. "They're a very slightly reflective three-kilometer blob in space. Can't see them on infrared, no radiation signature. If it wasn't for the illumination from the Russian cruiser's exhaust flare, we may have even missed them with the high-mag optics. Sons of bitches are really hard to spot at range if you don't know exactly where to look."

I've directed the data feed from *Indy*'s CIC display to the holotable in the ops center again and simplified the diagram for the ground-pounder officers a little. The Russian cruiser is a red blip on a parabolic trajectory toward New Svalbard, still a little over two AUs away and creeping along at a quarter-g acceleration. The orange icon representing the Lanky seed ship is less than two billion kilometers behind the Russian. The Lanky is decelerating at two-g and closing on the Russian cruiser rapidly. You don't need to be a space-warfare expert to see that the seed ship will overtake the SRA cruiser long before the Russians even get close to New Svalbard. They are no longer our enemies but a bunch of frightened fellow soldiers in a broken ship trying to run to the only other humans in the system for help, and they'll never make it. Our own units are still on an intercept course, 250 million kilometers away from the Russian on a reciprocal heading, and even if they could kill the Lanky seed ship, they won't get there in time.

"So much for turning off the Alcubierre nodes," Colonel Kemp says. "Backed ourselves up against a wall for nothing."

"Could be that they were in the system already when we shut the network down," Colonel Campbell replies. "Could be that they came through the SRA node, and the Sino-Russians didn't mine theirs. Could be the nukes made no difference even at transition. Doesn't matter now, though."

"No, it doesn't," Sergeant Fallon says. She's studying the plot with her hands crossed in front of her chest and her lips pursed. "What matters is what we do about it once they get here."

"Like there is anything," the civilian admin says. He looks at the orange icon representing the Lanky ship like a mouse watching the cat approach. On the whole, all the civvies in the room look like they'd rather be somewhere else right now.

"Just because nobody's ever kicked their asses doesn't mean nobody can," Sergeant Fallon says.

"We can't let them land," I say. "That's a given. There's hundreds of those things in a seed ship. Once they land, we're fucked. We have two battalions and whatever they stuffed into Frostbite, but we have no anti-Lanky weapons. They're too hard to kill with the other kit. They'd eat us for lunch with numbers, even without gassing us."

"Then we have to figure out how to keep them from landing," Colonel Campbell says over the tight-beam line. "I'll do what I can with *Indy*, but we're an OCS, not a heavy cruiser. We could at least do kinetic strikes on their landing sites from orbit if we can avoid the seed ship long enough."

"There may be another way," I say. The colonel and the civvie admin turn around to look at me.

"And what's that, Sergeant?"

I look at the holotable, where the orange icon for the seed ship creeps closer to the red symbol representing the SRA cruiser, slowly but steadily. The little orange lozenge-shaped icon represents a three-kilometer-long ship, black and shiny like a bug carapace, impossible to kill even with atomic warheads, and stuffed with hundreds of eighty-foot creatures who consider us a nuisance at best.

"Can you call Dr. Stewart down here?" I ask the admin.

"I don't know if that's the most idiotic or the most brilliant plan I've ever heard," Sergeant Fallon says dryly when Dr. Stewart ends the basic rundown of the idea we tossed around the night before.

"You want to use half of our spaceborne capability and fly it into a Lanky ship?" Colonel Campbell asks.

"It's not like the *Gordon* is doing us much good right now anyway," I say. "She delivered her payload, and right now she's just a target. She's not big enough to load up all the mudlegs, even if we had a place to take them. But she has docking collars and arrestor clamps for standard-sized cargo pods."

"And we have plenty of those here on the moon," Dr. Stewart continues. "We can fill them with water, shoot them into orbit, and load up the freighter with them. Increase the mass, give it extra reactor fuel. Maybe even flood the interior. Water doesn't compress. She'd be able to pull a lot of acceleration."

"And the crew? Are we going to have them run the ship in vac suits? And who's going to volunteer for that one-way trip?"

"Nobody needs to," I say. "She has fleet standard neural-networking gear, right? I can get together with your NN admin and the weapons officer, and we can send the *Gordon* off from the *Indy*'s CIC."

"You're talking about hitting a bull's-eye from, what, two AUs?" Colonel Campbell asks. "Even at one-g acceleration, you're talking close to relativistic velocities. You won't be able to correct the trajectory very well if the Lanky sees us coming."

"It's stupid." Lieutenant Colonel Decker shakes his head. "Really stupid. You can't hit anything at that range just by throwing a *freighter* at it."

"Yes, you can," Dr. Stewart says. "You're talking about a three-kilometer target that's a few hundred meters in diameter. Even at two AUs, that's not an impossible shot for a computer."

"If you're wrong, we'll be wasting that ship for nothing."

"If I'm *right*, we'll be hitting that Lanky ship with a few hundred gigatons' worth of impact energy," Dr. Stewart replies. "I don't care what kind of nukes you've shot at them before, but I *guarantee* you that a twenty-thousand-ton freighter moving at a tenth of light speed is going to vaporize that Lanky."

"A few hundred gigatons, huh?" Sergeant Fallon looks at the plot again and smiles a little. "I don't know about you people, but I really like that number."

There are a few moments of heated conversation in the ops center as all the civilians and soldiers in the room share their opinions of Dr. Stewart's idea at the same time. From the sound of it, half the personnel in the room think it's a workable plan, and the other half concur with the admin's assessment that it's criminally stupid. Then the chirp of the tight-beam connection from orbit cuts in as Colonel Campbell interjects.

"My weapons guy says it's not even a difficult shot. Providing they stay on trajectory, of course."

"Doesn't matter even if they deviate," Dr. Stewart says. "We send that ship off with four times the acceleration of the Lanky, we'll have the edge no matter what they do. We can always adjust, and they won't be able to avoid us."

"You're awfully sure about that stuff for a civilian," Sergeant Fallon tells her.

"I may not know anything about weapons, but I know mathematics and physics," she replies.

"If it's such a sure thing, why hasn't anyone ever had the same idea before?" Colonel Decker asks. He's clearly not enamored with the idea, and his body language is somewhere between frustration and defiance.

"Because it's nuts," Colonel Campbell says from orbit. "And because we usually don't see them coming. Besides, you never put all your cash on one hand unless you're desperate."

"I don't know about you folks," Sergeant Fallon says, "but I think *desperate* pretty much hits the nail on the head right now." She looks at the administrator. "Of course, I'm open to other ideas, if anyone has any. Right now the Freighter of Doom plan sounds a little nuts. But if the only alternative is to let them land and hope we can nuke them, I'll take *a little nuts.*"

"I concur," Lieutenant Colonel Kemp says, and his sergeant major nods his agreement.

"Let's have a tally," Sergeant Fallon says. "All in favor of the Freighter of Doom, raise your hands."

Colonel Kemp and I raise our hands. Dr. Stewart looks around the room as if she's unsure whether she has a vote as well, and then raises her hand, too. The administrator joins us.

"All opposed to that crazy-ass idea, raise hands."

Colonel Decker's hand shoots up. After a few moments, the sergeant major of the 309th also votes against the plan. The deputy administrator of the colony adds his vote to the "opposed" tally as well.

"Mark me down as 'for,'" Sergeant Fallon says. "That's five to three. I guess it comes down to you and the *Gordon*'s skipper, Colonel Campbell."

For a few moments, we hear nothing over the tight-beam line. Then Colonel Campbell comes back on with a sigh.

"*Indianapolis* and *Gordon* concur with the crazy option," he says. "And the *Gordon*'s skipper says his new boat is a piece of shit anyway, and he hopes it will make a better missile than a freighter."

CHAPTER 25
— OPERATION DOORKNOCKER —

Outside, the weather has improved a little over the zero-visibility blizzard that kept us inside yesterday. The snow has slacked off, but the cold winds that are whipping through the spaces between the reinforced concrete domes of the airfield buildings are still bitingly cold.

I walk out of the airfield's control building and immediately have to suppress the urge to lower the visor of my helmet. Dr. Stewart, who is following me onto the tarmac, is wearing a borrowed military vacsuit that looks about five sizes too big for her.

Out on the landing pad in front of the main hangar, one of our hijacked Dragonflies is standing with the tail ramp open and the engines running. Even though the fleet units are out on an intercept trajectory several hours out from New Svalbard, using a third of our offensive air power to shuttle two people up to the *Indianapolis* seems exceedingly wasteful and unwise, but the *Indy*'s stealth birds don't have passenger capability and can't pick us up.

"When's the last time you've been up in space?" I ask Dr. Stewart as we walk up the Dragonfly's ramp. She is eyeing the interior of the cargo bay, which is lined with the usual complement of sling seats for fully armored combat grunts.

"Not since I arrived here," she replies. "Three years, nine months. I've never hitched a ride in one of these, though."

"Dragonfly-class drop ship. It's a mean little beast. Holds a full platoon of Spaceborne Infantry in armor and does the fire support once the troops are on the ground."

"It *looks* mean," she concurs.

There's no loadmaster, just the two pilots up front. I walk over to the loadmaster console and tap into the cockpit comms.

"Passengers loaded. Give us thirty seconds to strap in, and then let's get her upstairs. Are you sure you're qualified to do orbital docking maneuvers?"

"Yeah, no sweat," the pilot replies in the lazy drawl they seem to teach in Combat Flight School. "I've read the manual. Can't be all that hard if the fleet jocks can do it."

Dr. Stewart is struggling with the harness of one of the passenger seats, and I walk over and help her with the straps.

"Thanks," she says. She looks about as nervous as I felt when I took my first drop-ship ride in a Territorial Army Wasp, five years and half a lifetime ago on Earth. I check her helmet seal and plug her suit and helmet into the ship's oxygen and comms circuits.

"If we get decompression, your helmet shield will lower automatically. That won't happen, though. There's nothing around that can shoot at us. So just sit back and enjoy the ride."

I take the seat next to hers and strap myself in. The pitch of the engines changes, and I can feel the Dragonfly lifting off the deck. Then we're in forward motion, and a few moments later the pilot goes full throttle and points the ship into the sky. I tap into the optical systems of the Dragonfly and watch the feed from the multitude of external sensors on the hull.

"You want to see your little moon from above?" I ask Dr. Stewart over the intercom link.

"Can I?" She looks around. "This thing doesn't have any windows."

I reach over and lower the visor on her helmet. Then I share the camera feed with her and cycle it through the multitude of views from the optical array. The sky over the settlement is the color of dirty snow. The cloud cover stretches from horizon to horizon now, and as we ascend through the low clouds hanging over New Longyearbyen, the seventy-ton drop ship gets buffeted by the winds.

"We really weren't meant to live in places like this," I say.

"Why not?" she asks.

"So much effort just to stay alive," I say. "Ten years of terraforming, and if I step out of the admin building without heated armor, I'll be dead from exposure within fifteen minutes."

"That's what we do," Dr. Stewart says. "As a species, I mean. Earth is no cozy womb, either. Never has been. This is no worse than Antarctica, and we've had cities there for half a century now. You've been around the colonies, haven't you?"

"You could say that."

"Then you know how much we can adapt. We *have* to. Earth is getting too small for all of us."

I think of the place where I lived until I joined the service—humans stuffed into concrete shoeboxes and stacked a hundred high, then crammed next to each other for dozens of square miles. Weekly food allowances, occasional treats through vouchers for better food, and a small hope for a shot at a better life, the colony lottery. I know damn well that Earth is already too small for us, but I also know how small the colonies are, how long it takes to make a planet or moon even minimally habitable, and how quickly the population grows back home even with mandatory birth control in the food for welfare rats. We were running out of time long before the Lankies started to take everything away from us again. As a species, they seem much better at the adaptation game.

The cloud cover on New Svalbard seems to extend forever. When we finally break out of the zero-visibility layer of white that covers this part of the moon like a shroud, the altimeter readout from the computer shows twenty thousand feet. The sky is the color of cobalt, with the far-off sun a small but bright sphere near the cloud horizon, and the much closer blue orb of Fomalhaut c taking up a quarter of the sky behind us. Fomalhaut c is the gas planet around which New Svalbard orbits, twice as far away from its parent sun than Neptune is distant from the sun in our home system. It's a pretty sight, but it reminds me of the mind-boggling vastness of the universe, and how far away from other members of our species we are right now.

The pilot takes a conservative ascent into orbit to save fuel, so we have thirty minutes to gaze at the scenery before we approach the *Indianapolis* in orbit. The orbital combat ship is built for stealth, and I don't even see it until the pilot calls in docking clearance, and the *Indy* lights up her positional illumination. Twenty degrees off our port bow, a sleek ship appears out of nowhere, a vague indication of shape only illuminated by blinking station lights. As we draw nearer, I get my first look at the exterior of a Constitution-class OCS. It looks a little like a Lanky ship in miniature, all curves and streamlined surfaces, almost organic in appearance. The drop ship draws closer and positions itself underneath the *Indy* for the automated docking procedure, but even from just a hundred meters away, I can't make out any exposed antennas or exhausts, just a series of openings near the tail end that look more like gills than thrust nozzles.

A few minutes later, the hull shudders slightly as the docking clamps attach to the Dragonfly and pull the drop ship up into the hangar of the *Indianapolis*. The status light on the loadmaster's panel across the aisle turns from red to green, and the deployment light above the tail ramp follows suit. I shut off the sensor feed from the sensors and raise my visor.

"You can unbuckle," I tell Dr. Stewart.

"Is there a procedure for stepping on a navy ship? Like, do I have to wipe my feet or something?"

"I'll handle that," I say, and return Dr. Stewart's wry smile.

I get out of my seat and walk over to the loadmaster console to unlock the tail ramp. It comes open with the familiar soft hydraulic whining and reveals the small craft hangar of the *Indianapolis* beyond.

The *Indy*'s hangar is claustrophobically tiny. As we walk down the laminate steel ramp of the Dragonfly, I look around and see that the drop ship fills out most of the available space. I see a refuel probe, an automated ordnance loader, and very little else aside from two deckhands stepping up to the ship to check for ordnance to secure. There's a corporal in fleet fatigues with a PDW slung across his chest standing by the bulkhead in front of us. I stop at the end of the tail ramp and salute the NAC colors painted on the bulkhead above the corporal's head.

"Permission to come aboard to report to the CO," I say.

The corporal returns my salute. "Permission granted," he says.

I step off the ramp and onto the deck, and Dr. Stewart follows me. "That is one small hangar," I say to the corporal as we step up to the hatch. "Smallest one of any boat I've ever been on."

"We don't have an air/space complement except for the two stealth birds," the corporal says. "And those have their own berths in the hull. Hangar's just for ferry flights and visitors."

"I see." I look back over my shoulder and see that the wingtips of the Dragonfly are barely far enough away from the walls to let an ordnance cart squeeze past.

"Well, it's not a carrier," he says. The hatch in front of him opens silently. "But everything's new and shiny. Best galley in the fleet, I guarantee it."

Colonel Campbell stands at the tactical display with his arms folded when I enter the CIC with Dr. Stewart in tow. He turns around and briefly returns my salute before offering his hand.

"Welcome aboard, ma'am," he says to Dr. Stewart. "You're the first civilian on this ship since the shakedown cruise."

"Thank you," she replies. "Your ship is, uh, impressive."

"Hardly," he smiles. "We're a glorified patrol boat. But thanks for the compliment." He offers his hand to me as well, and I shake it.

"Mr. Grayson. Good to see you in one piece. Looks like you've been around since I last saw you."

The last time I saw Colonel Campbell, he was a commander. They changed the service structure around us about a year after our first tiff with the Lankies on Capella Ac, where both the commander and I had a ringside seat to First Contact. The commander was the executive officer on my first navy assignment, and that ship ended up scattered all over Capella Ac as fine debris.

"Yes, sir," I say. "Couldn't leave well enough alone. Combat controller for the last three years."

Colonel Campbell nods. "I knew you'd get bored as a console jockey. First time you reported to me on *Versailles*, you already had a drop badge and a Bronze Star on your smock."

The CIC is a very intimate little affair, just like everything else on this ship. It has a half dozen people in it, less than a third the staff of a carrier's nerve center. *Indy*'s XO is a short and stocky sandy-haired woman who is introduced by Colonel Campbell as Major Renner. She returns my salute and shakes hands with Dr. Stewart.

"I guess we ought to get down to business," I say. "Mind if I call home and then set up with your Neural Networks and Weapons guys?"

"She's all yours," Colonel Campbell says. "And I think I speak for everyone in our sorry little excuse for a fleet when I say 'aim well.' We have one round and no reloads."

"Fallon, this is Grayson. I am set up on *Indy* and ready to kick off Doorknocker."

Operation Doorknocker is our fancy term for the Freighter of Doom plan that is still under revision even as we are getting ready to send the *Gary I. Gordon* on her way. I never understood why the fleet likes to name non-martial ships like fleet tenders after ground-pounder war heroes, but I think that her namesake—a Medal of Honor winner who defended an air crew to the death in some police action in the pre-NAC days—would approve of us using his ship to try to score the first Lanky seed-ship kill in history.

"Grayson, Fallon. Understood. The ground crews are still filling the last batch of cargo pods with liquid refreshments. They should be on the way into orbit in about ninety."

The colonial ground crews are doing their usual jobs of filling standard fleet cargo pods with water and launching them into orbit to be picked up for replenishment. The fleet uses water as reactor fuel and for the usual human uses, and New Svalbard is one of our intergalactic watering holes. Once they are in orbit, the freighter uses its orbital tugs to collect the pods and attach them to the pod clamps on the outside of the ship. The crew of the *Gordon* rigged a system that will allow us to remotely flood the interior spaces of the ship with the contents of one of those cargo pods, using transfer pumps and the ship's own cargo redistribution lines in a highly irregular manner that required the overriding of every major and minor safety protocol. According to the science crew, the incompressible water will make the ship a more effective projectile and more resilient to withstand the four-g sustained acceleration needed to intercept the Lanky seed ship at its calculated turnover point.

"Bogey is now two mil kilometers from the Russian," the tactical officer says behind me. I turn to watch the plot, where the red icon for the SRA cruiser and the orange one for the Lanky have almost merged on the holographic display.

"Uh-oh," Colonel Campbell says. "Looks like the fleet has picked up our hard-shelled friends. Battle group is changing course and acceleration."

On the plot, the icon cluster for the fleet task force—the *Midway* and her escorts—breaks away from the intercept trajectory it has been on for the last twelve hours. They're a half AU away from New Svalbard, seventy-five million kilometers, and still two hundred million kilometers from the Russian and its Lanky pursuer.

"Are they reversing?" I ask.

Colonel Campbell shakes his head without taking his eyes off the plot. "No. They're running."

He magnifies the relevant section of the display and spins it to orient the tactical symbols in a plane I can see.

"They've accelerated. I'm guessing by the rate they're going for maximum burn. And they're headed ninety degrees away from our incoming party guests. Into deep space."

"They're running," I repeat. I want to get angry at the fact that the task force commander has chosen to make discretion the better part of valor instead of returning to us to defend the only NAC settlement in the system from almost certain annihilation, but part of me can't fault him. Part of me would rather be on the *Midway* right now. They may just be the last humans alive in the Fomalhaut system once we've all played our hands.

"Smart," Colonel Campbell echoes my thoughts. "Not brave, but sensible."

"Bogey will intercept the cruiser in fifteen minutes," the tactical officer announces. I notice that he doesn't refer to the SRA ship as a bogey as well. I watch the red icon on its futile, limping run away from the monster that's chasing it. A week or a month ago I would have cheered the prospect of blotting a Russian space control cruiser from the plot, but now my stomach clenches at the thought of the poor bastards who have fifteen minutes of existence left before the Lanky overtakes them and shotguns their ship from bow to stern with yard-thick spikes that will crack open every pressurized compartment they have left.

We keep watching the plot as the minutes tick down on the CIC's clock. It's like watching a condemned prisoner squirming on the gurney as the executioner approaches. The distance between the icons decreases until they look like they're on top of each other even at maximum display magnification.

"Two hundred and fifty thousand," the tactical officer calls out. "Two hundred . . . one-fifty . . . one hundred . . ."

He brings up the video feed from the central optical array and superimposes it on the tactical plot. The Russian cruiser is a little gray dot in the middle of the segment. I don't see the Lanky at all.

"Fifty. Twenty-five. They should be overtaking them right . . . about . . . *now.*"

I still don't see the Lanky ship on the screen, but suddenly there's a bright flash of light, searing and white-hot even at this distance and magnification. Then the Russian cruiser is an expanding ball of fire that rapidly scatters and disperses into the blackness of space.

"What the hell was *that*?" the tactical officer asks.

"Nuclear detonation," I say. That wasn't a fusion bottle letting go after battle damage, but a high-yield atomic warhead going off in hard vacuum.

"Son of a bitch," Colonel Campbell says, with something akin to respect in his voice. "They launched their nukes at contact range."

"Did they kill the Lanky?" Dr. Stewart asks. She looks nauseated.

"Not likely," Colonel Campbell says even before the tactical officer checks the optical feed to answer her question. "That wasn't their goal anyway, just a possible fringe benefit."

"They went out on their own terms," I say. "Launched the nukes to kill themselves and possibly the Lanky, too."

"That is *insane*," Dr. Stewart says.

"You've never seen a ship that was hit by a Lanky broadside," I reply. "People getting sheared in half by a Lanky penetrator. Running out of air. Those are some shitty ways to die. Nuclear fireball? Instant oblivion."

"And a last 'fuck you' to the other team," Colonel Campbell says.

"I have the Lanky back on optics," the tactical officer says. "He's backlit from the nuke right now. Same speed and heading. Didn't even slow down for the intercept."

"Or from getting twenty megatons right in the kisser," Colonel Campbell says. "Keep tracking him until you lose him, and then have the computer track his trajectory with the optical array, same speed. He'll turn invisible on us again sooner or later. Let's make sure we can find him again."

"Well, there we have it," I say to the CIC in general. Then I send a transmission down to New Longyearbyen.

"Fallon, Grayson. The Lanky has overtaken the Russian. He's coming our way now, same trajectory." I don't have to mention that the SRA cruiser is now a cloud of debris vapor still traveling at one-quarter-g acceleration.

"Copy that," Sergeant Fallon sends back. "It's all on you now. Doorknocker commences in sixty minutes. Keep me posted. Fallon out."

There are no windows in the CIC—the combat information center is always deep in the center of a warship, where it's most protected—but I can tap into the numerous optical sensors on the outside of the hull. Below us, New Svalbard is a cold, white ball of frozen ground and ice, barely more hospitable than the rest of this system. Fomalhaut c looks ethereal in its almost translucent presence, blue storm swirls the size of entire Earth continents rippling on its surface. Somewhere in the black void beyond, toward the Fomalhaut star that is twinkling brightly in the distance, there's a Lanky seed ship coming for us, and all the plans we're making right now feel a little bit like the battle strategies of cockroaches who see the boot coming down on them.

Still, we gear up to throw our rocks and give them the finger because that's what we do. The Russian cruiser captain, or whoever had survived to remain in command over there, did exactly that when the boot came down on him, and if our water-laden kinetic missile fails to hit the target, I hope to go out in a similar way. Not that anybody would ever know.

We spend the last hour before the launch double- and triple-checking all the numbers, and then starting over and checking them again from scratch. Dr. Stewart has gotten the same response from the computer every time, and she still verifies everything by hand and with her data pad. The Neural Networks guy on the *Indy* is a sergeant who looks to be about my age. He graduated Neural Networks School the same year I did, two classes before me, and it occurs to me that he is exactly where I would be at this point in my career if I hadn't opted to go for the combat-controller track because I got bored watching progress bars all day long. In an alternate universe, I may be the one sitting in the Networks Center of the *Indianapolis* right now, with some other combat controller looking over my shoulder. Maybe in yet another alternate universe, we're still in the task force that's running away, or we're part of the debris cloud that's now dispersed behind the approaching Lanky.

I watch as the *Indy*'s Networks administrator systematically disables all the fail-safes and security protocols on the *Gordon*'s shipboard network. I went to Networks School and had his job for over a year in the fleet, so I know that some of the things he's doing are supposed to be impossible to do, and very definitely in violation of fleet regulations. It's also how I know that he is good at his job and not just one of the bottom 10 percent of his tech school class.

"I'm probably the first Neural guy in the fleet who has ever gotten to do this in real life," he says as he digs his way through yet another subsystem of the *Gordon*'s central computer. "Pissing on every safety reg in the book."

"They'll bust you back to private and drum you out without your end-of-service bonus," I say, and he grins.

"*Please*," he says.

Without the crew on board and with all her hollow spaces filled with water, the *Gordon* will be able to pull much more sustained acceleration, and the reactor won't need to spend any of its energy budget keeping the artificial-gravity deck plates energized. What we're about to do has never been done, not even with a target ship, and it's only even possible because the *Gordon* has military-grade propulsion and computer systems, to keep up and interface with the fleet units she was built to support. Still, nobody has ever thought of pushing a military freighter to four gravities of sustained acceleration and keeping her there for thirty-five hours. We are truly on the cutting edge of desperate measures.

"That was the last one," the Networks admin says. "The reactor output fail-safe and automatic shutdown. *Unhackable*, they said in tech school."

"There's no such thing," I say.

"There's only the fear of a court-martial." He taps his screen and initiates the reactor warm-up. "Fifteen minutes to one hundred and ten percent. This baby will go out of the starting blocks like a fighter."

I watch through the external feed as the automated tugs wrestle the two remaining cargo pods into position and lock them into place. The freighter itself is a long, knobby hull with a command section at the front and an engine section aft, connected by a long spine. The external cargo pods all connect to the spine of the ship and form the bulk of the *Gordon*'s hull. Each cargo pod can be jettisoned separately for orbital drop—an easier and cheaper method than ferrying everything down to the surface with atmospheric craft.

The Networks admin lets out a low whistle.

"Gross weight is forty-three thousand metric tons," he says. "I think that's a class record. The water in the main hull added damn near eight thousand tons."

Dr. Stewart taps around a bit on her data pad and lets out a whistle of her own.

"If this thing hits—*when* it hits—we're going to need some heavy-duty eye protection back here. Because the impact energy will be two hundred *gigatons*. Give or take a few depending on how much water she burns along the way."

There are general sounds of amazement and appreciation in the CIC. The nukes in the tubes of all the task force ships put together probably total less than a thousandth of that yield.

"If we miss that shot, it will be the biggest waste of ordnance in the history of space warfare," the tactical officer says.

"Then let's not miss." Colonel Campbell looks up at the time readout on the CIC bulkhead. "Is the Lanky still where we want him to be?"

"He's skipping in and out. Sensors keep losing him, but the computer is tracking his projected path with the optics. Every once in a while, we get a reflection, and he pops back into the visible spectrum. He's right on track. One-gravity acceleration. Thirty-six hours, eleven minutes, and three seconds to turnaround. Unless the Lankies have a way to negate physics and stop their ships on a dime without having to counter-burn," the weapons officer adds.

"Well, let's hope they don't. XO, reset the shot clock. Prep for send-off. Weps and Networks, whenever you're ready."

At minus thirty-six hours and three minutes, the Networks administrator opens the throttles on the *Gordon*'s fusion rocket engines and increases the reactor output to 110 percent, emergency military power. The *Gary I. Gordon* leaps out of her orbital parking spot like a MARS missile popping out of the launcher tube, faster than I have ever seen a warship accelerate from a dead start, let alone a fifty-year-old freighter. We had debated using the gravity well of Fomalhaut c by slingshotting the freighter around it, but with all the reactor power being available for the engines, we concluded that the risk of losing telemetry and having an unfortunate freighter/planet interface wasn't worth the extra acceleration out of the starting block. We've slaved the navigation system and thrust controls of the *Gordon* to the neural network on the *Indianapolis*, and now the freighter is a giant guided missile, unmanned, with the remote control sitting in front of me in the CIC.

"Send a courtesy message to the *Midway* and her entourage," Colonel Campbell says. "Tell them to stay clear of that neighborhood. Not that they'll need the encouragement."

The comms officer does as instructed, and I take the opportunity to contact the ops center down in New Longyearbyen's admin center.

"Fallon, this is Grayson. Operation Doorknocker is in progress. Time to target is thirty-six hours."

"Rolled the dice and bet the house on one throw," Sergeant Fallon replies. "Are you staying up there, Andrew?"

"Affirmative. Thirty-six hours to go, I'll be backing up their Networks guy so we don't have to pop a bunch of go-pills."

"Makes sense. I'll inform the troops down here." There's a brief pause. "If we miss, how long until our party crashers arrive?"

"They're going a steady one-g, so once they flip and accelerate the other way, seventy hours."

"One hundred and six hours, then. Guess I don't have to have everyone lock and load just yet. Good luck, Andrew. If we miss, get your butt back down here so we can do our epic last stand together."

"That's affirmative, Sarge," I say. "Grayson out."

I turn around and watch the tactical display. The *Gordon* is out of sight of the low-power optics already, but on the plot, she has barely moved toward the Lanky. Blue icon accelerating toward orange icon, irresistible force hurling itself against immovable object.

Don't you fucking miss, I think. *I'll be in deep shit if I don't make it back for my own wedding.*

CHAPTER 26
—— PRESUMED HOSTILE ——

The combat-stations alert on the *Indy* is a very well-mannered low electronic trill that yanks me out of my sleep instantly nonetheless. I open my eyes to find that the berth is illuminated by red combat lighting. It feels like I had just fallen asleep, but when I check the chrono on the bulkhead, I see that I've slept for almost six hours. I drop out of bed, put on my boots again, and rush to the CIC.

"We're picking up radiation signatures from the Alcubierre node we mined a week ago," Colonel Campbell says as I step across the CIC threshold and almost fall on my face as my boot catches. "Several nuclear detonations in the triple-digit-kiloton range."

"Sounds like someone tripped the minefield," I say.

"Or *something*," the XO suggests.

"Anything come through?"

"Can't tell yet," Colonel Campbell says. "At this range, the nuclear noise is blotting out everything else. We'll have to wait a little until the dust settles, so to speak."

I look over at the running shot clock on the CIC bulkhead. It shows twenty-eight hours left to go until the freighter meets the Lanky ship. The newcomers, if they are coming from the bearing of the Alcubierre node, will be coming in almost from the opposite bearing of the incoming Lanky. Our fleet combat units are playing chicken in deep space, so whatever just entered the system through Alcubierre only has to push aside our little OCS to take control of New Svalbard.

"Maybe it's reinforcements," the XO says. "They're coming from our Alcubierre node."

"They wouldn't trip the mines," I say. "Unless their IFF transponders went to shit."

"Could be the SRA has figured out the location of our node," the colonel says. "Could be *their* node just happens to be close to ours. I'll take all of that over another Lanky coming our way from the other direction. At least we can *surrender* to the SRA, and they'll leave our colonists alive."

The sensor package on the *Indy* is the best on any fleet ship, and it doesn't take very long for the computer to sort out the clutter between optical arrays, infrared, and radar.

"Can't make out who it is, but there's a bunch of 'em," the tactical officer says. "Too far away for comms, but I don't get any IFF verifications." He cycles through a few windows on his display. "Three . . . four . . . five . . . six . . . make that eight, maybe nine."

"Can't be Lankies, then," I say. "I've never seen more than one of theirs at a time."

"Not Lankies," the tactical officer says. "Too small for that."

"I'm not sure that having to face an entire SRA task force would be a great improvement," Colonel Campbell replies. "But I'll take small blessings right now. Get me an ID on those guys the second they get close enough for an IFF ping."

A short while later, we're all congregating in the CIC again, watching the holographic orb projected above the tactical table like some sort of high-tech fortune globe. The icons for the newcomers are the pale red of "UNCONFIRMED, PRESUMED HOSTILE" contacts. They are steadily accelerating away from the Alcubierre transition area and straight toward New Svalbard.

"Still too far away for comms, but I'm getting some optical recognition matches now," the tactical officer says. Both the XO and Colonel Campbell step over to the tactical console to look over his shoulder.

"It's a whole mess of ships. System's still drawing a blank on most of them. But the computer says the lead ship is definitely a Chinese 098D-class destroyer. There's a seventy percent certainty the second is an Indian Godavari-class frigate."

"Well, *great*," Colonel Campbell sighs. The icons on the tactical display turn from faded red to the bright red of "HOSTILE" contacts.

"New contacts are designated Raid One. Two point five AUs, proceeding in-system at two gravities and accelerating."

Colonel Campbell glances at the shot clock on the CIC bulkhead. "They'll be in range right around the time the *Gordon* is at the turnaround point for the Lanky," he says. "This will not do."

"Can we explain the situation to them?" Dr. Stewart asks. "Surely they'll see that blasting us out of space just when we're about to take out a seed ship isn't exactly in their best interests."

"Maybe," the XO says. "But I'd rather not reason with a Chinese task force commander right around the time we need to be glued to the remote in here."

"If they don't just blow us out of space the second we enter their long-range-weapons envelope," I say.

"As long as we're sitting here and maintaining telemetry with the *Gordon*, we can't even go stealthy again," the XO says.

"They'll see us from a long ways off with our active gear running," Colonel Campbell concurs.

"Then we need to run," the XO suggests. "Follow the *Gordon*; keep out of range of the SRA task force as long as possible. At least until we've hit or missed our target."

"You want to leave our troops down there without orbital cover?" I say, a flash of anger welling up in me. "Run like the rest of the task force?"

"If we had the *Midway* and her escorts here, we may have a chance," the colonel says. "Against nine ships, maybe not a realistic one, but at least they'd think twice before taking on a carrier group head-on. With one OCS that can't go into stealth? Forget it."

He studies the plot for a few moments, lips pursed and hands on his hips. Then he shakes his head.

"Helm, get us out of here, flank speed. Same trajectory we sent the *Gordon*."

"They have the acceleration on us, sir," the tactical officer says. "They'll overtake us sooner or later."

"We're not running indefinitely," the colonel replies. "We're just keeping out of reach until the *Gordon* does her job. Then we can drop off the plot again and figure out something else."

I know he's right. The combat power bearing down on us is far too much for one orbital combat ship to handle, even one as new and capable as *Indianapolis*. But I know what we're leaving behind down there: three thousand troops without air/space support that will be easy pickings for a spaceborne regiment of Chinese marines with a full battle group in orbit.

I walk over to the comms console and tap into the network to raise the ops center on the moon.

"Colonial Ops, this is Staff Sergeant Grayson on *Indianapolis*. Do you copy?"

"Loud and clear, Sarge," someone replies. "What gives?"

"Get me Sergeant Fallon. It's urgent."

There are a few moments of silence on the line, and then Sergeant Fallon's voice comes on, sounding slightly out of breath.

"Fallon here. Go ahead."

"We have an SRA task force headed our way from the Alcubierre node," I say. "They'll be on top of us in less than a day. Nine ships at least."

"Goddammit," she says, with what sounds like annoyance in her voice, and I smile. "Can't catch a break, can we?"

"Not lately," I say. "*Indy* is bugging out for a while, which means you'll be without spaceborne cover."

"Guess I'll be sounding the alarm early after all. Where are you going?"

"We need to stay out of their range until we've hammered that Lanky, or everything is fucked to hell. Once that's done, we'll come back around and see what we can dent."

The hull of the *Indianapolis* vibrates ever so slightly as the nose of the ship swings around and the engines go to maximum acceleration. Even with the artificial gravity compensating for the sudden three gravities of acceleration, I still have to hang on to the side of the comms console for a moment.

"They'll find this place a tough nut to crack," Sergeant Fallon says. "At least our guys have weapons for the job."

"You don't have any air support except for three Dragonflies," I reply. "You may just want to negotiate terms with them."

"That doesn't sound like you at all, Andrew," she says flatly. "POW orange doesn't go well with my complexion."

"Hold out one way or another. Until we're back. Last stands, and all that."

"We'll be here," she says. "One way or another. Just kill that alien son of a bitch." She cuts the comms link.

We speed away from New Svalbard at flank speed, which is pretty swift for a warship of *Indy*'s small size. The guilt I feel when

I watch the dirty white globe of the ice moon recede behind us is almost debilitating. I should be on the ground right now with Sergeant Fallon and the rest of the troops, and dig in for the inevitable battle with the SRA landing force. I try to recall how many troops a Chinese or Russian carrier has on board. They like to stack their marine regiments troop-heavy, so if they come equipped for a spaceborne assault, they probably have four thousand troops getting into combat armor right about now. And that's if they didn't bring along a second carrier, which is very likely considering the size of their task force. We have four thousand troops on the moon, but they're split up into two factions, and ours is split up over several dozen terraforming stations. We are in a horrible tactical position, but we will fight if we are attacked, and I should be with them. Instead, I am running away from the impending battle. I know that the *Indy*'s mission is vital to our survival, but I still feel like I made a terribly wrong call by coming up here.

The tactical display is a conga line of icons—the *Gordon* in the lead, with the *Indianapolis* behind, and finally the cluster of SRA fleet units bringing up the rear. We're all headed right for the Lanky, who has been on the same stubborn course and acceleration since we first spotted him against the exhaust flare from the now-dead Russian cruiser. I take turns standing watch at the neural-networks station with the *Indy*'s administrator. The display in the middle of the CIC changes its resolution and scanning range automatically to keep the units in sensor range in their proper spatial relationships on the tactical orb, and the kilometer scale next to the sphere shrinks with every passing hour. The *Indy* is running, but the SRA task force is slowly gaining because of their acceleration advantage. The shot clock on the CIC bulkhead is ticking down, but it seems like the minutes and seconds take much longer to pass than usual.

In the middle of the third watch cycle, something changes. The SRA task force is a 150 million kilometers from New Svalbard, and their acceleration numbers are steady, but all of a sudden we're gaining range again and pulling away.

"They've gone for turnover," the XO says. "They're not chasing us. They're just going for the colony."

Their turnover point means they'll spend the second half of their approach to New Svalbard accelerating in the opposite direction, which means they're definitely planning to coast into orbit instead of letting us lead them on a wild goose chase.

"Small consolation," I say. "That's too much combat power for our troops to take on. They want the place, it's theirs already." I have no doubt that Sergeant Fallon and her HD troops will extract a hefty toll for the SRA victory, but I know orbital assault tactics, and if the Chinese or Russian in charge of that battle group has been awake for just half his lectures in war college, they will take New Svalbard away from us.

"Two hours, sixteen minutes to impact," the weapons officer says.

"Let's see if all of this is even going to matter in the end," the colonel says darkly.

CHAPTER 27
—UNPRECEDENTED EVENTS—

"*Gordon* is doing forty-eight hundred kilometers per second," the tactical officer says. "Time to impact: three minutes, thirty seconds."

"Do they not see us coming?" Dr. Stewart asks.

"Maybe not," the XO replies. "Maybe they don't care. I doubt anyone's ever rammed one of theirs at relativistic speed."

The Lanky on the plot still plods down the parabolic trajectory toward New Svalbard at the same one-g acceleration he's been pushing for the last forty hours. Nobody knows how their tech works, or if they even have tech, but whatever they use to sense their environment seems to leave them completely ignorant of the kinetic projectile hurling its way toward them at planetoid-shattering velocity. Either that, or they are aware of us and don't consider the *Gordon*'s stored-up hundreds of gigatons of kinetic energy a threat, which is not a happy thought right now. I know just enough about physics to know that I understand the subject very little, and I sincerely hope Dr. Stewart is right about the destructive potential of the *Gordon.*

"What if they have a close-in weapons system like our ships?" I ask.

"Won't matter a bit," Dr. Stewart says. "It would take terajoules of energy to break that freighter apart and boil all that water away. And even if they blew it up right now, all the debris would still hit them at the same speed. Physics," she adds with a slight smile. "Nobody's immune to physics. I don't care how big and tough they are."

I watch the icons on the tactical display, the kilometer scale contracting with every passing second, and the dread in my middle is almost balanced by the excitement I feel. If we miss, or the Lanky dodges the bullet at the last second, we are as good as dead. If we don't miss, we will have pulled off something that has never been done before, and we will get to live on. Maybe only until we get back to the colony and decide to take on the SRA force that will be moving into orbit there soon, but at least we will be going out on our terms and while putting up a fight, not exterminated like a bunch of cockroaches at the bottom of a garbage collector.

The CIC now has all hands on deck. Most of us are standing in a circle around the holotable. Dr. Stewart looks like she wishes she had something a little stronger than galley coffee right about now. Colonel Campbell's expression is unreadable as he stands motionless with his hands behind his back. The tension in the CIC seems thick enough to refract light.

"Two minutes," the tactical officer says.

We all watch the holographic display like it's the last minute of the last episode of the world's most interesting Network show.

"Come on," the XO says under her breath. "Come on."

The *Gordon* is still visible through the optical feed, a tiny speck of glowing fusion-rocket exhaust streaking through the blackness of space over 150 million kilometers in front of us. The Lanky on a reciprocal course is all but invisible to us, his presence and position only guessed by the computer based on sporadic sightings of reflections on his hull, or the occasional blacking out of star's light in the distance. Without the Russian cruiser making a futile run for New Svalbard, we never would have known about the Lanky ship until it showed up in orbit over the colony and started landing its advance party.

"One minute."

The shot clock on the CIC bulkhead jumps to its final two-digit seconds readout. The tactical icons on the orb are now so close together that they look like they're on top of each other. I hold my breath as I watch the optical feed where the *Gordon* hurtles toward her target like an angry firefly.

Don't miss, I think. *Don't miss, don't miss, don't miss.*

"Ten. Nine. Eight. Seven." The tactical officer's voice cracks with stress.

". . . four, three, two, one. Impact."

Nothing happens on the optical feed. We all still see the exhaust flare of the *Gordon* shooting downrange at close to five thousand kilometers per second.

"Fuck," Colonel Campbell says.

Then the display turns white with noiseless fury. The computer kicks in lens filters to prevent frying the optical array and zooms out the scale automatically. Out in deep space, a white-hot sphere expands, much brighter and closer than the far-off sun.

The *Gordon* didn't miss.

The CIC erupts into cheers and shouts.

"*Impact*," the tactical officer calls out over the noise, jubilation in his voice. "One point one five nine AUs."

Next to me, Dr. Stewart lets out a long, shaky breath and runs both hands through her hair. I grin at her, and she laughs.

"Science," she says to me. "It works."

"That is the biggest fucking fireball I have ever seen," Colonel Campbell says. I look at the camera feed again. The Fomalhaut system now has two suns, however briefly. Even from 150 million kilometers away, the fireball from the released impact energy makes all the vacuum detonations of nuclear warheads I've ever seen look like someone briefly flicked on a helmet light.

"I've never seen anything like it," I say.

"Nobody has," Dr. Stewart says. "We just caused the largest man-made energy release in history."

"It's going to be hours before I can get anything on optics or radiation tracking again," the tactical officer says.

"That fireball is fifty-five thousand Kelvins," Dr. Stewart says. "We just caused a two-hundred-gigaton energy release. If there's anything left in that area of space other than vapor, I'll eat every last diploma on my office wall."

Colonel Campbell sits down in his command chair and activates the *Indy*'s 1MC.

"Attention, all hands. This is the skipper. You are now crew members of the first fleet ship to ever destroy a Lanky vessel. Operation Doorknocker was successful. Our extermination has been postponed. Not bad for a little OCS, people. Carry on."

Another cheer goes up in the CIC.

"I don't suppose alcohol is allowed on military ships?" Dr. Stewart asks the colonel. "I could really go for a strong drink right now."

"No, it's not allowed," he replies. "And of course we have some."

It takes a while for the *Indy*'s sensors to poke through the noise from a two-hundred-gigaton explosion. All that's left in the vicinity of the Lanky ship's projected turnaround point is a superheated debris cloud that is slowly expanding. The light from the fireball gradually decreased after the collision, but even a few minutes later, it's still impressive to look at.

"All right, people. Helmsman, bring us about and back on course toward New Svalbard," Colonel Campbell orders. "Tactical, get me the word on our SRA friends. Weapons, check stores and warm up the nukes. We're going stealth again."

The thought of an imminent hopeless engagement with the far superior SRA force approaching New Svalbard is like a cold shower after the heated excitement of our destruction of the Lanky seed ship. We may have bought the colony some time, but if we have to take this ship into battle against an entire carrier group, there's no question we'll lose.

"There they are," the tactical officer says a short while later. I watch as the tactical orb display expands in scale. New Svalbard is a hundred million kilometers away, and the SRA task force pops up on the screen almost a hundred million kilometers on the opposite side of the moon.

"We have the acceleration advantage," the XO says. "We'll be back over the moon before they get there, but not by much. For whatever good it'll do."

"This is odd," the tactical officer says. On the plot, the tags for the tactical icons change as the computer starts to identify the first of the SRA units conclusively.

"What's that, Lieutenant?" Colonel Campbell asks.

"Well, the ELINT profiles are strange for some of those ships. I know for sure that the lead ship is the Chinese 098D. That's that Godavari right here." He marks the icon on the tactical display briefly. "That third one there? The computer doesn't have it yet, but I'm eighty percent sure it's one of their older assault carriers. Maybe Kiev class."

He highlights two of the ships in the back of the group.

"But those right there? I could swear that one of them looks like a Hammerhead cruiser."

The display changes, and the icon he is pointing out changes to the pale blue of an "UNIDENTIFIED, PRESUMED FRIENDLY" contact as the computer appears to concur with the lieutenant's assessment. It's impossible for us to capture one of their warships in space, or for them to capture one of ours—there are multiple safeguards in place, right down to DNA locks on the control consoles—but seeing friendly units in a task force with enemy ones seems even less likely.

"Captured and forced to tag along?" the XO wonders aloud.

"Possible," Colonel Campbell says. "That would explain why they came through our Alcubierre node."

"But why would they have to set off the minefield on the way in?"

"Beats me." The colonel scratches his chin as he watches the plot.

"Go to turnaround and decelerate for New Svalbard," he orders. "We'll see what's going on when they're in comms range. Any sign of our carrier group?"

"No, sir. They're not within two AUs of us or the moon."

"Smartest sons of bitches in the system right now," the XO mutters.

———————

A few hours later we're in communications range with the colony again, and I contact Sergeant Fallon as soon as I can get a stable comms link. At this range, the signal takes five minutes to get to New Svalbard, and my excitement over the news makes the wait for a return reply agonizingly frustrating.

"The Lanky ship is destroyed," I send. "Fine stardust. We are coming back to the barn to assist with the defense."

"That's the best news I've heard all month. Hell, year. Make that 'decade,'" she sends back. "I'd buy that science crew a shitload of drinks if they had any to buy down here."

"Dig in and hold on. We are coming. We'll get there before the SRA battle group."

"Hope you like Chinese rations," she sends back. "The civilian admin wants to surrender the moon rather than risk destroying half his terraformers. I'll be the first to pick a fight, but on this one I think he's on the right track. No point winning if we have no infrastructure left."

In *Indy*'s CIC, everyone looks as if Sergeant Fallon has just voiced some particularly offensive sacrilege, but I know that everyone present also understands that the admin is completely right. For better or worse, we subjected our little force to his control, and I realize with some shame that I am actually relieved at not having to fight yet another hopeless battle.

"We're getting IFF transponder signals," the tactical officer says. "Computer is sorting them out."

The display on the holotable shows a flurry of activity as the computer updates the icons of the approaching battle group with names and hull numbers. One assault carrier, three supply ships, two frigates, and one destroyer, all SRA. One of our Hammerhead cruisers, the NACS *Avenger*. And one of our supercarriers—NACS *Regulus*, CV-2154, sister ship to the *Polaris*, the ship I pulled out of the hat in the assignment lottery at the end of Neural Networks School. I traded that assignment off to a fellow graduate so I could be on the *Versailles* with Halley, five years ago when all this started. The Navigator-class supercarriers are prized fleet assets, the biggest and most powerful units we have, and I can't conceive of a scenario where one of them would be flying around with an SRA battle-group escort. In the *Indy*'s CIC, everyone just gawks at the tactical display, trying to make sense of it.

"Get me the *Regulus* on tight-beam," Colonel Campbell finally says to the comms officer.

"Aye, sir." The comms officer plays his console for a few moments. "Go ahead, sir. You're on tight-beam package."

"*Regulus*, this is the NACS *Indianapolis*, *Indy* Actual, in deep space beyond New Svalbard and under stealth. We show you in the middle of a shitload of confirmed SRA warships. What gives, over?"

Under normal circumstances I'd have to chuckle at Colonel Campbell's cavalier radio etiquette, but under the current ones, I almost have to laud his restraint.

We wait for the reply from *Regulus*, almost ten minutes delayed because of the two hundred million kilometers between our ships. It's a gamble to be sending at all, but with a tight-beam link, the SRA ships shouldn't be able to pin down our transmission, especially not at this range.

"*Indianapolis*, this is *Regulus*. SRA units in our company are not hostile. Repeat, SRA units are not hostile. Do not take offensive action. Proceed to New Svalbard and rendezvous with the battle group."

"*Regulus*, *Indy* Actual. Like *hell*. I won't do any such thing until I know that you don't have a squad of Chinese marines in your CIC and rifle muzzles pointed at your heads."

The next few minutes are almost unbearably tense as we wait for *Regulus* to reply to the colonel's declaration. When the transmission arrives, it's a different voice.

"*Indy* Actual, this is *Regulus* Actual, Colonel Aguilar. We are not compromised. I understand your concern, but you've been out of the world for a little while, and you're unaware of the latest developments." There's a pause in the transmission, during which my heart pounds like it wants to leap out of my chest through my ears.

"We have a truce with the SRA units in our attendance," Colonel Aguilar continues. "They are not a belligerent task force. They are refugees. And so are we. The Lankies are in our solar system."

EPILOGUE

"First time I've ever seen one of those this close," I say as we watch the SRA drop ship come in for a landing on the colony's repaired drop-ship pad. The Sino-Russian designs are bigger than our Wasps and almost the size of a Dragonfly, but they look much meaner, all angles and armor plates and cannon muzzles. The SRA drop ship carries no attack ordnance on its wing pylons, but it's still a little unsettling to stare right down those autocannon barrels. I've spent the last five years fighting the people who crew those ships, and now the moon is crawling with them.

Sergeant Fallon pulls up another chair and plops her boots down on them. We are sitting in the control tower of the airfield in front of the patched polycarb windows. In the last hour, we've watched a highly irregular mix of SRA and NAC drop ships, ground-attack birds, and civilian craft land and depart.

"Must really be the end of the world if we're taking warm showers with these people after beating the shit out of each other for fifty years," Sergeant Fallon says. Down below us, the tarmac is crawling with activity as ground crews unload cargo holds and refuel spacecraft.

The reports we got from the crews of the newly arrived NAC ships have pretty much announced the start of the apocalypse. The Lankies showed up in orbit around Mars, our main fleet yard

313

in the solar system aside from Earth. The Battle of Mars ended in a total defeat. The fleet yards are gone, and so is the entire colony—twenty-five million people. What's left of the fleet is scattered all over the solar system. The Lankies aren't advancing for now, but they've blockaded the Alcubierre nodes, and the task force that made it through to us had *sixteen* ships in it before they battled their way through the node past half a dozen seed ships. There are no SRA or NAC fleets anymore, just small groups of humans on the run. At least we've finally stopped shooting at each other.

"What are you going to do?" I ask her. "Stay here or join the counterattack?"

"I don't know yet," Sergeant Fallon says. She takes a swig from the coffee mug she's been repeatedly draining and refilling for the last few hours. "They say it's a crapshoot whether any ship will be able to run that blockade and make it back to Earth. I'd like to have a fighting chance, not get blown out of space with no way to shoot back. Maybe I'll stay here and wait for them to come to me."

She puts down her mug and leans back with a tired sigh.

"What about you?" she asks without taking her eyes off the SRA drop ship settling on its skids outside.

I consider her question—not that I hadn't made my decision pretty much the moment they put the options in front of us. We're free to decide whether to stay part of the garrison force on New Svalbard, or join the combined NAC/SRA ragtag battle group to go back to the solar system and try to force the blockade.

"If any ship can make it through to Earth, it's the *Indy*," I say. "Colonel Campbell says we're welcome to tag along for the run. Stealth dash back to the inner solar system."

"You're going back *there*?" Sergeant Fallon smiles. "Whatever happened to wanting to breathe the free air of the colonies? I thought Earth's a shithole?"

"You're staying *here*?" I say, aping her tone exactly. "Whatever happened to sticking with the shit you know? I thought the colonies are desolate wastelands?"

She rolls her eyes, but the smile doesn't leave her face.

"Last time I tried to do my job right, they shipped me off into exile. They've been barely holding it together as it is. What do you think Earth's like right now, with the Lankies on our doorstep?"

I try to imagine the PRCs, perpetually in unrest anyway, gripped in end-of-the-world hysteria, hundreds of millions of frightened and hungry people aware of their imminent extermination. I know that that's about the last place in the universe I really want to be right now. But I can't help thinking of Mom and Halley and Chief Kopka, and my former squad mates in the 365th AIB at Fort Shughart. If our species is going to end anyway, I want to make my stand with the few people I care about. I want to be in charge of my own fate, not wait for my death in a frozen hole at the ass end of the settled galaxy.

"Earth *is* a shithole," I say. "But it's *our* shithole. And they can't fucking have it."

Sergeant Fallon looks outside again and picks up her coffee. She takes a long, slurping sip.

"Come to think of it," she says. "The apocalypse is at our door. The survival of our species is in doubt. That's going to be one bitch of a fight. I'd hate to miss it."

Outside, the snow flurries have stopped. As we watch the latest arrivals swoop in low over the runway and set down on the snow-swept concrete with blinking position lights, there's a sudden break in the cloud cover, and the light from the distant sun paints the mountaintops on the horizon in shades of pale blue and white.

"Let's go and pack for one bitch of a fight, then," I say.

——— ACKNOWLEDGMENTS ———

The list of people to thank gets longer and longer.

Thanks to Marc Berte, who made sure the science in the book isn't total and utter handwavium.

Thanks to my developmental editor, Andrea Hurst, who suggested ALL THE CHANGES. She made me rewrite the stuff that sucked until it didn't, and it's a much better novel for that.

Thanks to my local Upper Valley writer posse: Laura Bergstresser, Patricia Bray, and John Murphy. I know none of you ever got to critique this novel, but our regular chips-and-beer shop talks have done a great deal to keep me going when I considered hanging up the pen and exploring a new career as a store greeter.

Thanks to my agent, Evan, who brokers my novel deals in the smoke-filled, shady backrooms of the publishing world where a clueless newbie like me would get shanked and left to die in the gutter next to remaindered copies of Fifty Shades novels.

And a big "Thank you" to everyone who bought *Terms of Enlistment*, especially those of you who took time out of your day to write a review or recommend the novel to your friends. You are all beautiful people, with exceptionally good taste and OK I'LL SHUT UP NOW.